Praise for

ᚦAUGHTERS OF THE STORM

❖ ❖ ❖

"This fantastic series opener, powered by an engaging, female-led cast of characters, is riveting from page one right through to the end, with almost every scene bringing new excitement and intrigue. All of the five leading women are richly drawn, with distinct voices and multidimensional personalities that never slip into caricature. Wilkins sketches these royals with nuance and sensitivity, making even the vexing characters like careless Ivy and the villainous Wylm feel worthy of our sympathy. . . . Wilkins has struck gold with her thrilling high fantasy world! Book two can't arrive soon enough!"
—*Romantic Times*

"Readers who enjoy epic journeys and strong female protagonists will enjoy Wilkins' first installment of her new Daughters of the Storm series." —*Booklist*

"A twisty high fantasy . . . exploring political machinations and the relationships between sisters; betrayal lurks at every turn."
—*Washington Post*

DAUGHTERS OF THE STORM

KIM WILKINS

Del Rey | New York

2018 Del Rey Trade Paperback Edition

Published in the United States by Del Rey, an imprint of Random House, a division of Penguin Random House LLC, New York.

Del Rey and the House colophon are registered trademarks of Penguin Random House LLC.

Originally published in Australia and New Zealand by Harlequin/ Mira, Sydney, in 2014. Originally published in hardcover in the United States by Del Rey, an imprint of Random House, a division of Penguin Random House LLC, in 2018.

This book contains an excerpt from the forthcoming book *Sisters of the Fire* by Kim Wilkins. This excerpt has been set for this edition only and may not reflect the final content of the forthcoming edition.

LIBRARY OF CONGRESS CATALOGING-IN-PUBLICATION DATA

Names: Wilkins, Kim, author.
Title: Daughters of the storm / Kim Wilkins.
Description: New York: Del Rey, [2018] | Series: Daughters of the storm; 1
Identifiers: LCCN 2017058635 | ISBN 9780399177491 (paperback) | ISBN 9780399177484 (ebook)
Subjects: LCSH: Quests (Expeditions)—Fiction. | Family secrets—Fiction. | Sisters—Fiction. | BISAC: FICTION / Fantasy / Epic. | FICTION / Fantasy /
General. | FICTION / Action & Adventure. | GSAFD: Fantasy fiction.
Classification: LCC PR9619.3.W547 D38 2018 | DDC 823/ .914—dc23

Printed in the United States of America on acid-free paper

randomhousebooks.com

9 8 7 6 5 4 3 2 1

Book design by Virginia Norey

For Oliver: the best of men

DAUGHTERS OF THE STORM

PROLOGUE

A thousand times he had murmured her name in the soft darkness; now, though, he didn't know her name. He didn't even know his own.

The rain had set in outside the bowed wooden shutters. Endless mornings under dark-gray, swirling clouds that unburdened cold water from one end of Almissia to the other had turned the roads to stinking mud: Gudrun could not send for a physician, and she could not tell anyone he was ill, because he was the king. She could not even tell Byrta, his counselor, because Byrta would send for his daughters.

Gudrun knew his daughters hated her.

And so she had been trapped for three long days in the gloomy bowerhouse with him as he raved. The wild man in the looking glass made him quiver with fear; he shouted obscene words at her; he wept like a babe over a loose thread on his robe. She soothed him with soft words and firm touches, even when he pummeled her with his fists and accused her of trying to steal his food. The fits came suddenly, and left just as suddenly. Then he would sleep for hours among the crumpled woolen blankets while she watched his face, barely recognizing his sagging skin and gray beard.

Where was the noble, strong man he had been? The warrior king, the Storm Bearer, Athelrick of Almissia?

And where was the woman she had been? Whose were these thin-skinned hands, fearfully stroking an old man's troubled forehead?

Finally, the rain cleared, and she sent for Osred, the physician who had accompanied her more than three years ago when she came to marry Athelrick.

She should have known word would spread quickly.

The bowerhouse door opened, gusting air against the tapestries so they swung then settled with a clatter. Three figures stood there. Osred, tall and finely dressed; Byrta, the crone who had attended Athelrick since she was a young maid; and Dunstan, a grizzled war hero who was so old the hairs on his meaty fists were silver.

Gudrun's stomach coiled. Osred was her only ally. The others were natives of Almissia. No matter that they had always been friendly to her; she knew they thought her an interloper. She felt old, frail. Far from home. The person she loved and depended on the most was lost to her; lost, it seemed, to the world.

"Why didn't you tell me?" Byrta admonished, though gently, as she hurried to Athelrick's side. He was sleeping now—the deep, impenetrable sleep that measured out the hours until his next fit.

"I hoped he might get better on his own." Oh, how she had hoped it. She had hoped so hard, her ribs ached at night.

Osred came to Gudrun and laid his hand on her forearm. "You mustn't worry," he said in a cold, flat voice.

Dunstan closed the door carefully and pressed his back against it, arms folded across his round belly. "No one must know," he said. "If our enemies thought our king could not rule . . ." He trailed off, his voice tripping on tears he refused to shed. He straightened his spine. "We must send for Bluebell."

Bluebell. The name turned Gudrun's stomach cold. Athelrick's eldest daughter, with her sinewy tattooed arms and her crushed nose and her unsheathed hatred.

"It is premature, surely," Osred said smoothly. "Let me examine the king and prescribe him a remedy. Then we will see. He may be better in a few days." He advanced to the bed, gently but firmly pushing Byrta aside.

"I have medical training," she said, bristling.

"I have trained in the Great School."

"Which is run by trimartyrs. Their faith is not welcome in Almissia."

Gudrun's scalp tingled with fear and anger. "Enough!" she said. "Byrta and Dunstan, you must leave. My husband's dignity does not allow for any but his wife and a trained physician to see him." As she said it, it became urgently true. The room smelled of sour sweat and trapped stale breath, the bed a mess of dirty blankets. "Wait outside. Osred will advise you when he has finished his examination."

Dunstan set his jaw forward, but Byrta quieted him. "My lady," she said, her bright-blue eyes locking with Gudrun's. "I understand you are uncertain and sad. I would not add to your misery. If you want us to leave . . ."

Gudrun nodded, chest pounding. Byrta smiled at her slightly—there was stone beneath it—and took Dunstan with her. "We will be in the great hall," she said as she closed the door behind her.

Alone with Osred, with Athelrick sleeping, Gudrun felt her desperation wane. Osred led her to the carved wooden chair by the bed and helped her to sit. Then, crouching in front of her, he said, "Tell me his symptoms."

She described the last few days to the physician, and gradually his expression softened with a pity that terrified her. Her heart grew colder and heavier. At last he said, "Dunstan is right. You should send for Bluebell. You should send for all his daughters. They will want to see him."

"You think he will die?" The words rushed and mumbled against one another, but he understood her nonetheless.

"A malady that comes upon the brain this way is serious. I have heard of such an illness before. The fits will grow shorter, the sleeps will grow longer. Until . . ."

Her veins hardened. The forgotten certainty of death was upon her with steely force. But through it glimmered self-preservation. If Athelrick was to die, what would become of her, surrounded by enemies who masqueraded as friends to please the king? She needed someone on her side. Someone *by* her side. And long before the king's daughters arrived, greedy to turn her out of the king's bowerhouse.

"My lady?" Osred's voice roused her from her dark reverie.

She turned her face to him, forced her swimming eyes to focus.

"Shall I send for his daughters?" he asked.

"No." The strength of her voice surprised her. "Send for my son."

CHAPTER 1

B lood. It smelled like the promise of something thrilling, as much as it smelled like the thrumming end of the adventure. It smelled like her father when he came home from battle, even though he had bathed before he took her in his arms. Still the metal tang of it lingered in his hair and beard, and as she smashed her skinny, child's body against his thundering chest in welcome, he smelled to her only of good things.

Now that she was a woman and knew blood intimately, Bluebell loved and feared it—and appreciated its beauty splashed crimson against the snow.

The air was ice, but her body ran with perspiration beneath her tunic. Her shoulders ached, as they often did if the skirmish was fast and intense. Around her, twelve men lay dead; ten men stood. *Her* men still stood, as did she. Always.

Thrymm and Thrack, her dogs, nosed at the bodies delicately, their paws damp with powdery snow. They were looking for signs of life, but Bluebell knew they would find none. The ice-men hadn't had a chance: They were on foot, trudging up the mountain path, no doubt to attack the stronghold that managed the beacon fire and kept watch over the northern borders of Littledyke. Bluebell's hearthband were mounted, thundering down the path from the stronghold. They had speed and momentum on their side. Four of the raiders had fallen to the spear before Bluebell had even dismounted. Swift, brutal, without cries for pity. Death as she liked it best.

Bluebell crouched and wiped her sword on the snow, then rubbed it clean and dry before sheathing it. Her heart was slowing now. Ricbert, whom she had collected from his shift at the stronghold, called to her. She looked up. He was kneeling over the body of one of the fallen raiders, picking it clean of anything valuable. She rose, stretching her muscles, joining him along with the others, who had been alerted by the sharp tone of his voice.

"Look, my lord," Ricbert said. He had pulled open the tunic of the dead man to reveal a rough black tattoo beneath the thick hair on his chest. A raven with its wings spread wide.

Sighere, her second-in-command, drew his heavy brows together sharply. "A raven? Then these are Hakon's men."

"Hakon is dead. His own brother murdered him," Bluebell said sharply. Hakon the Crow King, they called him. The only man who had come close to killing her father in battle. Brutal, bitter, the ill-favored twin of the powerful Ice King, Gisli. The man whose face Bluebell herself had mutilated with an unerring ax throw before helping to deliver him into Gisli's hands. Hakon had been perhaps the man who hated her the most in all of Thyrsland, though it was admittedly a long list. "It's an old tattoo."

Ricbert called to her from another body. "No, my lord. They all have them."

"It means nothing. He's dead." He had to be dead. Gisli was cruel and brutal, but a man to be reasoned with; Hakon lacked his brother's intellect, acted on every raw impulse. Dangerous as an injured wolf, in love with war and chaos. Thrymm and Thrack had loped over to join her, their warm bodies pressed against her thighs. She reached down and rubbed Thrymm's head. "Come on, girls," she said. "Let's get off this mountain."

She turned and stalked back toward her stallion, Isern. His big lungs pumped hot fog into the chill air. Bluebell mounted and waited for her hearthband.

Gytha, a stocky woman with arms like tree branches and a brain to match, was last to her horse. As they moved off into the snowlit morning, Gytha said, "They say Hakon is so favored by the Horse God that he escaped his brother's dungeon by magic. They say he has a witch who makes him war spells that—"

"No more of this talk," Bluebell commanded, "or I'll cut someone's fucking tongue out."

Her thanes fell silent; they couldn't be certain she wasn't serious.

Bluebell longed for her father's calm company and good advice, and determined to lead her hearthband home before pasture-month was upon them. If Hakon was alive, then he had to be found and stopped. Her father would know what to do.

A noise in the dark. A furtive knocking.

Bluebell sat up, pushing the scratchy blanket off her body and feeling under the mattress for her sword. It took a moment for her to orient herself. She was in a guesthouse that huddled in the rolling green hills of southern Littledyke. They had ridden a long way southwest of the snow-laden mountains that day, into warmer climes, and were half a day's ride from the Giant Road, which would take them home. In truth, Bluebell would have preferred to push on into the evening, but her hearthband were tired and sick of the cold. When they spied a guesthouse in the dip of a valley, under a fine blanket of twilight mist, she'd agreed to stop for the night, even though the rooms were small and dark and the wooden walls whiskery with splinters and sharp malty smells.

"Declare your name and your business," she called, her voice catching on sleep. She cleared her throat with a curse. She didn't want to sound weak or frightened: She was neither.

"My lord, it's Heath. King Wengest's nephew."

Bluebell hurried from the bed. She was still dressed: It didn't pay for a woman of physical or political power to be half dressed in any situation. She tied a knot in her long, fair hair and yanked open the door. He stood there with a lantern in his left hand.

"How did you get past my entire hearthband to the door of my room?"

"I bribed the innkeeper to let me in the back." He smiled weakly.

"Hello, Bluebell. It isn't good news." He paused, took a breath, then said, "Your father."

Her blood flashed hot. "Come in, quickly." She closed the door behind him and stood, waiting. Anything she could endure: The world was a chaotic, amoral place. But not Father. *Don't let Father be dead.*

"You must keep your head when I tell you," he said.

"I can keep my head," she snapped. "Is he dead?"

"No."

Her stomach unclenched.

"But he's ill," he continued. "A rider was sent from Almissia to our war band up on the border of Bradsey. Wylm was called away urgently by his mother."

"Gudrun," Bluebell muttered. The flighty idiot her father had chosen to marry. "She sent for Wylm?"

"I overheard their conversation. King Athelrick is sick, terribly sick."

"And she sent for Wylm instead of me?" Misting fury tingled over her skin.

"Don't kill her. Or Wylm. Rose wouldn't want you to kill anyone. Least of all your stepfamily."

She glared at him. The beardless half-blood in front of her was her sister's lover. Bluebell had assigned him to a freezing, sedge-strangled border town to keep him away from Rose. Three years had passed, and still he went soft and sugary when his tongue took her name. "I'm not a fool," she said. "I'm not going to kill anyone. Despite what my itching fingers tell me."

He nodded. "Wylm left on foot. I don't know if he managed to horse himself since, but he'd be on the Giant Road by now in any case. You're directly above Blickstow here. You can catch him."

Sleep still clung to her so she had to shake her head to clear it, as though the early-morning dark was only given to dreams and this must be one. Why had Gudrun sent for Wylm and not her? What purpose would it serve to separate Bluebell from her father if he was dying? Did she have plans for Wylm to lead Almissia? The thought was ridiculous: Wylm was untried in war, and Bluebell was well loved by Almissia's people. She dismissed the thought as quickly as it crossed her mind.

"Do you know anything else about my father's illness?" she asked, fear clouding the edges of her vision. "Will he die?" He couldn't die. He was too strong. *She* was too strong. She would get the best physician in the country and march him down to Blickstow at knifepoint if she had to.

Heath shook his head. The two lines between his brows deepened. "I know nothing more. But if she has called for her son . . ."

"She should have called for us."

"Perhaps she has. Perhaps she's sent for the others, but didn't know where to find you."

"Dunstan knows where I am. There's only one good route between the stronghold and home. *You* found me." Her heart was thundering in her throat now. "What was she thinking?"

"Perhaps she wasn't."

Bluebell fixed her gaze on him in the flickering dark. "I'm going home. Now."

He helped her pack her things, then followed her out into the early cold. She saddled and packed her horse, who whickered softly. He was a warhorse, not afraid of the dark, but still getting old enough to miss his sleep. She rubbed his head roughly. Thrymm and Thrack sniffed at her feet, straining against their chains.

"At first light, tell Sighere where I have gone, but ask him not to speak of it. We don't know what the future holds for my father, or for Almissia. If an idiot like Ricbert got wind of the idea that Father was . . ." Curse it, she couldn't say the word.

Heath pointedly looked away.

"People would panic. Just don't tell anyone. Urgent business. That's all." She let the dogs off the chain and vaulted onto Isern's back.

Heath grasped Isern's reins. "Wait," he said. "Your sisters?"

Her chin stiffened. He was right: They needed to be told. A chill wind rattled through the trees. She spat hair out of her mouth. While she didn't want to send him to Rose—it was better if they were apart—

she was sensitive to her sister's feelings. This news shouldn't come from a stranger. "Ride at first light to Rose. Tell her to join me in Blickstow immediately."

"And Ash?"

Bluebell frowned. "Get Rose to send a messenger. Ash will likely feel us on the move." Her words turned to mist in front of her. She dropped her voice. "Perhaps she already knows."

"My lord." Heath nodded and stepped back.

Bluebell picked up the reins and urged Isern forward, thundering down to the moonlit road with the dogs barking in her wake.

The night began to lift as Bluebell approached the Giant Road. She glimpsed the first curve of the bright sun as she galloped over a wooden bridge and down toward the wide road. In some ancient misted past, gray paving stones—the length of two men and easily as wide—had been lined up five across for hundreds of miles: from here in the midlands to the far south of Almissia. The giants had laid them in a time before recollection, but now they were cracked and worn, with grass and wildflowers straggling up through the gaps. Bluebell's heart breathed. From here to Blickstow was two and a half good days' ride, directly south. She was almost home.

But Isern would not go farther without rest and water. He was huge and powerful, but she had no desire to drive him into the ground and have to run home on her own legs. Once, a witch princess up in Bradsey had offered to sell her an enchanted horse faster than a hare, but Bluebell had kept Isern: Speed mattered less, in battle, than courage and weight. She reined him in at the edge of the stream and jumped off to let him walk awhile. Her dogs realized they were stopping and ran barking into the stream. When Isern had cooled, she led him to the water and spoke soft words to him. He dropped his head to drink, and she lay herself out on the dewy grass to close her eyes. A beam of sun hit her face, and she could see her pulse beating in her eyelids. She was tired and sore, her thighs aching, but the constant frantic movement had kept her thoughts from growing too dark.

Bluebell wasn't a child. She knew one day her father would die and she would take his place. She had prepared her whole life for the moment, but it had always been abstract, like a story. The real moment—hot and present—had lit a fire in her breast. She wished she had her sisters with her. They would understand. Well, the oldest two would: Rose and Ash. She barely knew Ivy and Willow, the twins. They'd been raised a long way from home after they'd killed her mother by being born. Bluebell wondered if anybody had sent for them; wondered when Rose would hear, when Ash would hear.

"Ash," she said, soft under her breath. She was closest to Ash, who was away at the east coast in Thridstow, studying to be a counselor in the common faith. Ash had glimmerings of a second sight. She wasn't supposed to; she was far too young. Nevertheless, Bluebell had made use of her sister's premonitions once before battle. "Ash," she said again, drawing her eyebrows together, wondering if Ash could feel her words across the miles, vibrating on the sunlight.

Sleep caught her gently, and she dozed lightly against the growing dawn. Then a shower of water made her sit up and open her eyes. Thrymm stood by her, shaking water from her coat. Bluebell pushed the dog away with her foot and rolled over on her side. The dawn light made her stomach swirl. A new day. Perhaps he was already dead. But surely she would have felt it: the sudden absence, a new quiet where his breath had once been. She sat up and rested her long arms on her knees. Isern wandered over and nuzzled her shoulder with his big hot nose. He was keen to be going, too. As keen, perhaps, as she was to catch up with Wylm and find out what dangerous ideas he and his mother were brewing.

The Giant Road was the main trade route through Thyrsland. Even during war, it was busy with traffic. But there hadn't been war this far south since Bluebell's sister Rose had married Wengest, the king of Nettlechester. Ill will had evaporated overnight, and Nettlechester and Almissia, the two largest kingdoms of the seven in Thyrsland, had raised a joint army to keep out the much greater threat of raiders from the kingdom of Iceheart, the icy lands in the far north of Thyrsland. The sparsely populated northern kingdoms of Bradsey and Littledyke were most vulnerable to incursions from Iceheart, but raiders would think nothing of marching south to take the wealthy trimartyr kingdom of Tweening, or the trading hubs of Thridstow. If raiders ever got as far south as the Giant Road, blood would flow freely.

The road wound in and out of woods, wearing sunlight in shifting patterns. The chestnut leaves were thick and green, and the trees bristled with creamy catkins. Pink and white soapwort grew in profusion on either side of the road, ivy crawled across fallen logs, blackbirds and robins sang in the sycamore trees. Life bloomed around her, even as she made this journey toward death. Bluebell urged Isern to canter, then let him walk, then pressed him forward again. Every two hours she stopped—her stomach itching the whole time—to rest him. The day drew out. Around dusk, Bluebell flagged a caravan to stop. The woman at the front of the caravan grudgingly reined in her horses. She wore gold rings on every finger, and a richly dyed robe of red.

"Have you seen a young man, traveling south alone?" Bluebell asked.

The woman's eyes narrowed. "I've seen many travelers today."

"A young man. Dark-haired." *Mean-spirited. Dull-witted. Snide.*

"Less than an hour since I saw a dark-haired man on a bay horse." The woman shrugged. "Could have been your man." She eyed Bluebell's baggage, the dented shield that hung on Isern's rump, the ax and the helm. "Are you going to kill him?"

"No," Bluebell said, kicking Isern forward. With his big stride and some speed, surely she would catch Wylm.

Poor Isern. Even the dogs were exhausted. Even Bluebell was exhausted.

At the crest of the next rise, she thought she saw Wylm. But then the road wound into the trees.

At the trees, she thought she heard his horse's hoof-falls. Long shadows drew across the gray-green road. Robins returned to their beds. Isern began to slow. Bluebell's heart was hot. She didn't want to kill her horse, but she wanted to catch Wylm.

Through the other side of the wood, she saw him on the open road.

She whistled the dogs forward and they streaked ahead, barking loudly.

Wylm slowed and turned as the dogs caught up with him, yapping at his horse's feet. His horse shied, but Wylm held steady. He glanced up and saw her approaching. She urged Isern forward, but he slowed to a walk. This wasn't how she had imagined approaching Wylm. She had imagined thundering down toward him, terrifying him. But Isern had had enough.

Wylm waited. He recognized her now. Was probably carefully thinking up excuses to give her. He would lie. She would be unforgiving.

"Princess," he said as she approached. "Are you looking for me?"

"Don't call me princess," she snarled. "My lord will do. Or Bluebell." She pulled Isern's reins and he gratefully stopped. She dismounted and let him walk to cool down.

Wylm dismounted, too. He extended his hand for her to shake, but she refused it. She took pleasure in the few inches of height she had over him.

"Well, my lord?" he asked.

"My father is dying, and your fucking mother sent for you and not me."

He blinked his dark eyes slowly. Now the lies would start. "Yes," he said.

It took her a moment to realize he'd admitted it. "Why?" she spluttered.

Wylm shook his head. She watched him carefully. Her greatest skill was to judge fast and well, but her greatest failing, she knew, was not to notice change. And Wylm *had* changed. She had in her mind's eye a picture of him from their first meeting. Back then, he'd been a slippery, spotty youth. Now he was a man—not tall, but dense with muscle. Not a child she could push around with ease.

"I've no idea why Mother didn't send for you," he said. "I can't read her mind."

She wanted to kill him for being so flippant: remove his greasy head from his wretched neck. She fought down her anger and nodded once. "We'll travel back together."

He shifted his weight from one foot to the other, the only sign he wasn't comfortable with the suggestion. "As you wish, my lord. It's twelve miles to the next town. I intended to stop there for the night."

Bluebell glanced about. Her dogs had found a soft patch of long grass, and both lay on their sides panting. Isern sagged, his eyes pleading with her to take off his saddle. They could travel no farther.

"No, we'll camp nearby." She indicated the edge of a lake, a mile off. "Over there," she said.

He began to protest, but she interrupted him. "You're not afraid of the dark, are you?"

Wylm lifted his shoulders lightly. "No."

His calm coolness was like a burr in her blood. "Follow," she said. "I have to tend to my animals."

Wylm took a long time to get to sleep. It wasn't the cold night sky above him; cold had long since ceased to worry him. Bluebell had shipped him off to the northern borders the day he turned eighteen, six months ago. It had been an instruction in hardship, as well as an instruction in how his stepsister felt about him.

Rather, what kept him awake was how he felt about Bluebell.

She lay three feet from him, on a rolled-out blanket by the fire. She was on her side, her back turned to him, her hair tied in a knot on top of her head. She'd barely spoken a dozen words to him since they met on the road, and sleep had come to her as though she commanded it. Now he watched her pale neck. It was the only part of her that looked as though it belonged to a woman.

He loathed Bluebell and yet was fascinated by her. There was no more famous soldier in Thyrsland, unless one counted her father. Up at the border camp, they told tales of her reckless courage, of her famous sword, of her ability to take on three or four armed men and still be standing while they lay dead. They called her unkillable. And yet, staring at that bare, white neck, he believed her very mortal indeed.

In the dark, distant woods, a mournful bird cried. The fire crackled softly. The night was still, apart from the occasional soft shudder of the uppermost branches of the ash trees that formed a semicircle around them. Soft, gray dark settled like mist. His face was hot and tight from the fire. Slowly, his eyes fell closed . . .

He woke with a start to a different kind of night. Darker, colder. The fire had dwindled to embers. The sharp-sweet scent of earth rose strongly as the dew fell. And Bluebell was no longer there.

A moment passed, or perhaps only half a moment. He wondered what had woken him, then decided it must have been Bluebell moving off to find a private place to relieve herself. He smiled, wondering if she shit steel. His bones ached from being in the one position, so he rolled on his other side. And fear slashed his heart.

A foot away, a beefy man with a long, tangled beard and a weatherworn mail shirt held a spear point toward him. Over his shoulder, he wore Bluebell's pack.

"You want to die?" the man said in a harsh whisper.

Wylm's hand tightened at his side, looking for his spear. But of course, his spear was an inch away from his nose, in the bandit's hands.

And then Bluebell was there. It happened too quickly for him to put in order. One moment he was alone with the bandit, the next she was towering over the both of them, her face grim in the shadows: a giant, grisly thing fashioned from blood-rusted iron. She made a noise, somewhere between a grunt of exertion and a guttural roar of rage. It was the most terrifying sound he had ever heard, doubling back on his ears as the dogs barked harshly and the sword came down with enough weight and speed to bruise the air.

The bandit fell, onto Wylm, his head split from crown to nose.

The dogs were on the body in a second, at the throat, their fast, eager paws in Wylm's face. He gasped for breath, then sat up and pushed himself to his feet.

Bluebell retrieved her pack and bent to check the body for any further spoils.

"What happened?" Wylm asked.

"I couldn't sleep," she muttered, her bloody fingers closing over a gold shield-boss. "I saw him from over by the road."

"It's a good thing you were awake," he said.

She fixed her pale eyes on him. "I wouldn't have slept through it. As you did."

Wylm thought about defending himself, but saw no point in wasting his breath. He was satisfied, though, that he needn't doubt the stories of her abilities. Perhaps she was unkillable after all. Who had the courage and skill to defeat such a monster?

chapter 2

D*on't dream.*

Ash hauled herself up through leaden sleep to wake gasping in her dark room. The soft hush of the moving sea in the distance. The slow breathing of the women in the other beds. The twitch and pull of her own blood pressure.

But she had done it. She had avoided the dream that had been trying to press itself into her mind for the last six months. She filled her lungs. The room was dim, dawn swallowed by early-morning rain, but Ash didn't dare fall back to sleep in case the dream was still waiting for her. So she rose, tiptoed past the beds around her, and went to the shutter. She pushed it open an inch, letting in a fist of cold air and the smell of damp earth. Rain fell between the bowerhouses in the gray light. Early-morning rain was common here on the southeast coast. It would clear to a fine day, the gulls would spread their wings to dry on the gable finishings of the great study hall, and the grim darkness would be forgotten. But the clouds in Ash's mind would not lift so easily. Only two days had passed now since the last time she stopped herself having the dream. Before that four days. Before that eleven. It was becoming more urgent; of that there could be no doubt. But if she let herself dream it, then she would know what it was about. And every sign told her she did not want to know.

Knowledge was irreversible.

Ash closed the shutter and sat on the end of her bed to plait her long, dark hair; hand over hand in practiced movements. A gust of battle-keen north wind buffeted the shutters, and one of her bower-sisters stirred, then settled again into untroubled sleep. Ash opened the chest at the end of her bed and pulled out a dress to go over her shift; she belted it on tightly and pinned on a long, green jacket. Then she slipped into her shoes and quietly left the bowerhouse, closing the door behind her. She stood for a moment under the gable. The sudden rush of damp cold pierced her warm clothes, and the rain fell steadily. Head down, she dashed across the muddy wooden boards to the great study hall, careful not to slip. She pulled open the heavy doors and hurried inside. The doors thudded closed behind her, shutting out the cold and the wet. In the dry, firelit room, she listened to the rain falling on the tiles, above the high, arched ceiling. Rain spat down the chimney hole and hissed onto the fire, freshly lit by the new scholars. Ash remembered her first year here, how much she'd hated rising early to light the fires and change the rushes and cook the breakfasts. Her father was a king; for her to be servile was unnatural, like speaking in another tongue. But she'd soon grown used to it and come to appreciate the lessons it taught her. To know the common faith and practice it in the community—whether it was offering medicine or advice or a soft shoulder for sorrow to spill upon—meant understanding how the common people lived. Besides, the first difficult year had passed soon enough. Now she was in her fifth and final year of study.

She sat heavily at one of the long tables where they took their lessons. Behind her were shelves and tables overflowing with vellum scripts, but Ash read only grudgingly, and most of their lessons could not be captured in words. Here at this scarred wooden table, she'd listened to the accumulated wisdom of many counselors, earned from their many years of practice. The stories she had heard would never leave her: the crushing grief of mothers who had lost their children; the ordinary cruelties men and their wives were capable of toward each other; miraculous cures for diseases and daring rescues of babes from their mother's body. Of course, they had talked about the common faith, too: the observances that structured their year, how to prepare for mother's night, or the proper way to honor the Horse God on his festival day. They had even talked about the trimartyrs, the new faith that was growing roots in Thyrsland, and how they could work alongside these pilgrims if they had to—though pilgrims were notoriously narrow of mind and dismissive of women. Bluebell was fond of calling the trimartyr religion a woman-hating death cult, and it was true that their stories were grim, their practices relished hardship, and they had deposed and beheaded a queen before taking over the kingdom of Tweening. It was no wonder Bluebell hated them.

But one lesson Ash had never learned at study hall was how to manage a prescience so insistent it threatened to drown her. Because she wasn't supposed to have any prescience. She was far too young and inexperienced.

"You're up early, Ash."

Ash looked up. It was her teacher, Myrren, a tall woman with an age-spotted face the shape of a perfect oval. Ash's pulse quickened in her throat, as though Myrren could read her thoughts. But Myrren couldn't read thoughts: She had been clear about that at their very first lesson together. "We are not magic," she had said. "We are only people who read other people well. Do not make the mistake of thinking you are a seer. It takes many, many years to become a seer. And some of you, like me, will never feel the stirring of the sight."

The stirring of the sight? For Ash, it had never *stirred*. It had sprung up like an ocean squall on her fifteenth birthday. Some said that the sight was a forerunner of other, greater powers. Ash found that notion terrifying.

"I couldn't sleep," Ash said, rubbing her eyes as evidence.

Myrren looked at her closely. "A poor night's sleep is a troubled woman's burden. Is something on your mind?"

"No." Ash kept her face studiously blank. "Alice was snoring."

Myrren's mouth twitched into a smile. She placed a knotted hand on Ash's shoulder. "I'm going to see a woman in town. She has a fever and is managing on her own with a small child. I promised I'd call at first light. Do you want to come with me?"

Ash nodded and rose. Most of her studies now were given over to working in the field, mostly in the town of Thridstow but often enough in the countryside. She preferred the town. She preferred to be around people and movement, and her dearest hope was that—at the end of her studies—she could return home to Blickstow and be near family and friends. Her post was yet to be decided, though. A wise and fearsome counsel of crookbacked men and women would make that judgment on her final day, based on her history here.

She and Myrren each took a cloak from by the door, the gray-green cloak that signaled their profession, and headed out into the drizzly morning.

Somewhere behind the clouds the sun was rising, and blue burned through on the western arch of the sky. The study hall and its buildings lay on the outer edge of the town. They picked their way through muddy paths, past the butcher and the cobbler, the alehouse and the smith. The town smelled of damp, of sea salt, of coal smoke and fermenting flowers. Layers of smells; sweet, muddled evidence of people and their lives.

Myrren led her to the front door of a little boardinghouse with cracked wooden boards that were chinked with moss. She let herself in and Ash stood for a moment behind her, eyes adjusting to the dark. Myrren closed the door quietly, but a bleary-eyed woman with her hair tied tightly in a scarf bustled out.

"Can you be no quieter?" the woman said.

"I thought I was being quiet," Myrren answered, drawing herself up very erect. "I'm here to look in on Ingrid and the little one."

The woman indicated the corridor. "You know where she is. She coughed all night. I barely slept a wink."

Myrren thanked her and moved down the corridor. Ash smiled at the woman, but received no smile in return. She and Myrren entered a miserable room with a drafty shutter, a choking fireplace, and threadbare rugs. In a bed on the floor lay a young woman racked with coughing, and a little boy about three years old. Ash couldn't help but compare the child with her niece, Rowan, who had come with Rose to visit Ash on the first full moon of mud month. Rowan was plumparmed and tall, with shining dark eyes and rosy cheeks. This little boy was pale and small, a bird fallen too soon from the nest.

While Myrren knelt to tend to Ingrid, Ash stood back to watch. The itching started low in her stomach. She never knew why this ability was called the sight, for she always experienced it viscerally, not visually. It shuddered through her body, knowledge seeping into her mind the way seawater seeps into a sinking boat: always faster than one fears. Myrren's words became muffled behind a sussuration of whispering voices, none of them clear enough to hear properly. But in an instant Ash knew with absolute clarity the sick woman's Becoming—she would die by the end of the week. Worse, the child would catch her sickness if he stayed with her until nightfall this day. Then he would die, too.

As quick as the feeling came, it withdrew. The real world was clear and present again, but her body ached from calves to neck, as though she had held it tensed for hours. Myrren was giving Ingrid one of her remedies—Myrren was the acknowledged expert in herbal medicine—and reassuring her she would be up and about in a day.

"Do you not think," Ash blurted, "that the child should go somewhere else while his mother recuperates?"

Ingrid turned to her with anxious eyes.

Myrren frowned, her face still in profile to Ash, not meeting her gaze. "There's no need, Ash."

"But the illness—"

"No need, Ash," Myrren said forcefully, but quietly. She smiled at Ingrid and then the child. "You two are better off together."

"I don't want my boy to get sick," Ingrid said. "I can send for my sister. We've not spoken for many months, but she would come if it was urgent." Her words were punctuated by wheezes.

Myrren turned to glare at Ash. Ash forced a cheerful smile, even though her blood was thundering in her heart. "If Myrren says all will be well, then all will be well," she said tightly.

As they returned to the study hall, Myrren admonished her in a soft voice: Mothers and children belong together. The woman would recover quicker with her child to remind her of her responsibilities, and a separation at this stage would make her miserable and prolong the sickness. Ash heard, but didn't listen. She had long since realized that no elderly counselor—especially Myrren—would tolerate hearing about her premonitions. At best they would dismiss her; at worst their jealousies and fear would see her packed off to some dungheap community to learn humility. Ash went to her own room, waited ten minutes, then returned to Ingrid's house.

This time, the child was playing on the floor among the moldy rushes, pretending to make soup in a cracked pot.

Ingrid blinked back at Ash from the bed, fear making her pupils shrink. "You came back." Her skin was white and clammy.

Ash sat on the edge of the wooden bed frame and put a hand on the woman's shoulder. Her heart sped. "You are sicker than Myrren thinks."

"I know," the woman said. "I can feel it. A darkness . . . here." She pressed her hands into the triangle between her lower ribs, causing a long coughing fit. Tears welled in her eyes. "I'm going to die, aren't I?"

Ash turned her gaze to the little boy. He hummed a tune to himself.

Ingrid caught the direction of her gaze and began to sob.

"Is there somebody who can come for him?" Ash asked.

"How am I to let him go?"

"By telling yourself that, in him, you will live still. And in his children, and in their children." Ash measured her tone calmly, even though her own heart was clenching. "We all die, Ingrid. We are here but a brief bright moment then thrust out again into the darkness. To leave our trace in the light is the best thing we can do." Just as she had been told to say. The sentiment was supposed to bring much comfort, but Ash found no comfort in it herself. Perhaps when she was older she would feel it, but now she was as terrified to die as a cow in a slaughter pen.

Ingrid nodded, catching her breath. "My sister Gyrda lives outside town, behind the mill. Could you send for her?"

"I'll go to her myself." Ash rose. "But you must never tell anyone I came to you. Nor must she."

Ingrid shook her head. Her body trembled and hunched, struggling with terror and sorrow. "Can I cuddle my boy until she comes?"

"Of course."

Ingrid hesitated, then said, "When will I die?"

Ash looked at her. *The day after tomorrow, as the sun disappears behind the town.* But she said, "I don't know."

The little boy had scrambled onto the bed, and Ingrid reached for him with shuddering arms. "A lifetime of kisses," she said to him, her voice breaking.

Ash couldn't watch. She turned away and headed outside.

That evening she took comfort in the company of her friends, although she couldn't confess to any of them what she had done. Alice and Pansy, with whom she had started her studies four years ago, drank with her in the dining hall and cheered her with stories and comical impressions of their teachers. Ash flirted subtly with Conrad, one of the first-years. He was sweet on her, she knew, though she still wasn't sure she returned the feeling. The clatter and clamor of movement and voices both revived and soothed her, driving away her sadness, her fear of the dream, her growing apprehension that something dark crept behind her. Something uncontrollably expanding in every moment; a sentient, elastic thing not to be contained between her two small hands.

A rainy dawn broke two more times with Ash happily dreamless. On the third day, she woke early to silence: no rain. She plaited her hair and pulled on her cloak to walk down to the cliff's edge and see the sunrise.

The sky was pale and high, the morning cold, but not cruelly so. On the horizon, blue-gray clouds gathered, veiling the sun as it rose from behind the ocean. Ash followed the pebbled path up to the cliffs, then walked a little farther north where she knew of an outcrop of flat granite, perfect for sitting and watching the dawn.

Thyrsland was a large island, separated by icy straits from a sprawling continent where traders and second sons hunted their fortunes among the many towns and tongues of other kingdoms. It was a foolish person who did not come to love and respect the sea.

But for Ash, it was something more. The rush and draw of the sea always made her feel settled, as though it knew something about her that the sky and the earth did not. As a child, she had spent a month recuperating from illness at a family friend's house on the southern coast of Almissia. Every day she had spent hours sitting on the grass near the cliff's edge, watching the sea move, until it grew so cold she was called inside. She had no doubt the sea's rhythm healed her.

The wind picked up; the gulls screeched overhead. Ash closed her eyes and breathed the raw scent of the morning.

Light broke over the clouds and pressed gold on her eyelids. She opened her eyes to see the first orange-gold bow of the sun. A sharp shred of the dream flashed into her mind: a cliff, an orange light, fire and claws. She shook herself, put her hands on the rock to feel the earth and keep herself on it.

"Hello there!" A distant voice, calling.

Ash turned. Conrad was trudging up the path toward her, his hands in the pockets of his brown tunic, his shoulders hunched against the cold morning air. She was glad to see him, to have ordinary things to fill her mind. Her panicked heart slowed and she rose and came down the path to greet him.

"Good morning," she said with a smile.

He nodded once but didn't smile in return, making her cautious. The wind tangled in his soft brown curls. "I've been looking for you," he said.

"A fine clear morning." She gestured to the rising sun. "I couldn't stay in bed and let it go unwitnessed."

He glanced over his shoulder toward the study hall, as though he feared they were being watched.

"What is it?" she said.

He smiled weakly. "I overhead Myrren talking to some of the elder counselors this morning when I was lighting the fires. About you."

A coil of guilt in her stomach. "I see."

He wouldn't meet her gaze, squinted his dark eyes against the sun. "They say a woman in town died yesterday afternoon. Her little boy was nowhere to be found. They eventually located him at his aunt's house. The aunt said you had arranged for him to be there—that you had seen his mother's death, and his, too, if he wasn't moved."

Ash swallowed hard. "Yes." Why had Ingrid's sister gone back on her promise not to speak? She had probably crumbled the moment Myrren set her gray gaze on her. Old age was to be feared, and Ash was too young to frighten anyone into silence. "Did they sound angry?"

He hesitated, then said, "I couldn't read their voices. Angry, perhaps. Myrren certainly was. But the counselors sounded . . . puzzled." He shrugged. "Worried."

"For me, or for themselves?"

"Impossible to tell."

Ash chewed her lip, glancing away to the sea.

"Ash," he said slowly, "I've been taught one can't use second sight until . . . Well, you're only a year older than me. You saw her Becoming?"

She considered him in the golden light. The desire in his eyes was gone, squeezed out by fear. Magic was associated with age, not youth. The old counselors who had studied for years squeezed tiny drops of magic out of grand rituals. Power this young . . . Well, that was associated with undermagic: the same magic, but wielded outside rules, outside society, by brain-bent loners around whom superstitions and wordless dread grew.

"Thank you for the warning," she said.

He waited a moment, to see if she would say anything else.

"I need to think," she said kindly. "I'll see you back at the study hall."

Conrad nodded, his dark eyes careful not to hold hers too long. She watched him retreat then turned her attention to the sea once again, to the orange sun low on the horizon. Here it was, her chance to tell them what was happening to her. The dream, the constant interference of the sight, the hollow fear that inhabited her as strange powers woke in her. Only her sisters and Byrta knew of her ability, and none of them guessed at how fast and wild it grew. Perhaps the elder counselors might even help her.

The sea roared. The sun was bright on her cheeks.

And then a voice was in her head.

Ash.

Just one word: her name. But with it a cascade of sensations: Bluebell, lying on the grass by a stream. Her sister's body ached, but not from battle. Inside her heart beat a bruising dread.

Father was dying.

The sensations lifted off Ash, leaving only the fresh morning air on her skin. "Oh," she gasped, and her voice sounded loud in her ears. How could she not know Father was dying? Was the carefully undreamed dream about Father's imminent death? Or had her attempts to suppress the dream also suppressed any but the most immediate and close tremblings of the sight? It had taken Bluebell's direct address to break through.

She had to get home, but how was she to explain to Myrren why she had to leave? Myrren knew no messenger had come for Ash. And she couldn't wait for one to come: It might take days, and Bluebell needed her now. And she certainly couldn't admit she had received a vision as easily as other people took a breath. No scrying pool, as most of the old counselors used, no deep rumination, no sacred fire: just a sudden and certain overlaying of Bluebell's mind with her own.

Ash was overwhelmed with tender feelings toward her sister—her favorite sister, if the truth be told. Ash loved her father, of course, but nobody loved him as Bluebell did.

Another option waited, unconsidered, and Ash turned her mind to it warily. She could simply run. Put off indefinitely facing Myrren over the incident with Ingrid and her son. Her father was dying—and her father was the king of Almissia, the largest and most powerful kingdom in Thyrsland. And when he was dead . . . Well, what would they say? They could not caution her if she was grieving. A counselor's first law was that compassion comes before all else. And when Bluebell was queen, perhaps Ash could beg her not to have to go back . . .

Already her feet were moving. Home to her father's hall.

CHAPTER 3

R ose held Rowan's little hand and was led around the garden.

"This one?" the child said.

"Crocus."

"This one?"

"That's a bluebell."

Rowan nodded solemnly. "Like Bluebell."

"Yes, like your aunt."

"It doesn't look like her."

"No," Rose said, laughing, "it doesn't." Rose turned to see if Wengest was still watching. He was, a lazy smile on his face. He sat on a carved chair he'd had a servant bring out onto the grass. His legs were spread out in front of him, and Rose could see how indolence was making his body change. His torso had softened; it strained against his richly sewn tunic.

Rowan pointed to the next flower.

"Daisy."

"Clever girl," Wengest said. "Come here for a kiss."

Rowan turned and ran toward him, flinging herself on top of him so hard it nearly knocked him out of his chair. He laughed and turned her upside down roughly, while she squealed happily. Her skirt pooled around her middle, revealing two plump white thighs.

The garden behind the chapel had become Rowan's favorite place

since spring stretched awake, and Rose brought her here every afternoon if it was fine. It was unusual for Wengest to join them, though
not unwelcome. Rose lay back on the grass beside them, stroking the
cool blades with the back of her hand. The mingled soft scents of flowers and damp earth evoked layers of memory and anticipation. Spring
had its power.

Wengest wrestled with Rowan. The child should have been born a
boy: She was all wild energy, hot as the midsummer sun, and as strong
and willful as a little goat. She broke from him and bared her teeth and
claws. "I'm a dragon!" she shrieked.

"There are no dragons in Thyrsland anymore. They died out with
the giants," Wengest said, giving Rose a cautionary nod. Her own
father's standard bore a three-toed dragon. Family lore held that
Rose's great-great-grandfather had slain the last dragon in Thyrsland
and that her father's hall had been built upon the bones, and that
was why Almissia was the most powerful kingdom in Thyrsland.
Wengest preferred Rowan to learn about the kings of Nettlechester,
whose far less menacing standard bore the stinging nettle leaf.
Though, admittedly, Rose had been threatened by nettles far more
often than dragons.

"No! I found a dragon bone in the garden," Rowan declared.

Wengest looked at Rose, who shrugged. "I think it was a sheep
bone."

"It's a dragon bone. And *I* am a *dragon!*"

Wengest scooped her up again, tickling her violently. A clatter at
the chapel gate caught their attention. One of the gatehouse guards
stood there.

"Speak, fellow," Wengest said, righting Rowan and putting her on
her feet.

"Again!" Rowan shouted.

"My lord, your nephew has arrived."

Every drop of Rose's blood lit up.

"Heath is here?" Wengest smiled. "Where have you put him?"

His words were a thousand miles away. Rose's ears rang faintly.
Her breath moved roughly in and out of her body; she had never been
so aware of it. *I am alive, after all.*

"In the hall, my lord." The guard dipped his head toward Rose. "He has news from your sister, my lady."

Bluebell had sent Heath to Folkenham? That was a surprise: Her sister had kept them apart for three years. Perhaps Bluebell thought time and distance would cool her love for Heath. They had not. Some days she had tried not to love him but, inevitably, the ordinary misery of her life forced her imagination back to thoughts of him.

Wengest propelled her gently toward the bowerhouse. "Go, Rose. Take Rowan to her nurse. I'll meet you in the hall."

"Can I not come, Papa?" Rowan asked.

"Can she not meet Heath?" Rose echoed, somehow managing to keep her voice steady.

"You know I don't like to do business with the child around," Wengest said with a dismissive gesture. "If he stays long enough to eat, Rowan can meet him then."

Rose scooped Rowan up—the girl grew so heavy—and hurried out the chapel gate. Heath was here. Music in her veins.

Rose found the nurse in the spinning room, and left Rowan there playing with threads on the floor. Her heart sped and she dashed into her bower to tidy her long, dark hair in the bronze mirror. She stopped a second, steadying herself on the bed pole. Breathe in, breathe out. It wouldn't do for Wengest to see her with such a high color in her cheeks, to see the frantic desire behind her eyes. She had never stopped hoping Heath would come back. That she would be able to look on his face again and feel his touch on her skin. But she had carefully hidden those feelings. She mustn't let them slip out from under cover now.

The doors to the hall creaked open under her trembling hands. And there he was. Her heart caught on a hook. He was deep in conversation with Wengest, his back turned to her. His body, so familiar to her yet so long kept from her: his square shoulders, his lean legs. His clothes were dirty from the journey, his long golden hair lank with sweat.

Wengest glanced up and saw her and came to take her hand with a sad expression on his brow. Rose's vision darkened. Her bliss bled away. It was ill news; that's why Bluebell had sent him. Rose felt a fool, young and self-centered.

"What is it?" she said, her voice giving way.

Heath turned, his sea-green eyes fixed on her. "Rose," he said, and his voice was a breath on an ember that had never faded to coal. The heat of her heart was in her face, but cold dread weighed down her hands, gripped roughly in Wengest's fingers.

"My sisters?" she managed.

"Are all well," Wengest said quickly. "Your father, though, is ill."

"Ill?"

Heath tilted his head, almost imperceptibly, to the side, his mouth tightening softly. His adored cheek was lined faintly, not as smooth as it had been three years ago. What horrors had he seen in the intervening years? "Your father is dying," he said, plainly.

An image of her father sprang to mind: his tall, lithe body; his unruly fair hair; his boyish smile. "But . . . I saw him not two months ago. He was here with his wife. He looked well."

"I'm sorry, Rose." He spread his hands in a helpless gesture. "Bluebell rides even now for Blickstow. She wants you to join her immediately."

"Of course, of course."

"Slow down," Wengest said, dropping her hands and standing back. "I can't race off to Blickstow now. I have business here."

"I have to go," Rose said, indignant. "It might be my last chance to see my father. Your ally. The king of Almissia."

"You can't travel alone."

"I traveled here alone five years ago, when we married."

"Women can't wander about by themselves. It will set people talking."

"What do I care for such talk? If I don't go they'll talk, too. They'll say I didn't love my father." Rose became aware Heath was watching them squabble. She felt small.

"I can accompany Rose," Heath said, slowly.

Rose's skin hummed as Wengest considered. Her imagination formed the journey a thousand times in a moment: flashes of caresses, kisses, embraces that crushed her ribs . . .

"Wengest," Heath said, "when Athelrick dies, Bluebell will rule in his place. She would want her sisters about her."

A sour expression crossed Wengest's face. Rose knew what he

thought of women rulers. And yet he was as afraid of Bluebell's power as any of the kings in Thyrsland. She was capable of raising a passionately loyal army quickly and deploying it with devastating brilliance. And her ability on the battlefield was legendary: Rumors circulated that the raiders thought dying by her sword—known as the Widowsmith—was the only honorable way to die at the hands of a Thyrslander.

"You are right, Heath," Wengest said. "It's a politically important moment. I need you there to represent my interests. Rose can accompany you."

Rose was careful not to say anything at all, lest her desire be betrayed by her voice.

Heath nodded. "I'll speak to the stable hands and have two fresh horses for us to ride in the morning."

Rose took a deep breath. "Will you join us for a meal?" she asked Heath.

"I . . . I've been riding nonstop for two days," he said, glancing away.

Her heart thudded uncertainly.

"Not a moment to sit and talk to your favorite uncle?" Wengest said, slapping his shoulder.

Heath smiled weakly. "Let me bathe. Perhaps it will restore me."

Rose watched him leave. The promise of his presence over dinner was a delicious thrill in her heart. Wengest slid his arm around her. "You should go to Nyll. Pray for your father's soul."

Rose turned and caught him in her gaze. "My father does not believe in Nyll's religion." Athelrick ruled through love, not fear. Athelrick was a leader who rode out onto the battlefield to protect his people. Wengest sat at home and ate too much pork fat.

Wengest shrugged. "Your hot tone suggests you take offense. I mean none. But you *will* go to Evening Thought with Nyll tonight." He released her roughly and moved off, closing the doors behind him with a thud, and Rose stood in the hall alone.

The inside of the chapel was dim and smelled of mold. It was the last place Rose would have thought a soul could feel closer to the vast and powerful gods, and yet Nyll claimed all the trimartyrs built little chapels like this. And then they enforced daily, dreary observances like Evening Thought. Every afternoon at dusk, Rose, Wengest, and Rowan came to kneel on the bare floor of the chapel to contemplate each of their soul's fates. Nyll, the head of the faith in Nettlechester, knelt with them. He seemed to enjoy kneeling on the hard ground, as though the bruises on his knees provided the proof of his god that was lacking everywhere else. Maava was a lone male god who ruled with an army of punishing angels and a narrow definition of good behavior, compared with the fluid and nature-based tales of the Horse God and the Earth Mother at the center of Almissia's common faith. Little wonder the trimartyrs weren't catching on. They were no fun.

And yet this was the decision Wengest had made for Nettlechester three years ago. He had perceived the expedience of a religion that held kings as divine. The citizens of Nettlechester became trimartyrs overnight, but in name only. While the people here in Folkenham knew what was expected of them, most of the people in the countryside had no idea they were to believe anything other than the common observances. And most in the small towns quietly and subtly continued as they always had.

Rose glanced at Rowan. The trimartyrs also believed that women were unfit to rule. Rowan would never be queen of Nettlechester. The little girl's dimpled hands were clutched together in front of her, but her eyes wandered everywhere. Through her daughter's dark hair Rose had wound hawthorn blossoms to mark the first month of spring—Rose's own little protest against the dust-dry trimartyrs and their year-round misery.

"Rose," Nyll said with due gravity, rising to his feet, "I am told your father is dying."

No matter how often she thought it, Rose could barely credit it. Athelrick of Almissia's fate surely was not to die of a sickness in his bower, but on the battlefield with a gutful of iron. "They say he is sick, yes," she said.

Nyll licked his lips, as though tasting the sorrow. Lord knew he tasted everything else. He had grown as fat as a pig and as overconfident as a kitchen rat. He had once been deferential, even kind. But he and Wengest were close; they feasted and drank together. Now, Rose suspected, he thought himself well above her. And yet he wasn't brave enough to tell her to unwind the hawthorn from her daughter's hair. Her family was too powerful.

"We should pray for him."

Rose set her teeth. "If it is your will." She endured the prayer with good grace, taking particular delight in Rowan excavating her nose while Nyll tried not to notice. Her knees grew sore. Wengest had already given up kneeling and sat back with his legs stretched out in front of him.

Finally, the prayer was over. Wengest, still sour with her, gave Nyll a meaningful nod and strode off. Wengest was often sour with her, so it was of no moment. He would forget they'd exchanged heated words by bedtime, especially if he wanted to fumble against her body in the dark, which he had been doing often of late, pricked on by the pressure of having no male heir. Rose collected Rowan and attempted to exit. Rowan, deeply involved in picking candle wax drips from the floorboards, squealed indignantly. As Rose scooped her up, her little legs wriggled like fishes.

"Let her play a moment," Nyll said. "Wengest asked that I speak to you about something."

Rose set Rowan down, and the child immediately lay herself flat on the floor to cry a little more in protest.

"What is it?" Rose asked over the din.

Nyll folded his hands in front of him. "It's about the problem of Wengest's heir."

Rose's heartbeat doubled. "The problem . . . ?"

"Yes. You've not given him a son yet."

"Oh." Now Rowan had started to beat an angry rhythm with her skull on the floor. Rose was distracted, caring little for what Nyll was saying. "Rowan, stop that. You'll hurt yourself."

"Your little girl is three. Many months have passed without your belly swelling again."

Rose bit her lip so she didn't mention the way *his* belly had swelled.

"Are you seeking help from someone to avoid having a child?" he continued.

Rose was so infuriated by his meddling that she almost lost her ability to speak clearly by his accusation. "What? No!" She pushed Rowan gently with her foot. "Get up."

"Those of the common faith know how to prevent the quickening. It's an evil in Maava's eyes, though. Have you sinned?"

In truth, Rose knew how to take care not to quicken, as any woman who hoped to control her own destiny did. For a little while after Rowan, she had hoped for another baby and, yes, a boy. Wengest would be satisfied and he might thereafter leave her be. But Wengest couldn't father children, that much was clear. He only thought he could, because it was beyond imagining for him that she had presented him with another man's child. With his nephew's child.

"Your silence speaks to me," Nyll said.

"And what does it say?" she replied, too quickly for kindness.

Nyll forced a smile. "It would be much better for everyone if you accepted you are a trimartyr queen, not a heathen like your sisters. You oughtn't wander off to the village witch every time you need something." His eyes wandered to Rowan, to the small white flowers in her hair. "That is all I shall say."

Rose hid her amusement. How it must stick in his throat that one of her sisters was a common faith counselor and that another was a famous soldier. Then her mouth turned bitter. It stuck in her own throat. She was nothing more than a peace-weaver, a way for Almissia and Nettlechester to stop fighting long enough to secure the south of Thyrsland from raiders. A settlement so promised could not be unpromised without bloodshed. And so she was doomed to return to this chapel every day for Evening Thought and watch Nyll grow fatter and more officious.

"Mama? I'm still hungry."

Rose turned to Rowan. The child's face was awash in tears and snot. "You mean you're hungry again," she said.

"Yes," Rowan said with a solemn nod, "I'm hungry again."

Rose glanced over her shoulder at Nyll. "I shan't need any of your trimartyr help to get pregnant yet, though I thank you for thinking of me. I travel tomorrow to Blickstow with Heath." The words were round and full of promise on her tongue, like cool grapes in summer.

"Perhaps when I get back you can pray to Maava that my husband's arrow finds its target more fruitfully."

Nyll blushed.

She grabbed Rowan's hand and headed out into the twilit evening. At the door to the hall, she caught herself: Here she was looking forward to traveling to Blickstow, and yet it was a journey to say goodbye to her father. But to be away from the dark tedium of life as King Wengest's wife was to breathe again. To breathe so at Heath's side was happiness, no matter through what sorrow it was won.

By nightfall, the hall tables had been erected and a deer spitted over the hearthpit. Wengest's thanes arrived with their wives, who crowded together at the lower table so the children could run about in the empty space at the far end of the hall. The smell of roasting meat made Rose's stomach grumble. A small feast, but a feast nonetheless, to celebrate the return of the king's nephew.

Only the king's nephew didn't arrive.

Rose kept her eyes on the entrance to the hall, her mind only a tenth on the mundane conversation of the other wives. Rowan played with another little girl. They plucked hairs out of each other's scalps, then pretended to spin them on sticks: laughter and tears in equal measure. The mead was sweet and spicy across her tongue, but failed to relax her. Traveling tale-tellers had arrived a week before, and Wengest invited them to perform. One played the harp; the other recited a story about brave deeds and shining treasures. To placate Nyll, they always included a trimartyr tale: one of the gentler stories about the martyr Liava receiving Maava's wisdom from a colorful bird while in exile on an island surrounded by gray seas and skies. A much more palatable tale than the one about how she became a martyr with her twin baby sons, burned alive for their beliefs, pelted with rocks and spittle and insults, until all that was left of them was a pile of charred bones in a rough triangle shape among the ashes. The merry music played on, but eventually became soft and sad as they began a song about a faithless wife and her cuckolded husband. Rose's skin prickled.

Guilt, yes. She was always guilty. Wengest was a good man. She didn't love him, but that was not his fault, and he did deserve love. But it was fear that truly haunted her: fear she would be found out. She glanced at Rowan, firelight in her hair. The little girl loved Wengest so much. For Rose to be with Heath, Wengest would have to be out of their lives. Such an unhappiness to wish upon a child.

The song continued. Faithless wives were a common theme for tale-tellers and balladeers, and yet Rose didn't recognize herself in the description. She didn't have a wandering gaze, nor a sick yearning for young men, nor a sexual appetite that couldn't be fulfilled. She was simply a woman who had unexpectedly fallen in love with the wrong man. The affair, experienced from the inside, was honest and beautiful and completely real. Not a dark stain on a pure man's story.

The meal was served, and still Heath didn't come. Rose ate without appetite, throwing food on top of hunger for reasons that were only practical. Her eyes traveled again and again to the entrance, and her heart jumped at shadows. Finally, she excused herself and went up to Wengest's table. He was deep in conversation with one of his thanes, but looked up with a smile when he saw Rose approach.

"What is it, my dear?"

"Our honorable guest? Heath?"

"Ah, he caught me outside at sunset. He's too tired to join us."

All bright colors bled out of the world. "Oh."

"Don't worry about him." He took her hand. "Look, Rowan is having a lovely time."

Rose glanced over her shoulder. Rowan was playing a hiding game behind the carved wooden pillars with some of the smaller children. She squealed with laughter, and her face was shiny with excitement.

"I'll never get her to sleep tonight," Rose muttered. But then she wouldn't have to deal with Rowan's tired tantrums tomorrow, would she? And it mattered little that Heath hadn't come tonight, because soon they would be alone together for a long time.

Wengest didn't demand she come to his bower that night and for that she was glad. She would not have to endure his rough beard on her cheek while holding the image of clean-shaven Heath in her imagination. Rowan was curled against her side, sleeping fast. Rose would miss her; already she ached with thoughts of the separation. But she would be gone a few weeks at most, and she would have Heath's presence to comfort her. Certainly, at her father's hall there would be little chance for them to meet unseen, and so all her hopes were pinned on their journey. They would avoid the inns where spies lurked everywhere; they would sleep under the more forgiving stars. She closed her eyes tightly and imagined Heath's arms around her, the warm, male scent of him. Then other thoughts intruded. Her father, illness, death, sorrow. Sleep was a long time coming.

The sun did not smile on them. Drizzle oozed through the clouds as Rose and Heath stood in the courtyard waiting for the stable hands to bring them their horses. The leaden sky was in perfect tune with the blanket of gravity under which Rose had woken. Father was dying. This morning the fact was blunt and real.

Wengest stood under the eaves. Rowan stood next to him, clinging to her nurse's leg and whining loudly. The goodbye had already been said and Rose wished the nurse would take the child away and distract her somehow. She helped the stable hand adjust the saddle and was about to mount up when she saw the nurse picking her way across the mud with Rowan wriggling in her arms.

"I've already said farewell to the child," Rose said irritably.

"King Wengest said you're to take her with you."

"What?" She looked sharply at Wengest, who made a dismissive gesture.

"He said the child belongs with her mother."

All Rose's fantasies fell away, leaving behind the ordinary truth: She was a mother before she was a lover. "I see. Well, will you pass her up?" Rose mounted the horse, pointedly not looking at Heath. She didn't want to see her disappointment echoed in his eyes. Rowan was her daughter, after all. The separation would have been hard.

But the freedom would have been sweet.

Now Rowan wriggled and started crying about wanting to say goodbye to Papa while her baggage was hastily fetched. Rose wrangled her onto the saddle between her legs, pressing her close. "Don't fidget so, Rowan. You'll fall."

"Papa?" she said, mournfully, reaching chubby hands toward him.

"Hush, Rowan."

"But I want Papa!"

Rose caught Wengest's gaze and subtly indicated with a tilt of her head that he should come to give his daughter some kind of affection in parting. He shook his head. Rose was used to this: Wengest believed it wasn't wise for a king to show affection in public; that people would think him weak. Rose didn't mind for herself, but Rowan was working up into a fit, her voice growing more desolate. "Papa, Papa!"

"Let's make this quick," Rose said to Heath as soon as Rowan's pack had arrived.

Heath responded by urging his horse forward, and Rose moved off after him. Hot imaginings of intimacy were left on the muddy slope as they trotted down to the gatehouse and out into rain-drenched fields, with Rowan wailing all the way.

The rhythm of the horse settled Rowan eventually, and the rain eased. But distance and travel made talking difficult, and knowing that Rowan was listening constrained Rose to discuss only outward things with Heath. Rowan was famed for repeating what she had heard adults say, with unerring mistiming.

Rose spent most of the day measuring the breadth of Heath's shoulders from behind. She remembered those shoulders, bare and pale. She remembered the smudged black tattoo over his heart: a bird with its feet in its own beak. She remembered pressing her own naked flesh against him, the lightness of his fingertips across her nipples, and the sweet heat of his mouth against her stomach. She remembered it, yes, but the years had drawn a curtain between them. As the day wore on, as she stole glances at him while he kept his eyes resolutely in front of him, he grew to seem a character from a dream. This man, the real father of her child: a stranger at the center of a familiar longing.

The unpredictable weather drove them early to a tall, crooked alehouse in Doxdal, south of the great lakes of Nettlechester and still two long days from Blickstow. Heath stayed with their horses to cool them down, while Rose took Rowan inside to feed her and dry her clothes by the fire. The child always demanded to be held while she fell asleep; it had been scarce a month since she was weaned from the breast. Rose lay beside her on the blanket, watching her eyes flicker and sink, flicker and sink, until finally she was still. Rowan's soft, even breathing measured out the minutes, the first hour. Evening settled in. Perhaps by now Heath had eaten, too, and was sitting downstairs among the noise of men and the spitting fire, thawing his limbs from the long cold ride. He would be thinking of her . . .

Would he not?

But they had been apart a long time. Perhaps his feelings had changed. The thought staggered her. She had felt the proximity of him all day, feet away, her skin aware of his skin. She had assumed such feelings were shared, but perhaps she was being a fool.

A deep, sad current thrilled through her, making her gasp loudly. Rowan stirred and settled again. And why should Heath be constant for her? She was married to someone else. And not just someone: the king of Nettlechester, Heath's uncle. Her fingers went to Rowan's soft cheek, grasping for the last thing in the world unsullied by dissatisfaction. She was trapped, and the truth was crushing. Once, she had imagined that when Bluebell was queen, Rose could ask to come home to Blickstow, not to have to perpetuate this loveless marriage. In her imagination, her sister would raise war against Nettlechester to free her. But now that Bluebell stood poised to take control of Almissia, these imaginings revealed themselves for what they were: childish fantasies. Bluebell would give her life for Almissia. Rose had to give nothing but her womb.

And, it seemed, her happiness.

A creak on the floorboards outside her room made her sit up. She cracked the door open a fraction and saw Heath rolling out his bed against the wall. He had placed on the floor a stuttering lantern that made the shadows of the balcony rail leap.

"Heath?"

He looked up and saw her. Smiled. Love was still there; she knew it with an arrowing intensity. A sob caught in her throat. He came to the door and took her right arm in his hands, his desire compressed into the hot palms that circled her sleeved wrist, sending her heart into a frantic rhythm. But he dared not embrace her. From here, they were visible to whoever cared to look up. And she could hardly bring him into the room where Rowan was sleeping. Sleeping, but listening.

"This is torture," he whispered, dropping his hands.

"I know."

His glance went over her shoulder, to the warm lump of Rowan in the bed. Rose smiled and stood aside, so he could see his daughter properly.

"If she were my uncle's child, then I would know how to behave around her," he said. "But to know she is my blood . . ." He trailed off, glanced away. "I search her too often with my eyes. She's growing frightened of me."

"Be natural with her. She's a friendly child. She won't be frightened for long."

"I couldn't look at either of you today. Happiness so close, but forever denied." The rushlight lit auburn glimmers in his hair.

She gazed at his face, the beloved contours of his jaw, the shallow furrow in his brow. His hard shoulder inches from her soft shoulder. Warm waves of desire magnetized the space between them. Misery and longing mingled to such a high pitch that her chest burned.

"I still love you," she said.

A little sigh and yawn. Rowan. Rose stepped back, and Heath dropped her arm. Rowan sat up, looked around sightlessly, then fell back on the mattress with her eyes closed.

Heath withdrew, dropped his head. "Good night, my lady. I will sleep close to keep you and your daughter safe." He pulled the door shut reluctantly, and Rose returned to the bed.

"Mama?" Rowan murmured, reaching out her hand.

"Here, my love," Rose answered, curling up against her, yearning uselessly into the dark.

chapter 4

 he Giant Road led up and then down the rocky hillsides
and oak groves above the town of Oakstead: the closest
large town to Blickstow. At the end of a full day of travel with Wylm,
Bluebell was exhausted. Her bones and muscles and mind ached. She
hadn't slept properly since Heath had woken her with the news back
in Littledyke. She had been either in the saddle or itching to move,
and her thoughts were constantly turned toward her father. They rode
down the hill into the town—Wylm was twenty feet behind her—
while dusk gathered at the eastern rim of the sky and a thick flock of
starlings swooped low overhead. Oakstead was a forest town: a town
of hunters, not farmers. The people were harder, crueler, than in Blickstow, living in the shadows of wolves.

This was where they would stay the night. She couldn't push Isern
further, and she needed to sleep in a proper bed. The alehouse was
well known to Bluebell, but she had only ever approached it with a
full hearthband around her. Tonight, she had only Wylm to scare people with. She snorted a laugh despite herself. Wylm couldn't frighten
a cat.

A light drizzle started as Isern cantered between the tall front gates
of the town. The stables stood immediately on Bluebell's right and
already Harald, the stable master, was stepping out toward the road
waving to her. Thrymm and Thrack, recognizing him, rushed up with

tails thumping, pawing at his chest, their hot tongues seeking out his hands.

"My lord," Harald said. "Well met."

Bluebell dismounted and handed the reins over to him. "Be kind to him, Harald, he's exhausted." She put her mouth close to the horse's cheek. "Aren't you, my old friend?"

Harald rubbed Isern's nose with a big, hairy hand. "What has she been doing to you, big fellow?"

"We're heading for Blickstow at first light."

"We?"

Bluebell gestured over her shoulder toward Wylm, who walked his horse through the stable gate. "My stepbrother," she said, with a sneer in her voice.

Harald turned his attention back to Isern. "I'll have him ready for you, my lord."

"Can you feed and water my dogs? I want them nowhere near the hunting dogs that crowd the alehouse."

"Of course."

Bluebell waited for Wylm to dismount and hand his horse over.

"This way," she said to him, and led him up the grassy slope toward the alehouse, a dark, wooden building squatting on muddy, rutted ground. The smell of sweet yarrow steam and roasting meat met her nose, and her mouth grew wet at the idea of eating. She pushed open the front door. Every head in the room turned to look at her. Some men smiled, some nodded, others glared at her stonily.

"You've been here before, I take it?" Wylm asked her.

"Many times. I come here with my hearthband to hear cases and settle disputes." She smiled grimly. "There are always disputes. And after those disputes have been settled, there are always dissatisfied men. And more disputes."

The large main room was bathed in firelight, suffused with smoke, and heavy with the smell of damp dog. The wood and finishings were finely wrought: Oakstead was also a logging town, and Oakstead timber and carvings were known even beyond the seas of Thyrsland. Animal-hide rugs covered the floor in front of the roaring fireplace, while long wooden tables lined up beside the cooking pit where a deer was roasting on a spit. Bluebell took a seat, and Wylm seated himself across from her. He was grubby from travel and stank like a goat; she was glad she couldn't smell herself. The alehouse wife—a thin, harried woman named Sinburg—caught her eye, and Bluebell nodded. A few minutes later, warm ale and plates of food landed at their elbows.

"You're traveling light, my lord," Sinburg said.

"I'm hoping to be invisible," Bluebell replied.

Sinburg looked around the room at the many men stealing glances at her. "Not much chance of that." She returned to the bar, and Bluebell started on her meal.

Soon enough, Bluebell could feel the shadow of somebody moving closer. She longed then for Sighere's company, or even panicky Ricbert; for the company of thanes who had been hardened in the fires of battle and who knew how to keep a drunken fool at a distance. For a drunken fool had slid onto the seat next to her and was leaning on his elbow right over her meal.

"I remember you," he said, rubbing his patchy beard.

Bluebell glanced at Wylm. He did nothing.

"You and your father decided I'd been hunting over my boundary, but you didn't even go out and look. I asked you . . . I begged you. And you wouldn't even go and look."

"I have no recollection," Bluebell said, without emotion.

"Well, I have," he said, his voice growing louder, "because since then my neighbor is growing rich hunting on *my* land."

"If you have a dispute to settle, wait until the next King's Hearing and speak to me then." Bluebell didn't allow herself to imagine whether she would be running the next King's Hearing alone.

"That's not until summer." He stood now, leaning over her. She was aware a small group had gathered. "Your father is no wiser than a donkey, and as slow and stubborn."

"Shut your gob, fool!" This was another man, a willowy one with unusually pale skin. He shouldered through the small crowd and grasped Patchy-Beard by the shoulders. "How dare you speak like that to Princess Bluebell?"

"Don't call me princess," Bluebell muttered under her breath, turning back to her meal.

Patchy-Beard pulled back and plunged his fist into Pale-Man's gut. A shout went up, and the others surged forward. Bluebell watched them sidelong, always surprised by how men liked to use their fists. It was so base. Her first instinct was always steel. The room erupted with cursing and yelling, pushing and pulling. Dogs growled and barked. She calmly finished her food, then stood and drew her sword. The ones who noticed backed away quickly with their limbs drawn close, scuttling into corners like spiders. The others moved quick enough as she muscled them aside to find the two men who were the core of the brawl. Pale-Man lay on the floor while Patchy-Beard kicked his ribs. She grabbed Patchy-Beard by his greasy hair and jerked his head back, pressing the edge of the blade against his throat.

His eyes rolled toward her. "Let me go!" he shrieked, struggling against her.

Why couldn't Wylm get on his feet and help her? If she were traveling with her hearthband, there would be at least half a dozen pairs of hands on him by now. But then, if she were traveling with her hearthband, this fight might never have happened.

"Hold still or I'll fillet you, fucker!" she roared.

Patchy-Beard stilled. Pale-Man stood up, coughing and clutching his ribs. The crowd quieted, eager to see what would happen next.

"I don't care if you don't respect me," Bluebell said, "but you will not insult my father with your foul, toothless mouth." She thrust him away from her and he stumbled against an adjacent table. As he righted himself, she turned the point of her blade to the crowd. "Go and sit down, and leave me the fuck alone."

They dispersed, some with eyes averted in shame, some with chests puffed to show they weren't scared of her, even though they were. She sheathed her sword and sat down to return to her drink. The sweet ale hit the back of her throat with a light fizz. She became aware of Wylm considering her in the firelight.

"What?" she said.

"I'm sorry?"

"You're staring. What is it? Have I grown a second head?" He watched her too much. At first she thought he'd developed some misguided affection for her: Plenty of men and a number of women had in the past, despite the fact she had more scars than eyelashes. But there had been no affection in his words or actions.

"No," he said, "you have only the one head." His gaze was dark, oily.

"Then why must your eyes always follow me?"

His eyes didn't flicker. "I know not what manner of thing you are."

"I will be your king, so it would be better for you to choose your words with care."

He smiled. "You are a woman. You'll be a queen."

"I'll be what I damn well please," she said, with a shrug of her bony shoulders.

He snorted with laughter. "You will still be a woman. You cannot be a man."

"Nor do I want to be a man," she countered.

At this he shook his head in genuine bewilderment. "And so we are back to my first observation. What manner of thing are you, Bluebell?"

Bluebell's fingers crept to the grip of her sword, imagining the elastic resistance of Wylm's belly under the tip of the blade. Then there would be the shove and the gratifying give. Then there would be the smell of his blood, and it would be as hot and pretty as blood ever smelled. These thoughts made her feel better and she didn't draw her sword, but neither did she answer his question. The Horse God had given her speed and strength; what else was she to do but turn her arm to war? Not to do so would be dishonor. Why must people question her? Her father never questioned her.

The sadness—forgotten in her anger—returned. Life would go on without her father. She had her sisters; she had her hearthband. But without him, life would be sapped of its muscle and steel, a withered thing. She was only twenty-seven, but tonight she felt older than the Giant Road. Weariness infused her bones. She pushed her plate aside.

"I must sleep," she murmured.

"It's not even dark."

She shrugged. "Good night, worm."

Wylm smiled at her tightly. "Good night, *sister*."

Sinburg took Bluebell to a tiny bedroom at the top of the stairs, with a soft mattress on the floor and no shutters or fire. Dark and quiet. Bluebell turned on her side and, before she could draw a third breath, she was asleep.

Wakefulness came upon her too soon. The room was still dark. She could hear no men's voices, no creaking of floorboards as people moved about. Her body told her it was after midnight, but still long before dawn. She closed her eyes tightly, but she knew she was defeated. She was weary, so weary, yet sleep resisted her. So all that was left was to wait in the dark.

But how could she bear to be still, lying awake in an inn, barely five hours' ride from her dying father? Especially when she suspected they had enemies on the move toward them? The raven-branded raiders had unsettled her. Rumors were everywhere that the Crow King was still alive. The thought filled her with dread. If Hakon learned that her father was weak, that her country was weak, he would do anything in his power to exploit that weakness, and he would do it with all of the sadistic pleasure a disfigured man bent on revenge could feel . . .

Bluebell slipped from her bed—every muscle ached—and pulled on her cloak. She scooped up her pack and cracked open the door. Downstairs, low firelight moved across the walls. Wylm would be down there somewhere, stretched out on a deerskin, sleeping too hard. She wouldn't wake him. Let him realize in the morning that she had gone ahead. This way, she could speak to his wretched mother when he wasn't present to defend her.

Bluebell crept from the alehouse and out into the cool, dark morning. The stable door creaked open, and she approached Isern's stall. He had sensed her and his eyes were open. He walked up to the gate and pressed his nose into her hand. Bluebell's gut clenched. He looked tired and old, and suddenly she couldn't bear to make him go out on the road again in the dark. For the first time since she'd had the news about her father, her throat blocked up as though tears might be on their way.

"My lord?"

Bluebell turned to see Harald approaching. She cleared her throat roughly. "Harald?"

"I heard you come in. I sleep in the loft." He indicated Isern. "Don't make him go out."

"I won't," she said. "I won't."

"I can give you a fresh horse, and I'll bring Isern down to you in a few days."

Words wouldn't make their way into her mouth.

"My lord?"

"Yes," she said, hoarsely, "that would suit me well."

He eyed her in the dark. "You need to get home quickly?"

"I do."

"King Athelrick is a good king. You will be, too. May it be a long time before that comes to pass, though."

Bluebell patted his shoulder warmly. "We are of one mind, Harald."

Within half an hour, she was back on the road with her dogs, leaving Wylm sleeping like a small, pampered child.

The sour smell of ash and the cool chill of morning. Wylm prickled awake. His shoulder was sore from sleeping on it too hard. He rolled over and opened his eyes. Dawn glimmered through the cracks around the shutters. Next to him, a fat dog slept, snoring lightly. Wylm was still tired. He could easily have slept longer, but he wanted to be awake when Bluebell came down. He climbed to his feet and rolled up his pack, setting it by the door of the alehouse. A large bowl of porridge was hanging over the cooking pit, so he fished a bent silver coin out of his pocket to pay for a serving.

The sun was up, the shutters of the alehouse open, and Bluebell wasn't awake yet. This was wonderful. She had relished him sleeping through the thief's approach the previous night; perhaps he should find a disgruntled hunter to creep into her room and put his fingers under her blanket.

He wouldn't do it himself, though. He valued having a hand attached to each arm.

Wylm finished off the porridge and went outside to sit in the weak morning sun on a carved wooden bench. A strong smell of damp earth filled the air. He spent the time sharpening his blade and watching the town come awake for the day. The door of the alehouse creaked open and he looked up, expecting Bluebell. But it wasn't Bluebell. It was a silver-haired man in dirty hunting greens, a sleek dog pressed against his thigh.

"Morning," the man said.

"Morning."

He sat next to Wylm and put his pack between his knees. A few seconds later a woman, obviously his wife, joined him. She began going through arrows one at a time, checking for bent shafts and loose fletchings. The man waxed his crossbow string while his dog sniffed around the foundations of the alehouse and pissed every four inches.

Wylm was itching to get going. His mother was expecting him. Perhaps he should go and wake Bluebell. He stood. Hesitated.

"Where's your ugly friend this morning?" the silver-haired man said.

"She's not my friend," Wylm countered lightly. "She's my stepsister. She's the king's daughter."

The man laughed. "I know who *she* is. A couple of the men last night were speculating if you were her lover. But you're her brother, eh? No climbing aboard?"

Wylm shuddered. "No."

"She usually travels with a pack. Like a wolf." He lined his bow up with his eyes and ran a fingernail over the nocks.

His wife picked up the thought. "When she comes in with just one fellow . . . Well, we start to talk."

"Surely no man could be interested in . . . doing that. With her."

The silver-haired man raised an eyebrow.

"Oh, she has a lover," his wife said, "though nobody knows who it is."

Wylm laughed. "Well, I hope he wears a mail shirt in bed. And mail pants." The thought of Bluebell having any kind of love affair was hugely, hopelessly wrong. "I should go and wake her up," he muttered. The hunting couple didn't notice him leaving.

The warmth inside enveloped him. The fire was stoked again, and all of the sleeping bodies were up and off the floor and packing for travel or hunting. He found the alehouse wife tending to the porridge pot.

"Where's Bluebell?"

"Top of the stairs. You'd better knock."

"I will."

He took the stairs two at a time, then paused outside her door. Wondered for a moment. Did she undress to sleep? What was under those stinking travel clothes? White skin? A pair of small, firm breasts? He chased the thought away angrily. She was probably covered in scars and tattoos to match the ones on her arms. He lifted his hand and rapped hard.

No answer.

It occurred to him that she might be dead. She had enough enemies, after all. It was not the first time he had imagined her dead, but now, in the light of Athelrick's mortal illness . . . Why, he would have a claim on the throne, would he not? His mother would be the king's widow, the other daughters were not soldiers like Bluebell, and plenty of folk in this land were more comfortable with a man on the throne.

He pushed open the door, heart speeding.

Not dead. Gone.

Wylm cursed, turned on his heel, and ran back down the stairs. Let himself out and made for the stables. The silver-haired man's dog barked at him, snapped once at his heels. Wylm kept running.

"She left hours before dawn," Harald said as Wylm crashed through the stable gate. "You won't catch her."

"The sneaking dog," Wylm spat.

Harald eyed him coldly in the dim light. "I should cut your throat for that, but I won't. I'm sure Bluebell will do it herself one day soon."

Wylm reached for his saddle. "I'm her brother. She can't kill me."

"You may be right." Harald shrugged. "But there'd be few that cared if she did."

Wylm mounted up and urged his horse forward. He wouldn't catch Bluebell, but he could still get there in time to protect his mother from the worst.

chapter 5

B rimheath was one of the largest port towns in Thyrsland
and it lay twenty miles south of Ash's study hall. The sun
had warmed to high, bright yellow, casting an unforgiving light on
her decision to run back home. If it could be called a decision and not
an impulse. As her feet, swollen from heat and walking, carried her
down toward the docks, she wondered if she should return to face
Myrren and the elder counselors.

A thought shot across her mind: They wouldn't understand because they couldn't, because they were lesser than her. Then she chas-
tised herself for her pride. She was just a girl. Young, unschooled,
desperate to see her father before he died.

The sea roared, out past the cliffs, but was gentle in the estuary,
where dozens of ring-prowed longships skimmed past one another
on their way in and out of the river. Their bright sails and canopies
dazzled against the gray-blue water. The voices of the shipmasters,
shouting at the crew, were stolen by the wind. The docks lined the
estuary for two miles, the wide wooden planks standing firm against
livestock and barrels and baskets of goods—wood, furs, spices, deli-
cacies, treasures—being loaded on and off vessels. She watched it
from a distance and it was curiously quiet, although once she was in
among the jostling and noise she wouldn't be able to think clearly, so
she took a moment now.

A deep breath brought with it the choking odors of fish, carrion, and rubbish. She only had to find a vessel going upriver. The Wuldor River, wide and calm, led from here to Blickstow—the Bright Place—which sat between green fields and below the gleaming white ruins of the giants. She hadn't seen it in three years, since her father's wedding. Home. *Home.*

She started down the hill, jumping out of the way as a caravan of trading carts streamed past her, all horses' breath and clattering hooves. A hawk circled overhead, riding the wind, the sun on its wings. The grass on the shoulder of the road was overgrown, tipped with yellow seeds. It tickled at her ankles as she descended, and the sound of the docks grew louder and clearer in her ears.

The smells of the docks overwhelmed her. Seaweed and fish and spices. A crowd of men were rolling barrels onto a vessel with a striped-yellow-and-gold canopy, its sail rolled tightly at the crosstree. She approached hesitantly.

"Out of the way, please," one of the men said.

"I'm looking for a passage to Blickstow."

He gestured to an indeterminate place in the distance. "We're only going as far as Whitebyre. Try Alchfrid."

Ash looked around, confused.

"Farther up the docks. His ship has a green-and-white canopy and a hawk carved on the prow."

She stepped back onto the thoroughfare, nearly colliding with four men carrying a hefty wooden chest. She waited for them to pass, aware that somebody's eyes were on her.

Ash turned slowly. On the other side of the thoroughfare, under a dirty moleskin awning, sat a snow-haired woman with veiny hands clutched around a staff. Two men were queued up to buy journey charms from her, but her gaze was fixed on Ash. The sea wind gusted, rattling her awning and allowing shards of sun into the shadows. Gulls called to one another. Ash glanced away, moved farther up the docks looking for Alchfrid's ship.

She found it a few moments later. The vessel was long and sleek, with a bright, taut canopy and a belly full of chests and baskets. Even the crew looked well kept, in clean clothes and with neat beards. Now she only had to convince them to take her to Blickstow.

A tall, thin man with hair graying at the temples stood at the front of the vessel with a foot resting on the hawk's head carving as he oversaw the loading of the cargo. Ash presumed this was Alchfrid and approached the edge of the dock.

"Hello," she called to him. "I need a passage to Blickstow."

He turned and an expression of irritation crossed his brow and then was gone. "You're traveling alone?"

"Yes." For some reason, her heartbeat quickened in her throat.

"Certainly. We push off in one hour. You can sleep under the canopy with the goods."

Relief washed through her. "Really? Thank you! I'll pay you when we get there. I have a—"

"No need," he said, with a wave of his hand. He smiled, and his lips pulled back over his teeth. "A lady traveling alone is always welcome on my ship."

She was shoved out of the way roughly by a man backing into her with a large barrel. She sidestepped and moved back onto the thoroughfare to see if the old woman was still watching her. She was.

Ash moved closer, curious. The old woman was in the middle of a common faith working, muttering her charms onto colored stones and handing them to the sailor who knelt in front of her. And yet, through half-closed eyes, her focus was fixed on Ash.

The sailor took his charms and moved off. The old woman beckoned Ash with her eyes.

"You're watching me," Ash said, approaching.

"Because you're not watching yourself, counselor," the old woman said.

Ash realized she was still in her green counselor's cloak. Perhaps that was why Alchfrid was happy to have her on his ship. Some sailors thought it was good luck to have a representative of the common faith aboard.

"No," said the old woman, picking up the thread of her thought, "Alchfrid wants something quite different from luck. Make no mistake, little counselor, you will pay many times over for a journey with him."

Ash thought about that thud at her throat and knew the woman was telling the truth. She was too remote from her own prescience, had spent too much energy holding back the tide that threatened to drown her. "I have to get to Blickstow," she said.

"Four hundred yards in, there is a vessel taking donkeys upriver. They will take you." The old woman spread her knotted hands. "Though it won't be as nice as Alchfrid's ship."

Ash nodded. "Thank you," she said.

But before she could turn to leave, the old woman took a knotted hand off her staff and reached slowly for Ash's fingers. Ash offered her hand warily.

The old woman's touch was cold. "What are you trying not to see?" she said.

Ash's vision tunneled. The question felt like falling, and the sharp edge of the dream needled her with colors of fire and blood. "I don't know," Ash whispered, though she suspected she did. She suspected the dream told her something of her own life to come, something that would change her until she no longer knew herself.

The old woman narrowed her eyes and tilted her head to the side, like a crow sizing up a worm. "The greatest dishonesty is that which we serve to ourselves," she said. "Your Becoming belongs to no other, little counselor. What use not to look upon it?"

Despite the bright sun and blue sky, a dread like winter-death fell upon Ash. Her skin prickled into gooseflesh.

"Come on, you've had long enough," a gruff voice said.

Ash turned to see a sea-bitten sailor waiting for a journey charm. She stepped aside and finally the old woman's gaze released her. Ash was free to go.

She made her way down the dock, carefully avoiding Alchfrid's ship, though she still longed for the cover of the sturdy canopy. The ships grew less and less impressive the farther she walked down the dock, until she found a low, wide vessel being loaded with donkeys. She guessed, with a sinking heart, that this was the boat the old woman spoke of. No canopy, no carved hawk, no bright sail. Just a tattered oilskin, crudely hewn wood, and a dun-colored sailcloth. It smelled of pitch and donkey shit. She paused on the dock, contemplating two days on the vessel.

A gray-faced man herding donkeys saw her and stopped beside her. "You need passage?"

She nodded. "To Blickstow."

"You can pay me?"

"At the other end. I can pay you well."

He looked her up and down, rubbed his beard with cracked fingers. "I trust you. Climb on board. There's a seat under the oilskin and blankets behind if it gets cold." His eyes went to the sky to scrutinize it. "At least it doesn't look like rain."

The storm blew in after dark. Murky raindrops fell on the oilskin, rolling underneath until Ash felt damp spreading across the broad boards beneath her feet and seeping into her shoes. The donkeys brayed in protest. Ash would have, too, had she not been concentrating so hard on trying to keep her hands warm. Misery upon misery. The idea of her father's impending death burrowed into her mind like a dank worm. *Mortal, we are all mortal.* If Athelrick could die, then anyone could.

But she couldn't sit under a blanket of fear and sorrow all night, so she tried to cheer herself with memories of him. He had been away at war or counsel for much of her childhood, and when home he was more concerned with Bluebell than his other daughters. An image came to her mind: Bluebell had been fitted for her first set of armor at twelve. Ash had been six, and jealous of her sister. She had found her father's sword and dragged it behind her to the hall where he was briefing his hearthband before heading out. He'd looked up, momentary anger crossing his brow at the interruption. But then he'd laughed and swung her up in his lap, let her sit there while he talked. She'd listened to his voice rumbling in his chest and had played with his long fair hair until she started to doze. He'd lifted her up and taken her to the bower she shared with Bluebell and Rose, and let her sleep with his sword under her mattress, just as Bluebell slept with a sword under hers.

The memory made her smile, chasing away the moldering shadow of death for a little while. She wondered again how her father fared now, what kind of illness troubled him. Quietly, she closed her eyes and reached out with her mind . . . but before she could find him, something dark intervened. An image from the dream. Immediately she backed away, opened her eyes. Rejoined the sodden boat and the stinking donkeys.

Ash pulled her feet up onto the seat, wrapped her arms around her knees, and kept her head down. Sleep wouldn't come, but it was probably better that way. If she didn't sleep, she couldn't dream.

Rowan wouldn't stop fidgeting. Rose grew more and more exasperated as the little girl wriggled and twisted in the saddle, slippery as a fish.

"Will you *please* sit still?" Rose asked her for the eleventh time, tightening her elbows to stop Rowan from slipping off the saddle altogether. They were on a long, straight stretch of muddy road that cut between large flat fields. The sun was high in the heavens' hollow, sparkling off the previous night's rain and lifting green brightness out of the mossy rocks lining the road.

"I'm *tired*," Rowan declared, bouncing angrily against her embrace, getting her hair caught in the row of beads pinned to Rose's dress.

"But if you keep wriggling, you'll fall off and hurt yourself." As it was, they had slowed to a walk. The effort of trying to keep hold of the reins and Rowan at the same time was taxing her. Heath, in good grace, slowed his pace.

"Can't we stop?" Rowan whined.

Rose grimaced. She, too, wanted to rest. She had divided the night between mourning that she and Heath could never be together, and imagining in detail that they were. The world had cooled past midnight before she slept.

Heath reined his horse in and stilled Rose's with a gesture. She looked at him curiously. He turned his attention to Rowan, who shrank a little under his gaze.

"Rowan," he said, "would you like to come and sit on my saddle with me?"

Rowan shook her head, but slowly.

"Go on, Rowan," Rose said. "I'm exhausted."

Rowan looked up at her with big eyes. "I don't know that man."

"He is Papa's nephew."

A blank look.

"Papa had a sister. Heath is her son." Wengest's sister was famed for her affairs in her youth. Heath was her only child, and his red-gold hair told a tale: His father was First Folk, one of the original peoples of Thyrsland who had now been pushed to the margins of both land and thought. This was why Heath remained clean-shaven: His beard, when it grew, was fiery red. And there were still many people who would heap contempt on him simply because of his First Folk coloring.

Rowan was considering Heath now in the warm sunshine. The long grassy fields waved on either side of them, tiny insects caught sunlight on their wings, and dandelion seeds lifted and swirled on the wind.

"Come on," Heath said. "I will keep you very safe."

Rowan nodded once and Rose lifted her into Heath's arms with a sense of relief. Unencumbered, the ride would be infinitely easier.

Heath settled Rowan on the saddle in front of him. Rowan leaned back against him, seeming to enjoy the breadth and safety of his chest. They rode again, this time a little faster. Within twenty minutes, Rowan was asleep, her head lolling against Heath's heart.

"She's asleep," Rose said to him.

"I thought so," he replied, smiling. "She's very warm."

Rose chose her words carefully, aware at any moment Rowan might wake and hear what they said. "I envy her. She looks very comfortable." Which meant, *I would like to be pressed up against you like that.*

Heath was playing his own game of doublespeak. "She is very like you, Rose. Her dark hair and eyes." *Luckily she didn't inherit my coloring.*

"Wengest likes to think she looks like him." *He has no idea.*

They lapsed into silence awhile, the road disappearing underneath them. Then Heath said, "Wengest told me . . . He hopes for a son soon."

"When did he tell you that?"

"I spoke with him at length in his bower, the night I arrived. He was very keen to talk about your sister." Heath glanced down at Rowan.

"Still asleep," Rose said, "but always listening. What about my sister? I presume you mean Bluebell. What did Wengest say of her? Nothing good, I suppose."

"Oh, he is afraid of her, don't doubt it. And with good reason. But he has seen ahead further than I suspect you, or even Bluebell, have."

"What do you mean?"

"When King Athelrick is gone, Bluebell will be queen."

"Yes."

"But Bluebell rules by force of arms. She cannot both fight wars and bear children."

The idea of Bluebell bearing children was ridiculous. But the moment she expressed the thought, she knew what Heath was going to say next.

"Then who will her heir be? Who will rule Almissia when she is gone?"

"I'm the next oldest," Rose said.

"And you're married to Nettlechester. So Wengest will have a claim."

"Rowan could rule Almissia."

"Rowan can't rule. Wengest won't allow it."

"Almissia will allow it. Wengest can't have Almissia."

"Then Rowan would have to defy her father and the alliance would be broken. No, Rose, Wengest needs you to have a son. He needs that more than anything. It solves every problem he has."

Rose glanced at Rowan, who was still soundly sleeping. "He can't."

"I suspected as much."

"He does not suspect it, though. Do you see? He has Rowan: proof of potency." She shook her head. "But our speculation is meaningless. Bluebell will have thought of this, I'm sure. She will know what to do."

"Will she? When I brought her news of Athelrick, she looked as though she had never considered it possible that he might die."

With a pang of compassion for her sister, Rose fell silent, turning

Heath's words over in her mind. The weight of her own responsibility was crushing. Other women loved, married, bore children, and nobody cared how many or to whom. All her decisions, however, were chained to the fates of kingdoms. She wanted, more than anything in that moment, to run. She and Heath could bundle up Rowan and disappear. She pulled her horse to a stop. Heath rode a few yards ahead and then returned, reining in his horse and looking at her curiously. The sun was behind him, gold in his hair. His hands were folded across Rowan's chest protectively. "Rose?"

"There are bandits on these roads. Violent bandits. If we were . . . If all of us were to disappear, Wengest might never find us. Our horses, perhaps, some of our belongings. But . . . Eventually, he would stop looking."

Already Heath was shaking his head. In a low voice, he said, "You think I have not imagined a thousand times what it would be like to be"—he searched for a word—"free? But my happiness is not more important than Wengest's, or Bluebell's." He glanced down at his daughter's sleeping head. "Or Rowan's."

Rose felt chastened. Her cheeks flushed and tears pricked her eyes. "I am sorry, but . . ."

"But the longing is like madness," he said, his mouth pulling down at the corners. "I know. I have been so far from happiness."

She gazed at him, noting how deep the furrow in his brow had become. He had once been a farmer, but then the northern wars had intensified and he had been pressed into military service by Wengest, then sent to a stronghold on the freezing border by Bluebell. Duty was as heavy for him as it was for her. Heavier—because, for him, it smelled like death.

She risked leaning forward, reaching across the distance between them to touch his cheek. "Poor Heath. What have you been through?"

He leaned his cheek into her palm. "You cannot imagine the weight, Rose. We train for any situation, but then in battle unpredictable things can happen. Dust and blood blur my eyes. In a two-minute skirmish, all can be lost. I have seen . . . I could not repeat what I have seen near the ears of a child."

How she wanted to hold him, then. Against her heart. She dropped her fingers to Rowan's dark hair, shining in the sun. "She is precious. The most precious thing I have ever owned."

"And she loves her papa. I will return her to him safely at the end of this sad journey. Come." He picked up his reins and turned. "We still have a long way to go."

chapter 6

The first glimpse of Blickstow always filled Bluebell's heart with fierce pride. Across the newly plowed fields that smelled of lingering winter damp and up the fair, bright slopes where wildflowers were starting to bloom, the tall wooden gates with their fine carvings stood firm against the world. Behind the town stood the giant ruins of some other place now fallen into history. Tall, crooked teeth of dirty white stone—the remains of an arch no living man had the knowledge or skill to fix. When the rising sun touched the ruins, they flushed to orange-gold. Beneath them, she could see the high horned gables of her father's hall, like a pair of mighty arms crossed in defiance of the pale streaky sky.

With the last of her energy, she booted her horse forward at a gallop. Its hooves churned the muddy ground of the ring road that led around the back, through the rear gatehouse and to the stables, closer to the family compound so she wouldn't have to walk through the town. She wasn't in a mood for greetings. Her heart hammered against her ribs as she pounded up the hill and through the gatehouse. She didn't ride into the stables. She dismounted and let her horse drag its reins. Somebody would find it. She began to run over the wooden boards that led toward the back of the compound, her dogs a few feet behind her, barking happily. Past the back entrance to the hall, and straight to her father's bower. Then she stopped, her hand on the door. Perhaps he would be inside, sitting up, looking well again, laughing at her for rushing all this way. Or perhaps he would be dead already, laid out pale and cold. A spear of pain. She reached for her sword, unsheathed it, and flung the door open.

In the second before they moved, Bluebell saw two people by her father's bed: Gudrun and her pompous, oily-skinned physician, Osred, heads bent in urgent discussion. Then they saw Bluebell at the door and jumped apart. Gudrun swallowed a shriek.

From the corner of her eye, Bluebell could see her father. Not dead yet, but not well. He groaned and writhed; she shielded her heart. She would not look at him while these foreigners were in the room with her.

Bluebell turned her attention to Osred. "You will leave. This room. This town. This kingdom. You will return to where you came from, and you will never speak of your time here again."

"I'm only trying to help. Your father is mortally ill. He—"

She lifted the point of her blade, balancing its weight so it came to rest gently beneath his chin. His face was reflected and distorted in the welding patterns. "I do not repeat myself for anyone," she said.

Osred took a step away from her blade, then took a wide berth around her and out the door. Gudrun remained rooted to the spot, thin hands pressed hard into each other.

"Surprised to see me?" Bluebell said to Gudrun, keeping her voice low. "Expecting your son?"

"Bluebell, I . . ."

"Leave me alone with my father."

Gudrun set her chin. "He's my husband."

"He was my father before he was your husband. Get out."

"He needs me."

"You don't know what he needs!" Bluebell shouted. "Now get out or I will fucking kill you!"

Gudrun began to sob, but she scurried out nonetheless, covering her face with her sleeves.

The door swung shut behind Gudrun. Bluebell sheathed her sword and closed her eyes. Robins twittered outside; the wind played with a loose shutter somewhere in the distance. The room was still, quiet except for her father's soft moans. Then she turned and opened her eyes.

"Father?" She sank to her knees beside the bed. His fair, wavy hair was spread out on the pillow, streaked with white. His strong hands lay on top of the covers, clutching and unclutching. She focused very hard on the gold rings trapped behind his knuckles. Then she dared to look directly at his face. His eyes were fixed on a point above her forehead; they did not see her or know her. He was drawn and gray, his thin lips muttering words that were not words. His proud, straight nose looked too big for his face. She reached for one of his hands. "My lord, it's Bluebell."

And then, for a moment's moment, there was a flash of recognition: a pull of his eyebrows, a pressing together of his lips as though they might form a *B* sound. Warm relief crossed her heart and then went cold as his eyes rolled back and he slumped against his pillow, still now.

"Father? Father?" But she could see that his chest still rose and fell. He was asleep.

Bluebell laid her face against the rough blanket and allowed herself to sob. She tried to remember the worst pain she had ever felt. Once, three mail rings had been driven into the soft flesh of her belly during a skirmish with a band of Wengest's men, long before the peace deal Rose had secured. Four days and four nights she had sweated with an agonizing infection. Yes, that had been painful. Or there was her sixteenth birthday, when she'd commanded a friend to smash her nose to pieces during training. It had seemed an easy way to avoid a husband. That pain had nearly blinded her. She tried to hold on to either of those memories, to make the agony of this moment diminish. But it did not, and she was both appalled and amazed she could suffer so much without a blow having been struck to her body. Without an enemy she could see and repay.

But was that true? Was there really no enemy? The image of Gudrun and Osred, heads bent together in conspiracy, flashed into her mind, and the fury began to spark awake in her veins. What kind of illness was this, if not bad magic? If not an elf-shot?

A sound near the door had her lifting her head, palming away the tears she would allow no living man to see.

Byrta warily peered in. "Bluebell?"

Bluebell was relieved to see her. "Byrta," she said quickly, "I think—"

Then Byrta pushed open the door and Gudrun stood behind her. Bluebell clamped her mouth shut and climbed to her feet, her hand going to her sword.

"Please be calm, Bluebell," Byrta said.

"Don't tell me to be calm. Almissia's security has long depended on me losing my fucking temper. So don't ask me to drop my weapons and be soft and womanly now, when I have suffered such a great blow to my heart." With her free hand she pounded her chest.

"Yes, but our security also depends on you knowing when to keep your head cool."

"What is wrong with my father, Byrta? In your opinion?"

"A brain sickness of some kind. He raves, then he sleeps. Osred thinks—"

"Osred? Why should we trust him?"

"Because he has seen such an illness before."

"I believe he has. I believe he knows the illness intimately." She fixed a deathly gaze on Gudrun, who shrank behind Byrta. "Did you put him up to it?"

"Bluebell, get hold of yourself," Byrta said sharply. "This is your stepmother. You have flown past reason."

Bluebell was trapped in the hot moment, and she knew it. She was primed for battle, not diplomacy. She forced the muscles in her arms to relax, released her sword.

Gudrun stepped forward. "I'm sorry I sent for Wylm and not for you. I had need for comfort, and I thought of myself before I thought of the kingdom. Read nothing more into it."

"I do not know if I should believe you," Bluebell said, refusing to soften. "You may stay with my father, but only under watch. I will send Dunstan up here to sit with you."

"I don't want that man in the room with us! This is private, this is—"

"He is a king, you fool. There is no 'private,'" Bluebell spat. "What happens from now on is a matter of state. Should my father die, all of Thyrsland will shudder. Do not think you own him. Almissia owns him." She turned to Byrta. "I will fetch Dunstan. Stay with her until he comes, then meet me at the hall. We need to speak urgently. And get someone to send to Fengard for Ivy and Willow. Ash and Rose are already on their way."

"Yes, my lord," Byrta said, ushering Gudrun ahead of her.

Thrymm and Thrack waited outside the door and pounced on Bluebell when she emerged, tails thumping madly. "No, you stay here," she said. "I'll be back." Straightening, she headed toward the stables to retrieve her horse and ride to Dunstan's farm. Her father's former second-in-command had traded his shield for a plow after being speared in the thigh by a raider. He had four acres of land at the bottom of the hill and worked his own farm still, despite arthritic joints and half lameness. He would come quickly and do what she asked. The animosity between him and Gudrun was no secret in Blickstow.

As she entered the stable, the sunlight was swallowed by wooden walls and the smell of old straw. She saw a figure at the back door, saddling a horse. It was Osred.

"Where is Isern, my lord?" This was her steward, Tom. He and his father had served her family for twenty years.

Bluebell, distracted, took her eyes off Osred. "Hmm? Oh, he's back in Oakstead. He'll be home in a day or so. Did anyone find the horse I brought in about half an hour ago?"

"No, my lord."

"Go look for it, will you, Tom? He'll be wandering behind the hall, still saddled."

Tom nodded and slipped out, leaving Bluebell alone in the stable with Osred. Osred was concentrating very hard on saddling his horse, but Bluebell knew he was aware of her presence. She approached him, standing tall. He turned and looked up at her.

"I'm going," he said. He was terrified.

"What did you do to my father?"

"I tended to him. But there's little that can be done—"

"Did you give him an elf-shot?"

"Elf . . . ? I don't believe in elf-shots, Princess. I'm a physician, not a village witch."

"Then why do you know so much about his illness?"

"I've seen it before."

"I haven't. It's mysterious to me. He doesn't cough, he has no fever. It doesn't look like illness at all; it looks like bad magic. And that makes me wonder who administered it."

Panic crossed his brow. "Surely you don't think—"

"But I *do* think," she said, pressing two fingers against her temple. "I do."

"Princess, I would never—"

"Don't call me princess," she said. "I'm not a fucking princess, waiting to be married off to a foreign prince. I am the latest in a great line of warrior kings. I will rule this country as my father does, through skill in war and deathless courage. Whatever mad plan Gudrun has, she will not take this kingdom from me, with your help or anyone else's!"

He was frozen in front of her. She wanted to kill him. She wanted to kill him so badly it made her brain ache and her thoughts bend, and she was losing her grip on reason. *He is not armed, Bluebell, and if he is not armed it is murder.* Forcing breath into her lungs, she stilled her hands.

"I will go," he said in a little voice. "You will never see me again. I will go immediately." In his terror, he did not look like a man who could poison a king. And yet any overweening weakling like him would be afraid to taste steel. Innocence and desperation looked very much alike.

"You are too dangerous to let go," she said. "I am sorry."

Serpents and birds were carved into the round beams that held up the roof of Athelrick's hall. Bluebell thoughtfully traced the swirling patterns with her fingers, considering her dirty nails in the half-light. The hall was the largest in Thyrsland at forty yards long and seven wide, big enough for a great feast. But now it was quiet, the mead benches stacked away, the hearthpit cold, the cauldron on its long chain empty, the smell of ash and animal fat lingering in the air. The door opened and a shaft of light fell across the stone floor, then disappeared again as the door swung closed behind Byrta.

The older woman approached, then stopped in front of her with arms folded. "Gudrun is terrified of Dunstan."

"Good."

"You are cruel."

"It's my job to be cruel."

"Not to your family."

"She isn't my family."

Byrta made an exasperated noise. "You have never liked her, but she is a good woman. Your father loved her, so she can't be all bad."

"Perhaps that was also an enchantment."

Byrta narrowed her blue eyes. "What do you mean by 'also'?"

"Father is elf-shot, Byrta. Don't you see?"

Byrta's mouth opened and closed once. Then her soft hand reached out to encircle Bluebell's wrist. "Oh, Bluebell, no. He isn't elf-shot. He is sick."

"Then what kind of sickness is this? I've never heard of anything like it."

"The brain is mysterious, but some say it can block up and fill with pressure, with unpredictable results. I'm almost certain that is what's happening to your father. But I disagree with Osred that it will be over quickly. I think he will see out the spring with us. There will be plenty of time for you to say goodbye, to grow used to the idea."

Bluebell formed a fist with her right hand and punched the pillar. "I do not intend to grow used to it! I intend to find somebody who will make him better." Osred had just denied until blood was shed that he had elf-shot Athelrick, then denied until locked away that he could fix it. A week in a muddy hole in the ground with a festering wound and rats for company might change his mind. But if it didn't, she would need to find somebody who could cure bad magic.

Byrta was shaking her head, pity in her eyes.

Bluebell grew furious. "Don't you look at me like that, old woman."

"Respect somebody who has had feet in the world longer than you, girl," Byrta responded hotly. "Your father isn't elf-shot; he is brainsick. He will die, as do we all. You are familiar enough with death, surely."

"Pity if a soul heard you speak to me that way," Bluebell muttered. "I'm not a child anymore."

"You will always be a child to me. I was the first person who held you, covered in your mother's blood."

Bluebell crossed her arms tight over her body and shoved her hands in her armpits. "You are certain it's not bad magic?"

"I am almost certain."

"Almost?"

Byrta shrugged. "There is always possibility. But don't look to Gudrun. Gudrun loves your father."

"I don't trust her."

"You have never trusted her. Are you mad? Do you think she wants to harm your father? Take his throne? Give it to that oily boy she calls her son? She'd no more be able to achieve that than jump to the moon."

Bluebell fell silent. Those possibilities did seem remote, now they were voiced.

She needed her sisters here. She needed Ash. Ash could tell in an instant if it was bad magic or illness, as Byrta claimed.

"Bluebell," Byrta said, her voice softening, "I know this hurts. But he doesn't suffer. He doesn't know who he is, or what he has lost. And when the time comes, you shall be our king, as you have been preparing your whole life to be."

Bluebell thought about this awhile, then said, "He recognized me."

"Surely not."

"He did, I know it. For a moment, but certainly."

Byrta didn't respond, and Bluebell knew the counselor believed her self-deluded. But Bluebell cared little: She had seen her father's brow furrow at mention of her name. He wasn't so far from life as they all believed. And she would bring him back. Just as soon as Ash arrived.

After the second night with no sleep, Ash was raw behind the eyes. The journey seemed interminable as the river wove its winding pattern through fields and forests. She grew used to the smell of the don-keys, she ate the rough chewy bread offered her by the crew, she even managed to raise a smile at their overheard jokes. But she did not sleep. Because every time she veered close to sleep, the dream was waiting. It was inescapable now. And yet here she was, still trying to escape it.

She was nodding into her knees, pinching herself awake at dawn on the third day. The clouds had cleared and the sun was fiery orange as it can only be when rising directly over a cloudless horizon. The sail turned black in silhouette in front of the burning sunlight, and Ash's heart spiked. The color reminded her of something . . .

She stood, hurried to the side of the vessel, and grasped the heavy wood with her hands for safety. But it was no use. Sleep or no sleep, the dream was coming, roaring down on her . . .

The town is alive with panic. She doesn't recognize it, but it is a town built high above a harbor, like Thridstow. People rush away from the sea, from the wharves and the rough rocky beach, shouting and crying. The end of everything is here and Ash is among them, confused, blinking in every direction, crushed on every side by swarming, frantic bodies. The people look to the sea, where steam rises in a thin curl. They point and scream. Then the thin curl disappears and a mighty spout of steam shoots up; the noise grates against Ash's brain like iron against stone. The sea ruptures, and a scream tears her throat. Something vast and terrifying is coming. From within the churning ocean rises a great dragon, eyes dark as cinders, scales red as new-spilled blood, with cruel hooks tipping its tail and water sheeting off its wings as they spread and black the sky.

Ash is buffeted by the crowd but stands to watch as the dragon opens its jaws and spews sunbright fire, bloody amber across the crowd. Charred bodies fall.

Ash knows this fire is intended for her, and nobody else. As soon as the dragon sees her, he will leave the others alone. Her body is shaking to pieces with the fear. The dragon rises like the sun, mighty and cruel and scorching, and she turns to run with the crowd, before those ancient glassy eyes can see her.

But he will *see her, because it is only Ash he seeks. And she knows this as certainly as she knows she is breathing . . .*

"My lady?"

Ash startled back into the world, heart thudding. When she became aware of a pain in her hands, she looked down and realized she had driven her fingernails into the wood so hard that splinters had shafted up inside them. Her body ached from nape to ankle, as though she had been trampled. And in some way, perhaps, she had.

"Are you well, my lady?" the donkey trader said.

"I . . . I am . . ." Her mouth was dry, her head swam, her ears rang. "Not well," she said.

"We'll have you home within a few hours," he said kindly. "Come back to your seat. I'm afraid you'll fall and hit your head."

She allowed herself to be led back to her seat, and took a drink of ale from him. He returned to work and she found herself alone, icy-skinned and terrified. For certainly, she had seen her own Becoming, and it was blighted beyond redemption.

chapter 7

The weather held, and the afternoon was fine and clear as Wylm rode up toward the gatehouse and into Blickstow. He wasn't expecting the gatehouse guards to step out in front of him and shout for him to stop.

He reined his horse, skin prickling with irritation. This was Bluebell's doing, no doubt.

"The queen sent for me," he said. "I'm here to see my mother, the queen."

"Bluebell said we are to accompany you to the family compound," one of the guards said, while the other held his horse firmly around the bridle. "Dismount. My friend here will take care of your horse."

Wylm slid from his saddle. His mouth was dry. Damn his stepsister. One of the guards moved off with his horse; the other held him firmly but respectfully around the upper arm.

"Please," Wylm said, "I won't run. Let me go. Everyone will think I've committed some crime."

The guard released him but did not stand back. "Stay close," he said.

"Or what?" Wylm laughed. "Will you kill me?"

The guard didn't answer, and Wylm resigned himself to the shame of being walked through the main thoroughfare of Blickstow under guard. He kicked a passing chicken in frustration. It squawked and dashed off, shedding feathers in the mud.

Outside Athelrick's hall, the guard instructed Wylm to sit on one of the long benches beneath the overhangs and wait. Wylm slumped in the seat petulantly, expecting Bluebell to come and chastise him. Again, his thoughts turned to how things might be if Mother were free of both Athelrick and Bluebell, if he were the king. Nobody would dare treat him as though he were a naughty child. He passed the waiting minutes entertaining this fantasy in detail. Footsteps nearby. He turned. It wasn't Bluebell; it was his mother with the same gatehouse guard.

"My son!" she said, rushing toward him.

He stood and took her in his embrace. She seemed very pale and thin, her normally tidy hair working its way loose of its plaits. "Mother," he murmured against her hair, "are you well?"

"No, I'm not." She stood back and looked at him, and her eyes were moist. "I'm so glad you're finally here!"

Wylm looked over her head at the guard. "Go on. Leave us be."

He looked uncertain.

Gudrun turned. "Leave us," she said. "Neither of us is under arrest, are we? Or is unhappiness a crime in Blickstow?"

The guard inclined his head slightly to the side, then said, "I will leave you be, my lady. Remain in the town."

"I would not leave my husband's side," Gudrun said. "Don't offend me."

Wylm waited for the guard to move off, then said, "They marched me here like a prisoner."

"It is Bluebell," Gudrun said. "She has gone mad with sorrow."

"Bluebell is always mad. She needs no excuse." Wylm took her upper arms in his hands gently. "Mother, why did you send for me and not her? Who gave you such bad advice?"

"I took no advice. I wanted you near me, before *she* came." She glanced away, not meeting his eyes. "Now she thinks I mean her harm. Athelrick says I will come to love her, but she is a monster. And how is a monster to rule a kingdom as important as Almissia? Athelrick deserves an heir whom people will love, not fear."

"She commands a mighty army."

"And I am to be impressed? She has done nothing good for me. She has done nothing good for you, either. She sent you away, to a remote outpost, probably hoping you'd meet your death."

Wylm considered telling his mother Bluebell had saved him from death at the hands of the bandit, but decided not to. Everyone else sang her praises; why should he? "Was she cruel to you, Mother?"

"She only threatened me at swordpoint! She sent Osred away. She has me under watch in my husband's bower by that one-eyed monster who calls me the Twit from Tweening." She dropped her voice low. "I hate myself for being so afraid of her, Wylm. I am soon to be widowed for the second time; I want to be at my husband's side, to count his breaths. I should be thinking of him, but instead my thoughts are always on her. What will she do to me next? What will she do to me when Athelrick dies? I've nowhere to go . . ." She descended into sobs and Wylm pressed her close, shushing against her hair in the same fashion she had comforted him in his childhood. He led her to the long bench to sit and let her cry for a while.

"Where is Bluebell now?" Wylm asked, when her sobs had eased.

"I don't know. She hasn't been near her father since she first arrived. She must not love him. Perhaps she thinks her other business is more important." Gudrun snuffled against her sleeve and gazed up at the sky. "Why have I lost two husbands, Wylm? Am I careless or unlucky?"

Some childish part in him took offense. "You still have me, so perhaps you are neither."

A shadow fell over them, and Wylm glanced up to see that the guard was back.

"What is it?" Wylm asked.

"Queen Gudrun may return to the king's bower, but you are to accompany me now to lodgings above the alehouse."

"On whose orders? Bluebell's?"

"Yes."

"Am I under arrest?"

"No, but we can't let you go free until you've spoken to her. I'm not sure when that will be—"

"You won't treat my son like a prisoner!" Gudrun shrieked, shaking her pale fists. "I am your queen."

"He's not a prisoner, my lady. But Bluebell gave clear instructions that she wanted to speak with Wylm, and . . ." The guard dropped his voice. "It is a tense time for Blickstow. I mean no disrespect, my lady. Your good favor is important to me, too."

"But I'm unlikely to cut your head off. Is that what you mean?"

The guard didn't answer.

Wylm squeezed his mother's hand. "I'll go, Mother; don't spare a thought for me. I'm not a prisoner, for all I feel like one." He smiled at the guard, but it was his fake smile: the one where he crinkled up the corners of his eyes to feign warmth. Nobody ever picked it for a forgery. "Come, my friend, I've been traveling all day and I look forward to ale and rest."

He allowed himself to be led off, glancing back with a wave. His mother seemed very small, sitting by the hall. Bitterness hardened in his heart, and its name was Bluebell.

For Bluebell, rage and sorrow—or even great happiness—were best expressed physically, and that meant one of two things: fighting or fucking. Byrta had strictly forbidden her from the first until her head had cooled, so she found herself at Sabert's house on a millet farm half an hour's ride from Blickstow instead. She lay on her back on his straw mattress, body still tingling, and watched a spider spinning a web in a dark corner above the roof beams. Sabert lay on his side, running his rough fingers up and down her arm.

"Is something troubling you?" he asked.

She didn't answer him right away. She didn't feel like talking yet. Sabert had been a friend for many years. He was trustworthy and as stocky as a draft horse, four inches shorter than her, but it mattered little lying down, and the salty, spicy scent of his skin never failed to inflame her desire. Her secrets were locked inside his breast as well as her own, and she knew they were safe there. As safe as she felt now, lying under the warm blanket while a lark sang in the distance and a shiver of breeze muttered in the rowan tree outside the shutter. Her blood slowed and cooled. She let herself be still.

"It's my father," she said, at last, turning on her side to face him. "He's sick. They think he's dying."

Sabert lifted a strand of her fair hair and wound it gently around his fingers. "I'm sorry, Bluebell."

"He has fits of madness and fits of deathlike sleep. It looks to me like bad magic."

"He is a king; he has many enemies."

Bluebell nodded emphatically. "Yes. I suspected Gudrun, but you are right. It could be anyone." Stillness evaporated; her stomach knotted with anxiety. "I need to find somebody who can fix him. And then I'll find out who did it to him and make them swallow my blade."

"Are you sure he's not simply ill?"

"I'm sure. Byrta argues otherwise, but what if everyone accepts her opinion? Then nobody goes out to look for a cure."

He didn't respond, and she took his silence as confirmation that he agreed with her. Any shred of self-doubt vanished. She sat up and reached for her clothes. She dressed quickly, pulling pants over her long legs, tying up her gaiters, wriggling back into her shirts, encircling her hips with the familiar weight of her belt and scabbard. Sabert took his time. He was a person who moved at a different pace. Long-held sorrows had stolen any need for haste in his life.

"Papa?" A little voice from outside the door.

Bluebell turned to him and smiled weakly. "Eni's back."

"He's a good lad," Sabert said, pulling down his shirt over his hard, hairy stomach. "But he can only stay busy for a little while collecting sticks. Coming, Eni!" he called through the door.

Bluebell cracked open the door to the main living area, where Eni waited with a handful of twigs. Eni was Sabert's son; his mother, Edie, who had been Bluebell's closest friend in her youth, had died eleven years ago giving birth.

"Hello, Eni," she said, taking the twigs from him. "What a fine job you've done collecting these."

The boy frowned slightly. He was the image of Sabert, with his thick black hair and florid cheeks.

"It's Bluebell."

"Papa?" Eni said, in a quavering voice. The birth had been hard on Eni, also. He had gone too long without breath and now he was blind and simple. Many men would have pressed a folded blanket across his face by now, but Sabert adored his boy and was infinitely gentle with him.

"Sabert is coming, Eni. He'll make you some supper," Bluebell said. There was always a little guilt, but she knew Eni's mother would have thought this convenient relationship a great joke. Neither Bluebell nor Sabert had the stomach for love and promises. "Here, I have a present for you." She knelt in front of him and pulled out of her pocket a gold ring. Her father had given it to her in her youth: It was the dragon insignia of Almissia, curling around to grasp its own tail. She had found it last night, back in her old chamber, when she'd moved the dresser against the door in fear of imagined enemies. She placed it in Eni's hand, and his grubby little fingers ran over it carefully.

"It's a dragon," she said.

"Dragon," he echoed, and she had no idea whether or not he knew what a dragon was or what they were said to look like. He tried to give the ring back, but she refused it.

"No, it's for you," she said, sliding it onto the index finger of his left hand. She pushed it over his knuckle, and it sat firmly enough that she was confident he wouldn't lose it. "It's too small for me now."

Sabert emerged from the bedroom and squatted by the hearthpit to stoke the fire, then stood to stroke the boy's head.

"Dragon," Eni said, holding up his hand.

Sabert considered the ring by the firelight. "Very nice."

"How has he been?" Bluebell asked.

"He was terribly sick this winter," Sabert replied, going to the corner to fetch a block of wrapped cheese and a half loaf of bread. "Something got hold of his lungs. He coughed till he was blue. I feared he would die." He stopped, ran a hand over his beard. "I once thought it would be the best thing for both of us if he died. But when it nearly happened . . ." He shook his head. "I don't know what will become of us. I hope I outlive him."

"Your brother, Seaton, will take him."

"Seaton barely speaks to me."

"Take heart. Long life is in your family. Your aunt Lily is eighty or ninety, isn't she?"

"Aunt Lily died two months ago," he said.

Bluebell winced. "Sorry."

"I have used up my grief, Bluebell. Don't feel sorry for me. She left me her farm."

"The one up past Stonemantel?"

"Yes. Remember? We spent the summer up there, you, me, and Edie."

"Of course. When was that? Twelve years ago?"

"It must have been. Before you broke your nose."

"Before *you* broke my nose," she said. "Will you move up there?"

"No, I'm busy enough with this farm. And she gave most of the land over to flowers in the end. She was mad for them."

"It would be nice to take Eni up there. The farmhouse is so big. He might like the flowers. Spring is here."

Sabert fixed Bluebell in his gaze. "He can't see them."

"He can smell them."

"It will still mean nothing to him. It all means nothing to him. It's not worth uprooting him. Upsetting him." He sat on the stool next to the hearth and cut some chunks of cheese with the knife on his belt. Misery lined his face.

Bluebell considered him awhile, then said, "The child is lucky to have you. Let me help. Come live in the town. I'll find you a nice place, a nurse a few days a week."

He shook his head. "We look after ourselves, Bluebell. We need nobody's pity or mercy. He can still help on the farm, if only a little. I never stop hoping . . ." He trailed off, shrugged.

I never stop hoping. Bluebell thought of her father. The prickling unease made her restless. "I should get back. I've sent for Ash and Rose, and they will surely be here soon."

He looked up and raised his eyebrows at her. "Don't stay away so long next time. Remember, your old friend has needs."

She shrugged. "Use your right hand. Then your left when your right grows tired."

"Good advice, my lord. Give my best to your sisters."

Bluebell left, closing the door on the smoky little house behind her. The sun was low over the fields, catching the soft green plants. She had been away too long from Blickstow, from the malcontent that brewed there. But she felt a little better, a little lighter. And once Ash and Rose were here, she'd feel better again. Rose would believe her, as Sabert had, and Ash would uncover the truth.

Ash's bones rattled as the cart pulled her up the rutted hill and into Blickstow. She had been longing for the end of the journey, telling herself she wouldn't spend another thought worrying until she came to rest. But now the end of the journey was here and her tired brain struggled to comprehend what had to be done next. Father was dying. She had run away from Thridstow. Her future was blighted.

First, though, she had to pay the donkey trader. The cart driver waited as she dashed into the alehouse, intending to borrow a few coins from the alehouse wife. Instead, she saw Bluebell sitting in the back corner, elbows on a table, staring into a cup of ale.

Ash approached curiously. "Bluebell?"

Bluebell looked up blearily. Then recognition flashed and her face transformed into a grin. She leapt to her feet and squashed Ash in her arms. She was all bone and sinew. "You're here!"

Ash extricated herself. "I have to pay the man who brought me upriver. Do you have any coins?"

Bluebell turned out her left pocket and showered silver coins on the table. Ash scooped a few up and returned to the cart driver, paying him and giving him some for the donkey trader. Then she hurried back inside.

Bluebell sat in the same place, watching the door for Ash. There was an expression on Bluebell's face that Ash hadn't seen before, a vulnerability that gutted her. Ash had to stop for a second and take a breath. Everything else had to wait. For this moment, she had to be here for Bluebell and her father. She slid into the seat across from her sister.

"How is Father?" she said.

"He's . . ." Bluebell glanced away. "You'll have to go and see for yourself."

"He's very ill?"

Bluebell nodded, pushing the cup of ale across the table to Ash.

"Here, you have it. I've drunk seven already. I'll be pissing like a horse tonight. You look tired and you smell terrible."

Ash took a grateful sip, considering her sister in the late-afternoon light through the shutter. "Bluebell," she said, "why aren't you with him?"

Bluebell's voice was low. "I can hardly look at him, Ash."

"Why not?"

"Because he is so changed. And because . . . I know if he dies . . . life will be so different. And I'm afraid."

Ash nearly choked on her ale. "Afraid? Really?" she managed.

Bluebell's pale eyes turned icy for a moment, giving Ash a glimpse into the thrilling terror her sister was capable of inspiring. But then Bluebell laughed. "I'm talking with ale on my tongue," she said. "Don't listen to me." She pointed upward. "I've got Wylm under guard up there. Gudrun's physician is locked up in the pit near the latrine. And Gudrun is under Dunstan's watch in the king's bower."

Ash took a moment to understand what she meant. "Why?" she asked.

"Because I think Father is elf-shot. And I don't know who to trust."

"What does Byrta think?"

"Byrta thinks he is only sick. That he is dying and I am a sad fool."

Ash's heart stirred with pity. If anyone would refuse to accept a parent's death, it would be Bluebell. One of Ash's earliest memories was of her mother's death, and of Bluebell raging about the family compound hacking at trees and swearing at the moon.

"Perhaps he *is* only sick," Ash said.

Bluebell's eyes locked with Ash's; her voice grew urgent. "That's why you need to go to Father and reach out with your second mind the way you do. Then I will know for sure."

Ash shivered. She didn't want to use her sight for anything. If she could, she would dam up that river forever . . .

"Ash? Can you do it?"

Contend with each moment as it comes, she told herself. "I can try," Ash said, "but you must come with me."

Bluebell's face hardened. "Very well." She climbed to her feet, pulling on her cloak and pinning it at her right shoulder. "Come."

Ash quickly downed the rest of the ale, then hurried to catch up with Bluebell. They walked briskly through town, Ash trying hard to keep up with Bluebell's stride. The late sunlight ached on her tired eyes, and the aftershocks of the dream still flashed across her mind every time she blinked. She wanted to tell Bluebell about it, she wanted her big sister's comfort, but Bluebell was not herself. She was drunk and grieving and angry, and had a head full of mad thoughts. She was too preoccupied with her own pain even to hear Ash speak.

As they approached the bowerhouse, Ash's pulse quickened. She tended to ill people all the time, but none, so far, had been beloved. Bluebell pushed open the door roughly. In the shaft of light that entered the room, Ash saw Gudrun sitting by her father's bed and Father lying deathly still upon it.

Dunstan sat on a stool by the door. He stood and blocked their path in, dropping his voice low to say to Bluebell, "Where have you been?"

"Dodging my responsibilities," she replied shortly, "and don't give me a fucking lesson about it."

Dunstan glared, but then backed away huffing. Bluebell marched up to Gudrun and hauled her to her feet. "Go on, out. Ash and I need to do something."

"What are you going to do?"

"Dunstan, take her out. I've no time for arguing."

Ash couldn't bear to see the fear and misery in Gudrun's face. "Bluebell, stop." She gently pulled Gudrun to her side. "This is your father's wife. She is grieving." Ash rubbed Gudrun's arm affectionately. "All will be well," she said to her stepmother. "The shock is always the hardest, but it is usually brief. Bluebell will be calm again in a day or so."

"Let me go," Gudrun said. Ash didn't need to read her mind to know what she was thinking; it was written in her expression. Mistrust had grown deep roots. It was too late for kindness.

"Go for a walk, take in the afternoon air," Ash said to Gudrun. "Dunstan, wait outside. Don't follow her. She's not a prisoner."

Bluebell glowered drunkenly but said nothing. When Dunstan and Gudrun had left she said to Ash, "I don't trust her."

"She hates you."

Bluebell shrugged, then turned to Father. "Go on, Ash. Tell me what's wrong with him."

Ash sat on the mattress and invited Bluebell to do the same. She took her sister's rough, callused hands in her own. "Bluebell, I will do this for you, but only on one condition. You must get hold of yourself."

Bluebell dropped her head; her long hair hid her face. "I drank too much. That's all."

"Father would want you to be clearheaded."

"I know," Bluebell whispered.

"If I tell you this is simply illness, you must accept it. You must apologize to Gudrun and Wylm and Osred, and you must make preparations to be our new king."

Bluebell lifted her head, set her chin. "I will," she said.

Ash dropped Bluebell's hands and turned to Father. He was sleeping. Deeply, in some subterranean cavern a long way from the world. She smoothed his hair off his brow, bare of the usual gold circlet he wore. Not a king now, just a man. Ash tried to relax her body. Inviting in the sight made her stomach twinge with apprehension. She leaned forward, pressing her cheek against his chest. Closed her eyes.

His heart beat. Slow. Steady.

Her body trembled, the strange whispering began, and it grew and grew to a roar. Images flashed, one after another, aching and burning along her limbs. She knew in an instant, but waited until the sight had subsided. Ash swallowed hard, opened her eyes. The moment spun out; her heart thudded. She stood at a very dark doorway: Once she told Bluebell what she knew, only bad things could follow.

"What? What is it?" asked Bluebell as Ash sat up.

"I'm sorry, Bluebell, but there is no doubt," Ash said. "He *is* elf-shot."

chapter 8

Wylm woke and wondered where he was. Morning light through the shutter, sweet malty steam through the floorboards. *That's right: the alehouse.* And his head was throbbing from too much to drink and too much . . . He looked down. A tousled-haired woman slept beside him, on her belly, her blond hair spread out around her. He stretched his brain, but couldn't remember a single distinguishing feature of her face. She'd brought him his dinner, that much he remembered, then returned at his invitation. The stepson of the king never had any difficulties finding a woman to share his bed. The difficulty was in ridding himself of them the next morning.

Slowly, pieces of his previous day came back. Being detained, sitting here in the room above the alehouse with anger coiling tighter and tighter . . .

A brisk knock at the door. The woman stirred. He flung a blanket over her.

"Come," he said.

The door opened. Bluebell. She had cleaned herself up since he last saw her. Her hair was washed and brushed loose. She wore fresh clothes and a newly oiled mail byrnie over her tunic, and a red sash with a three-toed dragon coiling across it: the king's emblem. She was here on official business. The Widowsmith, as ever, hung at her hips. His stomach clenched. He feared her, and hated himself for fearing her. A brief memory from the previous night fluttered into his mind. He'd been imagining the woman in his bed was Bluebell, hadn't he? He'd imagined conquering her body, pounding it into submission. Now he squirmed with embarrassment—and distaste. The woman— a pretty-faced thing not more than sixteen—sat up, pushed the blanket off herself, and looked at him blearily.

Bluebell glared at the young woman, who saw Bluebell and went white with fear. "I'm leaving," she said hoarsely.

She gathered her clothes while Wylm gathered his wits. Bluebell would be full of questions now, maybe accusations. He had to tread carefully. When the door had closed and they were alone, Bluebell grasped a chair and sat down. As she moved, the chain mail rang pleasantly. She eyed him awhile, then said, "You can go."

Wylm took a moment to comprehend. "What?"

"I'm sorry. I shouldn't have detained you." She was practically choking on her words. "My sister Ash is here and she has given me good counsel." She even managed a little smile, and Wylm's spine crawled. Dark currents tugged and swirled beneath this conversation, though he didn't know where precisely they lay.

"You're sorry?" he said.

"No harm?"

"No more than usual."

She nodded. "King Athelrick is sick, as you know, but we mustn't assume he is dying and we mustn't spread fear and uncertainty. So don't speak of it to anyone. You are free to stay here in Blickstow to be with your mother until the situation is resolved, one way or another."

Wylm was speechless.

She cleared her throat, not meeting his eye. "Well," she said, "will you stay with her? Or will you return to the stronghold?"

"I'll stay with her. Of course."

"Good," she said. "I've settled your account here." Then she was extending a hand for him to shake, and suspicion burned in his belly.

He took her hand and shook it soundly.

"We have cleared a room for you in the bowerhouse, with your mother. There are people here to help care for my father, so she needn't feel it falls only to her. Ensure she rests."

"Thank you, Princess," he said, with as much silver on his tongue as he could manage.

Her eyes narrowed slightly, but she didn't correct him. "I shall leave you to dress. Give my best to your mother."

She backed out. Wylm lay down again, hands behind his head. He had never seen such a poor performance of forgiveness or generosity. It was clearly paining her to be nice to him. But why would she pretend? What was she up to? Wylm vowed not to let down his guard until he found out.

Ash found Byrta in her chamber at the back of the bowerhouse, directly across the way from the long wing that held the kitchen, stores, and infirmary. Byrta had lived in this room for nearly forty years: a dozen of them with her beloved companion Hilda, and many alone after Hilda had died. The smell of the room was achingly familiar to Ash after so long away. The powdery scent of the lavender bushels tied to the roof beams, the thick odor of lanolin, the sharp-sweet dried herbs that sat in pots on every surface. Ash had spent many hours in here, learning to spin and weave—none of her sisters had the patience for it—and taking comfort in Byrta's company. Byrta had been, in some ways, a reluctant substitute mother to Ash, who craved such connections in a way her sisters hadn't. She had always talked over her problems with Byrta and taken her advice seriously.

Byrta was at her loom. She gave Ash a welcoming smile. "I'd heard you were here."

"I arrived late yesterday. It was a long journey."

"Did you sleep well last night?"

"Like the dead," Ash said, sitting on the stool next to Byrta.

Byrta patted her shoulder lightly. She was not a woman given to displays of affection. "I'm sorry about your father's illness."

Ash took a deep breath. "Byrta, he's not ill. He's under the influence of bad magic."

Byrta huffed. "Bluebell has gotten in your ear, I see."

"No. I reached out. I . . ." She trailed off.

Byrta had put down the shuttle. "I sense you have a lot to tell me."

"Oh yes," Ash said. "I'm in all kinds of trouble."

Byrta waited in the silence. A fly caught at the shutter buzzed against it before finding a crack between two slats of wood and flying free. Ash collected her thoughts.

"You remember I told you about my . . . ability?"

"Yes, of course." Byrta's fingers tapped against her lap once, and then were still; the only sign the topic was uncomfortable for her. "I'm very proud of you, and when you are older you will—"

Ash shook her head. "No. Not when I'm older. Now. In the last three years. It has grown so big, too big for me to see the edges."

Byrta pulled her eyebrows close together, and the soft light from the shutter illuminated two deep furrows. "I see. And you think your father has been elf-shot?"

"I don't think it. I know it."

Raised eyebrows. A wary tone. "You are very sure of yourself."

"I am."

Byrta exhaled slowly. "This is very serious. I hope you are not mistaken."

"I am not mistaken." Still Ash could feel Byrta's resistance, and even jealousy. Byrta had a little sight, yet she had not sensed the bad magic around Athelrick. She couldn't be blamed for that; bad magic tried to hide itself. It had certainly hidden the identity of the person who had dispensed it, much to Bluebell's agonized frustration. "We have to move him, and soon. He will die if he stays where he is. Bluebell is making arrangements."

"So Bluebell knows?"

"Yes."

"And she hasn't yet skewered a member of her stepfamily?"

Ash had to smile. "There is no way of telling who has done this to my father. But I have assured her it isn't Gudrun."

Byrta did not return the smile. "I have been tending, this morning, to Gudrun's physician, who has just been released from the pit. He is very ill with an infected wound. I don't find Bluebell's behavior funny."

Ash grew irritated. Byrta still saw them as children. It was difficult for her to imagine Bluebell as anything but the wild young woman she had been in her teens. "With my father sick, Bluebell is the most important person in all of Almissia, if not Thyrsland. Even I would not think to judge her."

Byrta waved dismissively. "She will do as she pleases, I imagine."

"Indeed, she will, but she requires your silence. We are not telling anyone where we are going, and none but the most senior in the army will know he is ill. Nobody except his daughters, Dunstan, and you will know he's elf-shot."

"Not even Gudrun?"

"Not even Gudrun."

"And when she notices her husband is missing?"

"She will have her son for comfort. Gudrun isn't our concern. Though Bluebell worded it more colorfully than that."

Byrta picked up her shuttle again, her lips disappearing as she set her mouth in a line. "Well. It sounds as though you have both made up your minds. I must do as Bluebell says, so you'll have no argument from me. I'm surprised you're telling me at all. You didn't need my advice."

"We would not leave you in the dark. You have always been my father's counselor and companion. You are family. Your wisdom has ever been a great comfort to me . . ." She trailed off. She wanted so badly to tell Byrta about the vision, about the terrible fear it had woken in her. Her ears began to ring faintly and her head felt light, as though the awful knowledge woven into the vision was a presence in the room, pinching her skull.

Byrta sensed her distress. "Ash? You're trembling."

Ash looked at her own pale hands in her lap. "So I am."

"Is there something wrong?"

"No." But forcing a smile was as difficult as building a bridge over a raging river. She took a deep breath.

Byrta kept weaving. "Go on. I'm listening."

"I . . . Do you think it's possible to know your own Becoming?"

"No. You can't turn your sight on yourself."

"What if it comes in a vision?"

Byrta shrugged, clearly at the end of her knowledge, and Ash decided not to say another word—not to say that she had always felt she was destined to die young, that she had been so fearful of death and so desperate to surround herself with company. The ringing in her ears became momentarily deafening. Byrta was moving her lips, but Ash couldn't hear her.

"What did you say?" Ash said, once the ringing had subsided.

"All of you girls are given to too much drama," Byrta said, but her voice was kind. "Ash, you are so young. The path toward being a counselor is a long one, and you'll likely be a crone before anything you think or feel is reliable in the world. Go and be with your father, child. He's dying."

Ash stood, pushing away the irritation. "Very well. Thank you for listening to me."

Byrta's brow was soft. "You will become what you will become, Ash," she said.

Ash left her, still weaving hand over hand in the dim room.

Bluebell watched Gudrun, and Gudrun watched Bluebell. Between them: a wooden bed with a wool mattress and a king on the verge of waking. He muttered, his brow furrowing deeply, almost as though he could sense the tightly drawn mood in the room.

Bluebell had apologized, though it had nearly split her tongue in two to do so. She had sent Dunstan away so Gudrun didn't feel she was under guard. She was doing, she thought, a very good imperson-ation of a woman who had accepted that her father was sick, that there was nothing she could do and nobody she could kill. But it made her ribs ache that this woman was sitting across from her still, tending to the king, because Bluebell didn't trust her.

Athelrick's hands started to twitch. Gudrun sat forward, making a soothing noise, stroking his fingers. Bluebell stood and paced toward the window, cracking open the shutter and taking deep breaths. She could bear his long, silent sleeps, but his raving was like needles under her skin. Sometimes he wept; she had never before seen her father weep, not even when her mother had died. She hadn't even thought it possible he could weep, and it loosened every nerve in her guts to hear it. She gazed out across the square to the hall, watching a sparrow clean its feathers on the corner of a tile. Spring drizzle fell on the tight little buds that covered the hawthorn hedge below the window. Life renewing itself.

A loud noise from behind drew her attention. Her father was moaning and thrashing now, calling out words with urgent precision. Only they weren't words; just noises, as though he were commanding an imaginary army of madmen. Gudrun leaned over to touch his hair and he sat up fast and flung his arm out, pushing her off. She landed in a heap on the floor, crying out. Athelrick kicked off his blankets and rolled out of the bed, shouting and hurling his arms around, making for the door.

Bluebell was fast on her feet, intercepting him. "No, Father, you can't go out there."

He turned to her, eyes blazing, and released a spittle-laden stream of meaningless abuse in her face. He pushed against her, unbalancing her, and reached for the door.

Bluebell didn't think. She launched herself at him, grabbed him around the waist, and tackled him to the floor. He shouted and lashed out, but she sat astride him, pinning him down, bony knees nailing his arms. "Stop it!" she shouted at him. "You're not going anywhere."

I'm stronger than him. The thought was sudden and piercing. She had brought her own father down. Beneath her, Athelrick went soft. She glanced down. His eyes were fluttering closed.

"Fuck," she spat, climbing to her feet. She turned to see Gudrun behind her, her lip split and bleeding. "Go and see Byrta," she said. "She'll tend to your lip. I'll get him back in bed."

"You'll need help."

"I don't need help. I can manage. You're bleeding on your dress."

Gudrun touched her lip, then glanced down at Athelrick. "I can lift his legs if you—"

Bluebell leaned over, scooped her sleeping father into her arms, then took him back to his bed. "Go and get your lip fixed," she said, settling him on the mattress and smoothing the blankets back over him. "Take a rest. I can look after him."

Gudrun wavered. The dark rings under her eyes told Bluebell she was longing for proper sleep.

"Go. I know you don't like me, but you cannot deny I love him and will care for him well."

"Very well. I will rest." And Gudrun slipped out.

Bluebell dropped her cheek onto Athelrick's hands, closed her eyes, and lay still a long time while her heart slowed. She could hear birds, hooves and wheels, shouting from the marketplace, the clang of the smithy ringing a rhythm. And in the room, her father's breathing, her breathing, winding together. A memory stirred. She had been sixteen, on her first real campaign with Athelrick; finally he had relented, after she'd begged him for years to be able to see battle. Her mother's death had unleashed in her a violent restlessness, and fighting alongside her father—her lord, her king, the famed Storm Bearer of Blickstow—was the only thing she could imagine would soothe her. They were stamping out small incursions by some of the lower lords of Nettlechester. At the end of the first week of the campaign she became tired. She was barely out of her childhood, still growing an inch a year. Somebody should have noticed she was too tired to fight; perhaps *she* should have noticed, or at least admitted it. Somehow, she had gotten herself cut off from the hearthband with three enemies surrounding her. She killed the first while fending off blows from the other two, but her hot heart told her she wouldn't survive five more breaths.

And then, he came. Athelrick had seen her, fled his place in the skirmish. She took a blow to the leg, fell to the ground, only to look up and see her father. Death in a whirlwind: his bright sword weightless, two bodies thudding to the blood-soaked grass next to her. And then he was gone, back into the fray, leaving her nursing her bleeding thigh.

The desire that infused her then was monumental. She wanted to *be* him, not be *like* him. This mighty bond with her father was more than love, more than kisses and comfort; indeed she could not remember the last time he had kissed her. Instead, it was how she assembled herself. Without him, how would she know how to live, how to rule, how to grow old?

The door opened, startling her from a near-doze. A little girl's voice rang out clearly: "It smells bad in here."

Bluebell leapt to her feet. It was Rose, with Rowan and Heath.

"You're here," Bluebell said, crushing Rose in an embrace.

"Enough," Rose said, laughing, pushing her away. "The oil from your byrnie won't wash out of this dress."

Bluebell crouched to Rowan's level and grasped the little girl's upper arm. "Your muscles have grown, little chicken."

"I'm not a chicken," Rowan said defiantly. "I'm a bear. *Roar!*"

Bluebell feigned fright and fell on her backside among the rushes. Rowan shrieked with giggles.

Bluebell climbed to her feet, dropped her voice, and rested a gentle hand on Rowan's head. "I don't want the little girl in here with Father. He's unpredictable."

Rose turned her eyes to Heath. "Could you take Rowan to Byrta?"

"Of course."

Bluebell couldn't bear the soft voices and hot eyes they shared with each other. Did they not know it was obvious they were saying one thing and thinking another? She took a short tone with Heath. "Find Ash for us. She's likely with Byrta, anyway. And then take a room above the alehouse," Bluebell added pointedly. "Only family will be near the king."

"As you wish, my lord."

"I'll speak with you tomorrow. You can either go home to Folkenham for a few weeks, or go straight back up to the stronghold. But we don't need you here any longer."

Rose's eyebrows drew down in annoyance with Bluebell, but she offered Heath a smile. Bluebell returned to Father. She could hear Rowan complaining all the way down the lane.

A moment later, Rose was kneeling next to her. She and Ash were very alike in some ways—the same dark hair and eyes, the same pretty smile—but Rose was soft and curvy like their mother, and always wore her hair loose.

"How long has he been like this?" Rose asked, reaching out for Father's forehead.

"He's been ill for over a week, but he's not always sleeping. He's often raving." Bluebell dropped her voice low. "There are matters of extreme urgency to discuss."

"What matters?"

"Not now." Bluebell glanced around. "When Ash comes." Bluebell returned her gaze to Rose. "Are you still cock-charmed by your nephew?"

"He's not my nephew, he's my husband's nephew." Even in the dim room, Bluebell could see Rose's cheeks color. "And, yes, I still love him."

"After three years apart?"

Rose's heavy-lidded eyes grew dark. "Yes," she said shortly. "And if I wasn't stuck in this arranged marriage with Wengest—"

"You would never have met him," Bluebell pointed out quickly.

"*You* have never loved," Rose said.

"And I don't expect to. That would fuck up just about everything." Bluebell touched Rose's hand. "I've got my mind on Almissia's security, Rosie. Wengest won't be friends with me if he finds out you're being poked by his nephew, and it will start all over again. Skirmishes along the border, quarrels over trade routes. The ice-men will hear of it and take advantage, and then I've got a war on my hands. So be a little more careful, won't you? If the next royal bastard of Nettle-chester has red hair, you can count on thousands of lives lost."

A muscle beside Rose's mouth twitched. "I tried to do the right thing, but once I fell in love it wasn't clear what was right anymore." She glanced away. "You haven't told anyone, have you?" she said.

"Of course not."

"Father?"

"Why would I tell him? He'd be ashamed." Bluebell stood and strode to the shutter. Immediately she felt bad for what she had said, though Rose had given no outward sign of being hurt by it. "I'm sorry, Rose. We pay a price for our privilege. You're not a milkmaid, you're a king's daughter."

"Would I were a milkmaid."

Bluebell opened her mouth to argue further. Heath would not have looked twice at a milkmaid; he was a king's nephew and had a high opinion of himself. But she sensed Rose hadn't the heart for such an argument. Silence fell on the room for a few heartbeats. The light was dim, and Rowan was right—it did smell bad. Yesterday, she'd stoked the fire high and opened the windows to let the fresh spring air in, but still the staleness clung. It made her think of the bad magic Ash had sensed, clinging to his sheets and clothes and hair the way grass seeds clung to the hem of a cloak. Deep in her gut, the fury prickled, but she did not let it form. Plenty of time for that, once Father was well. She would find the person who did this. Their fate was rushing toward them even now, and it smelled like cold iron and hot blood.

The door opened. Ash stood there, dark circles drawn deep under her eyes.

"Ash!" Rose exclaimed, throwing her arms around her sister. They held each other tight for a few moments.

Ash pulled away and smiled weakly. "We have much to discuss."

"Here?" Rose asked.

"Someone has to stay with Father," Bluebell said. "And he won't hear us."

Ash went to the other side of the bed to sit on Gudrun's stool. Rose and Bluebell sat across from her. Athelrick slept on between them, oblivious.

"Father is elf-shot," Bluebell said. Every time she said it, it burned her afresh. "Ash says so."

Rose's eyebrows shot up. "But who?"

"We don't know," Ash said. "It could be anyone. He's a king, and kings make enemies. We mustn't jump to conclusions."

"But somebody must have been near him to cast a spell on him," Bluebell said.

"Not necessarily," Ash said. "It might have come with a package or a messenger."

"I think we should look to Gudrun," Bluebell said, "or, at least, we shouldn't take our eyes off her."

Ash shook her head. "It's ridiculous. She loves him."

"We know nothing about her. She's—"

"We've known her more than three years." Rose put her hand on Bluebell's wrist. "You know she's not capable of killing Father, surely. Examine the facts, Bluebell, not your feelings."

Bluebell noticed her heart was thudding at her throat.

Ash leaned forward. "Bluebell, if you keep too close a watch on Gudrun, you might not see who the real culprit is."

Bluebell vowed then not to mention Gudrun again. Nobody would believe her, so she would keep her opinions to herself. She was tired of being treated like a fool.

"In any case," Ash continued, "who did this to him is not as important as making him well again. Rose, we're going to move him in the hope it will dislodge the elf-shot."

"We're leaving Dunstan in charge of the city and telling everyone Father and I are going to a King's Hearing on the border," Bluebell added. "Nobody will miss us for a few weeks."

"Has Gudrun agreed to this?"

"Gudrun knows nothing," Ash said, indicating Bluebell with an upraised palm.

"The only people I trust with the king's life are my sisters, Dunstan, and Byrta," Bluebell said. "You cannot convince me otherwise."

"She will worry," Rose said. "She will fret."

"We'll send her word when we've arrived safely."

"Arrived where?" Rose asked.

Bluebell and Ash exchanged glances.

"We don't know yet," Ash said.

"Thridstow?" Rose suggested. "There are counselors there who might understand the magic."

But Ash was already shaking her head. "This isn't common magic. This is dark, powerful. It must be undermagic. Besides . . . I've sort of run away from study. There will be trouble waiting for me there."

Athelrick stirred, his eyeballs skittering behind his eyelids. Bluebell's body tensed. His hands moved on the blankets and she was about to warn Ash to stand back when he fell limp again, quietly sleeping. The adrenaline in her body, with no action to burn it up, ached along her veins.

"And all the undermagicians are in Bradsey," Ash continued.

"Do you know anyone in Bradsey?" Rose asked.

"Well, we don't know who we can trust," Bluebell said. "The underfaith is amoral. You can't predict what they'll do. And so we are undecided what to do next."

They fell to silence, watching Athelrick's chest rise and fall. Where was his dignity, when his daughters sat around him arguing for his future and he knew nothing of it? What Bluebell wouldn't give for this not to have happened, to be on the first morning of a campaign with him, riding out by his side on Isern with her weapons rattling against one another.

"I know someone we might be able to take him to," Rose said, but she said it slowly, as though she had been thinking it for a long time but was unsure whether she should say anything at all.

Bluebell eyed her suspiciously. As far as she was aware, Rose rarely left the bowerhouse.

"Who?" Ash asked.

"I think he has a sister."

Bluebell was sure, at first, she had misheard. "He doesn't have a sister," she said. And if he did, Bluebell would know about it before Rose would.

"He does. I mean, he might."

"What do you mean, Rose?" Ash asked.

Rose twisted her hands together. "When I was pregnant with Rowan, I had a sending from a woman who said she was Athelrick's sister . . . an undermagician named Eldra. She tried to warn me Wengest was going to take the trimartyr faith. She was right."

"Father doesn't have a sister," Bluebell said again. "He would have told us. He would have told *me*." She was less surprised that Rose had experienced a sending. The glimmers of magic tended to weave through a whole family, in greater or lesser degree. Bluebell knew she had little of it, but she was a blunt instrument.

"He may have had a reason to keep it secret. I asked him. He was . . . evasive."

Bluebell was torn between wanting to believe she had an aunt who could possibly cure her father, and not wanting to believe her father had kept such a secret from her. She was angry, but she didn't know who the anger was directed toward.

"Do you know anything more?" Ash said. "Where she is?"

"No. I'm sorry. I know nothing more."

"But they all live in Bradsey," Bluebell said, slowly. "They worship out on the plains and they live in the forest caves. Ash, can you reach out with your sight and find this woman?"

Ash wouldn't meet her eye. "I can try," she said.

"Do more than try," Bluebell said. All of a sudden she couldn't bear to be still. She rose and strode from one side of the dim room to the other. "We will head north then, the morning after tomorrow." She thought about Sabert's aunt's flower farm, seventy miles north. Quiet and well away from the road. "We can decide where we go next once we're moving, but we have to get him away from Blickstow. His life depends on it."

The night air was cool and soft, and the smell of damp earth and flowers rose up around her. Rose stood in the center of the garden, looking at the swelling moon and fighting a losing battle with good sense. Rowan was asleep in Byrta's bed. Bluebell was in discussions with Dunstan. Ash had pleaded a headache and taken herself away somewhere quiet.

And somewhere in the alehouse, Heath was alone. Tomorrow, he would be gone.

What was she to do with this turmoil of longing in her body, tugging her in seven directions at once? His long absence had not diminished the weight of desire, but it had dulled the edge of it. Yet when she'd seen him again for the first time in years, it had started again. Now, every moment, she lived in two worlds: the real one, and the one built of clouds. She could be eating supper, wiping snot off Rowan's face, having a conversation with one of her sisters, but in her mind she was bare-skinned with Heath, his mouth against her shoulder, his hands firm and hot on her thighs . . .

Rose made up her mind. The only way to make the turmoil go away was to give herself to him, just once. Then she could go back to the blunted yearning she was used to. It was misery, but it didn't threaten to tear her apart.

She slipped out of the garden and through the nighttime alleyways of Blickstow. Cold mud squelched underfoot. From inside the wooden buildings, warm firelight glowed and cooking smells brewed. The alehouse was ablaze with lanterns and noise. She opened the front door.

The room was smoky and brightly lit. She found the alehouse wife tending to a spitted deer at the hearthpit.

"Princess Rose?"

Rose's stomach rolled with guilt, a nausea that had been her constant companion since her arrival in Blickstow; then she opened her mouth to say the words she had rehearsed: *I have a message to deliver to the nephew of Nettlechester. Which room is he staying in?* But the words wouldn't come.

"How's that little girl of yours?" the alehouse wife said with a smile.

"I . . . She's well. She's strong and growing. Exhausting."

"Ah, they always are at that age. Might I suggest a little brother or sister will sort her out? That will make her realize she's not at the center of the world." She wiped her hands on her apron. "Now, how can I help?"

There: her womb, always a topic for public speculation. What went on between her legs could never be private, nor secret, nor truly her own. The danger of her situation burned on her lips as she tried to speak. Bluebell's words came back to her. *You can count on thousands of lives lost.* One shred of suspicion, passed from someone's lips to someone else's ears, and she would have let down her sister, her father, her daughter. The whole kingdom.

"It's nothing," she muttered, withdrawing, backing away. Her skin ached as though bruised from the inside.

She could feel the alehouse wife's curious eyes on her as she returned outside into the empty dark.

CHAPTER 9

Ivy didn't much care for travel. She didn't much care for the smell of horses or carts or the constant bumping or even the pretty countryside. She didn't want to be heading up the hill toward Blickstow to see her dying father; she wanted to be back home at her uncle Robert's in Fengard where she could keep an eye on William Dartwood's strong, suntanned hands. But here she was, sitting on a fur that did nothing to soften the shuddering bounce of the cart, sucking the last of the flesh from a plum, and confined to the company of her sister Willow, who had become duller than a brackish pool since their fifteenth birthday.

"Iron-Tits isn't going to like you doing that, you know," Ivy said to Willow.

Willow looked up from the silver triangle she was turning over between her fingers. "Isn't going to like what?"

"That trimartyr nonsense."

"It's not nonsense, and I'm not afraid of Bluebell."

"You ought to be. With Father dead, she'll be in charge."

Willow shrugged. "Maava is the only king I honor."

Ivy looked away, annoyed. The afternoon sun was warm on her face. She'd insisted the canopy be turned back this morning when they left, but now it grew too hot and she knew her face would be pink and flushed by the time they reached Blickstow.

"What are you praying for, anyway?" Ivy asked, not really expecting an answer.

"Father's soul."

Not so long ago, Willow had been a normal, if slightly quiet, young woman. Around their birthday she had become somber and withdrawn, complaining of sleepless nights and terrible dreams. And then, around the same time Ivy discovered men, Willow discovered Maava. All her strange anxieties had evaporated, and she spoke of nothing but the grim teachings of the trimartyr religion. Ivy could understand in a way: Her own mad obsession with men and all of their warm, hard, hairy parts gave her insight into passion out of control. Maava was such a morbid, boring thing to be obsessed with, though. Uncle Robert and Aunty Myrtle were at the end of their tether with Willow, which suited Ivy well, as it took the attention off her.

"Driver," called Ivy, "can we stop and put this canopy back on?"

The driver didn't respond. Ivy grew irritated. She was hot and flushed, and the sun was making her eyes ache.

"Driver," she said, wriggling forward in the seat and raising her voice. "Stop. I need you to put the canopy back on."

"We're half a mile from Blickstow," he said sharply. "It's been a long day and we've already stopped half a dozen times. You'll be inside out of the sun soon enough."

"Did you hear that?" Ivy asked Willow.

Willow looked up from her trimartyr chain and triangle, her face placid beneath her distinct widow's peak. "Hmm?"

"He won't put the canopy up."

"We're almost there. You already made him stop so many times on the way here."

"I did not."

"Yes, you did. You wanted to pick flowers, you needed to wee at least three times, then we had to stop so you could buy those plums. He's lame. Leave him be. He's done enough."

"But he's being paid, and we're daughters of the king. He should do as we say."

"It's nice to have a little sun on my face," Willow said.

"Driver!" Ivy said sharply. "Stop and raise the canopy."

"No," he said.

The anger grew so intense inside her that she wanted to scream. She raised her hand and released the plum stone. It cracked against the back of his head.

The cart shuddered to a halt.

"About time," Ivy muttered.

The driver climbed down from his horse, limped to the back of the cart, and hauled out their trunk.

"What are you doing?" Ivy asked.

He dumped the trunk on the ground. "Get out," he said.

"Nice work, sister," Willow said with an eye-roll.

"I won't get out! You've been paid to take us all the way to Blickstow. You have to take us!"

"I don't have to do anything."

"But my father is the king!"

He shrugged.

"And my sister is Bluebell the Fierce. I will tell her what you've done and—"

Willow clamped a hand over Ivy's mouth. "Enough," she said. "Get down."

Willow climbed over Ivy and down to the ground, but Ivy still refused to admit she was defeated. "No!" she said. "Wait!"

The driver reached up and lifted her down. She struggled against him, but as soon as her feet were on the ground, he stepped away unevenly. "I served with your sister," he said, "right up until I took a blow to my leg. I would die for her. Not for you." He spread his hands apart. "Enjoy your walk."

Then he was limping back toward the horse. Ivy stood speechless on the side of the sunny road, watching as the cart rattled away.

Willow had the silver triangle pressed to her lips, eyes closed, and was muttering softly.

"Well, you were a lot of use, weren't you?" Ivy said.

Willow opened her eyes. "You take one handle, I'll take the other."

They lifted the chest and began the walk toward the gates of Blickstow. Insects skimmed across the grass on either side of the road. Ivy could smell mud drying out and horse shit, and her shoes were pinching: her own fault. They were such pretty shoes—leather lined with fleece, and blue ribbon decorating the front seam—but they hadn't really fit her properly for a year. She hadn't expected to be walking in them at all, let alone half a mile in the sun.

At the bottom of the slope that led up to the gatehouse, Ivy stopped. Willow, her arm pulled backward by the sudden stop, turned to look at her irritably. "I'm not carrying it by myself," Willow said.

"We're going to end up with callused hands. My shoulder's aching. My feet are sore." What she really wanted to say was, *I shouldn't have to do this, I'm a princess.* But she didn't. Willow wouldn't be sympathetic.

"What do you suggest?" Willow asked.

"Go up and find some man in the alehouse to carry our chest for us."

"Why should I do it?"

"Because . . ."

"I don't want to go near the alehouse. Women have no place around drunken men."

"Does Maava say that?" Ivy had already grown tired of Willow's endless moral lessons.

"No. I say it." Willow lifted an eyebrow. "Go on. I'll wait here with the chest."

Ivy glanced at the sun, then back up the hill. One way or another, she had to walk up it. "Well, then," she said, but Willow had sat on the trunk and closed her eyes to pray again.

She slipped off her shoes and began to walk. Halfway up the hill, a golden-haired man on a white horse burst from the gates. Ivy waved madly. "Hello!" she said. "Hello! Wait!"

The man reined the horse in and Ivy approached. Her heart had sped up because it had noticed before her eyes had that the man was gorgeous. He was clean-shaven, with aqua eyes and a deep arch to his top lip.

"Can you help us?" she said, panting. "My sister and me? We are the king's daughters and . . . we have a chest we need to get up to the king's compound. We can't carry it ourselves."

The man hesitated.

Ivy dropped her head and looked at him from under her eyelashes. "Please?"

"I know your sisters," he said at last. "I'm . . . Bluebell has asked me to return to Folkenham."

"She won't mind if you help us. She'd appreciate it."

He nodded, then climbed down from his horse and tied it to the gatepost. "Where is the chest?"

"Back down the hill a little way. I'll show you." Any thought of waiting in the shade evaporated. "There, see? There's Willow. How do you know my other sisters?"

"King Wengest is my uncle," he said. "I know Rose very well. I'm sorry, I should have introduced myself. My name is Heath."

"Heath," she said, tasting his name and finding it appetizing. "I'm Ivy." She glanced at him sidelong. He was tall and well made. The lack of beard was a novelty, and not an unwelcome one. She had only ever kissed men with beards. Sometimes she liked it; she liked feeling her smooth softness in contrast with their roughness. Sometimes she hated beards. Scratchy and ugly. She wondered what it would feel like to kiss a man—hard and strong—without having to contend with whiskers. The thoughts kept her busy all the way down the hill and back onto the road.

She glanced ahead and saw Willow, with the silver triangle against her lips. She willed her sister to put the wretched thing down before Heath saw her and reported back to Bluebell. Sometimes she wondered if Willow knew how angry the rest of her family would be if they knew she'd adopted the trimartyr religion. But Willow seemed to care little for anyone's opinion. She had a steeliness about her that Ivy found unnerving.

"Ignore my sister's bad habits," Ivy said to Heath, trying to keep her voice light.

He smiled tightly. "I won't say a word."

"Willow!" Ivy called.

Willow opened her eyes, saw she had company, and had the good sense to tuck the triangle and its chain into the pocket on the front of her dress. She stood, smoothing down her clothes.

"Thank you," Willow said as Heath bent to lift the chest, his long hair falling across his face. "We'll pay you well."

"There's no need to pay me," Heath said softly. "I'm in service to your family."

Oh, he was perfect. Ivy dragged her feet, extending the time she could walk beside him even though she knew it meant he had to carry the chest for longer. He slowed to her pace. She glanced at his strong forearms, the light golden hairs on his wrists, and felt the familiar stirring of lust. Lust, surely, was wild and fifteen like her: a blind thing that hummed in the body like mad bees.

Then they were back up through the gates, fighting their way through the afternoon crowds on the paths between the wooden buildings, getting stuck behind a farmer herding two goats away from the marketplace. Ivy fell into step behind him, with Willow behind her. They approached the family compound. Heath slowed and came to a stop. Ivy took her eyes off his buttocks for long enough to register that Bluebell stood in front of them.

"I thought you were going home to Folkenham," she said to Heath, and Ivy heard the chill edge of threat in her voice. Interesting. Bluebell didn't like Heath.

"It's my fault, sister," Ivy said, stepping out from behind Heath, who had laid their chest on the ground. "The driver wouldn't take us any farther and Heath was riding past and said he'd carry our chest for us." She turned to Heath and beamed. "Thank you."

He didn't take his eyes off Bluebell. "I only wanted to serve your family, Bluebell," he said deferentially. "I meant no harm. I'll be on my way."

Bluebell softened, shaking her head slightly. "No, don't go." She sighed. "I need to speak with you. Go back up to the alehouse. I'll meet you soon." She bent and picked up Ivy and Willow's chest. "Come on, you two. You'll want to see Father."

Ivy didn't really want to see Father. She didn't care that much for him, but she did as she was told, glancing one last time over her shoulder at gorgeous, golden-haired Heath.

❖ ❖ ❖

Bluebell pushed open the alehouse door and scanned the room. There, in the back corner under a shutter open to let in the afternoon sun, was Heath. He looked glum. She suppressed a smile. Rose had been wearing the same expression when Bluebell left her ten minutes ago.

She straightened her belt and strode over to him.

"My lord?" he said.

"Heath." She sat down, tapping her hands anxiously on the table. "I need to speak to you seriously."

He nodded once, his mouth set in a line.

"My second-in-command, Sighere, arrived today. I've been taking his counsel." She sighed. "Look, there's no point in hedging. You already know King Athelrick is ill and we don't want that knowledge too widely spread. My sisters and I are taking him north, for reasons I'm not willing to speak of. But there are unarmed women and a sick man—a very important sick man—and . . . I need another set of arms. I am strongest when surrounded by other strong men, but I still must keep the spread of information to a minimum. Will you come?"

"Of course, my lord," he said.

"Do I need to say the next part?"

He dropped his voice to a whisper. "I'll keep my distance from her."

"Do I need to threaten you?"

"No, my lord."

She thought about threatening him anyway. Perhaps pulling her blade and pushing its tip into the soft space between his ribs, asking him to memorize how it felt in case he was tempted: Nothing like cold steel to discourage a hard cock. But she didn't. Heath was a good soldier, and Bluebell would make sure there wasn't an occasion for him to be alone with Rose. Rose wouldn't like it, but she would have to get used to it.

"We leave at first light tomorrow," she said. "Meet us at the stables."

Wylm hadn't meant to follow Bluebell. He had simply noticed her thundering out the front gates of the town on a black stallion in the early afternoon and wondered where she was going. Two hours later, he happened to be near the gatehouse—loitering, flirting with a creamy-skinned woman named Hazel—when Bluebell came back. She looked . . . Well, she always looked grim. Grimmer? Perhaps. But their exchange at the alehouse had aroused his suspicion and he wondered where she had been. He went to the stables for his mother's mare and set off to find out.

The rain had stayed away for two days, but the ground was not yet dry so he found her horse's prints easily. He traced them down the road and across a field, then north a little and onto a narrow lane between farmlands. He lost the tracks for a while, but kept riding in the same direction, and soon picked them up again at a stream crossing. Then it was easy to follow them down a rutted, overgrown path. A little farmhouse came into sight, and Wylm dismounted and tied his horse to an oak tree so he could get closer without being seen. He took cover behind an unkempt hedgerow. Across the field, a man with a head like a block and thick, black hair was mending a fence. Wylm watched him for a while. The hoofprints definitely led onto this farm and he wondered who the man was, what Bluebell had been doing here.

Was this the lover?

Wylm nearly choked on his suppressed laughter. Why, she must be a foot taller than him! They'd both have to be blindfolded to enjoy themselves, surely. He stifled a laugh, but then the door to the farmhouse opened and a little boy emerged.

A child! A flame ignited in Wylm's chest. Could this be . . . Did Bluebell have a child?

No, he was letting his tired brain run away from him. Somebody would have noticed if Bluebell's belly had swelled. She would have been forced out of men's clothes, out of battle, out of public life.

But then, this child looked to be about ten. He didn't know where Bluebell had been ten years ago, what activities may have been used to cover a secret, illegitimate pregnancy. His whole body flexed forward with eagerness. A child. And not an ordinary child. This one felt his way carefully along with his toes, his sightless eyes unblinking against the bright sunlight. A certain slackness around his mouth told

Wylm it wasn't only his eyes that didn't work right. The farmer pulled the boy close into a hug.

Wylm was electrified. Had he just learned something about Bluebell that nobody else knew? A cooler, duller thought: Was it of any use to him?

He stood and headed back to his horse and made his way home to Blickstow, through the gate and to the stables. The change from bright daylight to semi-dark made Wylm stop a moment to adjust his eyes. The stable smelled of straw and leather.

Bluebell's big warhorse, Isern, was being groomed carefully by young Tom. Isern was back? Then why hadn't she taken him to her lover's farm?

"Afternoon, Tom," he said, leading his horse to her stable.

"Afternoon, Master Wylm."

"Bluebell's horse is back?"

"He's been back a few days. We're giving him a rest. She's off again tomorrow."

"Is she? Where to?"

"King's business, I imagine." Tom put down his head and kept brushing.

"But the king . . ." Wylm fell silent. Nobody outside a handful of people knew about the king. The steward certainly wouldn't. So Bluebell was off somewhere tomorrow? Far enough away to need her horse rested? His spine prickled. He needed to speak to his mother.

He patted his horse's nose, but noticed his hand was shaking. "Tom, you'll take care of my mother's horse for me? I have to be somewhere."

"Of course."

Wylm found his mother in the little room Bluebell had assigned them. Wylm hadn't slept beside Gudrun since he was a chubby-fingered boy, so he had been spending nights at the alehouse. Gudrun sat in front of a bronze mirror, carefully combing and plaiting her hair. She looked tired. No: more than tired. She looked haunted. He stretched his mind back to his own father's death—her first husband's death—and couldn't remember her looking so drawn and pale back then. A childish feeling of unfairness pulled tight in his belly, and he took a breath to make it go away. He had been only ten when his father died; perhaps his memory was faulty.

"Mother," he said, "is there any chance that Bluebell has a child?"

Gudrun snorted. "Of course not."

"Athelrick never said anything that made you suspect?"

"I . . . He knew she had a lover. But I think it unlikely that a pregnancy would go unnoticed."

Wylm let it go. "Bluebell is up to something," he said.

Her hands froze and she dropped her comb. He pulled over a stool to sit next to her, picking up her comb and handing it back to her. She twisted it between her hands.

"What do you mean?" she asked.

"Tom said he's getting her horse ready to go away tomorrow."

"She's going away?" Gudrun's whole body relaxed. "That's a good thing."

"Why would she go away? Her father is dying, and her love for him is legendary."

Gudrun made a sour expression. "And legends are often exaggerated." She took a deep breath, combing her hair rhythmically. "I will be safe once she is gone, as long as you are here. You will keep me safe, won't you?"

"I'll do my best." He touched her shoulder lightly. "But Bluebell will return. She's dangerous, Mother, and I couldn't save you from her. I think we should leave. I have a feeling in my stomach . . . This will not turn out well for either of us."

Her face grew mournful. "I can't leave. Athelrick is dying."

"Athelrick doesn't know you anymore. His mind is already dead. You only wait for the body to catch up."

She shook her head. "This is such a mess, Wylm! All my happiness has fled." She fixed him with her pale eyes. "My son. Can I tell you anything? Everything?"

Uneasiness stirred across his back. "Of course."

Gudrun stood and began to pace. "I am in so deep . . ."

"What do you mean?"

Pacing. Pacing.

"Mother?"

"I meant . . ." She fell silent awhile. Then said, "I meant no harm. Not to him."

Wylm struggled to understand her with his mind, but his skin was already shrinking in fear. "I don't understand."

She stopped, came close. Knelt at his feet and put her head in his lap. "I'm so sorry," she said, against the fabric of his pants. "I'm so sorry, Wylm."

Wylm touched her hair lightly, fearfully. "What have you done?"

She raised her head. "I bought an elf-shot off a traveler, an under-magician. I was specific. I said I didn't want to hurt Athelrick, I merely wanted to change his mind about Bluebell. I wanted him to take up the trimartyr faith, so she couldn't rule." Here her face contorted and she began to sob, her voice coming out high and whining. "I never meant to hurt him. I love him! But I knew it would be better for me—and for you—if Bluebell wasn't here. Maybe he would have even made you his heir."

"But I didn't want . . . I don't want . . ." His heart was thundering. Because he *did* want. The closer such a fate moved toward his outstretched fingers, the more he saw that it was right and good. King Wylm of Almissia. And timidity would avail him nothing. He fell silent.

"The traveler gave me a stone. I put it under Athelrick's pillow. He found it when we went to bed and I said it was to give him sweet dreams and he . . . He smiled at me and put it back. The next morning, it was gone and he seemed confused and . . . he bumped into things and he said he needed to lie down and . . . he didn't get up. I tried to find the traveler, but she was gone." She palmed tears off her face. "It's done, Wylm. I can't undo it."

Self-preservation helped him find his voice. "Does anyone else know?"

"Osred. He says there's nothing we can do."

Wylm realized his stomach was rolling with nausea. He gently pushed his mother away and stood, went to the shutter and opened it for fresh air.

Behind him, his mother continued to sob. "Perhaps I deserve to die," she said, her voice raw and harsh. "Look what I've done to him! Look what I've done."

He turned to watch her. Her eyes streamed; her nostrils were gleaming wet. He was overwhelmed with pity, but then he imagined Bluebell seeing Gudrun like this. If she knew, she would feel no pity at all. "You don't deserve to die," he said. "Nobody will find out."

"She'd kill me, wouldn't she?" Gudrun said in a small voice.

"There is no doubt." And she would enjoy it. Bluebell was in love with death. Wylm approached his mother, put a hand on each of her arms.

She broke into sobs again, big enough to break her. "I can't see my way out. Wylm, I trust to your judgment because I have none. Consult with Osred. He's in the infirmary. Between the two of you, you must find an ally. Any ally. One who will not side with Bluebell."

"Gather yourself, Mother," Wylm said. "All will be well."

Wylm left her shaking and crying and made his way to the infirmary. The edges of his vision were bright and blurring. Fear, mortal fear, had hold of him. His mother had done a stupid, selfish thing, and unless he managed his next few moves very carefully, there was no doubt both he and his mother faced brutal deaths. The vision of Bluebell splitting open the head of the bandit replayed in his mind's eye, only this time it was his mother's face crumpling. His gorge rose. He stopped, thumping the wall with the side of his fist. What an idiotic thing his mother had done, what a grumbling storm she had invoked.

And yet it was done. Now he had to be man enough to walk into this storm, and emerge as Almissia's king.

Osred practically leapt from his bed when he saw Wylm.

"You must get me out of here! Bluebell is crazed and—"

"I've come to remove you," Wylm said. His own pulse snapped so hard in his throat that he was certain Osred would be able to see it.

"Oh, thank you." Osred's shoulders and chest were wrapped in blood-soaked bandages. "I know I'm probably too ill to travel, but I don't know what she'll do next."

Wylm stilled him with both hands. The other man winced against his grip.

"Osred," Wylm said, "you know what my mother has done?"

"Yes."

"And how do you think we should proceed?"

"We should take your mother and leave."

"Would our departure not be an admission of guilt?"

"No, it would be self-preservation."

"And you would do whatever it took to preserve yourself?"

Osred cocked his head slightly. "I am of no use to your mother dead."

Wylm considered him a moment. Osred would tell. Eventually. That he hadn't so far, even under torture, was no indication of how he might behave in a week, or a year, or a decade. As long as he was alive, he could reveal Gudrun's betrayal. And should his mother's crime come to light, Wylm's future was dashed.

But was Wylm the man who could silence Osred? Was he the man his mother needed him to be?

"Dress quickly," Wylm said.

"I'm not under guard."

"Nonetheless, I don't think we should be seen together, lest Bluebell assume we are colluding."

They were not even an hour out of town when Osred complained that he must rest, that the jolting of the horse's hooves on the poorly finished low road was making him bleed. Wylm's heart seemed too big for his chest. Osred knelt by the muddy stream, forcing breath into his lungs, scooping a handful of water to his mouth. Wylm felt at his belt for his knife, drew it slowly, noted his shaking fingers.

Then he strode through dappled sunlight to stab it hard into the muscle and gristle of Osred's back. He would have given all his riches not to have heard the noise Osred made—a thudding, coughing, gurgling noise—before he pitched forward, his blood pulsing into the brown water. Wylm waded into the stream, pulling the body into the current. He would wash downstream then be pulled under in the cold river. Nobody would find him; nobody would know.

Wylm retrieved his knife and waded back to the bank. Blood

dripped from the tip of the blade, a slow flat noise against the ground. Then it stopped. He wiped his nose with the back of his free hand. Not crying. He wasn't crying.

Find an ally. Any ally.

A strong ally. One that already hated Bluebell. She had plenty of enemies. Wylm turned the thought over in his mind as he left the glade without glancing back at Osred's body.

Undermagic was dangerous, and Ash knew that. She had learned a little about it during her studies: Always wear sweet violets to protect yourself from undermagic; don't turn your back on one of their conjured spirits; be aware that undermagicians say one thing and do another. She didn't feel like an undermagician. She felt the same as she always had: the third of five daughters who had long stood in her sisters' shadows, who was amenable, even biddable. She didn't feel as though great powers ran through her body and brain, powers that made her different, vast and mighty. Surely, if she was an undermagician, she would know it somehow, feel it with more clarity and force.

Ash wound the cold fear up tightly and kept it tucked away. Yes, she was afraid of using her sight again, especially for something as risky as traveling out of her body and across invisible miles, because that was bordering on undermagic. But there was a small part of her that wanted to know how easy it would be for her. And an even larger part that wanted to find her father's sister, this hidden aunt. For clearly, it was from her that Ash drew her talent. What if she understood Ash? What if she could save Ash from her blighted Becoming?

Bluebell had left Ash alone in her bower, so she could close up the shutters and stoke the fire. The smoke was thick and choking, but she knelt by the hearthpit and tore up the leaves and roots of an angelica plant. The milk stuck between her fingers as she scattered the pieces into the fire. A sweet, sharp smell rose with the smoke, and Ash closed her eyes. Her head pounded, the thrum of her blood against her temples. The smells were sticky in her throat and she felt as though the world were growing distant from her, as though time and light were swelling and stretching away, and she was shrunk to a hard, sharp pin in the middle of it. She breathed deeply and began to say her aunt's name over and over.

"Eldra, Eldra, Eldra . . ."

The word droned on, losing its meaning, disintegrating, floating apart and traveling on the billows of the sky. Ash lost sensation in her body, felt the pull and welcome snap of freedom as she left herself on the floor of the bower and shot upward with Eldra's name. North and north. She blurred out of the bower, out of Blickstow, up the Giant Road, then west over darkening woods and giants' ruins. North and north again, trees and roads flickering against her sight, then slower, slower, slowing down. Her breathing was audible again, and she was both in the bowerhouse and on the edge of a dark plain. A towering stone cast a black shadow against the gray ground. Ash reached out with her hands and, even though she knew they were held out toward the fire, she felt the cold rough surface of the monolith. She looked down and saw her bare feet on the dewy grass. She reached up to her unbound hair, checking that the crown of sweet violets was still in place. As she touched the petals, a sharp, hot shock leapt into her fingers.

"Eldra?" she called, turning in a slow circle.

There. A path leading into trees. She began to walk. Her lungs felt raw and she coughed. The path led upward, and the trees were sparse. She stopped. At the top of the hill, she could see a human figure. When she looked hard, there were two. Then three. Lined up, one after the other, on the side of the path. She had to pass them to get to her destination. A cold dread seeped into her chest.

She moved on and up, the rocks poking hollows in her soft soles. She drew closer to the first figure and realized it was made of straw and corn—an attenuated slender thing that lurched to one side for lack of strong support. She stopped, looking at it more closely in the gloom. Eyes made of dead beetles looked back at her. She turned and kept walking toward the next. There was a noise behind her.

She spun. The corn dolly had turned its head to watch her. Her heart frosted over. These were thralls, made of mud and straw and undermagic.

"Pull away, pull away," Ash told herself, lifting up off the ground and trying to see the corn dollies from above. She glimpsed a little lime-washed hut, a warm light in its window, then she was slammed back down to the ground with a bone-jarring thud.

The woman's voice came from everywhere. "What do you want?"

"Eldra, I am your niece."

"You are blighted. You are destined to take thousands with you into death. Come not near me."

A surge of invisible darkness began to push Ash backward along the path, carrying her along like a doll in the waves. She flung her arms out, flailing, then felt herself funneled roughly back into her body, on the floor of her bower.

Ash opened her eyes. The smoke was thick and choking; sweat ran in trickles from her temples. She coughed and coughed, then pulled herself to her feet and ran outside into the sweet evening air, gulping it down.

All her joints were swollen and sore.

Eldra's words circled her, their dark import pressing in on her. "You are destined to take thousands with you into death." She had known it since she'd seen the dragon's indiscriminate fire in the vision. She hadn't wanted to believe it, but it was true.

As she stood, aching and coughing, Bluebell emerged from the infirmary and saw her.

"Sister? Are you well?" Bluebell strode over, her face grim in the darkening twilight.

"I . . . I am well." Ash coughed again. "I found her."

Bluebell's eyebrows shot up. "Eldra? Is she father's sister?"

"I don't know. She is certainly a powerful undermagician." A bolt of jealousy, frosted with fear.

"Can you lead us to her?"

"I think so," Ash said, "but I don't know if we'll be welcome." *I certainly won't be.*

"Which way?"

Ash coughed again, pretending it was difficult to breathe. "I'm sorry. The magic takes its toll on me. We go north and northwest, into the heart of Bradsey. There's a stone on the edge of a plain . . ." Her heart stuttered again at the thought of it.

"We'll find it," Bluebell said, squaring her shoulders. "Go and get some rest. You look exhausted." Then she was striding on her way to finish organizing their journey, Ash's ever-capable sister.

Ash watched her go, then sank to the grass to breathe the soft evening air. Her mind whirled. If her Becoming meant the deaths of others, then the only way to prevent such horror was to take herself into exile. Away from everyone. Away from her sisters. She could lead them to Eldra's, but then she would have to leave them, lest her Becoming sweep them all away.

chapter 10

W illow took a deep breath and let her hands fall in her lap, the fine silver chain loose over her fingers, the triangle spilling down and swinging slowly. She sat on the grass, in the shadow behind her father's hall. Evening damp pressed against her skirts; a light in a lantern flickered beside her. *Breathe in, breathe out.* But no matter that she told herself to relax, she could not stop the whirling thoughts in her mind. Where *were* they?

Come to me, most beloved angels, messengers of Maava. Praise Maava, may his glory be great. Come to me, angels, let me hear your sweet voices. Where are your sweet voices? Forsake me not . . .

Their silence infected her heart. Why did they not speak to her? Once, perhaps a year ago, she hadn't yet known their voices could be heard and had not realized how empty time and thought were without them. But then the preacher who lived behind her village—the one people warned her to stay away from—had told her about the voices, about how he had been chosen by Maava to hear angels speak in his head. He had soft eyes and long, strong fingers, and Willow was drawn to him in ways that she didn't understand, but suspected Maava had marked him out that way to bring her to the fold. Willow had wanted so much to hear angels that she couldn't sleep at night for feeling her ribs and spine push against her soft flesh inside. Finally, finally, after weeks of prayer, the voices had come.

But here she was, far from home, and nothing but silence.

Come to me, angels, for Maava's love. For pity of sweet Liava and her doomed twins. I would die for Maava, too. You can't leave me alone now. Come to me, tell me what I should do.

Then, when she was about to dissolve into despair . . .

"Here, child. We are here." A chorus of sweet voices, whispering across one another. "We are here. Be not sad."

Oh, thank you. Thank you. I ask only what I should do, here, so far from home. My father is dying, my father by blood. I barely know him, but I love him as a daughter should, though he is not my lord. Maava is my lord. May all pray for his might. Praise Maava may his glory be great. The one god, the only god.

"Your father is a heathen king. Your father will pass, on his death, to the Blacklands."

Her father in the Blacklands? Maava would judge her by her father's fate, surely. Her heart spiked. *No! Can I not save him? Can I not pray for him? I will pray every second.*

"You may pray. You may hope he dies when you are with him, so that you may ask Maava to transport his soul into the Sunlands. But he is a sinner and may yet not be saved."

Then the voices turned into the snarling swirl they sometimes did, where words weren't clear but meaning bloomed in her belly, dark and cold. Maava was unhappy with her. She had a heathen for a father. Heathens for sisters. She hadn't done enough to bring them into Maava's light.

Self-hatred, despair. She took the edge of her trimartyr triangle and dug it into the soft flesh of her wrist. It did nothing more than leave an indentation in among the crisscrossing of faint scars. She pulled the knife from her waistband and lightly scored three lines across her wrist. Tiny beads of blood bubbled out. She put her knife away, licked the blood off her skin.

Then she brought the triangle to her lips and prayed and prayed until the feeling slipped behind her heart; there it would remain until the next time Maava decided to punish her.

No use moping. She had to do something. The angels had told her to be with her father, but Bluebell planned to take him away in the morning. She would have to make sure she traveled, too. Maava would want that.

Bluebell wouldn't.

She rose, picked up her lamp, then her skin prickled. She realized she wasn't alone.

Willow turned sharply. Her stepbrother, Wylm, was watching her from around the corner of the hall. She quickly tucked away her triangle. He smiled and nodded, the usual cruel set of his brow absent. Her heart hammered. Would he tell Bluebell? Perhaps he didn't even recognize her. She had been twelve last time they had met.

"Hello, Willow," he said, and his expression was almost warm.

She was taken aback and her tongue labored over an answer. Before she could say a word, offer a defense, he slipped away.

Well, perhaps it would be good if he did tell Bluebell. It was well past time Willow told Bluebell herself. Maava was the one god. Those who didn't accept that committed their souls to the Blacklands. That was precisely where Bluebell was headed if she didn't accept the trimartyr faith.

The dark feeling again. *I'm sorry, Maava, I'm sorry. I'm a poor sinner. I will do better. But if I tell Bluebell now, she won't let me travel with my father. I will save his soul. I will send him to you in the Sunlands.* With new resolve, she went to find Bluebell.

She wasn't in her bower, though Rose was there with Rowan, Ash, and Ivy.

"Have you seen Bluebell?" Willow asked. "I need to speak with her immediately."

Ivy's curiosity was piqued. She stood and approached. "Willow, what's all this?"

Willow ignored her. "Do you know where Bluebell is?"

"Over at the infirmary, I think," Rose said as she brushed Rowan's long dark hair.

Ivy caught her at the door, dropping her voice low. "Why do you need to see Bluebell?"

"That's my business." Willow kept walking, head down.

"Your business is my business. You know that."

"I'm going to make her take me tomorrow. With Father."

"Are you mad? Why would you want to do that? We could go home tomorrow."

"Don't try to convince me otherwise, Ivy. I've made up my mind and I'm going to ask her. No, I'm going to *tell* her. I have to go with Father. Maava wants me to."

Ivy stopped and pulled Willow to a halt with a firm hand around her wrist. "No. No, no, no. You *cannot* mention your trimartyr nonsense to Bluebell!"

Willow set her chin. How she despised it when Ivy called her faith "nonsense," as though she were as flighty and inconstant as Ivy herself. "Why not?"

"Because trimartyrs don't believe in queens. And Bluebell rather fancies she'll be one."

Ivy was right on both counts. It wasn't for Willow to question Maava's wisdom, and Bluebell herself would one day have to accept it: The last heathen queen that didn't, mighty Dystro of Tweening, had found herself without a head resisting the trimartyrs. "I can hardly choose to believe some of Maava's truths and not others."

"Your head is made of wood. The moment you mention it, she'll stop listening to you."

A few feet away, the door to the infirmary swung outward. Bluebell's shadow proceeded her, indistinct against the flickering lamplight. Willow caught her breath, then hated herself for being afraid of her older sister. Whoever stood in Maava's righteous truth had no need to fear.

Willow hurried forward as Bluebell shut the infirmary door behind her and slid across a bolt. "Sister, I would speak with you."

Bluebell looked up. "What is it? I'm busy."

"Tomorrow. You've said you leave at dawn. I want to come with you."

"No."

"Athelrick is my father, too. I want to be with him."

"Why?"

Willow's heart stammered, but she forced her voice to be smooth and strong. "Because he may die. Why should three of his daughters travel with him while the other two wait and hope? Would you be content to wait and hope?"

Bluebell tilted her head to one side, her eyes narrowed. Willow could tell she was struggling. Bluebell was nothing if not loyal to the idea of family.

"I could be of use to you. You, Rose, and Ash will need help on the journey."

"We won't need help. Sighere and Heath are coming," Bluebell said.

"Heath?" Ivy squeaked.

Willow ignored her. "Heath is not even a member of this family!"

"He is your sister's nephew, and he can wield a sword better than either of you."

Ivy piped up loudly. "We should be allowed to come. If you say no, we will simply follow you."

Willow turned and looked at Ivy curiously.

Bluebell pressed the heel of her hand into her forehead. "Find your own horses, pack everything you need, don't ask me to stop and rest along the way, and keep your eyes open for danger. I can probably use you somehow. And it goes without saying you don't tell *anyone* what's going on."

A muffled voice from within the infirmary. "Bluebell!"

"Coming, Dunstan," she called through the door. She sized up her youngest sisters. "Don't fuck up or I'll send you home."

"We won't fuck up," Ivy said, clearly relishing the curse.

"We will do the right thing," Willow said as Bluebell wrenched open the door and went back inside.

Willow turned to Ivy. "Why did you change your mind?"

Ivy smiled dreamily. "Heath."

"I thought you wanted to marry William Dartwood."

Ivy snorted. "I don't want to *marry* anyone. Although . . ." Ivy pushed her lip out, thinking. "Heath would be rather a good match."

Willow fished the neck chain out of her dress and pressed the triangle against her lips. Never mind her heathen sisters; she was doing

Maava's work. She was sure she felt his favor turn to her, and despite the cool misty evening it was like sunlight on her bones.

Bluebell watched Dunstan as he hammered the last of the nails into the shutter.

"No way out?" she said.

"She'd have to pull these out with her teeth."

"The door?"

"You saw the bolt."

"But you'll need a lock. So no do-gooder comes along and—"

"The smithy has made you a box padlock. He'll bring it up tonight."

Bluebell pushed her long hair off her neck and tied it in a knot, glancing around the room. She and Dunstan had spent today making it into a prison. A comfortable one, but a prison nonetheless. The comfort was a concession to her sisters' opinions, even though she hadn't mentioned to them her plans for Gudrun. She'd intended to lock her stepmother up in here with Osred, but Osred had disappeared earlier that day. Bluebell couldn't help but see it as confirmation of guilt, and had sent six men off to try to catch him.

"Tomorrow morning at dawn, I'll come for you," Bluebell said. "My sisters will be down at the stables, waiting with the cart. Sighere and Heath will be with me. We'll take Athelrick, and you take Gudrun. Don't let her scream. Do what you have to, but be careful with her. We can't harm her, in case . . . in case I am wrong."

Dunstan hid a smile.

Bluebell kicked his shin. "Fuck you, old man."

"I'll be sweet to her."

"Pick up her son, too. He's staying at the alehouse. Get Gudrun locked up first, then bring Wylm down. He's not to be underestimated. He's inexperienced, but wily." She dusted her hands against her tunic. "They can keep each other company until I get back." She tried not to think about how much ill will her actions would arouse. If she was right, then it was of no matter. But if she was wrong . . .

"I'm not wrong," she muttered. "I *know it*, Dunstan. I've always had a sense she's bad for our family."

He looked back at her. "Well, either you are wrong, or your father is."

She lifted her chin. Dunstan had been her first teacher. He'd dragged her out of bed on her tenth birthday and beaten her over the head with a wooden sword until she developed the muscles to lift her shield swiftly and precisely to block him. Six years later, she'd beaten him in practice combat for the first time. "Who do you think is wrong?" she asked.

"I wouldn't dare to say, Bluebell. Either answer would upset you."

Bluebell shrugged. "Dawn, then," she said. "Lock her up. And don't tell my sisters."

Rose woke late in the night, with Rowan's elbow firmly jammed under her ribs. She gently dislodged it and rolled Rowan on her side. Ash, sleeping on the other side of the bed, stirred softly. Rose closed her eyes. She didn't mind waking up; it meant she had another chance to fall asleep thinking of Heath. She conjured him in her mind. Somehow they would slip away from Bluebell's notice, find a sheltered glade to shed their clothes . . .

"Rose? Are you awake?" Ash's whisper was soft in the dark.

"Yes."

Ash sat up. "I can't sleep."

"Are you thinking about tomorrow?"

Rowan stirred, and Ash dropped her voice. "I'm thinking about all my tomorrows."

Rose reached out and rubbed the back of Ash's pale hand. Her sister looked very young tonight. But then, Ash always looked young: a softness around her cheeks and mouth, the slightness of her shoulders and hips. "Is there anything wrong, Ash?"

Ash fell silent awhile. A light rain started on the roof.

"Ash?"

"How much do you imagine the Great Sea weighs?" Ash said. "Lately, it has lain upon my chest."

"Why? What has happened?"

"This . . . ability of mine. It grows so strong and . . . I am afraid of who I might become."

"Have you taken advice from Byrta?"

"Yes. She isn't much use."

Rose shivered. "How strong is it?"

"It's bigger than I am. Rosie, do you think it's possible to control your destiny?"

Rose thought about Heath. "My heart hopes so."

Rose couldn't be sure in the dark, but thought Ash was smiling at her. "My heart hopes so, too. I'm sorry. I shouldn't keep you awake."

"Will you sleep?"

"I don't think so."

"You'll be tired tomorrow. And Bluebell won't let you rest."

Ash chuckled softly. "Night will come again. Even Bluebell can't hold it back. You sleep, sister. No doubt the little one will make your life impossible on the journey tomorrow."

Rose lay down and put a protective arm around Rowan.

"I love you, Rosie."

"I love you, too." Rose closed her eyes and tried to imagine Heath again, but darker thoughts intruded. *Do you think it's possible to control your destiny?* Her heart hoped so, as she had told Ash. But her head knew better.

Bluebell dressed by the light of a candle. She had woken nearly a dozen times throughout the night, each time with startlement in her heart. Had she missed the dawn? Was it late in the day already? She felt ragged and gritty-eyed as she pulled her byrnie over her shoulders. Its familiar weight settled on her. She didn't anticipate anyone trying to stop her taking Athelrick from his bower, but she had to be prepared for anything. She sheathed her sword and slung her pack over her left shoulder. She cracked open the door to her bower, letting in a swirl of cool morning air. Thrymm and Thrack roused, climbed to their feet with tails wagging. The sky was still dark, but softening to pale blue on the horizon. On the western horizon, clouds gathered. The morning smelled of woodsmoke and dew.

Bluebell crept down to the stables and left her pack outside, urging the dogs to stay. She could hear her sisters and Sighere, talking to one another in quiet voices. Birdsong clattered all around. She turned and made her way light-footed back to the bowerhouse.

Dunstan and Heath were waiting in the predawn gloom.

"Dunstan, you take care of Gudrun. Gently. She slept with Athelrick in his bower last night, so we'll be fetching her from there."

Dunstan grunted his assent.

"Heath, you help me with Father, and you don't tell anyone what we've done. Not even Rose."

Heath nodded.

Bluebell opened the door, took a moment for her eyes to adjust to the dark. Two sleeping shapes. She nodded toward Dunstan. He stalked into the room without flinching and lurched toward Gudrun.

Gudrun shrieked as he pulled her out of the covers, but then his big hand went over her mouth.

"Get her out, quick," Bluebell whispered. "You know what to do."

She had a brief impression of Gudrun's face, white with fear in the dim light. Then it flashed past her and was gone.

Bluebell gestured toward her father's body. "You take his legs." Then, quieter, "Don't hurt him."

She approached the bed and peeled back the blanket. Her hair fell over his face as she leaned forward.

"Father, it's me. It's Bluebell. I'm taking you somewhere so you can get better. I'm going to look after you."

His eyes flickered but didn't open. Was she imagining it, or did his lips move soundlessly, as though he was trying to answer? She pulled his upper body against her chest, and Heath caught his legs. Together they carried him out of the bower and down to the stables.

Sighere and the cart were waiting. They'd set it up the night before, lined it with a mattress and blankets. Bluebell laid Athelrick in the cart, then laid beside him his byrnie and sword, and a deep-red cloak folded neatly. A warrior king should not be without his weapons and armor, even one who slept as though dead. Then she folded the canopy over the top so nobody would see the precious cargo within.

Rose sat on the cart, with Rowan curled against her, sleepily sucking her lip. "Nobody saw you?" Rose asked. "Gudrun?"

"All is well. All has gone to plan," Bluebell said, slinging her pack over Isern's rump and pulling the rope tight. "Let's ride."

Wylm detached himself from the shadows behind the stables and watched as the band of figures disappeared down the hill that led to the back gates of Blickstow. They stopped a few moments there, voices hushed but bridles clattering, as Bluebell unlatched the gates. Then they were through, the cart rattling and bumping behind them. The gates closed. They were gone.

The cart. What did they have in the cart? Where were they going? Wylm hadn't made out all the voices, but was certain he'd heard Rose with her child, and Ash's quiet, measured tone. The other two quieter voices might have been the other two sisters. And two male voices he couldn't place: soldiers, perhaps.

Uneasiness stretched in his guts. He turned, fear making his feet clumsy, and began to run toward his mother.

Already he could see the door to her bower standing wide open on the empty black. Already he could see the rushlights blazing around the infirmary, hear her calling out, "Don't hurt me! Don't hurt me!"

And another, harsher voice telling her to be quiet and she wouldn't be hurt.

Wylm slunk back into the shadows. His heart hammered. What kind of man was he not to rush in there with his sword in front of him, demanding they let her go?

But he had no sword. It was back at the alehouse, along with his spare clothes, his knife, everything he traveled with. And no doubt, that's where they would be looking for him. He was as helpless as a boy who still pissed his pants, and that made him angry.

It was still dark. He could creep away now.

But his mother . . .

He couldn't help her if he was incarcerated with her. Nor could he help her if he was dead.

"I'll be back when I can, Mother," he whispered into the empty dawn. Then he ran.

chapter 11

The sun rose, but was soon swallowed by clouds moving in fast from the west. A strong, stiff wind that shouldn't have belonged to spring rattled the new buds and leaves, bringing the smell of damp earth to Bluebell's nostrils. Rain was coming.

Bluebell rode at the head of the group with Sighere. Heath rode at the rear. Rose drove the cart, with Rowan sitting next to her and Father asleep behind them. The cart was slow and would add at least a day to their journey up past Stonemantel to Sabert's flower farm. Within four miles, too, they would have to leave the road and travel over fields and forest tracks. Bluebell didn't want to be visible.

But even though the horses had to walk, the fact that she was on Isern, with Sighere nearby and her dogs loping beside her, made Bluebell feel positive for the first time in the week since she'd heard the news. They were doing *something*. They weren't sitting around in that stuffy, sunless room waiting for her father to die.

Then the rain started. Spitting, at first, and cold. Rain from a long way up. Bluebell wouldn't have noticed it but for the chorus of bleating behind her. Ivy was the loudest, followed by Rowan—who could be forgiven as she was only three. Even Willow, who seemed such a quiet, stoic creature, muttered about the damp.

Bluebell turned to Sighere and said quietly, "It will get worse."

Sighere glanced over his shoulder at the dark cloud eating the sky, his long black hair lifted by the wind. "Yes, my lord. Are we going to stay on the road?"

"We can't."

"There will be mud."

"I'm not afraid of a little mud," Bluebell said, smiling.

Then the rain deepened, fat cold drops thundering to the ground. Bluebell was wet through in moments, her hair sticking to her face, her mail byrnie weighing cold against her. She gave the signal that they were splitting off the road and the others followed, down onto rain-slippery grass. Before them lay muddy fields.

"Bluebell? Must we leave the road?"

This was Ivy, of course. Bluebell didn't know what her mother's brother had been teaching Ivy, but it wasn't how to endure ordinary hardship. Bluebell had long disagreed with Father on how to raise the twins. She wanted them brought back to Blickstow to shape them for public life. Willow looked as though she might have the steel and valor for war, and some arms training would put hard thighs on those skinny legs of hers. As for Ivy, she was insufferably pampered and needed to be married off as soon as possible in a peace deal. Bluebell had already made an offer to one of Wengest's cousins, a duke named Gunther in north Nettlechester who controlled an important port town. She'd always suspected he might get too powerful and try his luck against her. She was just waiting for Wengest to say yes. Until both girls were put in service to their family, they would blow around like leaves on the wind.

"Yes, Ivy," Bluebell replied, "we must leave the road."

"But—"

Bluebell raised her hand to signal no further discussion, but Ivy paid no heed. She rode up next to Bluebell and said, "Only, it's terribly muddy."

Bluebell didn't say anything. She made a habit of leaving stupid requests unanswered.

"Bluebell?"

"Please go back and ride with your sisters," Sighere said to Ivy.

Ivy's eyes blazed. "And who are you to tell me what to do?"

Bluebell shook her head at Sighere, and Ivy's question was met with more silence. Ivy harrumphed and turned her horse around. Bluebell heard harsh whispering behind her as Ivy complained to Willow. She shrugged it off.

It took an hour for the complaining to ease—even Ash was cursing the mud—but then the wind picked up and drove icily against their wet bodies. Rowan's whining grew louder and louder, until finally Bluebell couldn't stand it anymore. She hadn't wanted the child here, any more than she'd wanted the twins. But Rose had insisted, as Ivy and Willow had insisted. And if there was one weakness Bluebell had, it was her family.

She pulled her horse to a halt, and the rest of the party clattered and stopped behind her. She turned her horse around and rode up to Rose and Rowan sitting at the front of the cart.

Rowan looked at her with huge, round eyes. She had seen the grim set of her aunt's mouth.

"Princess Rowan of Nettlechester," Bluebell said. "Are you crying?"

Rowan nodded.

Rose intervened. "Bluebell, be kind. The child is cold, the cart is rattling our bones, and she's too frightened of Father's muttering to go in with him and sleep."

Bluebell waved Rose's words away. She reached over and plucked Rowan from her seat, dumping her on Isern's back.

"Mama!" Rowan cried.

"Bluebell, please . . ."

Bluebell turned and rode back to the front of the party. Rowan sobbed for her mother. Bluebell leaned over and whispered harshly in her ear: "Stop it. I'm not your mother, and I won't put up with your nonsense."

Rowan took a deep, shuddering breath.

"I'm going to tell you a secret," Bluebell said softly. "Can you keep a secret?"

Rowan nodded, turning her face up to Bluebell.

"One day you'll be a queen."

"Yes," said Rowan, clearly enraptured by the idea.

"I have very big plans for you, little one."

Bluebell was almost certain Wengest couldn't father another child, and she was also certain she'd outlive him. If she managed his relatives well and kept them from getting too powerful, Nettlechester could be hers with the application of only a little force. And as she would have no children of her own, Rowan was her obvious heir. The little girl was sturdy and strong, with fire in her eyes. On her seventh birthday, Bluebell planned to have her brought to Blickstow under the pretense of giving her an education. Wengest would let her go; he didn't care for girls and wouldn't be interested in educating her himself. And then Bluebell would herself train the child in arms and strategy.

Of course, Rose knew none of this. It wasn't right to tell her, when the child was still so soft-skinned. No mother wanted to think about their little one taking up an ax.

"You'll be a warrior queen," Bluebell said. "Beautiful and terrible and mighty."

Rowan bounced in the saddle, all tears evaporated. "Yes!"

"But you mustn't tell your papa."

"No?"

"Your papa doesn't believe in warrior queens." Bluebell hesitated, then decided to go all the way. "He'd stop you from being a queen. That's for certain. So you mustn't mention it."

"Does Mama believe in them?"

"It doesn't matter. What matters is this: Warrior queens don't cry at a little rain and cold."

Rowan set her chin. "I'm a warrior queen."

"That's my good girl." Bluebell rubbed her head roughly, then urged Isern forward. Rowan was quiet for the rest of the day's journey.

Around midafternoon, they came across an abandoned stable with a piece of its roof missing. The rain and mud had tired everyone, including the horses and dogs. They had traveled as much as they could for the day, so they stopped.

"Horses outside, people inside," Bluebell said. Sighere and Heath unlatched the cart and brought it inside, and the weary travelers tended to their horses in the rain.

Ivy couldn't remember ever being so uncomfortable. Her clothes were damp and stiff, her thighs and back were aching, and her waterlogged hands were white and puffy. And now, for comfort, she sat on moldy straw next to a fire made with kindling so damp it could hardly warm her. Choking smoke poured off it. At least the hole in the roof allowed a little air in . . . not to mention rain. Night was approaching, and somehow she would have to sleep. Sleep! Unthinkable.

Added to this, Iron-Tits was cranky and casting a black cloud over everyone. She was displeased they hadn't gotten as far as she'd hoped. In Ivy's view, they had traveled halfway across the world: She simply couldn't think about the fact she had to get back on the horse tomorrow. If she thought about it, she would break down into uncontrollable sobbing.

Somehow she made it through the evening. She chewed halfheartedly on a piece of bread and some salted meat, found a quiet place outside to wee in the rain, and got her clothes barely dry. Everyone agreed they were exhausted and began to roll out their blankets. That's when Ivy realized she hadn't packed a blanket.

"Can I share yours?" she quietly said to Willow.

"No," Willow said, "it's too small for both of us. Why didn't you bring one?"

"I didn't think of it."

"What *did* you pack?"

Ivy didn't answer. She couldn't admit she had two pretty dresses and a selection of bead chains. Willow would make her sleep on her dresses, but Ivy didn't want mud on them. Those clothes were for when they got there, wherever "there" was. Bluebell had said something about a flower farm and Ivy had imagined herself in her blue dress with the gold embroidery at the sleeves, out among the flowers with the sun in her fair hair. Then Heath would see her and want her.

Ivy glanced around the room. Everyone was settling down for the evening except Bluebell, who was taking first watch by King Athelrick's cart. The cart! Ivy wagered there would be spare blankets in there. She approached it happily.

Bluebell, whose sword was drawn, frowned at her. "What?"

"I need a blanket," Ivy said, reaching for the edge of the cart.

Bluebell's sword whipped out in front of her, blocking her hands. The steel caught the firelight.

"Hey!" Ivy protested. "I'm your sister."

"You stay away from him."

"Why?"

"Because the Widowsmith says so," she replied with no trace of a smile.

"I need a blanket."

"You're not taking his."

"He has more than one, surely. You would've padded the cart with them."

Bluebell narrowed her eyes but didn't answer.

How Ivy hated her and her silences. "Please, Bluebell. I'm so tired, but I can't possibly sleep without a blanket." Her heart beat hard in her ears. She was aware everyone was watching this exchange, including Heath.

And still Bluebell stared at her silently and stonily, the sword barring her way forward. Ivy knew, though, what Bluebell was thinking. Bluebell had warned Ivy to prepare herself properly, and she hadn't. Ivy wanted to cry, but not in front of Bluebell. She took herself back to the other side of the stable and tried to plump up some straw. It smelled cold and damp. A tear rolled down her cheek and she palmed it away. Then a shadow fell over her. She looked up, expecting Bluebell.

It was Heath. He smiled and crouched down next to her, holding out a rolled blanket. "Here," he said. "I have a spare."

All her body and blood lit up. Heath was giving her a blanket. She smiled at him adoringly, gazing at the red sheen of his hair in the firelight. "Thank you," she said. "How can I repay you?" She knew how she wanted to repay him, and the thought made her shiver.

"By sleeping warm and safe," he said, patting her shoulder once and then moving away.

She watched him go. Now, there was a man. Not like the other men she had fancied herself in love with. Not selfish, or proud, or talking ill of her behind her back the moment she pulled her dress back on. Her heart squeezed up against her ribs. If she couldn't have him, she would die.

It was night, and Wylm was soaked through, muddy to his knees and terrified. Creeping around behind the king's compound, sticking to shadows, ears strained for the slightest sound. He knew they were looking for him. He'd been hiding in a hollow log that day when three armed riders thundered past, calling to one another. Lying there— elbows cramped against his ribs, dirt in his mouth, bugs in his hair—he had been so overwhelmed by misery and uncertainty that tears had formed. He'd blinked them back with rage. Bluebell had brought him so low.

Now, poised breathless with his back flattened against the back wall of the bowerhouse, any self-pity was squashed down into a hard brick inside him. He had to rescue his mother.

There was a pit near the latrine in the main street where Bluebell liked to put prisoners, and he assumed Gudrun was in there. The pit was out in the open, but the hour had slipped well past midnight and only the alehouse would still be lit up. He slid along in the shadows, stopping every few feet to listen. Crickets. Laughing voices on the wind. A soft steady drip from the eaves . . .

And a woman crying.

Wylm froze. Was it his hopeful imagination or did that sound like his mother? The sound was coming from the infirmary.

He turned back, scanning around for signs of life. All was still. He approached the infirmary. The crying had stopped now, and he doubted himself. Then he saw the bolt and box padlock on the outside of the infirmary door. Somebody was locked in there.

He went to the shutter, got his fingers underneath it. It wouldn't budge.

Heart thundering, he glanced around, crouched, and put his mouth at the gap along the bottom of the shutter. "Mother!" he whispered.

Nothing.

Helpless fear. His senses on high alert.

"Mother!"

A querulous voice. "Wylm?"

Relief washed through him. She wasn't in the pit; she was somewhere warm with a bed. He let his heart relax a little. Her footsteps approached the window, and the tips of her fingers appeared under the shutter. He brushed his own fingertips against them.

"Are you well?" he whispered.

"I am imprisoned!"

Her voice was too shrill. His skin was alive with tension. "Hush, Mother. Not so loud. Have they hurt you?"

Her voice dropped low. "No. In fact, they are very careful with me. But I am trapped in here. Can you get me out?"

"There's a lock on the door. If I tried to break it, somebody would hear."

"They're looking for you, too, Wylm."

"I know."

"And Osred. Where did he go?"

Wylm didn't allow himself to feel the small, cold thrill of guilt. "Perhaps he has gone home. Where we should have gone." As he said the word "home," he was moved by a surge of homesickness. His childhood home, Tweening, the smallest kingdom of Thyrsland, landlocked amid Almissia, Littledyke, Nettlechester, and Thridstow. Geography had made its people conciliatory, good at getting along; girls and boys from good homes learned diplomacy, mediation, the languages of the southern traders and the northern raiders. If only his mother had never met Athelrick. Would his life have been carefree? For a moment he was winded by the thought that, back home, none of this would ever have happened. He wouldn't have formed an ambition for the throne. He wouldn't have to face this test of what kind of man he was. Or would manhood, wherever it bloomed, have inevitably brought its burdens?

"They threw me in here. I think Bluebell took Athelrick," Gudrun said, crying. "My husband."

"Perhaps she believes she can fix him." Fear narrowed around his heart again. "If Bluebell does somehow find a way to make Athelrick well, then your secret will be exposed."

"No, Athelrick would forgive me. He wouldn't tell Bluebell."

"How can you be so sure?"

"I'm sure. He loves me."

Wylm dropped the topic. Athelrick would not forgive her. Athelrick would tell Bluebell, and then his mother would die and so, too, would Wylm. He wasn't about to let that happen.

She broke into sobs. "And this is my own stupid fault. I am truly the unluckiest woman in the world. Find somebody who can help us, Wylm. Somebody from Tweening who remembers me fondly."

Wylm pressed his fingertips against hers. Did she not understand? Nobody could kill Bluebell; or certainly, nobody from Tweening. A noise of a door opening and footsteps had him shrinking back against the wall. Without a chance to say goodbye, he dashed off in the dark. He heard voices: Dunstan's, his mother's. He paused behind the stables. Young Tom would be asleep inside. Had he been instructed to call out if Wylm came in, looking for his mother's horse? Of course he had. There was nothing for it. Wylm would be running away on foot.

No, not running away. Running toward something. His destiny as a man and as a king. He would not be the weakling; he would not be the man who floated helpless on the tide of Bluebell's will. He would be a different kind of man: a man of strength and cunning, a man who could bring down the crown princess of Almissia. Certainly, he could not do it alone. But there were rumors on the road and in the alehouses that a mighty enemy of Blickstow yet lived.

Hakon, the Crow King.

Ash woke on the edge of dawn from a confused dream about being back in Thridstow. She opened her eyes and lay still a few moments. Somebody was snoring loudly. She gradually remembered where she was. Her back was tight from sleeping on the hard floor, and she was bursting to wee.

She climbed to her feet. Willow sat by Athelrick's cart, head heavy in her hands. She smiled weakly at Ash. "I got the last watch," she said.

"We'll all have to take turns, I expect." Ash made her way out of the stable. Outside, blue light lay over the sodden fields. The clouds had shredded apart and pale, clear sky promised a more comfortable ride today. This was a flat part of the country, heading west toward the sea. Not the ship-friendly sea of the east, but the thundering cold ocean. Ash yawned. Her belly felt watery and crampy. She hoped she wasn't coming down with a loose stomach: That would be sheer misery while traveling. She trudged through the mud to the low hedgerow that lined the field, in the hope of finding a private place to relieve herself.

Her belly twitched again. She climbed over the hedgerow and squatted on the other side. A few feet away, a tight grove of elms stood, holding the shadows close.

It took a moment to realize the discomfort in her stomach wasn't an illness, but a warning.

She tried to gather her clothes quickly, but the dark figure was already rushing toward her, tackling her to the ground and clamping a rough, dirty hand over her mouth. She bit down hard on his fingers. He jerked his hand away long enough for her to scream her sister's name, but then his hand was back, under her chin this time, pushing her jaw closed. He flipped her over and fumbled with her skirts.

Time slowed. He said something to her. She couldn't understand, then she realized he was speaking the language of the northern raiders. Her heart squeezed into a stone. He wasn't speaking to her at all; he was speaking to his companions: Raiders never traveled alone.

But Bluebell was alone as she vaulted over the hedgerow, blade already swinging. The raider took his hands off Ash and she rolled onto her back in time to see four others emerge from the shadowy grove. Her blood froze. She scrabbled back out of the fray, her back against the rough hedge, and watched in horror.

Bluebell's dogs were there a moment later, leaping on one of the raiders and taking him down. Bluebell skewered a second man, but the other three were on her in a flash. Ash heard Bluebell's name passed from one to the other, as the raiders realized who they were fighting. Bluebell, grunting and shouting like a man, held firm against them until her foot got stuck in mud and she went down on one knee. The dogs rallied around her, snapping and snarling, but the raiders surrounded her. Ash tried to clamber to her feet, knees too weak to comply, eyes searching for a rock or a branch or anything to help, but then Heath and Sighere were there. Events became confused, overloading her senses. The clatter of arms, barking, groans of death; the blur of steel, the effusion of blood, black in the early light, loosened every nerve in her body. She closed her eyes and clamped her hands over her ears.

A few moments later, Bluebell was helping Ash to her feet.

"Did he hurt you?" Bluebell asked, puffing warm air into the cold dawn.

Ash shook her head, holding back tears. Bluebell was covered in mud, and a smear of blood—someone else's—colored her left cheek. It would be one thing to have been the cause of her beloved sister's death, and another altogether to have caused the death of Almissia's only heir when the king's fate already hung in the balance.

"My lord, what are raiders doing this far south?" Sighere asked, crouched next to one of the fallen bodies to search for anything of value.

Ash shivered. She had spent so long trying not to open up her second sight, she was becoming blind. Here, in the predawn gloom, surrounded by blood, with her heart returning to its normal temperature, clarity came to her. Ash had nearly led Bluebell to her death, because she wasn't paying attention to her instincts. Because she was blighted, and doomed to blight others with her. Getting Bluebell killed would plunge Almissia into uncertainty, Nettlechester would make a claim, the raiders would come . . . Was this the Becoming she so feared?

Ash made two vows. The first was never—no matter how much danger she was in—to call for Bluebell's help again.

The next was to keep her second sight open—no matter the cost.

chapter 12

Wylm watched Bluebell's lover's house all morning, the blockheaded farmer and his simple son. Possibly Bluebell's son. The more he thought of it, the more he convinced himself it was true. Why else would a simple be tolerated to live? How it must embarrass and shame her that this child would never be a warrior. He took comfort in imagining her distress, but then told his tired brain to concentrate. He needed to discover where Bluebell was and what she planned, and any man who loved something as vulnerable as a sick child was a man Wylm felt confident he could bend to his will.

The farmer plonked his boy onto a stool in the sunshine, where he sat unseeing and unspeaking while the farmer mended a basket and talked to him. It was almost relaxing, sitting here in the damp grass behind an elder hedge that bristled with marjory vine, watching them go about their ordinary lives. Fat, furry bumblebees buzzed around, and the grassy smell of horse shit in the distance tickled his nose. He might have felt sorry for them; but then he thought about Bluebell and pity vanished.

The right moment came, as he'd hoped it would. The farmer stood and stretched, touched his son's dark hair and muttered something inaudible to him, then moved off toward the fields. As soon as he had vanished from sight Wylm stood, brushed damp leaves from his pants, and climbed the hedge to stalk across the grass. Moments later, he stood in front of the boy.

At first he thought the child hadn't noticed him. He was clearly blind. But then Wylm bent toward him, so his face was only inches away, and the child's face twitched softly.

"Papa?" he said.

Wylm straightened, turned toward the house. Inside, on a low table, a loaf of bread was cooling. Beside it lay a heavy knife. He picked it up, tested its weight in his hand. Then he dragged a stool outside to sit with the boy.

The boy's shoulder turned slightly toward him. "Papa?" he said again.

"Papa's not here," Wylm replied.

The boy fell silent. Wylm kept his senses alert for the return of the farmer. Minutes crept past. The boy grew agitated, whimpering a little. He tried to stand, but Wylm grasped his wrist firmly and sat him back down. "Stay here," he said.

The boy did as he was told, but his skinny shoulders were pulled tight and he began to shake. His tension was contagious: Wylm's stomach twitched. A cloud moved over the sun.

Minutes dragged by. The boy fiddled with a ring on his left hand. Wylm glanced at it, saw the royal insignia of Almissia. He smiled to himself.

Then he was there: the farmer. Wylm saw him; he saw Wylm.

The farmer shouted something: not a word, an exclamation. He began to run toward them.

Wylm stood behind the boy, gently pushed his head forward, and pressed the knife against the side of his throat.

The farmer stopped. "Eni!" he cried.

"Come a little closer," Wylm called. "I'll need to talk to you."

The farmer approached, his hands spread in a gesture of peace. "Please don't hurt my boy."

"Where is Bluebell?"

Wylm watched the farmer's face closely. A barely perceptible tightening of his jaw told Wylm he did indeed know where Bluebell was. But now he would deny it.

"I don't know what you're talking about."

"Bluebell. Your lover."

Eni trembled. "Bluebell?"

"It's all right, Eni," the farmer said in a soothing voice.

Wylm's heart was thundering. "I will not play games with you! Tell me where Bluebell is, or I will cut your son's throat."

The farmer's eyebrows squeezed together, an exquisite expression of emotional pain. Wylm could almost see him weighing up his options: Bluebell could protect herself, his son could not.

"Two miles north of Stonemantel, take the first track after the road southwest to Littledyke. It's a flower farm. There is a long stable at the front edge of the farm. You'll know the farmhouse because it is large and the sills are carved with flowers."

"And what has she planned?"

"To heal her father."

"How?"

"I don't know." He shook his head, a tear squeezing out onto his cheek.

Wylm hated him for crying. "You do know."

"I swear I do not. I did not ask. It is not my business."

"Is this child hers?"

A look of brief incomprehension. "Is . . . ? Eni? No. He is not Bluebell's child."

"But of course you'd say that." Wylm's disappointment made him cruel. He yanked the boy's hand into the air roughly. "What about this ring?"

"It was a gift from Bluebell. A trinket that no longer fit her. Let him go."

Wylm dropped the child's arm.

"His mother's name was Edie," the farmer said, and the sorrow, the love on his tongue, convinced Wylm where no other evidence could. This child was not Bluebell's. He nodded once and stood back, releasing Eni. The farmer fell to his knees in front of the boy, the curve of his hard back exposed to Wylm.

His vision tunneled. The man was Bluebell's lover. Would he go ahead of Wylm to warn her? Surely not, with his blind child to look after.

More important, he mattered to Bluebell. She cared about him.

He brought the knife up, then drove it hard into the famer's upper back. The man twitched, his hands flying upward, knocking Eni off the stool and onto the ground.

"Run, Eni!" he grunted.

The boy yelped, scrambled to his feet, and ran off unevenly.

Wylm removed the knife and brought it down again, this time into the back of the farmer's neck. He fell still and silent on the ground.

Wylm retrieved his knife, wiped the blood on the edge of the farmer's tunic, then tucked it into his waistband. He looked around but couldn't see the boy. Should he give chase? The boy was neither a threat nor, sadly, a treasure. No, he was itching to get away from Almissia to pick up the next thread of his destiny. He quickly raided the house for food, stuffing it in his pack, then stalked off across the fields and headed northwest, toward the sea.

The air smelled of damp earth, smoke, and roasting meat. Bluebell paced near her father's cart, Thrymm and Thrack soft at her heels hoping for food, as evening closed in. The rain had cleared, and they would sleep under the stars tonight. Ash had scouted ahead and found this semi-sheltered place, against the wall of a rocky valley; they had wound down a muddy road to its floor and camped among the ancient roots of an ash tree. Moisture still clung to the grass, but had evaporated off the flat rocks and gravel. A fire burned at the center of their camp, and over it Sighere held two wild rabbits on a spear. The firelight created sinister shadows among the mossy roots. Bluebell was famished: Traveling always made her hungry. But Athelrick hadn't eaten today and it bothered her. His sleeps were becoming longer, impossible to rouse him from. And when he had been awake and Rose had tried to feed him, he'd thrown his arms about and knocked the bread into a muddy ditch, shouting half-coherent accusations that she was a poisoner. It was one thing to drip water from a cloth into his mouth, but she couldn't force food into him.

Willow approached tentatively with a handful of rabbit intestines. Thrymm whimpered.

"Bluebell? For your dogs?"

"Thank you."

Willow knelt and the dogs sniffed the air warily.

"It's all right, girls, eat up."

The dogs fell on the food. Willow rinsed her hands in a puddle then wiped them on her skirts. She gave Bluebell a shy nod and returned to Ivy's side. Bluebell watched her go. Willow had been surprisingly useful, willing to do the tasks the others shrank from, such as changing and cleaning Father and his bed. She had a simple manner and an artless compassion that impressed Bluebell.

Bluebell sighed and stopped pacing. She climbed up on the cart and sat next to her father, pulled her long legs up, and rested her cheek on her knees. When they'd left the previous morning, she had been full of hope. But now hope dwindled. The long, deep sleeps were deathlike. She raised her head and glanced toward Ash, who was feeding the fire from a bundle of small logs held in her skirt. The firelight made her soft face seem almost childlike. Bluebell wondered if Ash would be able to divine, with her other sight, whether or not Father's condition was worsening.

As she had the thought, Ash slowly turned her head to look at Bluebell. Bluebell saw something flicker in her eyes, and Ash stood and dropped the bundle, then came toward her.

"Did you know I wanted to ask you something?" Bluebell said, a shiver of awe passing over her skin for her sister's uncanny talent.

Ash shrugged. "Nothing so clear as that. But I looked up and you were watching me."

"Come up here with me." She shifted over to make room in the cart for Ash, who climbed up and sat next to her. A stiff breeze shook the branches above them, showering them with the rain that had been held in their leaves. Bluebell wiped a drop of water from her nose.

"What did you want to ask me?"

"We've been away from Blickstow for two days. Has he . . . improved? It seems to me as though the opposite is happening. He's barely awake anymore," Bluebell said.

Did Ash's mouth tighten, or was that an evening shadow? "You want me to open up my mind to him again?"

Bluebell nodded.

Ash took a breath, then reached her hands out to Father's sleeping form. She closed her eyes.

Bluebell watched Ash, a tiny note of dismay thrumming along her nerves. Below the soft, young skin, Ash looked tired. Desperate. As though her bones were struggling to hold their shape. But then Bluebell shook herself. She, too, was tired and desperate. Their father was sick, possibly dying. These were difficult times.

Ash sank back, lifted her hands away, and opened her eyes. She offered Bluebell a little smile. "He's no better, but he's no worse."

"The illness hasn't progressed?"

"No."

Bluebell's heart felt warm. "That's wonderful." And she knew she'd done the right thing, getting Athelrick away from Blickstow, from the site of the bad magic.

Ash rubbed Bluebell's hand. "Don't raise your hopes too high, sister."

"Too late." She glanced at Father's sleeping face. "If he gets no worse, then I'm sure Eldra can fix him."

"If we can find her."

"We'll find her."

Ash tilted her head to the side, and her long plait fell over her shoulder. "Bluebell, have you not wondered why Father has never told us about Eldra?"

Bluebell blinked. No, the thought hadn't occurred to her. She had been too busy thinking of other things.

"Perhaps she won't help," Ash continued.

"Why would she not help? She's his sister." Whatever else Eldra was, she was family. And to betray one's own blood was to betray oneself. Nobody would willingly do it, surely. Not even an undermagician.

Ash smiled. "I hope you are right, Bluebell."

Rose lay with her eyes closed long after the rest of the camp became still and quiet, although she didn't sleep: tired in her bones, but unable to drift off on that soft tide. She tried her left side, then her right.

Sometimes sleep veered close, but then escaped before she could grasp it. She heard the owls in the distance; she heard the watch change over; she heard the late-night breeze pick up.

Finally, she opened her eyes.

Warm firelight reflected off the rocky walls and gray tree trunks. Around her, bodies were wrapped tight against the midnight chill. She couldn't see Heath from here: He slept on the other side of the camp. Beside her lay Rowan, her little chest rising and falling rhythmically, her long dark hair falling over her face.

Rose sat up and glanced over to the cart. Ivy was on watch, but she had nodded off into her chest and was slumped uncomfortably against the side of the cart. Rose pushed off her blanket—the air was cool and damp—and went to her.

"Ivy," she whispered, shaking her softly.

Ivy startled awake. "Oh! Oh, it's you." Her gaze went to Bluebell's sleeping form.

"Do you want me to sit with you awhile? Keep you awake? I can't sleep anyway."

Ivy nodded and shifted over to make space, and Rose climbed up into the cart. Athelrick's stillness was uncanny: a warm version of death. Still, it was better than his periodic fits, which terrified Rowan.

Ivy palmed her eyes and yawned. "You won't tell Bluebell I was asleep on the job, will you?"

"As long as you try to stay awake next time."

"I will."

Silence for a few moments. Rose realized she and Ivy had little to talk about.

"Rose," Ivy ventured, "Heath is your nephew, is he not?"

Rose bristled. "My husband's nephew," she said quickly. Her gaze drifted to the outer edge of the camp where Heath slept on his side, facing away from her. Firelight in his hair. She turned her eyes back to Ivy, and realized Ivy was staring at Heath with unabashed longing. "Why do you ask?" she said, careful to keep the suspicion out of her voice.

"I think he's rather lovely," Ivy said.

The hard fist of jealousy made her unable to speak for a few seconds. "I see," she managed.

"Does he belong to anyone?"

And what was she to say? Heath belonged to her, of course. The thought of his hands touching another woman's body burned her to ashes. Those caresses, those kisses were hers. Nobody else's. Certainly not Ivy's. "He's not married, no," Rose said gruffly, "but he's a highborn thane in Wengest's family: the son of the king's sister. Wengest may very well have plans for him to marry someday. It would be foolish to develop any ideas about him."

"He's a soldier?"

"He was a farmer. He has twenty acres down by the river below Folkenham." A flush in her belly, remembering the smoky little farmhouse where they had made love. "Though I believe he hasn't seen his home for a long time. Bluebell has had him strongholded in the north for three years."

Ivy's lip curled. "She is cruel."

"Wengest put him into the army in the first place." Rose watched Ivy. She had hardly taken her eyes off Heath. "Bluebell only does what she thinks is right for the safety of her family and kingdom."

Ivy was silent a few moments. Then she slowly turned her eyes to Rose. "What kind of woman might Wengest choose for him?"

"I don't know." Her stomach twitched. The day would come, of course. And why shouldn't Heath have a wife? Rose had a husband.

"When you married Wengest, Almissia had peace with Nettlechester at last," Ivy said. "Now Bluebell commands an army that is made half of Nettlechester's warriors. Perhaps Wengest would consider cementing this goodwill with another marriage." She beamed. "What do you think?"

It took Rose two heartbeats to understand what she meant. "What? No! Ivy, you are barely out of childhood. Do not be in a hurry to marry. This is nonsense anyway. Don't you dare to mention it to Bluebell." For fear Bluebell would think it a very good idea.

"Well, I hadn't thought to marry yet," Ivy said, tossing her blond hair over her shoulders.

"Good."

"But I should like to get to know him."

"He is a good man," Rose said softly. The best of men. She was foolish to think no other woman would notice.

Willow woke to voices. Angel voices. Mad, spitting in her ear, poking her and prodding her in the soft places of her brain. *"Get up get up get up get up."* But as soon as she opened her eyes, the angel voices abruptly disappeared, sucked into a hushed midnight quiet. Instead, she heard the whispered voices of two of her sisters, Rose and Ivy, sitting in the cart. She couldn't hear what they were saying.

But she knew the angels had woken her for a reason. She screwed her eyes tight and prayed hard for a sign. *What do you want from me, Maava?*

No answer. She listened into the dark for a little while. Ivy and Rose murmured softly to each other.

She was being a fool. Maava wanted only one thing from her: to save her heathen father's soul. And even though she was tired and wanted to drift back to sleep, she climbed to her feet, relishing the effort and ache it took as proof she was Maava's good servant.

"I will take your watch, sister," Willow said to Ivy.

Rose shook her head. "You took a watch last night. You will be too tired to travel tomorrow."

"And that tiredness will prove my devotion to my father." A dozen echoing angel voices sighed in her head. Were they angry, or happy? She clenched her fists. "Please, let me."

Ivy shrugged. "I'm happy to go back to sleep. Do it if you like." She climbed down from the cart. "Go on."

Rose helped her up. "Do you want me to sit with you awhile?"

"I want to do this myself," Willow said, although she could hardly hear her voice over the angels. They were happy. Such relief! They were laughing along with her. How easy it had been. "Please, take your rest. I will do everything that is good for him."

Rose smiled and climbed down. "If you get tired, let me know."

Willow nodded. Her sisters departed. Minutes later, the camp was still and quiet.

She turned and glanced over her shoulder at Athelrick. He was only her father in blood. She barely knew him. Uncle Robert—her mother's brother with whom she had grown up—was not her father, either. He was a shallow, impatient man who cared more about his horses than his family.

But when she thought of Maava . . . Ah, he was the father she had longed for. Strong and good, infinite in wisdom and power. The voices in her head stilled as she fished her triangle out of her pocket and let its chain drape through her fingers. With her shoulder turned against curious eyes, she began to pray.

Maava, deliver my father to the Sunlands. Forgive his heathen soul . . . Over and over, surrendering her errant thoughts to the words, bending her mind to the single purpose. She let her lips move, let the words emerge as soft sounds on her breath. A wind stirred in the trees high above her, cool air rippled over her skin, she lost herself in the dark, sacred pool of prayer.

An hour passed, and her mind began to wander. She took a deep breath and opened her eyes. Five minutes of rest, then she would go back to it. By firelight, she counted the sleeping bodies around her with her eyes. Long Bluebell on her side, the narrow hard line of her thigh visible through the blanket. Rose and Rowan, a tangle of dark hair and white limbs. A tuft of Ivy's fair hair peeking above the blanket next to them. Ash, asleep very straight on her back, one hand clenched into a loose fist below her breasts. And Sighere and Heath. She couldn't look at them. She closed her eyes. Men were strange to her. So big and hairy and smelling of sweat and leather. She hoped Bluebell would never ask her to marry. How she despaired at the idea. Some heathen ape who would crush her. Sometimes, she let herself daydream about the kind of man she could love: someone smaller and softer of skin, someone who loved Maava as much as she did. But finding such a man in her father's kingdom, or under her family's protection, was impossible.

The thought made her lonely, but just for a moment. Then the angels spat to life in her head and she remembered her purpose. It wasn't to sit here, pitying herself. Once again, she prayed. This time, harder than before. Prayed until her ribs ached and her fingers were raw around the silver chain. Dimly, she became aware she was drifting away from the camp, from the popping fire and the spring breeze. The words were leading her into a different place, a soft place where she could lay down her burden . . .

Then she snapped awake. Birdsong, pale light. It was dawn. She had fallen asleep.

Quickly, she picked up the chain and began to pray again, in time to hear Bluebell's voice strong behind her.

"What are you doing?"

Willow plunged the chain and triangle between her knees, folding it between layers of her skirt. She turned to Bluebell, heart thundering. "I'm . . ."

"You're not supposed to be on watch. Ivy is."

Relief was warm in her heart as she realized Bluebell hadn't seen her praying. "Oh. Ivy was tired and I wanted to be there for Father."

Bluebell smiled—an expression that made her scarred face look cruel. "You can help Father best by being fit to travel." She touched Willow's shoulder lightly. "You do enough. Ivy needs to do more. Please let her." Then she was striding off while Willow wound up her chain and placed it carefully in her pocket, away from judging eyes.

chapter 13

They smelled the farm long before they saw it. A soft breeze from the north in the late afternoon carried the sweet, creamy scent of flowers. Ash took deep breaths. The change from one season to another always made her ache pleasantly. Yes, it was a farewell to the stark splendor of winter, to the bare trees and pure glistening snow. But that first kiss of warmth on the breeze, those first green shoots on the chestnut trees, made her heart cheer.

Soon they would rest and eat and have a roof over their heads. Bluebell had dispatched Sighere and Heath to Stonemantel for supplies. The rest of the party rattled wearily down a rutted track beside a stream where trees created a cold shade. Then over the rise Ash saw it: a sea of flowers. Creamy meadowsweet and blue wolfsbane, white daisies and yellow cowslip, all growing gloriously in the sunshine among the long, waving grasses. She caught her breath.

She urged her horse forward so she was riding alongside Bluebell. A flurry of white flower seeds, like snow, was beaten up by her horse's hooves. "The whole farm is like this?"

"It used to be a barley farm, but the woman who lived here loved flowers and turned the fields over to them."

"What happened to her?"

"She died a few months ago."

"It's very pretty," Ash said.

"You can't eat flowers," Bluebell grumbled. "But there are chickens and bees. And lots of room."

As the stable and the farmhouse came into view, Ash understood how true this last statement was. The house was long and sturdy. One end was constructed of stone, but the largest section was constructed of dark wood. The doorframes and windowsills were decorated with carvings of creeping vines and flowers. They rode through the wide front gate, under a carved arch, and around to the stables.

Bluebell ordered a horrified Ivy to tend to the horses, and Willow offered to stay and help her. Athelrick was in one of his deep sleeps, so Bluebell left him outside the stable in his cart and led the rest of them inside to see the house.

They came into the main part of the farmhouse, where the cold hearthpit sat. The interior was cool and dark, musty with the smell of dust and mouse droppings. Posies of dried flowers hung from the ceiling beams. Rose and Rowan stayed to light the fire while Ash followed Bluebell as she explored behind other doors. One small room was a larder, where they found barrels of grain and salt. The next door led to a bedroom, where the ceiling sloped dramatically low. A wooden bed had been built on the floorboards, and a large chest stood beside it. Ash opened the chest. It was full of women's clothes.

"This must have been where she slept," Ash said, a hollow sadness ringing over her body for this woman she had never known.

"Athelrick can have this room," Bluebell declared, characteristically indifferent to the shadow of death, testing the mattress with her hand. "This is full of feathers. He'll be comfortable here. There's plenty of room for the rest of us around the hearthpit."

She strode out, Ash scurrying after her. The next room was a kitchen. Knives and bowls, jars of pickled food and jams were stacked on benches. A large pot hung on a chain over the hearth. A low door stood opposite the one they'd come in. Ash unlatched it and found herself looking out over a soft carpet of meadow grass and flowers, down toward a deep-green strip that unribboned across the fields.

"A stream," Ash said. "Nice and close."

Bluebell was examining the jars. "There's a lot of food here already.

I'm told there are chickens." She looked up. "Ash, could you go out and look for eggs?"

Ash nodded, then ducked under the threshold and outside. She followed her ears to the chicken coop. Two hens were still out in the soft light, scratching in the dirt. Ash bent to enter the coop. Eggs were everywhere. Dozens of them. She collected as many as her skirt would hold and emerged into the twilight.

She stopped a moment, drawn by a prickling sense somebody was watching her. Her gaze went across the fields and toward the stream. A breath half caught in her lungs.

Nothing.

Then, something. A dark silhouette on the opposite bank of the stream, flickering into visibility. Ash blinked hard, but already the muffling hush against her ears told her that her second sight had opened up. She focused hard. The figure turned slightly, enough that the last light of the day caught her features. Then the figure dived into the water and disappeared, leaving a silvery flash behind her. It dissolved, and then nothing.

Ash knew she had seen a water spirit. She had never seen one before. She had never seen any kind of elemental before. Nobody saw elementals.

But she had seen one. And in that moment when the light had hit it, the creature had looked as surprised as she was.

The aching in her joints had started and Ash cursed this decision to keep her senses alert. Already, it seemed, she was attracting attention she didn't want.

The wood where Wylm decided to stay the night was thick and overgrown. Little dark berries and pale flowers hung from vines that wove themselves around rough hedges. He was too tired to hunt and cook, so he unrolled his blanket on a patch of soft undergrowth and lay down. The tendons behind his ankles throbbed softly. Late-afternoon shadows stretched cool throughout the wood. He closed his eyes and tried not to think about the sharp stone under his hip, the chilling damp that was beginning to seep through his blanket. Exhaustion overwhelmed these other discomforts, and he plummeted into sleep before the blackbirds stopped singing for the night.

The dream was as dark as the wood, though in it he was standing, not lying down. In front of him was a high stack of branches and twigs: a funeral pyre. He approached slowly. In the gray shadows, he could see a man's hand hanging over the edge of the pyre. A gold ring on his index finger glinted dully and Wylm knew this man was his father. Inconsolable childish grief returned to him with full force. He struggled against the dream, but was caught fast in its web. The pyre burst into life, sending up a spray of bright embers. He stepped back.

Then the skin on his back shivered as he sensed something behind him. Someone was crying. He didn't want to look around, for he knew when he looked he would see something so terrifying it would make his heart stop. The firelight made shadows leap and shudder.

"Please?" a little voice said, almost inaudible over the whoosh of the flames.

He turned. A boy stood there. The boy from the farm: Eni. Sightless eyes. Wylm's heart flashed hot. Eni reached his hand toward him.

Wylm woke up. His heart was thudding and his feet tingled. The quiet that engulfed his ears was sudden and shocking. It was fully dark now, and his eyes took a moment to adjust.

He shivered. A light rain fell. He sat up, pulling his knees close in the circle of his arms. The shivering wouldn't stop; even his breath shuddered in his lungs. The soft tissue under his ribs felt raw. The boy. He had left the blind, simple boy alone, probably to die slowly of starvation, wondering where his father had gone.

The distress he experienced at this thought was blunt and hard, and it made him loathe himself and fear for himself, and at the same time it made him stand and grab his pack and head back onto the road the way he had come, to retrace his steps.

He could not endure the boy's misery. He had to end it, one way or another.

Bluebell hated the hour before dawn blushed the sky. Quiet. Absolute quiet. Everyone slept, even the birds and the horses. The world had stopped. She sat on the floor next to her father's bed, her chin resting on her knees. Father slept, too.

She glanced at him in the candlelight. He was no better; he was no worse. Experience told her things would go as they would go, that hoping and fearing would make no difference to the outcome. Her spirit was weary of the hope and the fear.

The door opened, and Sighere stood there. "My lord. Your watch is over."

"Close the door," she said.

Sighere did as he was told and sat cross-legged next to her. He was a tall man, with bony knees, very dark hair, and thick eyebrows. Not a great brain, but a great heart.

"Why are we still watching him, Sighere? We're in no danger now."

"We are watching him because you willed it, my lord."

"You didn't question me."

"I never do."

"Yes, you do. If I'm about to ride into an ambush." She smiled.

"This is different, Bluebell," he said quietly. "This is your father."

She turned her eyes to Athelrick. "I want him watched, Sighere, because I'm afraid he'll die alone."

Sighere didn't answer.

"I have been listening to the quiet," she said. "It is the quiet of death, but not glorious death in battle. The death of old age and winter. And I have been imagining his hall, when we have returned from a campaign and the mead flows and laughter and firelight warm everyone's faces and the harps clang. Father with his arms outstretched, giving gold and love." She mimed the movement, her long arms sending spindly shadows across the bed. "Then I am back here in this wretched, silent darkness and I cannot bear it."

"I would bear it for you. If I could."

She shrugged. "We must look to the future. He can't travel. He is better here. I will take my sister Ash and we will go up to Bradsey alone. We'll bring back the witch."

"If she will come with you."

"I will make her come."

Sighere nodded. "I don't doubt you."

"You will stay in command here and protect my sisters, and my sister's child especially."

"When will you leave?"

She glanced at Athelrick again. She opened her mouth to say *Today*, then hesitated. What if he woke up with the dawn, clear-eyed and asking for her? Should she not allow a few days for any magic to weaken? "I'll wait until he's been a week away from Blickstow," she said.

Sighere's eyes flickered almost imperceptibly, and she knew he thought she had made a decision from the heart and not the head. "As you wish it, my lord. That way you can be certain you've decided well."

But certainty would continue to elude her, she knew, until he was well again. Or until he was dead.

Rose was meant to be collecting water from the stream behind the house, but it was too beautiful a morning to return inside. She put her bucket down and sat on a flat rock at the edge of the stream. She slid off her shoes and dipped her feet into the soft water, letting it lap around them. Bright-green streamers of weed were pulled by the current, tickling her toes. The air was warm and the sun shone. A fresh breeze drove fine white clouds across the sky. The stream bent away to the east, disappearing into an oak wood, while to the west lay fields of unfurling flowers. On the other side of the stream were grassy hills. Sweet smells of creamy flowers and damp grass. She closed her eyes and listened. The stream running over rocks. The cheep and chitter of sparrows. Leaves rushing in the wind. And dogs barking.

She opened her eyes. The barking was close, around the bend of the stream. Happy barking. It must have been Bluebell's dogs, but Rose had left Bluebell back at the house. She climbed to her feet and made her way barefoot along the rocks—avoiding sharp points—and into the cover of the wood to investigate.

Almost immediately Thrymm was barking happily at her ankles, shaking water off her coat and soaking Rose's skirt. "Bluebell?" Rose called. She moved a little farther in, where the stream widened and the trees opened up. It wasn't Bluebell with the dogs. It was Heath, stripped to the waist, standing in the water.

"Oh," she said.

"Oh," he said, seeing her.

Thrack, who was Thrymm's mother and a much calmer animal, raised her nose to sniff the wind, then returned to drinking from the shallows.

"What are you . . . ?"

"Bluebell sent me to take the dogs swimming. They were still muddy from the trip." He shrugged. "It seemed like a good idea to go in with them."

The breeze allowed a shaft of sunlight to break through the trees. It caught the red-gold in his hair, illuminating his white skin, his hard muscles, the black tattoo on his chest. A flame ignited, low in her stomach.

He must have seen the desire in her eyes, because he raised his hands and said, "Don't, Rose. We can't be found together. Bluebell has made that clear."

Bluebell. She hadn't stopped bossing everyone since they left Blickstow. She treated them as though they were her army, not her sisters. Rose approached Heath. "I'm not afraid of Bluebell."

"I am." He waded out of the stream and up onto the bank, where he pulled on his tunic. "You should go."

Embarrassment made her angry. "Don't be afraid of her," she snapped. Then, softer, "She's my sister. She won't hurt you."

Heath didn't look up. "I believe she will. You haven't seen her in battle," he said, belting his tunic. "I know what she is capable of." He whistled to the dogs, who ran to his side with their tails thumping. "You go back the way you came and I'll head back to the house separately, and we'll—"

How was she supposed to bear this? Three years apart from him and then, in their one moment alone, he was shutting her out. Wretched, wretched Bluebell. "Heath, please." Her voice cracked. "Please."

He wavered. Glanced around.

"I cannot bear this. Why have I been chosen for such great unhappiness?" She began to sob.

"Hush, Rose, hush," he said, touching her shoulder lightly. This touch—the kind that could pass between any two people, not lovers—made her cry harder.

"Let me hold you," she said, reaching for his wrist. He didn't move. "Nobody will see us," she said urgently. "The dogs can't talk."

Slowly, he turned his hand over and caught her fingers in his. Rose's feet tingled, and she breathed back her tears.

"I can't bear your unhappiness," he said, "but I can do nothing to prevent it." He squeezed her hand.

"The blame is not yours."

"Can you not see? Here I am, willing to do anything for you. But nothing I do will change the situation. We cannot be together. And still I cannot accept that. I cannot feel it as truth in my heart, because surely such a love should . . ." He trailed off, words stuck in his throat.

They stood like that a moment, eyes locked together. Her skin burned. He reached for her. His clothes were damp. Her breath flew from her lips. The scent of his skin overwhelmed her as she pushed her body against his, her cheek into his shoulder. Her hands spread out across his hard flanks. She felt his fingers in her hair. Her skin hummed.

Then, a whistle in the distance. Thrymm and Thrack immediately turned and began to bolt. It was Bluebell.

Heath pulled away from Rose as though stung. Her body missed his immediately. "I'm sorry," he said, and his sea-colored eyes grew sad. "I'm so sorry."

"Don't worry," she said. "I'll disappear. Go on."

He took her hand, squeezed it once, then went running after the dogs. She watched him go, then pressed her palm to her lips. She imagined she could smell his skin on her fingers: salty, male. It smelled like endless sorrow.

CHAPTER 14

The shoulders of the day were best avoided if Ash wanted to stay clear of elementals. Like birds and ants, they were on the move at dawn and dusk. But Ash wasn't sure she necessarily wanted to stay clear of elementals, and that surprised her.

It had been a glorious day: sunshine and pale-blue skies, the air heavy with the scent of flowers and damp earth. She had cleaned the farmhouse floors and laid fresh rushes, been in charge of mucking out the chicken coop, and helped Rose cut up vegetables for soup. The house was filled with the smell of cooking, and she was looking forward to a meal and a good night's rest.

But first, this.

As she left the farmhouse, the sky was pale pink along its western rim, shading to dusky blue. She headed for the stream, in particular the oak grove that stood to the north. A chill in the air coaxed goosebumps from her skin. Behind her, at the house, she could hear Rowan crying, Heath and Sighere laughing. She felt a long way outside everything, head down, hurrying for the dark grove.

She moved far enough into the trees that she was certain she would be undisturbed. Then, heart thudding, she closed her eyes and opened up her senses. Her skin fluttered. At first she could only hear her pulse, but then other sounds came to her. A breeze among the leaves, birds chattering as they settled in their nests, the soft pop of a twig deep in the wood as a small animal scurried about . . .

And the faint ringing of magic. Slowly, Ash opened her eyes. In her normal vision, the wood looked as it had before. Rocks, undergrowth, dark ivy-wound trunks, the flat stream. But her second vision picked up indistinct shadows nestled inside the ordinary shadows. Now the magic was growing louder, drowning out the other sounds.

"Come," she said, "show yourself."

Under the lowest branch of the closest tree, a shadow began to shiver. Ash kept hold of her focus, even though her heart was thumping hard. A figure began to form, visible only if she didn't look on it directly. Small and brown, a pointed face and black eyes, wild hair and two tiny horn buds. A tree elemental, with an expression of hostile curiosity on its face.

It spoke, its voice appearing in Ash's head even though its lips did not move. "Who are you?"

"I am Ash."

"I am oak."

"Why can I see you?"

"All is unveiled to you, woman. You can see behind the workings of the world."

This statement made Ash's stomach roll over with fear. Undermagic. It must be. Which meant that she was . . . No, she was just Ash, as she had always been. The elemental turned around to move away.

"Wait! Come back," she said.

It did as she said, stood in front of her. She moved closer, and although it flinched, it didn't run away. Ash raised her hand and reached for its face, but found only a freezing pocket of air under her fingers.

The creature's face twisted in scorn. "I wish you would not touch me. I wish you would let me go."

"Let you go?"

"You command me."

"I certainly don't."

"You told me to come back."

Ash hesitated a moment, then said, "And why did you?"

"Your voice is inexorable."

"Are you saying . . . ?"

"Whatever you tell me to do, I must obey."

Ash caught her breath. "But why?"

"I do not know."

She gazed at the creature, her mind too full of her own fears to recognize that it, too, was frightened. Then she shook herself. "I am sorry. Go. I set you free."

Almost before the sentence was finished, the elemental had dissolved back into the shadows of the wood. With its disappearance came the abrupt cessation of the ringing in her ears. Everything seemed quiet, suddenly. Normal. Her roiling stomach drove her to the edge of the stream to throw up.

Ash sat on a rock and wiped her mouth with a shaking hand. Always at the outer edge of her thoughts was the knowledge that her Becoming was blighted, and that she was a danger to others. Was this why? What kind of uncanny ability was possessed in her slight body?

And how long before that unwieldy power began to shake her to pieces?

It was well past time to leave and Bluebell knew it, but she put off departing day after day because she feared that, the moment she left, Father would die. As though her presence, her will, could keep him alive. But cooped up in the farmhouse, she felt unhappy and unsettled. Her sisters were sore with her for ordering them about, and their reluctance made her bad-tempered. At the end of the third day, she could bear it no more. She had to get out and kill something.

Of course, there was nothing to kill, she realized as she stalked through a carpet of daisies. A few badgers maybe, but that would hardly satisfy her. Besides, killing animals was not sport. They were not armed. In the distance, she could see an old scarecrow. She drew her sword and hefted its weight in her right hand, loosened her wrist by flourishing the blade, then began to run at the scarecrow. Moments later its straw head was lying among the daisies. Still not satisfied, she hacked off its left arm, then its right. She lifted her sword above her head, ready to bring it down and slice the damned scarecrow in two, when she heard a rustle behind her.

She turned. Rowan stood there, looking at her with frightened eyes.

Quickly, Bluebell returned the Widowsmith to its sheath. "What are you doing out, little chicken?"

"You killed him!"

Bluebell glanced over her shoulder at the headless scarecrow, bent shafts of straw poking up out of its collar. She turned back to Rowan and shrugged. "He was looking at me funny."

Rowan's little mouth turned upside down.

"Why are you crying?"

"He was my friend!"

Bluebell winced. "He was?"

Rowan nodded. "I played with him every day."

"Ah, I see. Well . . ." She bent to pick up the scarecrow's head and balanced it back on the body. "Now he's fixed, you see?"

Rowan didn't look convinced. Then a stiff gust of wind swept across the fields, making the head fall with a thud to the ground, and she started to wail.

Bluebell crouched in front of her. "Please don't cry. Shhh." She loved the little girl, but had scant patience for her. Always whining and crying. Rose was far too soft with her. The child needed a firmer hand. "Come on, hush."

Rowan threw herself toward Bluebell, her little arms encircling her neck. Bluebell put her right arm around the child and lifted her up. "Let's find your mother."

"I miss my papa!" Rowan wailed. "Where is Papa?"

Bluebell tried giving her a comforting squeeze, but perhaps it was too hard; Rowan began to cough. The coughing descended into more sobbing.

"Quiet now, little one," Bluebell said, hurrying back toward the house. "Rose! Rose!"

Rose was at the back door already, her arms outstretched. Bluebell handed the child over.

"What happened?" Rose asked.

"Bluebell killed my scarecrow!" Rowan blubbered.

"I killed her scarecrow," Bluebell said.

Rose kissed the top of Rowan's head, stroking her hair.

"I don't like this place. I want Papa. I want to go home to Papa."

Realization dawned. "Was she pretending the scarecrow was Wengest?" Bluebell asked.

"I'm not sure," Rose answered, "but she's been down there every day talking to it."

Bluebell was torn between guilt and annoyance. And, admittedly, a small thread of amusement. She patted Rowan's back. "Your mama is here now, please stop crying. Warrior queens don't cry."

This made Rowan cry harder. Bluebell had had enough. The endless round of domestic duties, the crying child, and through it all her father lying silent and still. It was time to leave and find Eldra, even if it meant leaving Athelrick behind.

It was a sodden gray dawn when Wylm arrived back at the millet farm. The farmer's body was little more than a red-brown smear that had been feasted on by wolves. Wylm entered the house. The hearth-pit was cold. Which meant that either the lad wasn't here, or he didn't have the ability to light a fire.

Guilt's clumsy touch on his ribs again.

"Hello?" he called softly. "Eni?" He listened into the silence.

A soft noise from the back corner. Wylm saw a little door. He went to it, touching the knife on his belt gently. "Eni?" he called again.

He pushed the door open. The boy was curled under a mound of blankets on a mattress on the floor. His face was pale, and his dark unseeing eyes rolled uselessly.

Already, he knew he wasn't going to kill Eni. That, in fact, he never would have been able to kill Eni. He was going to rescue Eni. It was a difficult thing to admit about himself. He liked to think of himself as the kind of person who could do whatever dark thing needed to be done, but perhaps he was not. The acceptance of this idea immediately released the knots of anxiety in his stomach. He didn't have to kill Eni. The gray clouds outside no longer seemed oppressive. He felt light.

"Eni," he said, making his voice as gentle as he could, "my name is Wylm."

The child's brows knitted and Wylm tensed. Could it be that he recognized Wylm's voice? That fear would make him run or scream or some other thing that meant Wylm had to silence him forever?

Wylm cleared his throat and continued. "I am Bluebell's brother."

The boy's lips moved, but no sound came out. Still, his body loosened at Bluebell's name.

"You must be hungry."

Eni nodded.

"I am going to take you from here now. There is nothing for you anymore. Your father is gone. Do you understand? Papa is gone. I am going to take you with me and find you somewhere warm and safe where you can eat and be cared for." Wylm carefully lifted the blankets back. "Come on, lad. Show me where the stables are. Let's be away."

"Papa."

"No. No Papa. He is gone."

The boy's face worked as he struggled with this, but he let Wylm pull him to his feet nonetheless. Eni made a soft mewling noise, pulling away. But Wylm held him firm. "You see? I am not hurting you." There would be an inn farther north, somewhere he could leave the boy, some woman whose womb had never quickened who would take him in. Wylm noticed the boy grip his hand tightly, fearfully, and he almost couldn't stand Eni's vulnerability. That he had to trust his father's murderer because there was simply no other way for him to survive.

Wylm held out hope that Eni didn't know who he was. He'd never seen Wylm's face, and he was too simple surely to tell between voices. "Let's find you some wet-weather clothes," he said, slipping his hand out of the boy's grip. "It's miserable out there."

It was well past midnight when Ivy saw her chance.

She had been lying very still, not sleeping, on the floor next to the hearthpit. Heath, a few feet away, had been shifting and rearranging himself; not sleeping, either. Finally, he rose and went outside, closing the carved wooden door softly behind him. The rest of the room remained still, even little Rowan who was disturbed at the slightest sound. Ivy waited a few moments, then got up and went outside to find him.

He sat on a bench a few feet from the front door. Elbows on knees, head in hands.

She approached. The dark was cool on her face and hands. A cricket chirruped and a breeze rippled across the long grass.

"Hello," she said.

He looked up, startled. "Ivy?"

She moved to sit next to him. "Shift over, make room," she said, laughing lightly. Men, she had found, liked women who laughed.

He shifted and she sat as close to him as she could, her thigh pressed against his. She imagined she could feel his blood, thundering up and down his veins. So hot and close to hers. "You couldn't sleep," she said to him. "Is there something on your mind?"

He looked at her, his mouth drawn into a tight line. "You should go back to bed."

"Oh, don't worry about me. I couldn't sleep, either." She paused, smiled, and dipped her eyelashes. "Something on *my* mind."

He was silent. She looked at the sky. Starlight broke through clouds. What a shame most people missed this time of the night. It was beautiful. She wondered what her skin would look like, bare under starlight. No doubt Heath would find it intoxicating. She enjoyed the feel of the warmth of his thigh against hers, but he wasn't talking.

"Do you want to know what's on my mind?" she prompted.

"You have plenty of sisters. Perhaps tell one of them," he said gently.

"They aren't awake."

Silence.

"And you're here now and . . . it's about you."

Heath stood. The sudden withdrawal of his warmth made her shiver. "Ivy, you ought not speak to me in such a way. Go back inside. Leave me be." He turned and took a few steps away.

Ivy leapt to her feet and caught him at the wrist—a fine, strong wrist—and said, "Don't go. Or if you do go, let me come with you. Let me show you how a woman can please a man."

He spluttered on his words, then finally managed to spit: "You are barely a woman, Ivy. And I am not the man for you."

Barely a woman? Her hot fantasies shriveled and went cold.

"Please leave me with my thoughts," he said, more gently. Then he moved off into the dark.

Ash sat by the hearthpit plaiting Rowan's hair. The child wriggled and complained, but Ash kept working, hand over hand, making soothing noises as she went. The fire popped softly and moisture dripped outside. Pine-sweet smoke collected against the ceiling. Rose watched Rowan with an amused smile on her lips.

"Is Ash hurting you?" Rose joked.

"You do it too hard," Rowan replied.

The drizzle fell unremittingly, as it had all day. They had been stuck inside, on top of one another. Ivy sat by the door, unusually quiet, sewing with Willow. Heath and Sighere had taken to the kitchen to inspect and repair their gear. Every now and then, the wind outside drove the rain harder, and a thin, icy breeze would creep under the door. The dogs slept curled together.

"There," Ash said, tying a piece of colored wool in Rowan's hair. "Now it won't get so wild."

The door to Athelrick's room opened a crack and Bluebell looked out. "Ash," she said, "I need you." Then the door closed.

Rose raised her eyebrows at Ash. "I'm a little tired of her ordering us about."

"She was born for it," Ash replied, giving Rose a gentle touch on the shoulder. "I don't mind."

Rose pulled Rowan into her lap and Ash went to Athelrick's room, closing the door behind her. Bluebell was pacing. Lately, Bluebell was always pacing.

"What's wrong?"

"I can't get him to eat."

Ash looked closer and saw the spilled soup through Athelrick's beard. She picked up the cloth beside the bed and gently wiped him clean.

DAUGHTERS OF THE STORM 163

"He's never awake anymore," Bluebell said. "If he doesn't eat, he'll die."

"It looks as though you managed to get some food in," Ash said, touching her father's warm forehead. "And we get enough water in. He doesn't need much. He's only lying here."

"It's been a week since we left Blickstow. My greatest hope, that the elf-shot would dislodge, has not come about," Bluebell said. "Tomorrow, you and I will leave to find Eldra."

Ash's ribs tightened. "Just you and me?"

"Yes. Rose will have to take Rowan back to Folkenham. The child misses her father."

Ash battled with her conscience. Eldra had made it clear Ash wasn't to come close, yet she couldn't tell Bluebell that. Ash was still struggling to accept herself that her fate was so stained.

"You ought to take Sighere."

"No, I oughtn't," Bluebell said, irritation husky in her voice. "I can't turn up there with armed men. I must go with family. Ivy and Willow are idiots, so it must be you."

"We have to take Rose," Ash blurted, and told herself she did it to protect Bluebell. So she would have somebody on the last dark miles of the journey.

Bluebell stopped pacing, narrowed her eyes. "Why?"

"It can't just be the two of us. I . . . I have a strong sense . . ."

"Ash? Your second sight?"

"Yes." It wasn't really a lie.

Bluebell nodded. "All right, we'll bring Rose. But Rowan must go home. I'll not have her whining for three weeks while we travel. Willow and Ivy can stay here and look after Father. Although they may be all but strangers to him, they are of his flesh and blood."

"Who will take Rowan home?"

"Sighere."

"Not Heath?"

Bluebell raised an eyebrow. "Heath will stay here with Athelrick."

"I only ask because that is what Rose will ask."

Bluebell paced again. The wind outside gusted strongly, rattling the roof tiles. "I do not make bad decisions, Ash. I make the very best decisions I can, based on what I see in front of me. My father is ill; he is probably dying. The security of Almissia is at risk. I have no heir. Rowan is Almissia's future. My best man will go with her. Heath is not my best man. But he is a good man, good enough to protect Ivy and Willow and to know what to do if Athelrick dies."

"Rowan is Almissia's future?" But as she said it, Ash knew it. A vision of Rowan, grown to a fine, strong woman, flashed across her mind.

"Rose doesn't know," Bluebell said. "The child is too tender, still. She won't see it." She paused a moment, seemed to be choosing her words carefully. "I want you to tell Rose she's coming north with us."

Ash's stomach dropped. She didn't want to be the bearer of ill tidings, especially not to Rose, who already had so much weighing on her mind. "Why me?"

"Because she is tired of hearing orders from me. I see the contempt in her eyes."

"You are too hard on her. Love isn't subject to reason, Bluebell. At least try to understand how difficult it is for her."

"Love? Rose's problem isn't love. It's desire." Bluebell sat on the edge of Father's bed, her knees spread wide, her elbows resting on them. Her body, which always seemed so alive and vital, seemed even more so next to the wax figure of her father. Bluebell always ate up space, blazed like lightning. "If she was married to Heath, she'd want Wengest. The only thing she's in love with is her yearning. She's always been like that."

Ash studied Bluebell across the dim room. "She has?"

"Oh yes. Give her one thing, she wants the other. Never happy with what she has. As a child, she would pine for a plaything until she got it, then start immediately pining for a different one. Usually the one I had. I'll never forget the day she begged Mother to give her my wooden donkey. I loved that thing."

Ash suppressed a smile, unable to imagine Bluebell ever having played with anything other than axes and spears. "But toys are trivial things," she said. "She has married against her heart."

Bluebell shrugged. "The day she met Wengest she was breathless and wet-eyed, and as flushed as Ivy when she sees a chest hair. She told me she loved him."

"Really?"

"Wengest was fit and handsome then. He was a king, she was going to be a queen. She was happy to become his wife. Do you not remember?"

And now Ash thought of it, she realized it was true. An image came to her memory of Rose, her cheeks glowing as she stepped into the deep-blue gown Byrta had sewn for the exchange of her marriage vows.

"But as soon as she had him, she lost interest," Bluebell continued. "The next I heard, she was pregnant to the nephew."

Ash felt as though she should defend Rose. "I think you misread the situation. I've glimpsed her feelings. She really is miserable."

"If I permitted her to leave Wengest for Heath, she'd be miserable a year later, Ash. Rose can be miserable under any circumstances. She's very good at it. And she has put Thyrsland's peace at risk for her misery. I can never forget that." Bluebell stood and patted Ash's shoulder affectionately, but far too hard. "You have to tell her she's coming north. She will take comfort from you. She takes no comfort from me." She spread her long arms. "I'm not formed for comfort."

Ash swallowed the guilt. It was her fault Rose had to come north. "Of course I will tell her," she said, "as gently as I can."

chapter 15

At the first break in the rain, Bluebell took the dogs out to exercise them. It was late afternoon; the fields were damp, and the flowers hung their heads under the weight of the water. Thrymm and Thrack barked and bounded after sticks, crushing daffodils with muddy paws. Bluebell's feet and ankles were damp, but she gulped at the fresh, clean air after long hours cooped up in Athelrick's room. She could hardly wait to be moving again.

Thrack returned to Bluebell's side and pressed against her thigh, ears pricked. Bluebell turned to see that Rose had emerged from the house and was approaching, a thunderous look on her face. Thrack had read Rose's body language and was growling low in her throat.

"Easy, girl," Bluebell said, dropping her hand to rub the dog's ears. "She won't hurt me."

Rose stopped a few feet away, eyes blazing. "I don't want to go to Bradsey."

"Ash has foreseen—"

"Let me finish. I don't want to go, but I recognize I must. I hate to leave Rowan, but I know I have to. But . . . Could you not send her home with somebody she knows and loves?"

"She doesn't love Heath. You do. She hardly knows Heath."

"I know you want to keep them apart, but you are not thinking of a small child's happiness." Here Rose's bottom lip began to tremble, and Bluebell's exasperation spilled out as a noisy sigh.

Rose continued nevertheless. "She is only three. She can't travel with Sighere. She's afraid of him."

"She oughtn't be. Sighere is my best and most skilled thane. She would be safer only with me."

"She doesn't understand that. She would rather be with somebody familiar."

Bluebell took a deep breath and swallowed her impatience. "Four days at most, then she will be home with her papa. If she can't endure four days of discomfort—"

"She is a little child! Have some pity!" Rose shouted. Her face was flushed.

Thrack growled again. Bluebell patted her side. "Off. Go on."

The dog padded away warily and sat among the daffodils a few feet away, watching.

"I'll send Ivy with them, then," Bluebell conceded. Ivy wasn't much use here anyway.

"Ivy? She prefers Willow."

"Willow will stay here. I can trust her with Father."

Rose balled her hands into fists. "Why is nothing negotiable with you, sister?"

"Have you forgotten we are kings?" Bluebell snapped. "I haven't. This isn't a small family matter to be sniped about at the supper table. Has becoming a mother turned your brain? Do you not feel the weight of the many lives beyond your bower?"

"You know nothing of being a mother. You know nothing of the love or the terror."

Bluebell held up her hand to silence Rose. "You anger me."

"Need I be afraid of your anger?"

Bluebell fell silent.

"Oh, so here is Bluebell's famous silent treatment? Am I to quiver?"

Bluebell blinked back at her.

"You cold bitch," Rose said, pushing past her and stalking off toward the stream.

"Where are you going?"

"Away from you," she called over her shoulder.

Bluebell watched her go. The dogs ran up, tails thumping. Bluebell knelt to scratch their ears. "Never mind," she told them. "She'll do as I say."

Rose climbed up across the rocks and sat at the edge of the stream. She pulled her knees against her chest and rested her head. She breathed deeply as the angry thump of her heart slowed. Bluebell would have her way, of that there was no doubt. Rose remembered a time when she was nine—Bluebell must have been eleven—when they squabbled over the last apple in the bowl, the last of the season. A year between apples was a long time for a child, and Rose had gotten to it first. Bluebell had tackled her and sat on top of her, threatening to spit on her face if Rose didn't hand the apple over. It had always been so with Bluebell: She had the ability to make her will manifest in the world. And not just by strength, which she had in large measure, but by sheer doglike persistence. Because it always seemed Bluebell got her way, Rose became fixated and envious of anything Bluebell owned. Rose would steal Bluebell's hair ribbons and tuck them under her own pillow, not that Bluebell ever noticed. But what triumph Rose would feel, having Bluebell's things. She would slip her hand under her pillow at night and clutch them jealously. Only once had Bluebell noticed one of Rose's small thefts: a wooden horse or donkey or some such thing. As ugly a toy as one could imagine, and yet Rose wanted it simply because Bluebell loved it so much.

Rose sat for a long time while the sun fell low and the birds, one by one, ceased their song. She breathed the smell of the muddy water's edge and the sweet waxy flowers as the sky cooled. She knew she should be getting back. Rowan adored Ash, but would soon start asking where her mama was. It had been nearly an hour since she left. When she heard movement behind her, her skin prickled and she realized she was a long way from the safety of the farmhouse. It was dark and she was alone.

Rose swung around and climbed to her feet, peering into the dark.

It was Heath, dusk in his hair. Her heart caught, stuttered back to life.

"I thought I might find you here," he said.

"Where is Bluebell?"

"She's with her father, trying to get him to eat. I overheard her telling Ash you'd fought with her then run off."

She folded her arms across her chest. "Have you come to take me back?"

"It grows dark," he said, patiently. "You are alone."

"You're here," she said. Yes, he was. Here alone with her. And she knew exactly what to do to get back at Bluebell.

He held out his hand. "Come on."

She gave him her fingers and climbed down, then stopped, tugging on his hand.

He turned to look at her. He already knew. His eyes were black with desire.

"Now," she said, "for there may never be another chance."

"If Bluebell finds out . . ."

She leaned into him, her breath mingling with his. "She won't find out."

Heath smiled, then leaned back and laughed. "I don't care if she kills me. Come." He led her farther upstream, deeper into the trees. Night was nearly upon them, and she stumbled over tree roots in the dark. He steadied her and they crossed the stream at a narrow point and moved into the wood on the other side. A small clearing opened before them.

Heath stopped and turned to face her, brought her hands to his mouth, and kissed her across the knuckles. Deep and low inside her, desire fluttered. The moment felt hot and present compared with the lonely and substanceless imaginings she had comforted herself with for three years. Her knees shook.

He stepped back, untied his belt and pulled his tunic over his head, then caught her against him. She ran her fingers over his warm shoulders, down into the light-golden hair across his chest, tracing the outline of his tattoo. Being so close to his body—his *real* body, not the imagined one—made her feel intensely vulnerable. Mortal. Lightly, with his fingertips, he lifted her chin and kissed her, his hot mouth claiming hers gently yet insistently, his tongue sliding between her lips.

Remember to breathe.

He released her and reached for the sash on her dress. It dropped to the forest floor with a thump: keys and scissors and comb and mirror lost among the leaves. Twilight fell away, as if in an instant, and night was left in its wake. As he slipped her dress over her head, a shiver traversed her body. Branches creaked, leaves shushed, forest creatures rattled in the undergrowth. She loosened her shift and let it slide over her breasts, which felt heavy and achey, then down over her hips and knees to pool on the ground. She bent to remove her stockings and shoes. Heath was scrambling out of his own clothes, then he spread them on the ground to lie on. She stood still and silent, her skin prickling sweetly, watching his strong pale body bent over. He pulled her down beside him.

"You are so soft," he said, losing his lips in the hollows along her collarbone. She lay back and beheld the velvet night. Her desire seemed at once to be of the sky, a divine thrumming beyond the knowledge of words; and of the earth, an impulse as base and uncomplicated as animals feel. His mouth moved to her breast and she swallowed a groan. Then she remembered they were far away from everyone, in the woods, and let her desire have its full voice. The bruising suction of his mouth on her nipple, the curtain of his golden hair falling over his face. Her spine arched, her hands ran over his ribs. He rolled her over so she lay on top of him, his mouth returning to hers. She propped herself on her hands, her knees falling either side of him, brushing her breasts across his lips, the searing wetness between her legs drawing down on top of him. Her breathing was so shallow that she began to feel dizzy. Dimly, she remembered Bluebell's warnings. No, and no, and no. But as Heath slid himself inside her, all she could think was, *Yes, and yes, and yes.* One bright moment, for who knew how long before they could steal another?

The angels were silent, but Willow knew what Maava would want her to do. Alone with Father, while he lay silent and still, she could almost see the heathen demons pulsing under his skin: at his throat, in his temples and wrists. She had to make this place, this dim room, a place where the angels would come and work their might, bringing her father's soul to Maava.

She pulled her knife from her belt. The tip of the blade caught a flash of firelight. She held open her palm and cut the fleshy part lightly, so that blood bubbled out. *I do not fear this pain. The pain magnifies your name, Maava. You whose mercy is bright and whose might is fearsome, glory be to you.* Willow returned her knife to its scabbard and pressed her palm so the blood flowed more freely.

The door swung in. Bluebell stood there. Willow hurriedly plunged her hand into her skirt and between her knees, hiding the wound.

"Bluebell? Is all well?"

"Your sister is an idiot," Bluebell muttered. Willow didn't know which sister she meant, but didn't ask for clarification. It could have been any of them.

Bluebell went to Father, leaned over and stroked his hair. "He looks less pale today, don't you think?"

Willow's palm stung. She pressed it between her knees. Father looked as pale as he ever had, but she knew better than to point that out to Bluebell. "You may be right."

Bluebell turned. The low sun through the window made her a silhouette, a big black shape, all arms and elbows. "We are moving on. Only you and Heath will stay with Father."

"As you wish." Perfect. It was easier to worship Maava without her sisters around.

"I feel I can trust you."

"You absolutely can."

Bluebell leaned forward and patted her head fondly, as though Willow were one of her dogs. "Good lass."

Then she was gone, the door closed again. Willow pulled out her hand. A hot red smear across her palm. She squeezed again, enjoying the pain. Remembering the martyred Liava's pain. Pain was good. Pain proved she loved Maava.

Willow carefully dipped her index finger in the blood and went to her father. She painted a triangle on the dark wood above his head. Barely visible unless one was looking for it, as Willow would be in the coming days. Then behind the door. Then under the mattress. Then the windowsill. Tiny blood paintings of the trimartyr symbol, undetectable to human eyes, but clear signs to angels. Finally, she leaned down and painted a triangle from the dip in her father's top lip, to the fullest part of his bottom lip. His mouth was left red, too obvious. So she leaned down and kissed him firmly, tasting her own blood. When she stood, the red stain had been absorbed into his skin.

He sighed, fidgeted, started his incoherent muttering. Willow's heart lifted. Had it worked already? Were the heathen spirits leaving his body? She glanced at her palm. It was bleeding heavily. She wrapped her hand tightly in her skirt and pressed down, heat and pain and deliverance shivering through her veins and lighting up her heart.

By the time Ivy realized she was probably in danger, she was already lost.

It hadn't been dark when she'd left the farmhouse, just bordering on dusk. She'd wanted to give Heath a good lead before following him. After all, her goal was for him to come upon her by accident in a flower field. She would look proud and beautiful in her yellow gown with the embroidered cuffs—a woman, not a girl—and he would be forced to admit he was wrong to speak to her as he had. But he had not headed into the fields, rather toward the stream. She didn't know that her embroidered cuffs would go particularly well with mud and rocks, but she gave him a head start and then made her way across.

But Heath wasn't there. She'd stood for a minute, listening. Thought, perhaps, there were footfalls in the oak wood. Hesitated. Perhaps it would be better to turn back to the farmhouse and wait for another opportunity to see him alone.

Then she'd moved off into the woods. And then, night had fallen. And now her yellow dress was barely visible in the dark.

It wasn't like Ivy to panic, though. She simply had to find her way back the way she came—if only she could be sure which way that was. She comforted herself with a fantasy that Heath would find her and have to rescue her. Perhaps she would fake a limp. Yes. Then he'd have to put his arm around her waist and help her home. Once he realized how curvaceous her body was, he wouldn't think her a girl. She wasn't a skinny, flat-chested thing like Bluebell and Ash and Willow.

She was comforting herself with these thoughts, trying to find her way through shadowy undergrowth, when she heard voices. A woman's voice, calling out. It traveled to her on the breeze, then faded. But at least she knew *somebody* was out here in the forest. Perhaps it was one of her sisters, looking for her. She was about to call out in return when she reminded herself she didn't know for sure if it was somebody she knew and could trust. So she warily set off in the direction of the voice, careful to keep her footsteps light, just in case.

Nearby, an owl hooted, startling her. She shivered and realized her heart was speeding. What if she'd imagined the voice? What if she was going to be stuck out here for the night, with the hooting owls and the wolves and . . . bandits, and whatever else was dark and evil and lurked in cold woods at night. Would Bluebell come for her if she didn't return home? The thought filled her with dread and relief at the same time. Bluebell would be cruel, but Ivy had no doubt she could fight off bandits with one hand and wolves with the other.

The voice again. Closer. And, unmistakably, the voice of a woman being pleasured. Ivy frowned. Not one of her sisters, then. Unless . . .

The thought made her burn. *Burn.* She hadn't seen Bluebell all afternoon. Heath had gone out. And now the sound of pleasure in the wood. Surely not. Bluebell could not possibly be a sexual being. Surely her orifices were riveted shut.

Ivy was determined to find out if her suspicions were right. She picked her way carefully through the trees. Now she could hear a second voice, a man's voice. She knew it was Heath's voice, and jealousy spiked her stomach. She had hoped to hear those sounds he was making, yes, but not in these circumstances.

Her heart hardened. They sounded like a couple of animals, grunting in a ditch. Then she got a clear sight of them through the trees.

Not Bluebell. Rose. Rose, queen of Nettlechester. Wengest's wife. Her white body arched under starlight, with Wengest's nephew between her legs, his hands over her breasts. She crept as close as she dared, but they were both lost to pleasure and heard and saw nothing.

Ivy slumped to the ground and gently and purposely knocked her head on a tree trunk. Why on earth did Heath prefer Rose? Rose was married. Rose had a child. That made her, surely, the least attractive woman in the party. She fought back tears. It wasn't fair. She had nobody and Rose had two men: a king for a husband and his nephew for a lover. Not fair. And Ivy was stuck in the woods alone, feeling like a fool. A little girl. Her only chance of finding her way home was waiting for them to finish and following them at a distance, and so she sat and waited while their breathing grew more ragged and they gasped, one by one, with the release of desire. She was sickened by jealousy, and appalled—no, fascinated—by her sister's dangerous infidelity.

Ash's stomach was hollow the morning they left. This would be the last time she would be together with the whole family. Once she had led Bluebell to Eldra, it would be time for her to take herself into exile. Away from light and laughter. And yet she couldn't tell anyone of her sorrow, so it was locked inside her, eating her away.

Bluebell looked much more positive as she mounted Isern. Her long fair hair was clean and brushed loose. Ivy, who had been told an hour before that she was accompanying Rowan and Sighere to Nettlechester, was red-eyed and sulking. They would ride in the other direction: back to the south, then across to Folkenham. The dogs barked happily, keen to be moving. Rose was fussing around Rowan, tightening the ties on her dress and pulling up her stockings.

"If you are cold, you tell Ivy."

"Mama, I want to come with you."

"Papa wants to see you, darling."

"You come to Papa with me!"

Rose gave Bluebell a cold glance. "I can't. But I will be home in a few weeks. It's only ten days north, then ten days back. Then straight home to you, my precious." She kissed the little girl's nose.

The cold that shimmered over Ash's skin then was intense, and she was seized by the sudden conviction Rose would not see Rowan for a very long time. Not weeks. Not months. Years. Ash caught her breath, but the feeling skidded away from her before she could pin it down. She intensified her focus on Rowan, but foresaw only happiness and safety, running in the garden outside her bowerhouse. Her gaze flicked to Rose, and she saw in her the shape of a mother, bountiful and bonny. Nothing to fear. Puzzled, she took up the reins of her horse.

Mist lay close to the ground, and the sky was leaden. The dark woods on the other side of the flower farm waited. They would head north, into the oldest parts of Thyrsland. Wild lands where ancient trees and fallen slabs of hewn rock marked the way; where undermagicians spun their spells; where elementals moved about on the plains, unafraid of the approach of men.

Bluebell looked to the sky. "The weather will hold," she said.

"Keep my baby warm," Rose said to Ivy, handing Rowan up to her.

Rowan wriggled and shrieked.

"Go, make it fast," Bluebell said to Sighere.

Rose stood with tears on her cheeks as Ivy and Sighere galloped off toward the road.

"The sooner we get moving, the better," Bluebell said to Rose. Perhaps it was an offer of comfort.

Rose mounted her horse without a word.

Bluebell smiled tightly at Ash. "I leave here with hope. I trust I will return the same. Can you see anything, Ash?"

"Not a thing," Ash said, relieved. "Just the trees and the sky and the road."

They moved off, northwest. Toward the undermagicians.

CHAPTER 16

Wylm hadn't spent time around children since he had been a child himself, so he was wary and impatient with Eni. Nor was Eni a normal child: He was a bundle of instincts with hands and feet—feet that kicked wildly to be let off the horse the moment he needed to piss, for example. The horse itself was a superb, broad-chested warhorse, no doubt a gift to the farmer from Bluebell. It eased the journey, and Wylm's feet didn't ache at the end of the day.

They were stopped now, in a soft grassy glade off the road. Wylm had kept them away from the main thoroughfares, which had made for a sometimes jolting journey. However, the roads to the northwest were not well traveled. The northwestern coast of Thyrsland was a dank place, with muddy beaches and hollow forests disfigured by prevailing winds.

But rumors and whispers had come to him that the Crow King had built his hall on an island off the northwest coast. He hoped for more than rumors and whispers in the northwestern inns: He hoped for a route, a map, a vessel to take him there. Wylm glanced at Eni, who was wandering around in the dusk collecting sticks. He also hoped to find somewhere to leave Eni.

"Watch out, lad, it's dark," Wylm called, then realized his warning was pointless. For Eni, it was always dark. He was sure-footed enough, mumbling to himself as he wove about, crouched over, feeling the ground for treasures. Wylm tugged at a slice of stringy rabbit meat with his teeth. What he would give for a soft bed and a proper meal, with turnips and beans and gravy. It wasn't that he didn't know hardship; Bluebell had had him stationed at a freezing stronghold for over a year, sharing a long, low hall with seventeen other soldiers. It was simply that he didn't think he should have to deal with hardship. His mother was the queen.

Now everything had been twisted out of shape, the threads of his destiny balled in a hopeless knot. It would be a measure of the kind of man he was if he could smooth things out, take charge of his future, shape the world to his will.

But sometimes, he didn't want to be that man.

Eni returned and held out his hands to Wylm. Wylm glanced at the collection of sticks and said nothing. Eni put the sticks down in front of him, crouched, and reached up for Wylm's head, taking it in his hands.

"Hey, what are you doing?" Wylm spluttered, then realized Eni was pointing his head toward the sticks, making sure he had seen them. "Oh, yes. Yes, they are wonderful sticks." He firmly moved the boy's hands away, noticing as he did that Eni still wore the gold dragon ring.

"You'll have to take that off, lad," he said, grasping the ring and tugging.

Eni's whole body spasmed in protest. He violently pulled away and threw himself on the ground, curling himself around the ring. "No!" he shouted.

"But I need to find an honest woman to look after you. I don't want somebody taking you for the gold ring then turning you out."

It was clear that Eni didn't understand this explanation. He flinched away from Wylm again and said in a very clear voice, "Bluebell."

"Bluebell gave you the ring?"

"Bluebell," he said again.

Hearing his stepsister's name put Wylm in a foul mood. "Suit yourself," he said to Eni. "Come and eat something."

The child didn't move.

"Eat," Wylm said, thrusting a hunk of rabbit meat toward him. "Come on. Rabbit. Rabbit."

But Eni stood and felt his way through the grass to the stream instead. Wylm watched as he bent to drink, then thrust his hands and wrists in the water, then stood and peeled off his shoes and stepped into the stream.

"What are you . . . ?" Wylm sighed, finished his meal, and stood. "What are you doing now, lad?"

Eni was smiling, giggling, as he trod on a spot in the water.

"What is it?"

Eni grasped Wylm's hand and pulled him toward him.

Wylm shook him off. "No, I'm not going in the water." He peered at the boy's feet, and realized he was squishing mud between his toes. "Come out. You'll be cold. You'll be . . ."

But the boy just kept giggling. Wylm remembered doing the same as a child, and was seized by the mad desire to join him. Impulsively, he slid off his shoes and stepped into the cold water. Mud squashed up between his toes.

"Ah, yes," he said to Eni, "you're right. It does feel good."

"Mud, mud, mud," Eni sang, surprisingly tunefully.

Wylm laughed, wriggling his toes in the mud as the sun disappeared behind the world.

Wylm woke to the sound of shouting in the distance. He sat up, addled for a moment by the morning light. Eni slept curled under a blanket next to him, arms wrapped around a bunch of sticks. It was their fourth morning together. The shouting continued, gruff voices arguing. He realized they were speaking the language of Iceheart, the language of the northern raiders.

"Wake, boy," Wylm said, prodding Eni. "We need to hide." The two of them out here in the open, barely armed, while raiders were on the road: Wylm had never felt so vulnerable. The stories of their cruelty were well known. He hurried Eni to his feet, packed swiftly, and led the horse off into the trees, where they crouched quietly among the saplings and the dewy grass. Eni seemed to understand instinctively that they were in danger and needed to be silent, his dark eyes rolling back and forth as they had the day Wylm had killed his father. An unexpected pang of guilt. But then Wylm brought an image of Bluebell to his mind's eye, and the guilt washed away.

The shouting continued. Wylm picked up a word here and there on the wind. They were arguing over the spoils of a raid. The thought that he would have to somehow make his way to see a raider king made his stomach hollow. Was he just to stroll up and greet the king of such men? Surely his throat would be slit before his greeting had left his tongue.

First, survive this close call. Second, get Eni to safety. Third . . . The desire to run. The desire to leave all this behind him. But his mother was imprisoned at Bluebell's will. A good son would not run away.

The argument stopped and their footfalls on the road drew closer. Five of them in dirty clothes, with long beards and hair. As they passed, just one hundred feet away, Wylm noticed one man had his hair tied in a long, tight plait. On the back of his neck, Wylm could see the tattoo of a raven.

Hakon's men. If, indeed, Hakon yet lived.

He opened his mouth to call out, but the words froze in his throat. It was not safe with Eni, he told himself. He was not prepared; he had not yet decided what words he would use, in their strange tongue, to explain himself.

But he knew he didn't call out because he was frightened.

They passed, and Wylm sat down heavily, his back against a tree trunk. The sun climbed higher and Eni sang a soft little song to himself. Wylm waited. Waited some more. Then when he was certain they would be safe, he grasped Eni's shoulder. "Time to keep moving," he said.

Eni understood the intent if not the words. Wylm saddled his horse and soon they were on their way.

The wind freshened from the west as the day wore on, and they moved due west out of the shelter of trees. They stopped to eat at an exposed place where the lungs of the ocean exhaled upon them furiously. Once again, Wylm tried to get Eni to eat the leftover cold rabbit, but the boy didn't want food. They mounted the horse and kept moving. Salt and seaweed were thick in the air. Wylm became alarmed that they hadn't seen another human since the raiders that morning. Would he find an inn soon? Or even a hunter's cabin among the rocks and growling pines? Any sign of life?

The sun was moving into its low position in the sky when the vista opened up and he could see beyond wild rocky cliffs to the gray sea. And there, finally, was a village. A white-painted inn sat in the middle of it, with little crooked stone houses huddled around it. Laundry and fish hung in equal measure on long ropes between houses.

"We are at the sea," he told Eni.

But Eni could already smell it. He had lifted his nose to the wind and was wrinkling it curiously.

"Do you think you'd like to live by the sea, Eni?" Wylm asked, and already his mind's eye was taken over by the fantasy. A cozy house, a warm maternal bosom, a wiry fisherman father, bleak weather outside the shutters, a warm fire . . . Then he wondered if the fantasy was for Eni or for himself. "I think you'll be happy here," he muttered as he urged the horse forward.

The alehouse was bright and full of folk and fire. Men who smelled of fish and seawater sat on long benches gulping drinks and laughing, while their wives chased fat children around or hung about their husbands' necks with shining faces. He had rarely been in such a happy place.

"Sit here," he said to Eni, finding a dark corner. "Now I must take your ring, but just for a day." He gently reached for Eni's hand and the gold ring.

Eni snatched his hand back. "Bluebell," he said.

"Here," Wylm said, withdrawing from his belt a trinket he had been carving over the last few days. He had taken a thick stick and turned it into a long, skinny rabbit. Eni's hand closed over it, feeling its contours eagerly.

"The ring, Eni," Wylm said. "Just for a day."

Eni didn't even notice Wylm slipping the ring off his hand, so delighted was he with the rabbit-stick. Wylm pocketed the ring securely, then went to the hearthpit, where the alehouse wife was turning a spit of fat fish over the fire. "Hello," he said.

She turned her plain, ruddy face to him. "Evening, sir."

"You are very busy tonight."

"The fishermen just came back. They've been away a week in deep water."

Wylm looked around with fresh eyes. Yes, a celebration. That's where the sense of merriment arose from. "I need a room and a meal for the young lad and me," he said.

She glanced over at Eni. "What's wrong with him?"

"He's blind."

"Looks more than blind. I've seen a two-year-old playing with a stick like that, not a big boy who should have been sent to apprentice."

Wylm felt a pang for Eni that he didn't expect. "He is as he is," Wylm said, "and I need to find a good, caring home for him here. I have to travel a long way and for a long time."

"Good luck," she said darkly. "If it can't catch a fish or bear a baby, it has no place in Greywall." She indicated around her with a free hand. "The whole village is here. You can ask around if you like. But we are too small to support somebody who isn't able-bodied."

Wylm scanned the room. Was there a couple without children? An older woman alone?

The alehouse wife's voice softened. "Go on, sit down. I'll bring you some food and ask a few questions for you. And I've got a room out the back for you and your lad if you don't mind sharing a bed."

Wylm returned to his seat. Eni was on the floor now, playing with the rabbit-stick, heedless of how his long skinny legs and jutting elbows marked him as a boy too old for strange noises and playing on muddy rushes. Wylm watched him awhile, thoughts turning over and over. What misplaced pity had brought him into this situation? He had killed the boy's father. He intended yet to extract revenge on Bluebell, the most famed warrior in the land. And here he was, minding a simple boy as though he were a softhearted woman. He should have killed the boy when he had the chance.

But he *couldn't* kill the boy. He had been incapable of it. No matter that his heart welled with dark thoughts, he wasn't pitiless.

How he longed to be pitiless.

The alehouse wife arrived with their meals—ale and fish and hot buttered beans—and said, "Old Florrie is going to come talk to you."

"Old Florrie?"

"She's my husband's grandmother. She wants to meet your boy."

Wylm nodded. Old Florrie would do. Once Eni was off his hands, he could get on with the next stage of his plans, unencumbered.

"Come on, Eni, sit up at the table. Food." He waved the plate under Eni's nose and the boy felt his way to his seat, carefully placing the rabbit-stick aside, and began eating with his fingers.

"Can't you even use a spoon?" Wylm said, forcing the spoon into his hand.

Eni could use a spoon, once reminded to pick it up, but it was still a messy affair. Wylm gulped his ale and waited for the arrival of Old Florrie.

She was nothing like he expected. No warm bosom and soft smile. She was all bones and hard surfaces, cheeks like scythes and a cold glint in her eye. "Is this the boy?" she said, without further introduction.

"Yes. His name is Eni."

She grasped Eni by the chin and forced his face up so she could examine it. "He's blind, then?"

"He can still get around very well."

"Boy, is that true? Can you still get around very well?"

Eni was silent, sightless eyes swimming. Florrie released him with a derisive sniff. "No, I'll not take him. Nobody here will take him. He's of no use."

"Perhaps a woman who's lost a child?"

"We don't mourn dead children long here," Florrie said. "I had six and only three lived. It's the way in these parts. If it's not the sea that swallows them, it's the creeping cold that gets in their chests."

Wylm didn't notice that Eni's hand had crept across the table until he felt it slip under his own, looking for security. Anger boiled up inside him. Anger at Eni, at Florrie, at Bluebell, at the whole world for putting him in this situation.

But then he remembered the ring. And it all fell into place in his mind—a way to both keep Eni safe and further his own ends.

"Never mind, then," Wylm said to Florrie. "I'll keep the lad."

Florrie shrugged and turned away. Wylm closed his hand over Eni's. "Never mind," he said again, more softly. "I'll find us a way through."

The raiders had been heading south, so that meant Wylm had to head south, retracing his steps. But they were on foot and he on a horse. He could catch them. It was a gray morning when they set off; the fog had barely lifted, and the seaweed smell in the air almost choked him. But he put Eni on his horse, the gold ring restored to the child's limp finger, and he rode hard and long.

A few hours back along the road, he stopped to rest the horse and give Eni a break. He stood by a narrow stream that ran over rocks, stretching his aching back and constructing the sentence over and over in his head in the northern language. But no matter how he said it, it could still be construed as an invitation to immediate and violent death. He changed the phrasing yet again. Better.

Wylm realized that there had been quiet for a while. He turned and scanned for Eni. Couldn't see him.

"Eni?" he called, heading toward the trees. No doubt the boy was collecting twigs again. "Where have you gotten to?"

A rustle in the bushes.

Wylm paused, his left foot flexed as though to take another step. "Eni?" he said, hating the note of fear in his voice.

Then they were around him, five hefty men in leather and fur, emerging from behind trees he hadn't even suspected as hiding places. And one of them had Eni hard against him, his hand over the child's mouth.

Wylm's lips tried to form words, but nothing would come out. White-hot fear sheeted through him.

The biggest in the group leaned forward, resting the edge of his ax against Wylm's shoulder. "Boo," he said.

❖   ❖   ❖

The raiders forced Wylm, hands bound, to march deeper into the glade, leaving his horse and pack behind. Every time he tried to speak, one of them would smack him around the head and shout, "Quiet!" so he did as he was told. Eni was being carried over a burly man's shoulders, crying quietly, every now and again saying the word "rabbit" mournfully, and Wylm presumed he had lost his plaything. At length they came to an encampment, and Wylm realized he was in much deeper trouble than he could have imagined. He counted twelve on the ground, sitting around fires, sharpening blades, fletching arrows. Who knew how many more were in tents, especially in the largest tent, which was painted with a raven insignia on a red sea?

"Ragnar!" the man who held Wylm called, throwing Wylm onto the ground and putting a foot on his chest to stop him moving. "Come and see this."

From the tent emerged a solid, muscular mass of a man with a giant red beard. To Wylm's surprise, the big man beckoned Ragnar not toward Wylm, but toward the boy, who stood uncertainly between them all.

The big man reached out and flipped Eni's arm into the air, showing Ragnar the ring.

Wylm saw his chance. "It is the ring of the royal family of Almissia," he cried, finally uttering the words he had been contemplating all day. "This child is the unacknowledged son of Bluebell the Fierce, the grandson of Athelrick Storm Bearer. I have brought him to you."

Ragnar turned and seemed to notice Wylm for the first time. "You speak our tongue?"

"I am trained in diplomacy. I am the son of Athelrick's queen, Gudrun of Tweening."

Ragnar nodded to the big man. "Let him stand. Unbind his hands." He crouched as Wylm sat up and offered his hands to be untied. "Why do you bring him to us?"

"I want to kill Bluebell. I have heard that Hakon still lives and I want an alliance with him to take her down. Her father is sick, dying. Now is the time to act." *Please don't kill us, please don't kill us.*

Ragnar considered him, lips pursed among the bright whiskers. "How do I know you are who you say you are?"

"He could be making it up," the big man said.

"The child has the ring," said another.

"So take the ring and kill them both."

"Hakon will want to see them."

Wylm caught his breath. So the whispers were true. Hakon hadn't died at his brother's hand.

"He has a randerman who could tell if they were lying."

"The boy can't lie. He's simple."

Laughter erupted. "Bluebell's son is a simple?"

"Hakon will enjoy that joke."

Their voices swirled around Wylm and he struggled to keep up with what they were saying. But he heard one word over and over: Ravensey. The Island of Ravens.

Finally, Ragnar made his decision. "If these two are who they say they are, Hakon will want them alive. We sail this evening."

"We are going to see Hakon?" Wylm asked.

"You'd best not be lying," Ragnar said. "For Hakon's randerman will know and it will be the ax's edge for you."

"I'm not lying," Wylm said boldly. "I fear no practitioner of magic." But he did. There wasn't a thing about this situation he didn't fear.

Their longship was pulled up on the muddy beach about five miles from where they'd intercepted him. From here, Wylm could see the smoke of the village of Greywall, where he had spent the previous night. Eni was at his wit's end, rocking from side to side and muttering as they tried to lead him onto the ship. Finally, they capitulated and let Wylm take him and sit with him under cover on the floorboards, with some barrels and a few skinny sheep. The raiders took an hour to organize themselves and pack their belongings. Wylm could feel the thuds and creaks of the ship as they did, while Eni's bony body trembled as though he might shake to pieces.

The fog had finally lifted and the sky was clear and pale blue as the raiders pushed the ship over mud and rattling pebbles and into the water. The ship found its weight in the water and bobbed softly. One by one, the raiders climbed in and took up oars, while Ragnar strode to the back and took the tiller. Wylm could see his legs from his place among the stored goods.

They lifted their oars and started to row, out past the currents into deep, dark water. A horn sounded. The sails came flapping down and they tacked against the wind, picked up speed.

Eni clung harder to Wylm, whimpering.

"Sh, now, lad," Wylm said. "All will be well."

The ship arrowed north, toward Ravensey.

chapter 17

Willow's throat was sore and her mouth was dry from praying. She no longer needed to whisper her prayers under her breath. Heath kept his distance from her, so when she sat in here with Father, it was as if they were alone in the world together. Sometimes she ran out of words to pray with and settled for saying Maava's name over and over. But then the angels would hiss and spit and she would start again.

"Take my father's soul. Forgive him his many sins. Take my father's soul into the Sunlands. Maava, great and good, listen to this poor sinner . . ."

And the angels' voices died away.

All except for one.

Willow felt the angel in her head, like a thorn lodged in the soft part of her brain. It waited for her, cool and disdainful. She stopped praying.

"What is wrong, angel of Maava?" Willow said, her heart speeding.

"Sinner," it said, its voice sizzling sharp against her ears.

"I know I am a sinner. I know. I pray for Maava's love."

"You are one of them."

Willow's fingers began to shake. "One of . . ." Then she realized the angel meant her family. "No, no. I'm not. I have come to Maava's light."

"Whores, witches, kinslayers."

"No, they are only heathens. I'm trying to bring them to Maava. See me? I'm praying night and day for the soul of the greatest heathen king in Thyrsland."

Athelrick began to stir, mumbling. One of his fits was coming on. She froze a moment, but knew she couldn't cope alone. She went to the door and opened it, calling out for Heath.

"Murderers, plunderers, adulterers."

Behind her, her father had begun to moan, low and long, like a wounded animal. She turned. His hands danced in spasms on the bedcovers. The angel laughed in her ears.

"He is no great king. And you are a sinner." Then the voice was gone.

Athelrick flung back his covers and tried to get up, shouting at her incoherently.

"My lord, you must be calm," she said to him, trying to smooth his covers over. "Heath! Heath!" But Heath wasn't in the house.

Athelrick had sat up and was struggling to push himself into a standing position. Willow threw herself on top of him, straddling him, using the weight of her body to push him back down. He grunted. She put her hands on his shoulders and leaned into him, and he slowly sank back down onto the bed. The knotted fingers of his right hand closed around her wrist.

Behind her, the door opened. "Willow?"

"He tried to get up," she said to Heath. "He's calm again."

"I'm sorry. I was in the—"

"Bluebell?"

Both Willow and Heath were stunned into silence. Willow looked down at her father, whose lips were moving silently now.

"Did he say . . . ?"

"'Bluebell,'" Willow replied. "He said 'Bluebell.'"

Her father's fingers went slack, drifting down from her wrist and landing on the covers. He slept again.

Willow climbed off the bed, her heart hammering. She could still feel the ghost of her father's touch, tingling cool on her wrist.

Heath couldn't hide his smile. "Do you think it's possible he might recover?"

Willow shook her head. "I don't know. Perhaps." Her heart filled with light. If he lived, Willow could convince him to take the faith. She could convince them all. Almissia would convert, and the angels wouldn't judge her anymore. Of course. Of course. This was why she had been born, why she had come to Maava. Through her father's illness, she would work a miracle. She would save the souls of her countrymen and make sure Thyrsland came to the trimartyr faith. She almost laughed, the giddy relief was so light.

Then she realized: All along she had been praying for the wrong thing. She ought not pray for his soul. A living man could save his own soul. From now on, she would pray for his life so that her glorious destiny might rush upon her, bright and clear.

From Stonemantel, the most direct route to Bradsey was to skim up along the coastline, but the west coast of Thyrsland was rugged and endured intense prevailing winds that had bent its trees into grotesque postures of submission. So Ash, Rose, and Bluebell stayed with the inland road, twenty miles from the sea—an overgrown track that led over the dramatic, heather-choked moors. They passed no other travelers, and Ash had the feeling they were riding off the edge of the known world.

Rose was silent, sulking. Bluebell responded by pretending she didn't notice. Ash lost herself in thoughts about her power, her Becoming, and how she was to try to make a future for herself. Now that she had spent so long allowing her second sight to be open—or at least, not actively shutting it down—she had realized her ability to read what was going on around her was patchy. Sometimes, the sight was wide ranging, intense, rolling over her like an ocean wave. Sometimes, it was like seeing through a chink in a wooden board: No matter how she positioned herself, she couldn't get a complete picture. And there seemed to be no pattern to predict it by.

How she longed for good advice. She knew she wouldn't find it at Thridstow, where the old counselors would be jealous or alarmed. She hadn't even found it with Byrta, and her hopes Eldra might help had been quickly dispelled. She had thought of asking Bluebell for advice but Bluebell, for all her knowledge and experience in war, would surely have nothing to offer beyond sympathy. Perhaps she would say, *What does it matter if you can't predict your second sight? Just use it when you can.* She wouldn't feel Ash's sense of urgency. *What is happening to me? When will it stop? Will I survive it?*

Out here on the lonely moors, far from the world of men, she could feel the creeping magic everywhere. It was skulking in the tangled heather, it was draping itself from the crooked rowan trees, it was slouching cool and dark in the crevices between rocks. The farther north they moved, the stronger this sense of organic magic grew— a force neither hostile nor kind, but coolly neutral. Indifferent. It was a feature of the landscape here, as much as rolling green hills were a feature of Almissia, or dense elm forests were a feature of Nettlechester. And today, they were still miles from the plains of Bradsey, where the magic was thickest, roiling across the ground like fog.

Rose slowed so she was riding alongside Ash, and said in a harsh whisper, "When do you think she'll let us stop for a rest? We've been riding five hours with barely a break."

As Rose said this, Ash became aware of the tired ache across her back and thighs.

"Even her dogs are nowhere to be seen," Rose continued, looking around. Her long hair was stuck to her face by the wind. "They're probably sensibly having a rest, a few miles behind us."

"They'll find us," Ash said. "But if you're tired, you should ask her for a rest."

"And give her another chance to put me in my place? I think not."

Ash urged her horse forward. "Bluebell, when are you thinking of resting?"

Bluebell stirred, almost as though from a dream. "Hmm? I suppose we can rest now if you want to eat. But I'd hoped to get to Shotley and stay there for the night. It's only an hour away, and then we're past the moors." She looked around, almost as though she was sniffing the air. "I don't like it out here. Something unseen lurks, as if it's watching us."

Ash glanced over her shoulder at Rose, raised her eyebrows to say, *See? You only had to ask.*

"Let's keep going then," Rose said. "I can stand another hour if it means a soft bed."

Ash's body had been preparing itself for rest and now she had to tell it to keep going. She shifted in her saddle, finding a new position for her back to settle in. She thought about Bluebell's comment: something unseen, watching them. This place would surely be crawling with elementals. Did she dare? But before she could even make up her mind, the sight was opening up.

What surprised her most was the stillness. She'd imagined elementals bustling about, darting between rocks and trees, going to ground as they felt her eyes on them. But they were motionless. Hundreds of them, lined up along the side of the track as though she and her sisters were a procession and they had come out to . . .

Watch. They had come out to watch Ash.

Wonder and fear boiled up in her gut. She looked at them with frightened eyes, and they looked back at her. Guardedly, sometimes hopefully, sometimes with angry apprehension. She moved past them, and they were perfectly still. Her sisters were unaware of the audience; her horse didn't shy.

Then she remembered what the oak spirit had said to her. *Your voice is inexorable.* She wanted very much to test if this was true, to feel that power, but fear kept her words inside. Besides, what would her sisters make of her shouting out commands to nobody?

So, in her head, she called to them: *Go to ground! All of you!*

And every single one of them dropped to the earth and disappeared. The air shimmered as it collapsed around them, and the ground shuddered as though a herd of invisible oxen had passed momentarily over it. Ash's bones shook.

"What was that?" Rose said, looking around, alarmed. Her voice came to Ash's ears as though muffled by layers of wool. Ash's horse put her head down and moved to buck. Bluebell stopped, her long tattooed arm raised.

Ash's heart thundered. She didn't say anything.

"The earth shook," Rose said, superstitious fear making her face pale.

"I felt it," Bluebell said, her mouth a thin line. "I think we should pick up our speed."

So they did, and Ash shut down her sight and clenched her stomach so she wouldn't throw up over herself. Her joints felt bruised. The physical discomfort was a welcome distraction for a little while. Stopping her from thinking about what all this signified.

She could command elementals. A storm of magic was gathering around her, and she had neither knowledge nor power enough to stop it.

But there was no longer any hiding it from herself. She was an undermagician, and she was riding directly into the land where undermagicians belonged.

Shotley was only a small village, but walled and gated from the wild woodland around it. It must have once been a town important to the giants, because the woods were punctuated by white ruins, crumbled to head height by time and weather. They reached Shotley by crossing a wide, wooden bridge over the Gema River—a turquoise-blue waterway that supported the village by way of trade and the abundance of Shotley trout, a delicacy throughout Thyrsland. The river marked the border between Almissia and Bradsey, and as they crossed it, they left behind the last shire in which Bluebell had direct rule. She and her father had not been this far north on king's business in many years. She doubted the people who lived in these parts knew they were ruled by anyone.

The stables were poorly kept: dark, with moldering straw. The dogs looked at Bluebell with pleading eyes as she left them in one of the boxes.

"Would they let me keep my dogs at the alehouse?" she asked the terrifyingly old stable hand.

He smiled at her with teeth worn down to stumps. "I'd say not, my lady. But I'll take good care of them here if you slip me an extra coin."

She did as he asked then reluctantly left, Rose and Ash behind her.

The sweet steam from the alehouse called her. How she longed to sit still and drink ale, then fall into a soft bed—if there was one in Shotley—and sleep for a long time.

As she was about to open the door of the alehouse, Ash tugged on her sleeve. "Bluebell," she said, "we ought not stay here too long."

"Here? At the alehouse?"

"Shotley."

Bluebell's stomach twitched. "We have to rest."

"Then keep your head low. Hide your weapons and wear a dress."

"Wear a dress?" She almost laughed. Then said, "You're serious?"

Ash nodded. "Come. Around the side here and away from eyes." She pulled Bluebell into the alley between buildings. "I have a strong sense it would be better if nobody knew Bluebell the Fierce was here."

Bluebell shrugged and turned to Rose. "Do you have a dress I can wear?"

Rose dropped her pack on the ground and pulled out a length of fabric. "Do you want a shift as well?"

Bluebell was already unbuckling her weapons and handing them to Ash, wriggling out of her tunic. "No, I'll just throw it on. Hurry."

The dress only came to her calves, revealing her gaiters and the leather straps that tied them on. Her tattooed wrists were also visible. Rose was trying not to laugh as she pinned the dress at Bluebell's shoulders with two amber-and-glass brooches.

"Will I do?" she said to Ash.

"Try to look a little less . . . fierce," Ash said, helping Bluebell back into her sword-belt and pinning her cloak: "And keep this covered."

Together, they entered the alehouse. Ash urged Bluebell to sit down with Rose in a dim back corner while she went to order food.

Bluebell eyed Rose across the table. They'd barely spoken since they left the flower farm. "Are you still sore with me?"

Rose gave a humorless laugh. "Sore? That's what you used to say when we were children, after you wrestled me into submission over something."

Bluebell shrugged.

"In case you hadn't noticed, Bluebell, we are not children anymore. I have a child of my own. And she is somewhere between here and the moon."

"They'd be in Withing. That's where I told Sighere to stop."

"We hope."

"I know. Sighere will protect her. That's why I sent him with her."

"If I knew she was home safe with those who loved her, I wouldn't mind so much . . ." Rose dropped her head. "But it feels as though that cord between her body and mine was never cut, and it pulls at my guts to have her so far away."

Bluebell realized she wasn't going to get any sense out of Rose and gave up, taking the opportunity instead to look around the room. A lot of smelly old fishermen and hard-faced women. No great threat. And yet Ash's eyes were dark with concern over some unseen thing.

Ash made her way back from the bar then and shooed Bluebell out of her seat. "You face the back wall," she said.

"I don't like to sit with my back to the door."

"I don't want anyone to recognize you."

Bluebell slid off the bench and swapped places with Rose. Now she felt uncomfortable. She couldn't see what was happening anywhere in the alehouse. "What is this about, Ash?"

Ash slid their cups of ale onto the table. "The moment we crossed the bridge, a cold feeling came over me," she said. "You are too bright a woman to come into this dark place. I can say nothing more than that. These feelings aren't always clear; they run beneath my skin like instincts. Wordless, but certain."

"Perhaps we should not have stopped. There are woods we could have slept in."

Rose shook her head. "The woods are wild. I saw no managed trees beyond the first few feet from the path. There would be wolves for certain." Rose's eyes flickered, catching sight of something over Bluebell's shoulder.

Bluebell resisted the urge to look around. "What is it?"

"It looks like a drunkard with love on his mind," Rose said.

Bluebell braced herself. A moment later, an oily man with a flushed face was standing by their table, his right foot propped on the seat next to Bluebell's thigh.

"Good evening, ladies," he said.

Bluebell turned her face to him. "We'd thank you to leave us be," she said.

"But three good ladies such as yourself must surely be in need of the company of a good man."

Bluebell bit back the retort on her lips, mindful of Ash's advice.

Ash smiled at him. "We sisters are all the company we need for one another. We simply want to have our meal in peace."

He scowled, then walked away.

"He smelled like trout guts," Bluebell murmured into her ale.

Rose laughed.

"Not so loud, Rose," Ash admonished. "He heard that."

"What's he doing?" Bluebell asked.

The serving woman arrived with their meals then, thumping the plates onto the table with the kind of dull force only deeply unhappy people can achieve.

Ash glanced up under her eyelashes. "He's talking to another man. A big fellow."

"We've not heard the last of our new lover," Bluebell said. "You'll see I'm right. Let's eat quickly and get to a room."

They fell on their food. Bluebell would have wolfed it down under any circumstances, she was so hungry from the day's travel, but she could also see in Ash's face the building panic. They had to get out of there.

A few minutes later, they were standing at the bar. Rose asked the alehouse husband for a room.

He eyed them one by one, taking special notice of Bluebell. "Yes, we have a room. One of you might have to sleep on the floor." He nodded toward Bluebell. "Your tall friend looks like she's well used to hardship."

"Give us the key," Bluebell snapped, earning a kick in the shins from Ash.

He handed the key to Rose and they turned to the door, only to find it barred by the oily man and his friend.

Bluebell bit her lip so she wouldn't swear. Her fingers twitched at her hip.

"Let us by," Ash said in a sweet voice. "We mean you no harm."

The larger man huffed. "You were laughing at my friend."

The hushed quiet behind them told Bluebell they had an audience.

"We weren't," Rose said. "We were laughing about something else. We offer you no disrespect."

"We see it differently," said the oily man, "and we don't take kindly to women who talk out of turn."

And, by fuck, Bluebell wanted to make him eat steel. Hot mist built up behind her eyes.

The larger man took a step forward. "You see . . ." he said, reaching for Ash's upper arm.

And that was it. Bluebell's sword was out and swinging down, its deadly edge stopping suddenly on his sleeve. "Touch her and you lose your hand. Then how would you fist your mister?"

Ash gave an exasperated groan. The man reached for his knife, but Bluebell grabbed him under the armpit and in seconds had him in an armlock, his back against her chest and her sword resting lengthways across his belly. His knife clattered to the floor. The oily man stood back. A long way back.

"Do I have to spill your guts?" Bluebell asked him.

He shook his head.

She let him go and sheathed her sword. Looked around. Everyone was staring at her. She readjusted her cloak. The alehouse husband was staring at her, and she could see the wheels in his brain turning. She felt the first cool touch of regret.

"Come," Ash said, urging her ahead. "Let's be away."

They found their way outside to the guesthouse, locking their room firmly.

"The alehouse husband recognized you, I'm sure of it," Ash said, pacing.

Bluebell pulled off her dress and handed it back to Rose. "So what do we do? Do you want us to leave?"

"We need to rest," Rose said.

Bluebell was climbing back into her own clothes. "What do you sense, Ash? Is danger near?"

"No. It's not . . . I can't control this. I'm sorry. We are both safe and not safe here, and I don't know why." Ash sat heavily on the bed, her head in her hands.

Bluebell considered her by the flickering lamplight. On the one hand, she took Ash's fears seriously, but on the other, she found it hard to conceive of a world in which she couldn't keep two of her sisters safe. She had sometimes kept her entire hearthband safe. "Ash? What's wrong?"

"I'm fine," Ash said. "Let's sleep and be away early."

Bluebell glanced around the room, spotted a large chest. She pulled it up to the door to bar it. "You two sleep, I'll keep watch," she said.

"You need sleep, too."

"I'll doze. I'll be fine."

She sat on the chest with her back against the door, the Widow-smith drawn, to wait for sunrise.

There were more appealing ways to be woken than being prodded by Bluebell's bony fingers at dawn. Rose opened her eyes, the comfort of sleep fell away, and she was left instead with the memory that she was far from those she loved the most. Ordinarily, she would take a few moments to remember Rowan's soft kisses and derive small comfort, but Bluebell was insistent.

"Come on. We must be away. Up and dressed, sisters."

Ash was doing as she was told, but Rose wasn't in the mood for Bluebell's orders. "In good time, Bluebell," she said.

"The good time is now," Bluebell said in reply. In the dim light, Rose could see that her sister's eyes were darkly shadowed. Had she stayed awake all night on watch? A small pulse of guilt.

Ash put a cool hand on Rose's shoulder. "Take your time, sister. I'll pack your things."

Ash's kindness galvanized her more than Bluebell's overbearing bossiness ever could. She rose and pinned on her dress, pulled on her shoes. Bluebell paced the whole time, clearly anxious to get away. She took Ash's premonitions very seriously, even when they were as inarticulate as this one. Rose wondered if it wasn't the dark wood and empty isolation of the village that had made Ash uncomfortable. They were beyond the border of civilization here. For Rose, the idea of being away from everything was not an uncomfortable one. Away from everything meant away from obligation and damning eyes and promises made in public.

The dogs met them gratefully at the stable, tails thumping, and soon they were saddled and on their way. Bluebell was in a foul mood, shouting at the dogs and scowling. Rose ignored it, but when they had been riding about ten minutes and Shotley was a dark shape on the hill behind them, Ash ventured to draw Bluebell into conversation.

"Is everything all right, Bluebell?" she ventured.

"I'm fine," Bluebell replied shortly.

"Did you have any sleep last night?"

"What does it matter?" Bluebell snapped. "Let's get on."

Rose clenched her teeth. Enough of Bluebell's foul humor, especially as Ash had done nothing to deserve it. "Leave her be, Bluebell."

"All is well, Rose," Ash said. "She hasn't slept. She stayed awake to protect us."

"All is not well. She isn't the only one who has a reason to be unhappy. Why should we indulge her? She doesn't indulge us."

"You mean I've never indulged *you*?" Bluebell said, pulling Isern up hard and turning on her. "And why should I? You were given one thing to do to earn your place in this family. One thing: marry the king of Nettlechester and be faithful to him. And you couldn't even do that. You barely made it through a year before you were riding your nephew."

"He's not my nephew!"

"Please don't fight," Ash said. "You're both tired, you both have a lot on your minds. This will get us nowhere."

"Stay out of it, Ash," Rose said, firmly. "Bluebell and I need to speak of this directly."

"I've already spoken to you directly. Many times," Bluebell said with a scowl. "Heath is Rowan's father, and for that he may live and be of use to us. But one more half-breed bastard will be too many for me, and certainly too many for Wengest."

"You speak as though all that matters is the business of kings."

"It is all that matters. What am I to say to you, Rose, that you have my blessing to make decisions from between your legs? Where does that leave the rest of us in Almissia? In the other territories that rely on us? What am I to say to the people on the borders of Bradsey: *Oh, I'm sorry that you are being slaughtered by raiders, but my sister was in need of a good fucking*?"

The temperature of Rose's blood surged that Bluebell had reduced something so beautiful to something so coarse. She had sent her daughter away with strangers. And her heart was as cold and hard as steel. Rose kicked her horse and galloped off, down toward the woods. Away, for fear that if she stayed her heart would explode with hot fury.

"Rose, wait!" Ash shouted, a thrill of desperation in her voice, though Rose didn't know why. It wasn't the first time she and Bluebell had argued and it would hardly be the last.

Then she saw the heavy, overhanging branch of a chestnut tree barring the road. She yanked the reins. A hard, black pain shuddered across her forehead. The sun blinked out.

She was awake, but not awake. Consciousness was not lost, but shredded into incoherent pieces. She seemed to see herself from far away, Bluebell lifting her limp form onto Isern's back. Then a long stretch of ringing darkness. Ash's hands, close and smelling of leather from reins. Voices. Shouting. Bluebell shouting, ordering people around. Rose felt the beat of her heart as a deep ache in her head. The darkness flickered on and off. A pungent smell, choking her. She fought against it, then Ash said, "Sleep now. We are here with you."

Then a long silence in the hum of life.

Rose's eyes flickered open. Long shadows and a chill in the air told her it was late in the afternoon. She was somewhere soft, and her head throbbed. She took a moment to remember what had happened.

Then Ash leaned into view. "You're awake."

"Where are we?"

"Back in Shotley."

"Where's Bluebell?"

"I'm here." A voice from the shadows in the corner of the room. Rose sat up to look around, but her neck and shoulders screamed with pain.

"Stay down," Ash said. "You hit your head and then you had a bad fall. You need to rest."

Rose did as she was told, reaching for her forehead where the branch had struck her. It was bandaged. "Have I been unconscious all this time?"

"I gave you something to make you sleep. I had to stitch your wound." Ash pointed to her own forehead. "It was bleeding badly."

Bluebell came into view. "When can she ride again?"

Ash turned to her. "Give her a day or two. She's badly bruised."

"This place . . ."

"I know."

Rose reached for Bluebell's hand. Her sister looked gray with tiredness and concern. "I'm so sorry."

Bluebell shrugged. She squeezed Rose's hand, then released it. A quick knock at the door made her head jerk up. Her sword was drawn in a second.

Ash put out a hand. "I'll open it. Stay out of sight."

"They've already seen me."

"Please, Bluebell."

Bluebell shrank back into the shadows. Ash opened the door. It was the alehouse husband.

"Good evening," Ash said.

"How long are you staying?"

"It will depend very much on my sister's recovery."

He peered into the room, his eyes lighting on Bluebell.

"Why do you ask?" Ash said.

"I have a lot of travelers come through here," he said gruffly. "I might need the room."

"I'll try to get better quickly," Rose joked weakly.

Once again his eyes went to Bluebell. "Would you like some food sent up?"

"Thank you, but we will keep to ourselves," Ash said.

He nodded, then backed out. Ash closed the door after him. "He knows who you are, Bluebell."

"Good. Then he might have the sense to be afraid." Bluebell moved the chest back in front of the door. "Well, Ash, you still have your bad feeling?"

"I do," Ash said in a soft voice.

Rose felt such a fool. If she hadn't stormed off like a child, she and her sisters would be far away, perhaps in another, safer village, or perhaps preparing to sleep under the stars. But she had lost her temper the way Rowan did—hot and violent. Thoughts of Rowan made her ache. Where was she now? Was she safe? A fall like the one Rose had would kill a child. Rose began to cry.

"Hush," Ash said, grasping her hands. "All will be well. The best thing you can do now is rest so we can leave tomorrow."

"But if you're not up to it, we can wait another day," Bluebell said, sitting on the chest with her knees folded up under her chin.

Rose knew what an effort it must have taken Bluebell to appear calm as she said those words. Bluebell was in a hurry—to get out of Shotley, to save Father's life. Rose's stomach clutched with guilt. She spent too much time in her own head, consumed with her own feelings. She blamed her heart: Surely it experienced love and fear and desire and guilt more steeply than anyone else's. That could be the only explanation for her selfishness.

She felt woozy and disconnected. Perhaps sleep was all she needed. She turned on her side—gingerly, trying to find a spot that wasn't bruised—and promised herself that, no matter how she felt, she would ride tomorrow. She had already caused her sisters too much trouble.

A rush of cold water in Ash's veins made her startle awake.

She sat up, heart thudding, and looked around the room. Rose was asleep next to her, face soft, lips slightly parted. Bluebell was curled on her side on the floor in front of the door. As she tried to focus on Bluebell, a scream behind her eyes began to vibrate through her skull.

Something very bad was coming. Coming for Bluebell.

"Up!" she cried, leaping out of bed. "We need to go now."

Bluebell was on her feet in a second, not a trace of sleepiness or confusion in her expression. "What's coming, Ash?"

"I don't know. But it's coming for you," Ash said. She leaned over Rose, who was struggling to wake up. The tonic Ash had given her the day before had made her brain sluggish. She was blue with bruises from shoulders to hips, and Ash knew it was going to be painful for her to move. "Rosie, I'm sorry. But we have to go. Right now."

Rose lifted her head and palmed her eyes. "Yes, yes," she managed. "Help me with my cloak."

Bluebell had cracked open the door and was peering out. "How far away, Ash?"

Ash shook her head, stomach clenching with frustration. "I don't know."

Bluebell hoisted her pack to her shoulder. "Can you walk, Rose?"

Rose was on her feet, leaning heavily on Ash. "Yes," she said, though Ash could tell she was lying.

Then they were outside in the cool, early-morning air. Dawn-gold sunlight lay on low mist down the valley and across the river. The stable door was closed and bolted. Bluebell's dogs barked madly inside.

"Where's the stable hand?" Rose said, alarmed.

Bluebell gave Ash a grim look, her mouth a hard line. "They've locked our dogs and horses in. We are to be served to these enemies on a plate."

"Do you want me to try to pick the lock?"

"There's no time. Leave it," Bluebell said. "We run. We can come back for the horses and dogs later. And the revenge." She put her hand out for Rose, who winced as Bluebell tugged her forward. They began to run down the hill and out the front gate of the town.

Ash saw them a heartbeat before Bluebell did.

"Raiders!" Bluebell shouted, skidding to a halt. Four of them on the road, clearly heading straight toward Shotley. She turned and ushered her sisters ahead of her—poor stumbling Rose, and Ash—with her heart thumping. They skidded off the main road and onto a worn track through grass, then dangerously vertical down a grassy slope. Rose cried out in pain and Bluebell stopped and turned.

Ash stopped, too. "Bluebell?" Her sister's long fair hair was lifted by the wind. The raiders were a hundred yards away, just beyond the dirty white ruins of an ancient building.

Bluebell waved to them with both arms, and shouted, "*Sansorthinn!*"

"What did you say to them?" Ash asked.

"I called them cocksuckers in their own language." Bluebell smiled grimly. "Go. Take Rose."

"What? Where?"

"They'll kill you both. Hide in the woods and if I don't come for you, head back toward Almissia. I'll draw them away from you. Here." She pushed Rose into Ash's arms, and then before Ash could say another word she was off, heading down toward the grassy banks of the river.

Ash put her arm around Rose's waist and headed around the curve of the town perimeter, then up the hill toward the road home. Then she stopped to watch Bluebell, in her light mail, pushing her helm down on her head. Alone. No dogs. Four men came for her, down the same grassy slope. She couldn't win this one. Ash felt the foreshadow of death across her skin.

Bluebell stood, silent and tall, between the river and an oak tree. Her sword was drawn and her round shield was on her left arm as they closed in on her. Ash's heart galloped. Rose clutched her hand.

"There are four of them," Rose said. "We must do something."

But neither of them was trained in arms, and to go down there now would probably make matters worse. Ash could only sit and watch as the thrill of premonition was made solid. The pale morning sky watched the fates of kingdoms impassively, as it always did.

Ash's skin prickled. But she *could* do something, couldn't she?

"Go back over there, near the town wall," Ash said, giving Rose a gentle push.

"Where are you going?"

"Nowhere. But I need to concentrate."

Rose did as she was told, sitting heavily on the sparse grass. Ash moved a few feet up the rise so she had the best open view of the happenings below. Stilling her thundering pulse, she opened up her second sight.

Shadows and shimmers, escaping from her vision left and right. Elementals in the water, the tree, the rocks, the earth. She fixed her attention on one with her mind. *Hear me,* she said in her head. It stopped moving and glared at her across the distance, its chalky, cragged face set hard and cruel.

Ash licked her lips. She didn't know what to say next. A distant roar as Bluebell lifted her sword, the first two raiders running at her. Then Ash realized she didn't have to say anything. Her eyes went to the elemental, then the gravelly ground beneath it. A thought, barely formed, left her mind, and then the ground trembled. Small stones jumped. The other two raiders skidded over, fell on top of each other. Bluebell had already finished off one of the others and was fending off the blows of the second. The fallen pair climbed to their feet, and Bluebell was pushed back toward the river, three men closing on her.

"Into the river, Bluebell," Ash whispered under her breath.

Bluebell's head snapped up, as though she had heard. She turned and clambered over the rocky bank, waded in up to her calves. The three raiders advanced.

Ash focused her energy, her power, drawing it up from the ground and down from the sky. Little hands reached out of the water, shadows slithered over the rocks.

Then a spout of water shot from the river between Bluebell and the raiders. Bluebell took a step back, alarmed. The rocks along the riverside shook in their places and one large flat one, bigger than a man's head, jumped and slammed between the shoulders of a raider. He fell forward. The waterspout opened up and dragged him under. Bluebell took advantage of the confusion, dealing a blow to another man. His severed arm fell into the water, which ran red with blood. Ash couldn't watch, closed her eyes. She was sickened, her body ached and yet . . . Her veins thrummed with something that felt dangerously like excitement. She had tasted the first thrill of her power.

When she opened her eyes again, the rocks were still, the water was red, and two bodies floated downstream. Bluebell had another body under her arm, dragging it out of the river. She thrust the raider's body, limp as a doll, facedown on the ground by the river and crouched next to it, searching it.

"Wait there," Ash said to Rose, hurrying down the grassy slope toward her sister.

Bluebell was wet, smeared with blood, and lifted off her helm to cast it aside. She pulled aside the raider's long, wet hair and revealed a raven tattoo on the back of his neck.

"Explain this, Ash?" she said, panting.

"You want me to touch it?"

Bluebell nodded, sitting back on her haunches.

Ash reached for the raven. She was already sick and aching from the magic, but found that opening up again was easy. All her inner sight focused down on the man's cold skin.

His father had tattooed this on him, in a stone house with a grass roof, north and west and over the sea. *Hakon is our king, now.* The Crow King, alive and hidden on a birdshit-stained island far from his twin brother who had imprisoned him because Hakon so zealously believed in war on the Southlanders, not trade and treaties. Hakon who was in love with battle and believed himself the rightful ruler of all of Thyrsland. On that island, he drew his followers to him: the hard, the bitter, the cruel. Third sons and murderers and failed farmers. Hakon stirred hate in their hearts—hate for Blickstow and everyone in it, but especially the woman who had brought him so low. He sent them in bands south, but not to raid: to assassinate Bluebell.

"The alehouse husband alerted them," Ash said. "Hakon is alive and he has gold on your head, Bluebell. The Crow King's followers won't rest until you're dead."

Bluebell sniffed, wiping her nose with the back of her hand. "Fuckers." She picked up her sword and touched Ash's shoulder. "I want you two to head for the woods. I'm going to get our horses and my dogs. And I'm going to pay a visit to the alehouse husband. It's best you don't see."

Ash nodded.

"And tonight," Bluebell said with a slight narrowing of her pale eyes, "we will talk about what happened."

"I don't know what happened. Not really," Ash said.

Bluebell stood, nodded once, and strode off.

Bluebell sat on a rock, sharpening her sword. The rhythm of the simple task soothed her. Today she had seen many strange things and she needed to speak to Ash about it. But Ash looked tired and shaken.

They had traveled a long way today, mostly through gloomy yew woods, picking their way over fallen branches on the road: It seemed few people came this route to and from Bradsey. Except, of course, the raiders who were paying good coin for information on her whereabouts. Assassins. She wasn't afraid of them, but Bluebell missed her hearthband. Even jumpy Ricbert and mouth-breathing Gytha. But mostly Sighere. People who could wield a blade.

They'd emerged from the woods into cleared, stone-scattered land. Nobody could farm here, so Bluebell didn't understand why the trees had been felled. But there was a steep incline, a rocky overhang, and a perfect place to sleep. Enough shelter to be safe, and a clear view of what was coming from the woods. Bluebell had built the fire and Ash soaked it in fire oil and lit it. The warm glow chased away the shadows under the overhang, but it could do little about the shadows that gathered around Ash in Bluebell's mind.

She watched as Ash gently cleaned Rose's wound. Rose had grown paler and weaker throughout the journey, her eyes great pools of dark pain.

"Is it feeling any better?" Ash asked.

"The stitches sting and my skull still aches."

"It was quite a blow," Bluebell said, passing the whetstone back and forth over the blade.

Ash touched Rose's cheek. "There, Rosie. All clean. I'll leave the bandage off it now. Some air might make it heal faster."

Rose looked up, touched the wound gingerly.

Ash leaned away, but Rose caught her hand. "Ash, can you tell me if Rowan's well?"

Bluebell glanced over. "I don't know that we should be asking her to use her second sight for—"

"Hush, Bluebell," Rose said. "I know you ask her to use it often."

"Rowan is fine," Ash said, quickly. "I have no feeling otherwise." Rose curled on her side.

Bluebell sheathed her sword and shifted closer, so she sat with Ash and Rose on the spread-out blanket. Her eyes returned to Ash's face. "And can you tell me if Ash is well?" Bluebell asked.

Ash smiled weakly. "Yes, I am healthy as a horse."

"But you did something today that frightened you," Bluebell said. "Perhaps you can tell me what happened."

Ash took a deep breath and her slight shoulders heaved upward, as though warding off a blow. "It seems I have some power over nature."

Rose looked puzzled. "What do you mean?"

"Can you show her?" Bluebell asked.

Ash shook her head. "I won't do it if I don't have to. It hurts me. It bruises me from the inside."

Bluebell's heart clenched. Ash's voice seemed so thin, so frightened.

Bluebell turned to Rose. "When the raiders were closing on me, Ash saved me. She made the rocks and water move." She rubbed her chin with the back of her hand, fighting off the small shiver of uncanniness. "I swear for a moment I thought I saw watery hands and fingers."

"How is this possible?" Rose asked.

Ash shrugged. "I have . . . abilities growing within me. I barely understand them. But today, I was desperate and I called on the elements . . ." She lapsed into silence, staring at her hands.

Bluebell considered Ash in the firelight. Her long dark hair was neatly plaited off her small oval face. She remembered Ash as a child, her bonny sweetness. She never made demands, had tantrums, or said hurtful things out of spite. Her face had barely changed since childhood, but the sunniness was missing from her eyes. "You look unhappy," she said simply.

Ash nodded. "I am unhappy."

"Many wouldn't be, with such ability at their disposal."

"I am not in control of it," Ash said. "I don't know when the sight will come and when it won't. If I try to focus it, it bends me as I bend it. I'm frightened by it."

Bluebell pushed her feet hard into the ground. *It bends me as I bend it.* What kind of power did her sister possess? For a cold instant, Ash seemed unfamiliar, a chill stranger who belonged to the shadows. But then the feeling passed.

"Don't be frightened," Rose said. "When the Great Mother made you, she made you this way. Nothing that comes from her is wrong; it only seems so until it is understood."

"But who can help me understand? The Thridstow elders disapprove. Even Byrta was afraid and unsympathetic."

"Perhaps Eldra can help you understand," Bluebell said. "It is probably from her you draw this talent."

Ash dropped her eyes to the fire. "I would give anything for good advice," she said.

"I can only give you a sister's advice," Rose said, "and that is to worry less. It will be fine. You will see."

Ash nodded, but her eyes darted away.

Bluebell shifted her position, her gaze going to the edge of the woods, a mile in the distance. "Ash, you know we are being followed, don't you?"

Ash nodded. "Yes. We've been followed since we left Shotley."

"It isn't raiders. I've listened to the hoof-falls. Somebody light, somebody alone."

"I haven't been able to focus my mind on it, Bluebell. Whether it's because I'm tired or because . . . the somebody doesn't want me to focus my mind."

"Do you think it's human?"

Ash spread her palms. "I can't tell. It is horsed, so probably human."

Rose's eyes were wide. "Are we safe?"

"I can't tell," Ash said again. "I'm sorry."

Bluebell returned to sharpening her sword. "You are safe as long as I still draw breath," she said, knowing that, among the under-magicians, sharp steel was not necessarily a ward against danger.

CHAPTER 18

Rowan had finally cried herself inside out and was sleeping in a heap in the middle of the bed. Ivy didn't dare move her, in case she woke again and cried some more. She was sick of the sound of the child sobbing. If she was ever forced to bear children, she would farm them out to somebody with much more patience than she had. What irrational little beasts they were, so selfish and one-eyed.

Ivy lurked near the door to their room at the inn. The first day of travel had gone well: no rain, not too many hills and valleys to negotiate. Sighere had said barely a dozen words to her and most of the time she simply pretended he wasn't there. Rowan had cried the whole way, of course, but as Ivy had no sympathy, the pain was only on her ears, not in her heart.

She ventured out to the landing and peered over the railing. From here, she could see the entranceway to the inn. Men coming and going. She could hear their voices from the alehouse. They laughed and shouted, they talked in low voices, they argued. Men. Dozens and dozens of them. And here she was, stuck in a room with the baby. She imagined herself descending the stairs with her shining fair curls catching the lamplight, her white bosom swelling invitingly from the low front on her gown. How their heads would turn.

Ivy retreated back into her room. It was dimly lit by greasy candles in metal sconces, and smelled of old sweat and damp wool. She wanted to be home. She wanted to be around William Dartwood and . . . No, she didn't. Already, she had grown beyond wanting William Dartwood. Her infatuation with Heath had finished off her desire for anyone back home. But she couldn't have Heath. The thought made her angry and sad all at once. She'd never much liked any of her sisters, apart from Willow. Ash, she supposed, was kind enough. But Iron-Tits was an arrogant thug, and Rose . . . well, Rose had Heath. That was reason enough to hate her.

But Ivy would get over Heath. Somehow. Though it would help if she could get downstairs and flirt with some other men.

A loud knock at the door made Rowan stir.

"Please, no," Ivy said under her breath. She opened the door to see a serving woman there, with a tray of food.

"Sighere sent food for you and the child," she said.

"Bring it in." She looked around. Rowan was sitting up, rubbing her eyes. "Are you hungry, child?"

Rowan nodded. She was staring at the serving woman, who was First Folk, with the typical ginger hair, green eyes, and freckled white skin. Rowan had clearly never seen First Folk before.

The woman left and Ivy closed the door and sat on the bed with Rowan to eat.

"She had orange hair," Rowan said.

"She was First Folk. There are small tribes of them around here. You don't tend to see them in Nettlechester or Almissia."

"What's First Folk?"

"You don't know?"

Rowan shook her head, chewing noisily on a piece of cheese. Ivy didn't want to be bothered making conversation with a three-year-old, but at least she wasn't crying for once. "Before our people came to Thyrsland, when there were still giants and dragons, the First Folk lived here. The first people. They were weak and disorganized and now there aren't so many left." Ivy smiled. "They are still weak and disorganized. That's why they always end up serving us food and cleaning our horses' hooves." Ivy took cruel pleasure in planting the notion in Rowan's mind. Rose, no doubt, would be horrified. Bluebell doubly so; she and Athelrick ruled on the basis all men were entitled to the same rewards, if they cared to take the same path to achieve them. What a nonsense, especially coming from the mouths of kings.

"Do they all have orange hair?"

"Mostly. Some half-breeds have golden hair."

"Like Heath?"

Heath. Of course. She hadn't really noticed. He must be a half-breed. "Yes, like Heath."

"I like Heath. I wish he could have come instead of Sibhere."

"Sighere," Ivy corrected her. "Yes, I rather wish he could have come, too." Though what use it would have been to her, she didn't know. Perhaps it was better she didn't see him or think of him again; didn't put her own body in place of her sister's when she reimagined that scene in the woods.

And now Rowan was prattling about Heath and riding on his horse and some other incomprehensible childish ramble, when Ivy's attention suddenly caught on something she was saying.

"What was that, Rowan?"

"Mama said Heath is a good friend of our family and he would help me if I'm scared."

Ivy's suspicion prickled. "Did she, now?" She was looking at the little girl much closer now. Dark hair and eyes like Rose, like Wengest. But was there an auburn sheen in her hair? Or was that the candlelight? And that dimple in her left cheek, so like the one in Heath's? And Bluebell's animosity toward Heath? Could it be?

Ivy smiled. She *knew*. She didn't need proof. Rowan was three years old; Heath had told her he'd been away at the border stronghold for three years. And Rose hadn't fallen pregnant again.

"Go on, stop talking and eat," she said to Rowan, sitting back on the bed to watch her. It felt so good to close her fist around a secret, especially one about Heath.

Just past noon on the third day, Ivy's mood lifted dramatically. Perhaps it was the sunshine catching on the wings of bugs that skimmed across the flower-dotted meadows and shining on the stained white ruins of a magnificent arch overgrowing with vines. Or Rowan's sweet observations now she had given up on crying. Or the knowledge that within a day, they would be in Wengest's court and she would finally come to rest for a while.

Rather than camping out overnight, Sighere had brought them to a village in northern Nettlechester with a small guesthouse that overlooked the stream and the watermill. Near the edge of the stream, the stable stood, and at the door to the stable, the stable hand stood.

He was her age, with thick dark hair that fell in untidy curls. His hands were clean and strong, and his cheeks were flushed. Most important, he noticed her straightaway, offering her a bold smile as she handed him the reins of her horse.

She smiled back, but then Sighere was there, ordering the boy around and waving Ivy and Rowan out of the way. "Go inside the guesthouse. Leave this to me."

Ivy didn't want to leave it to him and be hidden away from the world again, so she lingered near the stable door, stealing glances at the boy. He would be a good way to purge her unfulfilled desire for Heath.

Then Rowan squealed happily and ran away, directly for the stream, and Ivy had to give chase.

She caught the little girl easily when she stopped to examine a ladybird. Ivy crouched next to her and glanced across the stream to the mill, its wheel turning slowly in the sunstruck water. The long grass waved in the breeze, and a robin sang sweetly in a tree. Ivy realized she was behind the stable here, right about where Sighere and the stable hand were standing talking. She brought Rowan with her, told the child to crawl in the grass to find another ladybird, and positioned herself near the shutter to see if she could hear anything.

Sighere, in typical boring fashion, was giving the boy a rundown of the tasks that were expected and how much he'd be paid for them.

"I can't find any, Ivy," Rowan whined.

"How about over there?" Ivy said, waving her away.

A happy shout told Ivy that Rowan had been successful. She strained to hear the voices over Rowan's chatter. But then she was rewarded.

"Who is the lady that travels with you, sir? Your wife?"

Ivy lifted her chin slightly, flattered to be the topic of conversation. Sighere snorted. "Hardly. A friend's sister."

"Tell him I'm a princess," Ivy muttered under her breath. "Go on."

"She's a pain in the arse," Sighere continued. "Never stops complaining."

The stable hand laughed. "I feel for you, sir."

The heat rose up Ivy's neck and cheeks. She blinked back tears.

Rowan started crying. "Ivy, I broked my ladybird!"

Ivy strode away from the stable and grasped Rowan's arm firmly. The child was trying to wipe pieces of squashed ladybird off her fingers onto her dress. Ivy kept her head down and kept moving toward the guesthouse. The sooner this damned journey was over, the better.

The entrance to Folkenham was almost as impressive as the entrance to Blickstow. Two tall, carved pillars stood either side of the gate, and the road up the hill was paved in pale-gray flagstones that rang when the horse's hooves struck them, but the gate was smaller than Blickstow's, the wood darker, and the guards' uniforms a dull gray. It mattered little to Ivy. She had never been so glad to arrive somewhere. She fully intended to stay as long as it took for the memory of the slow, uncomfortable journey to fade.

Sighere led them to the king's stables and helped Rowan down as stable hands rushed about to tend their horses. Ivy climbed down and stood a moment, stretching her cramped back and legs. Sighere was barking orders at the stable hands. He was filthy from travel dust and sweat, his long black hair lank. She touched her own hair. It, too, was dirty. How she longed for a hot bath.

Then a booming voice came from behind her.

"My darling!"

She spun around to see Wengest, arms open. Rowan squealed and ran to him. Ivy watched as he swept her up and crushed her in an embrace. In contrast to all the dull, dirty people in the stables, he was dressed beautifully in a blue tunic, embroidered around the collar and cuffs with gold and red thread, and a dark-gray cloak pinned with gold brooches. His beard was trimmed neatly across his square chin, and his dark wavy hair was held back from his face with a gold band. His fine appearance and clean white hands impressed Ivy deeply.

Wengest put Rowan down long enough to approach Ivy with an outstretched hand. She noticed he wore gold rings on the first three fingers of each hand. "I'm sorry, I don't believe we've met. Who are you that have brought my daughter home safe, and where is my wife?"

She squeezed his hand gently. "We have met," Ivy said. "At your wedding. I'm Rose's sister Ivy."

He dropped her hand, blinked, and considered her more carefully. "Ivy? Could it be? Why, last time I saw you, you were a little girl." He spread his palms and smiled. "Now you are a woman."

Ivy beamed. "As to your other question, Rose and Bluebell and Ash have gone farther north, into Bradsey, to look for a cure for my father's illness. They expect a journey of three weeks."

Wengest's brow drew down in irritation. "Three weeks? And without consulting me?" Then he remembered himself and the smile returned. "Forgive me, but I haven't been quite the same without my wife and daughter here. Women are a welcome weight on a man's thoughts, so they don't fly everywhere."

Ivy wasn't sure what he meant, but smiled anyway. "Rowan missed you very much," she said. "Didn't you, little one?"

Rowan, who clung to Wengest's leg, nodded silently.

Wengest glanced down at his daughter. "Three weeks, eh? What am I to do with the child until then?"

Ivy hesitated a moment, then ventured: "I could stay."

He brightened. "Would you? Rowan has a nurse, but she needs someone to love and I am very busy. You could have Rose's bower, and we would treat you as a princess of Almissia deserves to be treated. You needn't do anything but keep the child company during the day."

Ivy needed no time to consider. "Of course. I would love that."

Wengest bent to hug Rowan. "Who wouldn't want to spend more time with this little darling? What do you say, Rowan? Shall we let Ivy stay a little while until Mama gets back?"

"I want Mama," Rowan said uncertainly.

"Ah, but when you were with Mama, all you spoke of was being with Papa," Ivy said.

"Is that right?" Wengest asked.

"Bluebell killded you."

Wengest's eyebrows shot up and Ivy had to laugh. "Bluebell beheaded a scarecrow. We didn't know Rowan was pretending it was you."

He smiled, but Ivy could tell it was forced. "Well. Here I am. Alive and well." He ruffled her hair. "Rowan, you show Ivy where you and Mama sleep. I'll send someone to bring you a hot bath and some food." He nodded, then turned his attention to Sighere and the stable hands.

Rowan took Ivy's hand. "Come on," she said, pulling hard.

Ivy followed her, glancing over her shoulders one last time to admire Wengest's beautiful clothes.

Traveling had exhausted Ivy. She slept deeply, heavy and soft, far beneath dreams: the kind of sleep one only achieves after hard labor or good works. Then a thin cry needled through the layers.

Ivy struggled to open her eyes, didn't recognize where she was, couldn't place the cry. Then it came again. She was in Rose's bower in Folkenham and Rowan was having a nightmare next to her.

"Shhh," Ivy said, rolling over and stroking her hair, "it's just a bad dream." She closed one eye as though it could help her hold on to sleep.

Rowan woke, looked at Ivy, and said, "Where's Mama?"

"Mama will be back soon. I'm here with you now."

Rowan's mouth turned upside down. Her bottom lip pushed farther and farther out, and then she took a deep breath and began to sob.

"Shhh," Ivy said again, and moved to pick her up.

Rowan shrieked and flung her hand away, kicking her legs. Her foot caught Ivy under the ribs, knocking the wind out of her.

"You little brat!" Ivy spat.

"I want Mama!" Rowan screamed.

Ivy leapt out of bed, fingers itching to smack her chubby white thigh. "There's no need to kick me."

But Rowan was incoherent with tears and shrieks.

Ivy wasn't sure what to do. She wanted to go back to sleep, but Rowan was winding herself up tighter and tighter. Ivy went to the shutter and opened it a little way. Perhaps if Wengest heard, he might come to settle her down. That was probably what Rowan wanted: one of her parents. She barely knew Ivy.

Ivy waited, but nobody came. She went to the door and opened it. The chill of midnight skulked in, making her hug her shift tight around her body. She took a half step out onto the dewy grass, peering toward Wengest's bower. She was sure she saw a finger of light under the shutter. Rowan's sobbing intensified as the cold reached her. Surely Wengest would hear. And if he heard, he would surely come.

Then the door to his bower opened and Ivy shrank back inside. She didn't want it to be obvious she'd tried to wake him. She heard a voice. A soft female voice. Curious, she leaned out again.

A woman was leaving Wengest's bower, her face turned away from Ivy. She said something inaudible, then turned and hurried back toward the town. Ivy recognized her as the serving woman who had brought her meal that evening.

Ivy realized her mouth was agape and shut it, withdrawing inside. She closed the door and pressed her back against it. Wengest was tupping the serving girl. Rose was being tupped by Heath. And neither of them knew about the other. Why, Ivy knew more about them than they knew about themselves.

Rowan was still crying. Ivy sighed and went to her. "Please. Will you stop? It's very late and I'm tired."

"No!" she shrieked.

The door opened and Ivy turned to see Rowan's nurse standing there.

"You heard?" Ivy said.

"Half of Nettlechester heard." The woman came over and forcibly flipped Rowan onto her front. "Here, this always works if you can get her to lie still."

Rowan wriggled violently, but one firm touch of Nurse's hands on her shoulders and she started to relax.

"Hush, hush," Nurse said, rubbing circles on her back.

The crying continued but was, at least, muffled by the blankets.

"I thought Wengest might come if he heard," Ivy said.

"The king? He doesn't attend to children."

"Too busy attending to somebody else."

Nurse didn't meet her eye. "He's a man. Men must find their pleasure or they bend out of shape."

A violent stab of unpleasant feeling landed in Ivy's guts. She considered it carefully and realized it was jealousy. Wengest, the king of Nettlechester, with his gold rings and his fine dyed clothes, was being enjoyed by a servant.

Nurse lowered her voice. "Don't tell your sister. It will only make her sad."

"But surely she should know if he loves another—"

"Love? Love has nothing to do with it. Do you think the king of Nettlechester would love somebody as low as her? A highborn man such as him could only love a woman of equal birth."

And Ivy thought: *I am of equal birth.*

"Forget what you have seen," Nurse said. "I won't speak of it again."

"Nor will I," said Ivy. But she could *think* about it as much as she liked.

CHAPTER 19

λsh woke with heavy limbs, as though all the blood in her body were sludgy sand. The sun had not yet risen, but the sky grew pale above her. Bluebell stirred, but Rose was still and quiet. Ash lay for a little while, gazing up at the rocky overhang that served as their roof. Lichen patterns and a stale smell of old earth. Her senses tingled. Ash sat up and looked back toward the woods.

Someone had been following them since they'd left Shotley the previous morning. At least, she hoped it was someone and not some-*thing*. She would be foolish to think her display of magical power down by the river would go unnoticed. Such an act didn't have to be seen to be known: Magic's wake stretched a long way. Since crossing the border, she had already felt the tingling, prickling resistance of magicians near and far. But this was different. This had intent, and was focused on Ash. Ash pulled her eyebrows down, trying to focus, to get a fix on what was behind them. No success. She rose.

Bluebell called after her sleepily. "Are you all right?"

"I'm fine," Ash said.

"I feel as though I haven't slept at all," Bluebell said, yawning vastly.

"Same. I'm going to walk awhile to wake up my blood." Ash climbed around the rocky slope and up onto the hard, flat granite, so she was standing directly above Bluebell. Now she tried again. *Who is following us?*

A flash on the edge of her mind. The figure, slight and limber, of a man. Then nothing. No, not nothing: a distinct feeling of being pushed away . . . gently, but firmly. Whoever it was, he didn't want Ash to know. He was cloaking himself in magic.

"Who are you?" Ash said, under her breath. It wasn't an ice-man. Ash had no sense of cruelty, or ill intent, and they always traveled in groups. This man was alone and very interested in them. Or at least, very interested in her.

She took a deep breath and turned in a slow circle, scanning around her. Over the tops of trees, birds were black shapes against the sky. The world was waking up. The path arrowed back into the woods, and that's where they would head today. She turned and moved to climb down, then froze as she noticed.

"Oh!" she said, her heart rate picking up.

Last night, when they'd emerged from the woods into this clearing, Bluebell had wondered aloud why the trees had been cleared. Now, from up here, Ash could see they had been cleared in a circle about a mile across. And within that circle were seven concentric circles, their circumferences marked out by carefully arranged small stones, which were pale gray against the dewy grass. Right in the center, at the highest point, was this large slab of flat rock she stood on.

She dropped to her knees and hung her head over the edge.

"Bluebell," she said, "we need to get away from here."

"Why?"

"We are sleeping in the middle of a field of magic. I think I'm standing on an altar stone."

Bluebell sat up. "What do you mean by a field of magic?"

"Somebody has cleared this area and used it for magic." Ash glanced down at the rock beneath her knees. Were they faint, rain-washed stains of blood? "And we slept right below its hub." She thought about her heavy limbs. "Are you more tired than usual?"

Bluebell's eyes grew flinty. "Yes."

"We need to get away from here, or else we'll become infected with someone else's magic."

Ash climbed to her feet and hurried back down the slope. Rose was hard to wake; even the dogs and horses were sluggish. Somehow they managed to get packed and moving, out of the magic circle and toward the path into the woods.

"Is it not a long way south for undermagicians?" Rose asked groggily as they moved out of the light and into the shadow of the trees.

"Not for an exiled undermagician," Bluebell remarked, glancing around. "Why is it, Ash, that the thought of a band of raiders coming for me while I'm without my hearthband does not unnerve me, but the knowledge I slept beneath an altar of undermagic does?"

"Don't worry, it unnerves me, too," Ash said. "Let's move away as fast as we can."

Bluebell did not like to doubt her decisions once they had been made. But as they moved farther into the dark woods, she wondered why she had brought her sisters on this journey instead of her hearthband. Certainly a fully armed retinue might have frightened Eldra, and of course she hadn't been able to predict the future: that raiders were on the move with the goal of assassinating her; that her sister would be forced to conjure up magic that left Ash looking like a ghost; that Rose would have an accident that had left an angry, oozing gash and a mind so groggy she was almost impossible to wake. Bluebell had never questioned her ability to protect her sisters before they left the flower farm. Now she was not so certain.

The road was narrow, a rut between trees. They had passed two milestones, their carvings eaten by time and weather, covered in thick, sharp ivy. Serpentine roots lined either side of the road, and Bluebell had the impression that they moved if they weren't looked upon directly. The green of the woods was a damp green, a sick, dark green, crowding the horses and filling Bluebell's nostrils with a smell of age and moisture. Most of the trees were yews, ancient and contorted, tangled branches bending low over themselves. Against this dark backdrop, it was easy to spot the little piles of white and gray pebbles, like signposts at regular intervals along the side of the path. For some reason the sight of them, so carefully placed by a human hand on the bracken, gave her a cold feeling in her stomach. She didn't like what she couldn't see.

"What are those stones for?" she asked.

"They are the same stones that marked the circle where we slept last night," Rose said.

"We are in somebody's territory," Ash said. "If we move straight ahead and swiftly, we will be safe."

So they moved in a single line, straight ahead and swiftly, even though the dogs were jumpy and the horses uncertain. The trees crowded out the morning light, chilling her. The horses' hooves kicked up a mist of dirt from the road. Bluebell had a distinct sensation something was out of place, unnatural, but she had no second sight like Ash so she struggled to divine the cause.

Of course. There were no sounds in the woods. No birds, no animal feet. Just the rustle of the leaves and the occasional sound of a branch falling, deep in the dark woods.

"No birds," she said.

"Keep moving," Ash replied from behind her.

Bluebell glanced over her shoulder. Ash was pale. Rose behind her wore a wary expression. But there was no other way north, unless they took a four-day detour out through Littledyke.

The road deepened, so the tree roots were now level with Bluebell's thigh. The knotwork roots created an embankment on either side of them, the branches a ceiling. They were deep in a holloway and even Isern was tense, his ears pricked, his head bobbing. He felt, no doubt, as she did: that they were trapped between inescapable organic walls. She muttered words of encouragement to him, but kept her eyes forward, her back tensed against the uncanny quiet of the woods.

An hour passed. Two. The landscape didn't change.

Then Ash gasped.

Bluebell, already tense, experienced the sound as a spike of hot blood to her heart. She pulled Isern up and turned in her saddle. "What is it?"

Ash's voice was thick. "Raiders. I can sense them. Companions to the ones you saw off outside Shotley. They are looking for their friends."

"And they are on this road?"

"Heading straight for us. And they are mounted."

"We can barely turn the horses around in here," Rose said.

Bluebell quickly ran through the possibilities in her head. Let the raiders chase them back to Shotley? They would lose another two days. Stand and fight? She didn't know if she could rely on Ash's powers to control the elements, and Rose looked ready to collapse.

She gazed into the yew wood. Nobody would find them in there.

"No, Bluebell, not in there," Rose pleaded.

"How far away are they, Ash?" Bluebell asked.

"I'm . . . Now I'm not so sure . . . I . . ."

Already, Bluebell thought she could hear the hooves. She dismounted, untied her pack. "Into the woods," she said. "Leave the horses."

"Wait, Bluebell," Ash said.

"Leave them," she said again. "The raiders won't know they're ours."

Ash and Rose followed her lead. Bluebell stayed on the road and helped them to clamber up the embankment and into the woods. Then she turned to the dogs. "Go on," she said, indicating with her hand they were to scramble up ahead of her.

Thrymm put back her ears and whimpered. Thrack sat down and growled.

Hooves.

She glanced toward Ash and Rose. Nowhere in sight. Bluebell frowned. They had disappeared too quickly. She turned back to the dogs. She could pick them up and throw them in, or she could leave them with the horses.

Bluebell pushed her palm forward, north up the road. "All right. All of you, keep moving."

The dogs rounded up the horses and drove them up the road. Bluebell vaulted up the embankment and then crouched low, moving off into the woods. Where were her sisters? She seemed to be making so much noise, but couldn't hear them anywhere. Ahead, she could see the remains of a yew tree. The last remaining curve of its trunk indicated it had once stood ten feet wide. But now it had collapsed on itself in its ancientness, and resembled a spider reared defensively: bent brown branches ready to strike. Were her sisters hiding behind the trunk? She didn't dare call them. She kept low and moved away from the road, around the curve of the trunk. A deadfall, as tall as a man, awaited her. Still no sign of Ash and Rose. But here, a small pile of white and gray pebbles. Gooseflesh rose across the backs of her arms. Hidden from the road now, she stood tall and scanned around her. A breeze lifted her hair, tickling her face. The woods were so quiet. Not a sound other than the sound of leaves moving in the wind; the thud of her heart. Her hand went to her sword.

She had the feeling she was going to have to kill something.

Bluebell turned slowly in a circle. Off to the northwest was another huge, crumbling tree. In its trunk was a fissure wide enough to step through. Sword drawn, she moved toward it. Closer and closer, hoping to see a flash of Ash's green cloak or Rose's red dress before she had to go In There.

The smell of mold. The smell of dirt. The smell of ancient water.

And another little pile of stones: These were kicked over, as though someone hadn't seen them. Perhaps one of her sisters, in the rush to hide.

Bluebell ducked her head and squeezed through. Inside the tree it was dank, but light came in through the crack and through another opening directly across from her. Ash and Rose weren't here. She moved through the empty trunk and out the other side.

"Bluebell!" It was Ash, rushing toward her, hands outstretched, almost as though she were trying to push her back into the tree.

"What is it?"

"We're trapped," Rose said.

Bluebell hadn't seen her. She turned.

Rose stood at the foot of a tall mud wall, perhaps twenty feet high, that stretched off in both directions. "No way out."

"What the . . . ?"

"Can you go back through?" Ash asked.

Bluebell ducked her head through the opening in the tree. Inside the trunk was now mud-black. No opening on the other side. She circled the tree. The mud wall ran behind it. The mud wall that had certainly not been there before. "Where are we?" she said. "What is this?"

Ash grasped her hand. "This is very bad magic."

❖ ❖ ❖

Rose walked carefully and slowly, one foot in front of the other, her hand trailing along the mud wall. She had set out in one direction, Bluebell in the other, to see how far the wall stretched and to discover where it ended. Even in her slightly addled state from the blow to her head, it had taken only a few minutes of walking before she realized it curved around, forming a circle. Still she moved on, checking the integrity of the wall, looking for trees close enough to provide climbing opportunities, all the time aware *somebody* had built this wall, *somebody* had created the doorway through the tree. *Somebody* had trapped them.

She tipped her face to look at the sky through the crowding branches. The ache in her head worsened every hour, and worry made it worse. Added to that, a gray blot on her field of sight blossomed. But she wouldn't mention it. Not now. Her sisters already had enough on their minds. The clouds swirled above, storm-beaten and gray-blue. But it had been a fine, clear day when they'd left the road. The odd quietness of the wood was enhanced by a strange smell. Perhaps it was the wall. She looked at her fingertips. Brown, powdery, dry mud. She held it to her nose and gingerly sniffed. Yes, that was it. A cold smell, like a room that had been locked for a long time. She brushed the mud off her fingers and looked up to see Bluebell approaching. They had reached the middle at the same time.

Bluebell cursed and kicked the wall.

"Nothing?" Rose asked.

"Nothing. I don't like the smell in here," Bluebell said. "It smells old. What if there are giants?"

"The giants died out long ago," Rose said, and her voice was even despite the quickening of her heart.

"Who else could build walls this high?"

"They are built of mud. Not white stone."

"I wonder if Ash had better luck."

They walked together through the woods, back toward Ash, whom they had left with the task of using her talent to open the door in the tree again. Rose was careful to keep pace with Bluebell's long stride, even if it made the pain in her head stab rhythmically. A cold wind shivered through the treetops, and Rose looked up. In her moment of inattention, she tripped over a tree root and stumbled forward.

Bluebell caught her under the elbow and Rose steadied herself. She could see now that it wasn't a root she had tripped over. She peered closely, around the gray shadow on her sight, and gasped. Half hidden in the undergrowth was a collection of brown bones.

"I've seen others," Bluebell said.

"Animal bones?"

"There are no animals in here. These are human bones."

Rose's blood cooled rapidly. She hadn't yet allowed herself to consider they might die in here.

Bluebell gently released her arm. "I won't let anything kill you, Rosie," she said.

But Rose wondered what use Bluebell's sword was against hunger or cold. Or whatever it was that was wrong with her head.

Ash was crouched at the foot of the wall, examining it.

"What do you think, Ash?" Bluebell said. "Did giants build the walls?"

"No," she replied, standing up. "An undermagician did. They are built of magic. None of this is real. Our senses have been charmed. I almost saw through the wall, to the woods. The real woods, which are still here."

"So we could walk through the wall?" Rose asked, hopefully.

"I tried it. I hurt my shoulder." She rubbed her left shoulder. "I don't even know if my premonition of raiders was real."

"But I heard their hooves," Bluebell said.

"A trick. I think we've been drawn here. We slept in the witch's circle, and somehow she has gained power over us."

Rose shivered. She thought about her ordinary life, of running after Rowan, or bickering with Wengest, or spinning and weaving in her quiet bower. Magic never touched her. It was a distant thing that belonged to other, more important people than she. She was lost in trying to understand it, and her mind was having trouble grasping even the simplest things since her accident. "But he will come, won't he? He's trapped us for a reason?"

"I'm certain *she* will come," Ash said. "And I'm equally certain I don't want to meet her."

Bluebell sank down on the undergrowth, circling her bony knees with her arms and resting her head. Her long fair hair covered her face. "Fuck," she said.

"Your ability, Ash?" Rose asked. "Does it count for nothing? Can you not bring the wall down?"

Ash gestured around her. "Whoever did this is immensely powerful. I have no idea of my power, of how to control it, or how I would even begin to bring down this grand illusion."

Bluebell looked up. "So we wait for her?"

"We wait for her," Ash said.

Hours passed, though the sky above them gave little indication of what time of day it was. The sun was a long way behind bruised clouds that swirled unnaturally. Rose watched as Ash paced slowly, lost in thought. She watched as Bluebell grew exhausted trying to bash her way through the wall—with her fists, her shield, her feet. And Rose thought about her little girl, about Rowan, so far away on an unknown road. To fear one's own death was already torment, but to imagine one's child motherless stung acutely.

Sometimes, too, a darker thought troubled her. Did she somehow deserve this? Her guilt over the years had become an ordinary, dull thing. Renewing her affair with Heath had sharpened it again. No woman could live in two worlds at the same time: one half of her heart bowing to obligation, while the other half of her heart thudded desperately to be nearer to a forbidden someone. She sank now to where the self-blame grew, wondering if the Great Mother herself was punishing Rose for raising her child so irresponsibly, letting Wengest think he was her father while Rose longed always for another. Her head ached and she longed to sleep . . . deep and dreamless. When she woke, maybe her mind would be clearer, her sight restored.

They ate grainy flatcakes late in the day, when the light was fading from the sky. The lack of birdsong created an uncanny quiet where the echoes of her own pulse thudded in Rose's ears. Bluebell had dark shadows under her eyes and Ash was quiet and serious. There was no way of telling how long they would be trapped, and the uncertainty was loosening Rose's nerves from their sockets.

Finally, when it was fully night, Bluebell told them to roll out their blankets and get some rest.

"I'll take first watch," she said.

"You're exhausted," Ash replied. "I'll do it."

"I'm not closing my eyes," Bluebell said forcefully.

As they were arguing, Rose became aware of a noise nearby. She turned. Her blood seemed to slow, pulling like a tide past her ears. Bluebell's and Ash's voices became muffled; time stood still a moment. A woman approached. An old woman who leaned heavily on a thick stick. She had around her an aura of sick light, no brighter than moonlight. On her other arm perched an owl. Rose tried to make her lips move, to alert Bluebell and Ash. Then she blinked and the woman was standing directly in front of them, as if she had moved a hundred feet in a second.

Time started again. Rose could see there was no halo anymore. Just an ordinary-looking old woman, her wizened face turned toward the three of them curiously. Around her waist, she wore a belt that bristled with a hundred dangling objects. Some of them Rose could recognize: scissors, a mirror, a proliferation of keys. Others were a mystery to her: glittering things and jangling things and mysterious, soft hanging things woven of leaves and vines. The owl's powerful claws were locked on her upper arm. It moved its head and didn't blink.

Bluebell's hand went to her sword, but Ash stopped her.

"Who the fuck are you and what have you done to us?" Bluebell said.

The old woman ignored her, fixing her gaze instead on Ash. Ash gazed back at her, her eyes widening as though alarmed. A moment later Ash looked away. The old woman smiled cruelly. "It will be a long time before you are more powerful than me, dear," she said to Ash.

Rose found her voice. "Please, let us free. We mean you no harm."

The old woman turned to her. "You will have to earn your freedom."

"What do you want us to do?"

The old woman glanced at Ash, lifting her stick and pointing it. "She knows."

Bluebell's eyebrows drew down, making her look grim in the dark. "Ash?"

"She is haunted," Ash explained, "and if we can make it go away, she'll set us free."

"So," said the woman, with a little nod.

"But she can't recall what is haunting her," Ash said. "If we can banish the ghost, she'll be released from it."

"Usually people wander in here and I let them starve to death," the old woman said. "But *she* is different. She knows." She indicated Ash with a bony finger. "She can read me."

Bluebell was growing impatient. She drew her sword. "Well, then, bring out this ghost and we'll cut it to bits, then be on our way."

Rose almost laughed.

The old woman raised her eyebrows in amusement. "We wait."

"Wait? For how long?" Bluebell said.

"It comes. The owl will alert us." She raised her arm and the owl flew to the nearest branch and sat there, black eyes shining in the dark. The old woman leaned on her stick, with her bottom lip pushed out as though thinking.

"I tell you, I'm tired of this shit," Bluebell grumbled.

The darkness was cool and primeval, settling quietly on the twisted yew branches and the undergrowth and making Rose's skin shiver into goosebumps. Or maybe it was the thought of confronting a ghost that was making her shiver. Ash sat and pulled Rose down next to her, but Bluebell stood, back against the wall, her hand always ready to draw her sword. Did she really think she could kill something that was already dead?

"What do we do?" Rose said to Ash.

"As she asks," Ash said with a shrug.

"Do you believe her?"

"I don't know. But stranger things than ghosts have troubled me lately."

The old woman gave no indication she heard or cared for their conversation. Rose pulled her fingers through her hair, accidentally

brushing the wound on her head. She winced. It always fell to Bluebell and Ash to sort things out. It seemed Rose was only good for riding off in a rage and getting herself injured. She leaned on Ash's
shoulder, and Ash touched her hair softly.

"Don't give up hope, sister," Ash said.

Bluebell drove her sword tip into the ground and crouched with
them. "Do you know how to banish a ghost, Ash?"

"I know nothing," Ash said, and Rose noticed she looked pale and
frightened, "but I'll do my best."

"I know you can do it," Bluebell said.

Rose left her sisters to talk softly, trying to focus instead on the
woman's face. She was turned away, her profile harsh and pale in the
dark. But it wasn't witchcraft or evil that had made her such a time-
scarred crone. There were lines of grief on her brow and around her
mouth. This woman had spent many years in misery. The woman
turned, caught Rose looking, and returned the gaze. In that moment
the blot on her vision evaporated, leaving her able to see clearly. The
woman gave her a short nod and, strange as it seemed, Rose felt a
sense of connection to her. A soft lock, as a bond formed in the dark.

Then Rose looked away, put her head on her knees to wait for the
ghost. Time passed. Perhaps an hour, though it was difficult to judge
with no moonlight.

And then the owl let out a hoot. After a day without the sound of
birds, it seemed unnaturally loud in the dark.

The woman straightened her back. "It comes," she said again, but
this time her voice trembled with fear.

Rose's skin prickled and the pain in her head grew sharp. She and
her sisters stood, close, the three of them shoulder-to-shoulder.

A noise. Rose's senses grew sick, topsy-turvy. Was she hearing a
noise? Or was she *seeing* a noise? Reality shivered. She could see the
woods beyond the mud wall, then they were gone again. Cold crept
across her skin. In front of them, a light began to grow, that same sick
light that had surrounded the old woman. And yet . . . Rose looked
again. There was no light. There was nothing but clear forest air. The
noise and the light were nothing, and yet they pressed on her senses
heavy as a millstone.

"It's a trick," Bluebell said, as ever made uncomfortable by what she couldn't kill.

"Let me," Ash said, stepping forward.

Rose watched as Ash moved toward the light that was there and yet not there. It became bright, formed into a vaguely human shape, and the sound of crying—a man sobbing—filled her ears. Rose had a strong sense, deep in bones and belly, of recognition. But thoughts wouldn't form chains in her mind; they were as confused as her senses.

Ash held up her hands. "Tell us who you are," she said to the ghost, "so we can set you on your way and this woman can be free of you."

The sobbing turned into a snarling, then tangled over itself and became a noise that could not really be heard at all, except as a violent echo in Rose's head. If she looked at the light directly, it disappeared, became merely a blue-green impression on the back of her eyelids. But if she looked just beside it, it was terrifyingly bright.

Ash's voice was calm. "Reveal yourself. Let us send you on your way." The shape compressed itself together suddenly and a blue-white arc of light—brighter than lightning—leapt toward Ash. It wrapped like a vine around her wrist and yanked her forward. She skidded to the ground with a yelp. The light left its trace on Rose's vision, even after it had rapidly extinguished, making it difficult to see. Bluebell instinctively rushed forward with her sword and raised it, but the blue-white vine of light flashed to life again and snapped upward, grabbing the point of the sword and tearing it from her hands. Bluebell cursed in shock as her sword flew away from her, landing with a dull thump somewhere in the woods.

The old woman laughed. "Two of you have failed. What does your other sister have to offer?"

Rose's heart sped. Ash climbed to her feet, rubbing her wrist. Bluebell stood back helplessly.

Rose thought about the skeleton in the woods, about the insides of her own body eventually being exposed to the wind and the rain. Ash couldn't help, Bluebell couldn't help. And yet her thoughts weren't clear. She felt something that would not jump onto her tongue. She felt the ghost; in her sinews and blood, a sense of knowing.

"You give up?" the old woman asked, and Rose realized the question was directed at her. This was her chance to save them.

"It's all right, Rose," said Ash. "We did our best."

"No, wait," Rose said. "It's just . . . I feel . . ." The strange, physical familiarity stirred inside her. She tried to concentrate, but when that didn't work, she tried instead to turn her mind away from the problem. Like the light, perhaps this feeling could only be identified if not looked upon directly.

It was her breasts. A prickling sensation deep in her breasts, like the sensations she'd had in the years she had breast-fed Rowan; the moment before the milk let down and started to flow. She put her right hand over her left breast, half expecting it to feel damp.

"It's a child," she said.

The old woman gasped and grew very still.

"That doesn't sound like a child crying," Ash said.

Rose closed her eyes and tried to hear and see with her body rather than her ears and eyes. Unfathomable grief opened up inside her; she stood uncertainly on the brink. Down there was only one thing, only one event horrific enough to pull her in.

"You lost her." The words escaped Rose's lips before she knew she was going to form them. Rose opened her eyes and pointed at the old woman. "You lost a child. An infant. The grief drove you mad."

"But the man crying?" Bluebell asked.

"The child's father. He left. He didn't recognize you anymore."

The old woman raised her hands and froze like that a moment, as though she didn't know whether to cover her face, or tear out her hair. Even in the dark, Rose could see that the tendons in her wrists were locked with terrible tension.

"Oh," the old woman said. "Oh."

Rose approached, moved by sympathy to touch her.

"Don't get close," Bluebell warned.

But Rose ignored her, grasping the old woman's hands and pressing them together.

As she did so, the light vanished, and the mud wall began to tremble like a dream upon waking.

"I remember," the old woman said. "I remember. But I don't want to remember!"

"It's gone now," Rose said. "The ghost is gone."

"Every night for fifty years," she said. "The torture . . ."

"Tell me about her," Rose said.

Bluebell was already pulling away. "The wall's down. Let's go."

Ash hushed her. "Let Rose do what she must do. She saved us."

"I'm going to look for my sword," Bluebell harrumphed.

Ash and Rose exchanged glances, then invited the old woman to sit with them in the dark woods and tell her tale. The woman told the story of her infant daughter's long illness and the unrelenting pressure of hope and despair; how she had been a great healer, renowned in the villages and towns, but how the illness had baffled all her attempts; how in the end nothing could be done and how she had buried the little body, and then been unable to lift her head for weeks, months, years. How the child's father had finally left her one snowy day to make a life among the living. Some time after that, she had forgotten herself, and all that remained were the hauntings. Her voice wove through the dark, and even Bluebell came to sit and settle and listen. Though Rose noticed she didn't cry.

Toward the end of the old woman's story, Rose realized the dark was not as complete as it had been. Then came a sound that Rose hadn't heard in here before. Morning birdsong. At first one tentative call in the dark, then, as the sun flushed warm behind the clouds, another and another, building to a chorus. The day reborn.

The old woman finished her tale bent forward on her own knees like a doll without enough stuffing. Bluebell, Rose could tell, was itching to be on her way. She stood and shifted from foot to foot. But Rose's head was feeling worse, the lethargy weighing down her limbs. She wanted to be still.

"You should go," the old woman said. "I have held you here long enough."

"So we can go straight out now?" Bluebell said, indicating where the wall had stood.

"Yes, the magic has collapsed." She managed a weak smile. "I have been very weary holding it in place all these years."

"How did you do it?" Ash asked.

"One part of my mind was devoted to holding it in place," the old woman explained, "but it was growing weak. It could keep a few people in, like yourselves. But it never would have kept an army out."

"I knew it," Bluebell said, patting the grip of her sword. "Come on, sisters. To the road. Old woman, do you know of an undermagician named Eldra?"

"I have heard of her. She lives much farther north. They say she was once a queen."

Bluebell frowned. "Perhaps a king's sister, but never a queen."

Rose climbed to her feet and helped the old woman to hers.

"You are not well," the old woman said, grasping Rose's soft white hands in her callused fingers. She looked fixedly into Rose's eyes, as though trying to see inside her skull.

Rose had the distinct impression of something stirring in her mind, almost as though the old woman were poking around gently.

"No," she said. "I hit my head."

"Your skull is cracked. Your brain is swelling slowly."

"Come on, Rose," Bluebell said, already a hundred feet away with Ash following her.

Rose glanced at Bluebell, then back to the old woman.

"I can heal you," the old woman said, rummaging on her belt and coming up with a little bottle. She uncorked it and made Rose drink a few drops of sludgy, gritty liquid. "Take this with you," she said. "It will reduce the swelling and the pain."

Rose took the bottle and the woman put her hands over Rose's skull, murmuring softly. Rose had the sensation of bright liquid light pouring from the woman's hands and down through her scalp, across the cage around her brain. The pain ebbed a little.

"You love," the old woman said.

"I do." Her heart squeezed tight.

"It's how you knew." The old woman smiled. Her worn teeth were gray with age. "You are apart from the one you love."

Rose thought about Heath and her heart felt heavy.

The old woman withdrew her hands and reached again for her belt.

It jangled as she felt along it, her fingers finally coming to rest on what she sought. She detached it from her belt and held it out to Rose.

It was a loop of bronze, with a piece of ice trapped in it. Rose touched the ice. The cold made her shiver. "What is it?" she asked.

"It's a seeing-loop. Every morning, from the moment when the first curve of the sun appears, to when it has risen fully, the ice will become water, suspended in the seeing-loop. You will be able to see your loved one even if you are parted."

Rose's heart lifted in her chest. "Really?"

"Yes. But first, you must name the one you love the most in the world. So I can enchant it properly."

Rose opened her mouth to say Heath, then remembered her daughter and cursed herself. All things being well, Rowan would be at Folkenham by now, safe in Wengest's arms, playing with Nurse and eating like a pig. Within weeks, Rose would be with her again, able to see with her own eyes every morning if she was well and happy. She remembered Heath telling her about going into battle. *In a two-minute skirmish, all can be lost.* Surely it wouldn't have been wrong to ask for assurance of his safety when they were destined to be apart?

But Rowan was her child. And she didn't know if everything was fine: if Ivy and Sighere had made her feel safe, if Wengest made her feel loved, and if she was crying on waking every morning because Rose was not there.

"Rowan," she said. "My daughter." And she fought selfish disappointment.

The old woman lifted the loop to Rose's lips and said, "Go on, whisper her name."

Rose did as she was asked. A wisp of steam rose from the ice. She handed it to Rose.

Rose pinned the bronze object to her own belt. "Thank you," she said.

"And thank you." The old woman raised her arm. The owl flew to her with a clatter of its giant wings. Rose stepped back, alarmed, but then the owl was still.

"Good luck on your journey," the old woman said.

"Good luck with . . ." Rose trailed off. "Good luck."

The old woman nodded, her mouth trembling. "Bless you. Get some rest when you can. Your skull will heal in time."

"Are you coming, Rose?" Bluebell called.

Rose looked up. Bluebell and Ash were waiting. Bluebell's lips were set hard with impatience.

Rose thoughtfully fingered the seeing-loop on her belt. "Yes, coming," she called, hurrying off toward her sisters.

The dogs and horses had not strayed far from where they had been left, and were fresh and energetic where the sisters were not. Bluebell wanted them out of the deep wooded path before they rested, and Ash's anxiety grew as the day woke up. Her belly felt loose, her scalp prickled. She thought, at first, it was a result of not having slept the night before, but as they wound their way out of the woods, she knew it was something else. Whoever was following them had waited for them and was now shadowing them again.

But there was nothing else to do but go forward, so Ash kept her gaze in front of her and kept going. The road grew shallow, and light ahead told her the wood was thinning. The grim yews gave way to young elms, strong saplings stretching up for sunshine. Bluebell increased the pace, despite Rose's protests.

"The sooner we're there, the sooner we can rest," Bluebell told her.

"Where's 'there'?" Rose asked.

But Bluebell didn't answer. They were hoping for a village, for an inn, for a bed. Especially as the earthy smell of rain behind them intensified.

Finally, the road widened and they left the woods behind. Stretching off on either side was overgrown farmland. Meadow grass and wildflowers grew unchecked. Ambitious hedgerows marked off fields that were too rocky ever to grow much. And in the distance were the dark shapes of buildings.

"A village," Rose breathed.

"A bed," Ash said, glancing at the sky. Dark-gray clouds were moving in. "Bluebell?"

"Yes, we'll stop. We'll rest this afternoon and have a good night's sleep. We are only a few days from Eldra now."

This time, they were careful. Ash, in her counselor's clothes, found them a room, and Bluebell was kept well hidden when Rose went to the inn for meals. They ate in their room—a dim space lit by one narrow shuttered window and smelling of moldy rushes—then eased their weary bodies into soft beds. Bluebell said they should only sleep an hour so they could sleep properly that night, but even she didn't sound convinced by her logic. Ash suspected they would all wake in the middle of the night when it was too dark to travel, but couldn't fight the tide of tiredness. *Sleep. Now.* She fell into a deep, dreamless slumber.

When she woke later, she was confused. It was daylight, but not morning. Dusk. It took her a moment to remember where she was and why she was sleeping in the day. Then the sound that had woken her repeated itself.

Somebody was trying the door.

"Bluebell!" she whispered harshly, sitting up and shaking her sister, who was asleep next to her.

Bluebell was awake and on her feet in half a moment. Rose sat up, bleary. "What's going on?"

Bluebell held her finger to her lips and approached the door silently. She reached for the latch.

Ash's heart stuttered. Something was about to happen . . .

She formed Bluebell's name with her lips, to tell her to stop, not let the future in.

Then the door was open and Bluebell was hauling in a small, thin man with one sharp brown eye and one useless one. Her hand went to her sword. "You've been following us," she spat.

"Stop!" Ash cried. "Don't hurt him!"

Bluebell's head snapped up. "You know him?"

The man looked at Ash. A thrill of light and heat passed through her and, impossibly, his name formed in her head: *Unweder.* "No," she said, "I've never seen him before." But she was absolutely certain she had been waiting for him her whole life.

CHAPTER 20

Wylm wore the contents of Eni's stomach more than once on the crossing from Thyrsland to Ravensey. The two-day journey was plagued by ill tides and rain, so that the boy had no hope of keeping any food down. He sat miserable, damp-chinned, pressed against Wylm for most of the trip. Wylm's exhaustion started in his marrow and extended out to his toes and fingertips. He needed a hot bath, a sleep in a comfortable bed, some space from the child. What he faced, though, on arrival at Ravensey, was neither so certain nor so comfortable.

They sighted land in the early morning as Wylm was rousing from a sitting doze. The sky was a blue-pink flush, diligent stars still twinkling dimly between clouds. Figures moved about in the grainy light, dropping the sails, taking up the oars. Cold shivered across his chest and he pulled the rough blanket up higher. The fresh smell of morning was spoiled by the sour smell of stale vomit. The water slapped against the side of the boat rhythmically as he tried to recapture sleep ahead of their landing.

Eni woke as the flat hull skidded over gravel and came to rest. His fingers were hard on Wylm's upper arm, and Wylm opened his eyes. The sun was low but shining warm. Seabirds cried as they skated overhead. Wylm gently put Eni's hand aside and crawled from under the storage area to look around.

The island was covered in birdshit; gulls and gannets had nested in the jutting outcrops that flanked the gravel beach, and the dark-gray rock was white with it. A pervasive smell of seaweed and rain trapped in rocks greeted him as he stole a glance up the beach and across the long waving grass. He could make out the gable finishings of a wooden hall, carved as the wings of a bird: Hakon's hall. The rhythm of his heart picked up. He stood and reached down for Eni's limp hand.

One of the raiders ran ahead, no doubt to prepare Hakon for their arrival. The others, who had barely spoken a dozen words directly to him the whole journey, were now full of orders and warnings. They both had to have their hands tied—Eni resisted this violently, but unsuccessfully—they had to walk close, they had to keep their eyes down. Wylm watched his own feet crunch over gravel and mud and feathers, listening to the soft mumbling whine Eni made when he was anxious.

"Hush, boy," Wylm said with a stolen sideways glance. "You'll be fine."

Eni wouldn't quiet, though, and Ragnar shouted at Wylm to be silent and keep his head down.

They trudged up a hill and onto rolling grass. No shadows of trees or rocks. The bitter ocean wind from the north surged freely over the land. The hall sat in a natural hollow, scarcely protected from the wind, and surrounded by rock huts with turf roofs. Wylm felt a hard hand on the back of his neck pushing his head down again; he fixed his eyes to the birdshit-speckled rocks and rotten boardwalk that his own feet trod up to the Crow King's hall.

The heavy doors slammed shut behind them, closing out the bracing sea air and forcing his lungs to fill with smoke from a low-burning hearthpit.

"Sit here," one of the raiders ordered, shoving him to the ground. Wylm dropped his head and closed his eyes a moment, catching his breath. The remembered waves still swelled and ebbed beneath him.

The raiders were more gentle with Eni, whom they helped to sit on the rough wooden floorboards. Eni immediately wriggled very close to Wylm. The smell of ale-soaked wood and peat smoke enveloped

DAUGHTERS OF THE STORM   239

them. Wylm heard the departing footsteps of his captors, the thudding of the door again. Then nothing.

Slowly, Wylm opened his eyes and raised his head.

A man sat on a wooden riser upon a deep, carved wooden chair with high arms, looking at him. "Yes," Hakon said. "Here I am."

Wylm had expected a much older man, but Hakon was probably not yet forty. His hair was white-blond, his beard in two neat plaits. But his face was something from a nightmare. A ragged hole in his cheek, the edges little more than scarred flaps, allowed a glimpse through to his teeth and cheekbone. One of his eyes was missing, leaving a sunken sallow pit.

"They say you can speak our tongue," Hakon said, having distinct difficulties with some of his consonants because of the strange, constrained movements of his mouth and jaw.

"I can," Wylm said.

"They say you sought me out, deliberately." Hakon gave a grin, which arrived on his deformed face in a nightmarish configuration.

"I did."

Hakon stood. He was impossibly tall, perhaps six and a half feet, with a lithe, muscular body and gigantic feet in stained leather shoes. As much as his face was ruined by battle, his body was clearly strong and fit. He circled them once, then stopped and crouched down in front of Eni. "Tell me about the blind boy," he said.

"Show him your ring, Eni," Wylm said.

At mention of the ring, Eni tucked his hands under his armpits. Hakon gently but relentlessly withdrew them with his own long, large hands and held the ring finger close to his face to inspect it.

"Bluebell," Eni said, his voice little more than an anxious whisper.

Hakon dropped Eni's hand and turned to Wylm. "Bluebell?"

"I found the child on her lover's farm," Wylm said. "The ring proves beyond doubt that the child is hers."

Hakon stood and stared down at Wylm with cold, pale eyes, and Wylm prayed he could not see the lie. "You see a death's head before you," Hakon said, long fingers touching his own cheek. "Your sister is responsible for that."

"Stepsister," Wylm said quickly, concerned he was to be punished for Bluebell's acts.

The edge of a cruel smile. "I had your *step*father at the point of my blade. I was half a breath away from spilling his blood. She saved him." Hakon spat the words. "She threw an ax from a mile's distance. It found its mark in the side of my face."

Wylm didn't show his skepticism.

"She delivered me to my brother's hands, to face charges of murder and treason. But he underestimated me—as did your sister, even with all her strength and fury." He shook his head. "She has some dark, secret hands helping her, no doubt. It has long been said that she is unkillable. But lately, we on Ravensey have started to say something different."

The door opened slowly then, and Wylm turned his eyes to watch as a stooped old man with only fluff for hair entered the hall. His clothes were sewn over with long feathers, and a band around his head sprouted feathers at the back that hung down his shoulders and spine. As he walked toward them, Wylm caught a scent of sweet burning herbs and fish oil.

"Ah, here is my something different now," Hakon said. "Welcome, old man."

The man's eyes were pale gray, pupils so small the irises were like mirrors. He made his way forward by leaning on a rattling stick and came to a halt beside Wylm and Eni.

"Look you," Hakon said to him. "Bluebell's stepbrother."

"Stepbrother?" the man said.

"This is my randerman. His name is Eirik," Hakon said, as politely as he might if they were sitting down to break bread together. "Eirik, Wylm has brought us a boy he says is Bluebell's son."

The randerman leaned hard on his stick, bending into a crouch behind Eni and taking a long sniff of his hair. *"Kyndrepa,"* he said, in a cold, guttural voice, but Wylm did not know the word.

"Bluebell can be killed only by her own kin," Hakon continued. "My randerman dreamed it, not twenty nights ago. And now . . . here you are."

"The three-toed drake," Eirik said, bursting suddenly into life. "It

clawed her to pieces. All that was left were crushed petals and blood."
He extended his hand to indicate both Wylm and Eni. "But which of
you will it be? The boy? Or the brother? Who will wield the trollblade?
Who will cut open her breast with *Grithbani*?"

Another untranslatable word. Wylm's heartbeat flickered hotly in
his throat. A sense of destiny was upon him, and it smelled like the
strange burnt herbs that clung to the randerman.

Hakon, however, didn't feel the import of the moment. "It's hardly
going to be the blind child who kills his mother," he said with a snort.
"Give the blade to the brother."

"Stepbrother," Wylm said again, softly, not sure why he was saying it.

"You have traveled far," the randerman said to Wylm. "You must
rest, for at week's end, when the moon fills, we must spill your blood
in the forge."

Wylm shuddered, but the randerman smiled and tapped him on
the heart with a crooked finger.

"You need no courage," the randerman said. "You need only *Grithbani*."

Hakon, meanwhile, had drawn Eni close to him and knelt in front
of him smoothing his hair. "Is it not a joke," he said, "that Bluebell's
son should be a dullard?"

"A fit punishment," Wylm said. Then, hesitantly, "Will you hurt the
boy?"

"What do you think I should do?" Hakon's eyes were cold, fixed on
Wylm's face. Was the question a challenge?

Wylm showed none of his fear. "I think he is of more value to us
alive."

"If I sent him to her in pieces, would it not kill her with grief and
wrath?"

Wylm's stomach clenched. He cursed himself for being weak, for
having developed a protective sympathy for Eni. "This is Bluebell we
speak of. The woman has no heart."

"Or at least no room to love anyone but her father," Hakon said,
stroking his plaited beard thoughtfully. "Yes, more value in him being
alive. Oh ho. I have it!" The nightmare grin split his face again. "I will

take him to apprentice. I will raise him as my own. Now, *that* will torture her." He leaned close to Eni, and his booming voice was remarkably warm. "You're mine now, little boy."

Eni's head moved from side to side. He didn't seem anxious. Perhaps puzzled.

It was all unfolding just as Wylm had hoped.

"Leave him with me," Hakon said, standing and stretching to his
full height. "Eirik will take you somewhere you can eat and wash."

"This way, *kyndrepa*," the randerman said, and Wylm climbed to
his feet to follow him out into the thin morning sunshine.

Eirik the randerman fed him and left him alone in one of the stone-
and-earth huts. The wind howled over the turf roof, but the hut was
warm and smoky from a low fire. Dark except for firelight. The walls
were carved with rough, shallow shelves, and Wylm presumed from
their contents that this must be the randerman's own home. Shells
and feathers and dried fish skeletons abounded. Runic inscriptions
peppered the walls, seemingly at random. The room had the same
smell as the old magic-man himself: that acrid and sweet and slightly
fishy aroma, as though he had spent many hours by the fire inhaling
the smoke from the herbs that gave him visions. Wylm stripped to the
waist, washed his face and upper body in a tub of cold, cloudy water,
then sat on the bed. A poorly angled piece of straw pierced up through
the blankets and poked his thigh. The water air-dried on his skin,
coaxing goosebumps out of him. He crossed his forearms and rubbed
his hands over his arms and shoulders to warm them, feeling his own
lean musculature. As a child, he had been a skinny streak of pale flesh,
just like Eni. Wylm pulled on a clean tunic that Eirik had left out for
him, which was too loose and gaped open at the front, revealing his
hairless chest. He laced it as well as he could, pinned on a cloak, and
went to the door of the hut to let in the daylight.

Wylm had to trudge out of the hollow to see the rest of the island.
Standing on a high ridge, he could turn in a slow circle and see the
cold sea stretching off in all directions. Down at the rocky beach, between a dragon-head ship with bare masts buffeted by the wind and

a collection of small round fishing boats, Wylm could see a group of five men practicing ax throwing. The sound of the waves on the rocks carried up to him with the call of seabirds, the occasional thundering grunt as a raider threw an ax with all his might—such strenuous effort that Wylm wondered their shoulders didn't dislocate. The ax would land in the sand, the raider would fetch it, then it would be the next man's turn.

Hakon had said Bluebell threw an ax from a mile's distance, and that was how his face had become so disfigured. Wylm turned this thought over. It couldn't be true. Could it? The burly raiders on the beach were throwing only a dozen yards. He supposed Hakon might promote the story of Bluebell's supernatural prowess to hide an embarrassing truth: that he had simply been bested by a woman of flesh and blood and bone.

Flesh. Blood. Bone. And Wylm would be the one to kill her. The randerman had been certain of it: He was the *kyndrepa,* a word he had come to understand meant "kinslayer." He shivered, told himself it was the cold sea wind, and went back inside to the warm smoky hut.

Deep, deep in the night, Wylm woke to a thudding noise. A moment passed, then another, as he tried to remember where he was. The roar of the cold sea told him.

The thudding again. It was at his door.

He stood, lifted the latch, and a big hairy man thrust Eni at him. "He won't stop crying. Hakon says he must sleep with you."

Wylm caught Eni before the boy fell to the reed floor, and the raider was gone before he could reply.

Eni's two cold hands clung to Wylm's wrist. "Rabbit?" he said.

"I don't know where your rabbit is."

Eni lifted his hand and felt his way up to Wylm's chest. Pressed firmly. "Rabbit," he said.

And Wylm understood: The child was calling him Rabbit. He had only told Eni his name once, and clearly it had been forgotten. Instead, he had become the man who forced roast rabbit on him, who carved a stick like a rabbit. He had become Rabbit to the boy.

"Yes, it's me. It's Rabbit," Wylm said. "Will you sleep in my bed?"

Eni hooked his arm through Wylm's and allowed himself to be led to the straw bed. Wylm lay next to him, trying to keep a few inches of space between them, but the boy wriggled across the gap and was soon sleeping peacefully with his bony knees curled into Wylm's ribs.

Wylm lay awake much longer. Rabbit. What a grim joke it was. He should be Wolf to the child, or Bear, or Fox. But Rabbit he was, and would remain until . . .

Well, Wylm could not conceive the boy's ultimate fate. It lay behind a veil of darkness, beyond his destiny as *kyndrepa.*

His destiny. Yes, he liked the sound of that. The randerman had seen it in a dream: Only kin could slay Bluebell, and who else could that be but him? Her sisters were in her thrall, and her own father loved her better than he loved Gudrun. He rolled the thought over in his mind, and it grew dull and round and pulled him down to sweet darkness.

Just as he was succumbing to sleep, he thought he heard a strange voice on the wind outside. Neither human nor animal. Alert now, he listened into the dark.

It was singing. A strange, howling song.

He rose, careful not to wake Eni, and peered out the doorway. Up on the ridge danced Eirik, the randerman. The moon had risen: just a sliver off full. The sky was clear and the sea boomed. The randerman was no longer a stooped, fragile figure. He was lithe and mobile, his joints as fluid as a child's. His movements were so at odds with his tufted hair and wrinkled skin that it gave Wylm an unnatural chill. The song continued, the hooting and dancing, his voice carrying away far, far out to sea as the moon shone down on Ravensey.

For four days and nights the same pattern unfolded. Wylm spent each day out of the hut so that Eirik the randerman could sleep among his smoking prophetic herbs and dream about the mystical trollblade that he said Wylm would wield against his stepsister. The sword was even now being forged and shaped with an ominous clanking rhythm that echoed through the settlement.

As for Eni, he was taken every morning to spend the day with Hakon and his men. Wylm caught a glimpse of them occasionally as he spent his day darting away from the icy curiosity of the raiders. Hakon firmly but gently led the child from forge to stable to bakehouse, as though assessing his fitness for any of these tasks, then muttered and clicked in exasperation. Wylm knew Hakon's patience would eventually run out. Not this month, or the next, but by the time winter came and Eni stood exposed as a mouth to feed in lean times, Hakon would tire of the game and a pair of rough hands would hold him under the sea until it was over.

They brought Eni crying to Wylm at night, every night, with thinning patience and hardening carelessness. After, Wylm lay listening to the strange howling song of the randerman, high and cold on the hill, drifting in and out of sleep. He knew that he couldn't leave Eni here with Hakon. Not because he had grown soft and worried about the boy: Traveling would be far easier on his own. But because, whatever sword they gave him to defeat Bluebell, he would still need a shield.

Eni would be that shield.

Late, late at night, the door swung open and Wylm barely woke, so used was he to Eni's nocturnal appearance. But the door remained open, and a cold prickle made him open his eyes and sit up.

The randerman stood there, wearing a strange crown of black feathers that hung down around his ears and over his brow.

"What is it?" Wylm said, his voice catching on sleep.

"It's time to come to the forge, *kyndrepa*. The blade needs tempering."

"I don't know anything about making a sword."

"You don't need to know anything. Just follow me."

Wylm pushed back the woven blanket. The sea-cold air licked over him and he shivered. The randerman had already gone ahead and Wylm had to hurry after him, barefoot, over the gritty earth and down into the hollow of the village, behind Hakon's hall to the smithy. Firelight glowed under the shutters.

The randerman pushed the door open, and the hot smell of iron rushed out. Hakon stood by the forge, along with a young, tall black-smith whose hands were wrapped up with coarse cloth. Wylm, just a few moments out of sleep, felt as though he were dreaming. The dark and the smells and the orange glow of the forge rose around him like phantoms.

"Here he is," Hakon said, as though it was perfectly natural that they were meeting in the forge at midnight.

The smith held out the sword, but it wasn't a sword. It was a dark unfinished blade, with no pommel or crossguard, just an exposed tang. Wylm's stomach dropped. He thought of Bluebell's sword, the Widowsmith. A fine, gleaming blade forged by famous swordmakers in Almissia, a kingdom of exceptional steel.

The randerman, as if sensing his concern, leaned into him. Hot breath flowed over his ear. "*Grithbani* is not finished. The magic has yet to be poured in."

Wylm took heart in the randerman's words, in the prophecy.

"Hold out your hand," Hakon said to Wylm. "The blade must taste blood."

Understanding, Wylm cautiously extended his right hand.

"No, your off-hand," Hakon barked, jerking Wylm's left hand toward him and turning it palm-up.

"No, I'm—"

In a blur that lasted half a moment, the smith brought the edge of the rough blade down on Wylm's palm. The blow was a hot sting. Blood flowed.

"First bite," the randerman said, still close to Wylm's ear. "Now see."

The smith shoved the blade back into the forge. Wylm's blood dripped steadily onto the dirt floor. He stared at the wound in alarm.

"Go with Eirik," Hakon said as the smith pulled the blade out and quenched it in a barrel beside the forge. "He will tend to your wound."

Out again into the night. "It is yours now," the randerman said. "Your blood is in the steel. Only you can kill her now. Only you or one of your blood."

"But I'm left-handed. You just cut the hand that needs to hold the sword."

The randerman didn't miss a beat. "That is how it will fall, then. Blood from your sword-bearing hand will only make the magic stronger. Destiny will rush upon us; you cannot escape what has gone before and what is to come."

A thin drizzling rain fell. But Wylm's blood was too hot and thudding with pain to feel the cold.

The wound was deep and long, and although Eirik had wrapped it, it seeped blood all that night and all the next day. The randerman told him that the healing would take as long as it needed to take. They were in no rush to kill Bluebell, but Wylm was. Every day that crept by was a day his mother might be in danger. He could hear the clanking and clattering of the smithy and knew that the time for him to take up the sword was drawing closer. He began to think about how he could slip away and take Eni with him. Hakon had made a claim on the boy, keeping him beside him most of the day and at every meal in the long hall. And when Wylm had raised the possibility of taking Eni with him, Hakon had been surprisingly aggressive.

"He's mine," Hakon had shouted, firelight making horrid shadows of his face. "I will find a use for him yet."

But Wylm needed Eni. Eni might not be Bluebell's child, but he was her lover's—and she clearly cared enough about the lad to give him her ring. So if she saw the boy's life at risk, it might make her hesitate just long enough to give Wylm the victory he needed. Because as much as he believed the randerman's *kyndrepa* prophecy, it was unclear whether killing Bluebell would result in his own death, too. And while it might suit Hakon to have Bluebell dead at the expense of Wylm's life, it certainly didn't suit Wylm.

So yes, he needed the boy, to make Bluebell weak.

Two times in the past week, Wylm had seen a small group of raiders go out to sea in a round fishing boat made of wood and leather. It was a big enough boat for four men to sit comfortably, with a covered end. As they rowed away from shore, one of them would erect a sturdy mast in the middle, and the sail helped them negotiate the tricky departure and return under strong prevailing winds. Often his mind returned to this boat, to the distance back to the mainland with the winds in his favor, to his capacity to sail the boat and navigate it to the place closest to where Bluebell's lover had said she'd taken Athelrick. He had sailed many times on the river near his childhood home, and knew how to handle a boat and a sail.

All he needed now was the sword.

But before the sword arrived, the pain did. Pain in his left hand, throbbing from one end to another, making him unable to stretch or curl his fingers. In the smoky half dark of his hut at night, he peeled back the bandage gingerly to see a cruel purple edge on the wound. An infection was setting in.

They came for him at dawn, Hakon and the randerman. Eni was with them, dressed identically to Hakon, in rough wool dyed green and a string of amber beads with a silver raven hung about his neck. He hadn't seen Eni for days; the boy looked tired and desolate, shadowed around his eyes. Wylm wondered what Hakon had been putting him through.

"It's time," the randerman said.

Wylm climbed out of bed and pulled on his breeches. "Are we going to the forge?"

At the sound of Wylm's voice, Eni grew agitated. "Rabbit?" he said. "Rabbit?"

"Silence!" Hakon shouted, and his voice cracked through the dark. Eni froze, collapsed in on himself, hands pulled up defensively against his chest.

Hakon rolled his eye in contempt, then said, "No, we are going to the crown of the island. Follow."

In the dim light, they followed. Eni stuck close to Hakon now, fearful of being shouted at again. Wylm came next, and the randerman behind. They crested the island, then descended into a shallow valley, then up again toward a rocky outcrop where a fire burned high. Wylm had seen the outcrop before, but had never seen the steps carved into its eastern face. They rounded the outcrop and began to ascend. Gulls circled. The smell was of seaweed and birdshit. Up and up they went, until they arrived at a half-sheltered plateau of dark-gray rock, where the smith stood with a sword that caught the morning light on one side and the firelight on the other.

Hakon caught Eni between his hands and pressed the child against him, standing back. The smith handed the sword to the randerman and stood back also. Up here, the wind gusted randomly—one minute flat, the next pushing salty air down Wylm's throat. The flame of the bonfire rode the wind, and Wylm was careful to keep his legs away from the heat.

The randerman threw some herbs on the fire, then stood tall and began to move with that lithe, unnatural movement Wylm had seen out on the ridge at night. It was as though his old age had fled his joints and left a young man in his place.

"*Kyndrepa,*" he said, holding out the sword on two palms. "Meet *Grithbani.*"

Wylm took the sword and hefted it in his left hand, wincing.

"Only kin can slay Bluebell the Fierce," the randerman intoned. "With the trollblade, *Grithbani,* forged with your own blood, you will meet her in battle. Go forward with this blade, *kyndrepa.* Though you may yet suffer injury or death, know that you can end her reign."

Eirik then began his strange song, dancing and howling as though he were an exotic bird. Wylm considered the craftsmanship of the blade in the firelight. No jewels or gold embellishment, but it was a strong, sleek weapon. And it was a weapon forged with magic. Forged to slay his sister.

Wylm caught his breath, purpose hardening and fusing in him. The moment seared itself on his mind's eye: Eni in green with his black eyes sightless and his face bathed in firelight, the first glimmer of dawn touching Hakon's fair beard, the strange dancing contortions of the randerman's body, the smith looking on in wonder. And the weight of the sword in his hands; the weight of his destiny in his hands.

❖ ❖ ❖

Wylm was rolling up his clothes, stuffing them into his pack along with some bread and dried fish he'd lifted from the pantry after breakfast, when the door to the hut burst in and Eirik stood there, once again a stooped old man.

"Let me see your wound," he said.

Wylm offered the randerman his hand. Perhaps he could be of some use; perhaps he would put a poultice on it. "It heals slowly," he said gruffly. The sword lay casually in its sheath on the bed beside them. He'd barely dared look at it since taking ownership. To see the grim runic inscriptions on its grip was to be reminded of the cold, dark task ahead of him, and his own possible fate. *Though you may yet suffer injury or death . . .*

"You were cautious with it this morning." Eirik unwrapped the wound, and Wylm winced as the cloth brushed against the swelling. Eirik clicked his tongue in concern. "It's infected."

"It will be fine."

The randerman drew close in the dim room, his pupils still unnaturally small as he eyed Wylm. "Fever?"

Wylm gulped. He had felt a little sweaty behind the eyeballs this morning. "No."

"To bed," Eirik said. "I'll bring you some ale and a bucket of salt water to soak your hand in." He eyed Wylm's pack by the door. "You won't be going anywhere until it's healed."

He was constrained to spend the day in bed and, in truth, felt the better for it. He'd had an infection once before as a child. A nail had caught his shoulder and the wound had pained him for weeks and healed in a swollen scar. He expected this would be the same, but he was itching to move, to be off this birdshit-stained island and on his way. Perhaps another day or two to grow well.

Late in the night, as had so often happened before, the door to the hut opened. Wylm opened his eyes and looked. Eni stood there, framed by moonlight. No Hakon, no retainers accompanying him. The boy hadn't been brought to him in four days. This was new.

"Eni?" he said, his voice catching on sleep.

"Rabbit."

"Did you come alone?"

The boy felt his way across the room to the bed and sat down, not saying a word, just hitching a sob. Wylm understood that Eni had gotten away from Hakon somehow, and had come to him for comfort.

"What is it?" Wylm asked, knowing that the boy neither understood the question nor could frame an answer. He grasped the child's shoulder, and Eni gasped with pain.

"What have they done to you?" Wylm muttered, and he opened the shutter to let a little weak moonlight in, then peeled up Eni's shirt to see dark shadows on his ribs. Bruises.

Now. The time was now. His heart beat with it. He had Eni, he had the sword, and he knew how to get off the island.

The time was now.

"Eni," he said in a low voice, "Rabbit's going to take care of you now. We are going in a boat away from here, but you must be very quiet and do as I say."

Nothing about Eni's demeanor or expression indicated he had heard or understood, but Wylm climbed out of bed and dressed anyway. "Come on."

Eni hesitated, then stood and reached out to find Wylm's hand. He took it firmly, and Wylm almost shrieked with pain. Eni backed off, frightened.

"No, no," Wylm said softly. "No, it's not your fault. I have a cut on my hand and . . . Here." He offered Eni his good hand. "See? Rabbit's not angry."

Eni nodded. Wylm dropped his hand and grabbed his pack, attached the trollblade and its sheath to his belt, and opened the door. "Follow my footfalls, boy," he said. "We're going on an adventure."

Down on the gritty beach, the cold wind caught his breath and enlivened him. He was filled with certainty—*Grithbani*, his sword; Eni, his shield; prophecy on his side. He would make fate bend to him; he would be that man who could change the course of history. He threw his goods into the little hide-skin boat and helped Eni in.

He was in cold seawater to his ankles, pushing the boat into the waves, when he noticed a shadowy movement at the corner of his eye.

Wylm turned. The randerman stood by, considering him in the pale sea light. A frisson passed between them. Wylm wondered if Eirik would shout for Hakon, or try to stop him. A held breath.

But then Eirik simply nodded and said, "Let everything fall as it must."

And Wylm was up to his shoulders in the sea, then climbing into the boat and taking up the oars, his left hand stinging thunderously.

He and Eni headed into the ocean.

CHAPTER 21

*T*his is a dream of searing pleasure that will turn to cold shame on waking. She clings to it, pushing herself under the layers of sleep.

Willow lies on the soft carpet of grass. She is completely naked. Cool green under her warm skin. Her hair is loose, snaking around her. The sun lingers on her nipples. She bends her legs and lets them fall apart, so the sun can find that other sensitive bud. Her back arches. She is a flower sprouting from the earth; wild, sweet feelings traverse her.

Sighing, she drops her burden. She need not be a good soldier for Maava. She is simply a thing of flesh and breath and blood.

But then the sun flickers behind clouds and the rising wind tears the tops of the trees. She tries to prop herself on her elbows but finds herself unable to move. Naked, pinned to the grass by her own mortal weight. The trees part and there are dozens of them. Men with beards and hairy forearms and blood-spattered armor. Raiders. Tattooed, savage raiders; the ones spoken of in horrified tones in the chapel. And they will see her, they will come for her, they will smash her soft virgin body beneath them. The dream swallows itself and turns into a nightmare. Frozen, she can do nothing but wait for the brutes to come at her.

But then one among them strides ahead. She can't see his face, in the way that dreams have of obscuring crucial details behind a silver-gray cloud, but he is not a bearded brute, not a hairy bear. He is a lean, olive-skinned beauty of a man.

"I won't let them harm you," he declares, and she notices he wields a large, gleaming sword whose grip is covered in strange symbols. He rams it hard into the earth near her feet, and the raiders evaporate. Now it is just the cool green grass and the distant sun and the scudding clouds. He kneels before her, and she realizes he can see every intimate inch of her body. The soft pink folds and openings, the whorls of dark-gold hair. Thumping, thrilling desire grasps her.

Willow woke, her pulse thudding hotly between her legs. She rolled over and pressed her face into her rough blanket. The fire had died and smoldered to nothing. Cold filled the air around her. She reached down with the side of her palm between her legs and pushed hard in the hope it would make the feeling go away. To her surprise, the feeling intensified, grew hard, and she thought she might wet her bed, which she hadn't done since she was a child. Then one, two, three big throbs pulsed through her, and the feeling withdrew.

Relief.

She listened for angels. Would they be angry with her? Or was the smooth-limbed man in her dream an angel himself? There was something familiar about him.

Cool embarrassment shivered over her as she realized. Wylm. Her stepbrother. She had dreamed of Wylm, but in such a way that it had some hypnotic effect on her blood and her shameful parts. She breathed deeply, her nose tickling against the rough threads of the blanket, willing herself back to sleep.

Hoping without hoping that the dream might return.

Why had Ivy never noticed before how handsome Wengest was? Perhaps it was the firelight, the company, the mead, and the music. But it seemed to her his profile was one of the handsomest she had ever seen. Manly, yet gentle, with a noble forehead and dark, expressive eyebrows. When he smiled, the corners of his eyes crinkled up, and Ivy found herself stealing glances at him, trying to see that smile. It was hard to believe Rose had ever looked elsewhere. Because Wengest was something Heath could never be: a king.

Wengest was deep in conversation with the man next to him, whom Ivy had figured out was the trimartyr preacher: fat as a pig and determined to finish every last morsel on his overladen plate. One of Wengest's cousins, a widower duke from northern Nettlechester, had arrived that afternoon with his retainers. Within an hour, the smells of roasting meat had been wafting from the hall and Nurse told Ivy to put on her best dress and get ready for a feast.

So here she was, sitting at the king's table in Rose's usual position, wearing her blue-and-gold dress pinned up with a silver brooch to show the bottom corner of her shift. She had a string of amber beads fastened across her chest, and her bright curls were brushed loose over her shoulders. Gunther, Wengest's visiting cousin, couldn't stop looking at her from across the table. She made sure that when she laughed, she leaned her head back so he could admire her white neck. Not that she wanted him particularly; he was far too old for her liking. But she didn't want him to look away. When somebody's eyes were on her that hungrily, she knew she existed in the world.

The preacher—Nyll, that was his name—got up from the table and half walked, half stumbled outside, probably to relieve himself. Ivy felt a shudder of distaste at the thought. He probably pissed like a goat. Wengest, now free, turned his attention to her.

"Are you bored?"

"Not at all," she said, lowering her eyelashes a fraction.

"Rose is always bored at these dinners."

"I cannot think why. New people are *so* interesting."

Wengest glanced at Gunther, then back to Ivy. He dropped his voice low and leaned in a little closer. "Gunther seems very interested in you, too," he teased.

Ivy felt the tickle of his breath near her ear, and it gave her an unexpected thrill. "He's older than my father."

Wengest smiled. "You are like your sister. You say what you think."

"Like Rose, you mean?"

"Who else?"

Ivy grimaced. "I thought you might have meant Iron-Tits."

The corners of his mouth lifted. "Who's that?"

Ivy raised an eyebrow. "Bluebell."

Wengest responded by leaning back and laughing loudly. Ivy felt the glow of being the focus of somebody's warm attention.

"I take it you aren't so fond of your oldest sister?" he said, reaching for his cup of mead.

Ivy was keen to say something else that would make Wengest like her. "She's an overbearing bully, and I've never seen an uglier face unless it was a pig's arse."

This sent Wengest into thigh-slapping convulsions. The others at the table—Gunther and his retainers—began to show interest in what the joke might be. Ivy entertained them with imaginative descriptions of Bluebell's face and body, provoking roaring laughter. She kept going, until Gunther said, with barely a hint of jocular tone, "We'd be better off if she was dead."

A short, tense silence followed, as they glanced at her to see if she would defend Bluebell. Ivy began to understand that Almissia's peace with Nettlechester was an uneasy one, and a little coil of guilt moved in her stomach.

"Come now," she said, with a smile as big as she could fake it, "surely you don't mean that."

Gunther hesitated a moment, then laughed. "No, of course not."

A ripple of forced laughter followed his words. Ivy gulped her mead. She felt very warm all of a sudden.

Nyll, who had returned, took the opportunity to speak. "She's a heathen. Almissia is full of heathens. We should not be in alliance with them unless they take the trimartyr faith."

"If they do that, then Bluebell won't rule," Wengest said with a dismissive hand gesture. "It will never happen. They won't convert, so we must let it go. And please, remember, Bluebell is my wife's sister; my daughter's aunt. We must speak well of her, especially in the company of Ivy." He gave her a sidelong glance, nodded once, then returned to his food.

Ivy pushed back her stool. She felt self-conscious and as though she'd said too much. "I'm very tired," she said. "I bid you good night."

"Let me see you to your bower," Wengest said, jumping to his feet. He nodded, with a serious expression, at Gunther.

Curious, Ivy let him take her by the elbow and lead her outside. The night was soft and smelled of flowers and dew. Behind a high hawthorn hedge stood a little stone chapel, with freshly stained wooden shutters and a curling green plant clinging to the stone. The hedge rustled as a bird or animal shrank from their footfalls. As soon as they were away from the hall, Wengest said, "Don't mind Gunther. He is not wise."

"I don't mind."

He cleared his throat, seemed to be struggling with words. "Don't think I harbor the same hatred for your father's kingdom."

Ivy began to understand that Wengest was afraid she would tell Bluebell what had been said at dinner. She almost laughed with relief. She wasn't in trouble after all.

"Wengest, be calm. I won't say a word to Bluebell."

He nodded, his mouth pulled in a tight line. "Our kingdoms were at war for a very long time. My grandfather was killed by your grandfather. The peace deal has saved many lives. I do not regret it. I do not regret marrying Rose."

Ivy detected real affection in his words, and for some reason it made her feel sad. She had been thinking this evening she had Wengest's full attention. She shook back her hair and smiled brightly. "Of course you don't. She is beautiful."

"As is her sister," he said softly. His gaze traveled to her mouth, then he quickly looked away. "Good night, Ivy."

"Good night, Wengest."

She watched him go then opened the door to the bower. She thought about what Nurse had said to her: *Men must find their pleasure or they bend out of shape.* As she unpinned her clothes, she found herself turning that warm, promising idea over and over in her mind.

Ivy woke, wondering why she felt so rested. Ah. Rowan wasn't in bed with her. She must have gotten up early and run off to find Nurse. Ivy stretched like a cat. The shutter was half open, letting in a beam of sunshine that fell across her bed. She loosened the front of her shift, opening it up so that her breasts were bare in the sunshine. She closed her eyes, enjoying the warmth, the decadence. She dozed like that for a little while, but then a grumbling tummy told her it was time to get up. One foot on the rushes. Then the other. She laced her shift again and reached for last night's dress.

No. Rose would have many fine dresses here, surely. She was a queen, and they were much the same height and figure. Ivy walked across to the chest and flipped the lid open. She pulled out a few dresses and lay them on the bed. Then she turned her attention back to the chest. Under the dresses were other things: a little statue carved of stone, a wooden box with beads in it, a bronze hand mirror. Ivy pulled it all out curiously, laying things on the floor to look at each more closely. Rose had so many lovely things. It was hardly fair. So much jewelry! Rings and brooches and bracelets and necklaces. Bolts of cloth from far and exotic places; cloth Rose hadn't even bothered getting made into dresses. Jealousy pinched her. Ivy pulled a length of fabric against her cheek. The smooth silkiness of it. Farther down in the chest was a tiny carved box. She reached for it. It was locked. This far into the bottom of the chest would surely be where Rose hid her tokens of love, the ones Heath must have given her. For who had a lover but didn't receive presents from her beloved? Colored ribbons or polished stones: things that meant nothing to those who didn't know that they had been given with love? Ivy became desperate to know what was in the locked box. She sat on the bed with it, grabbed the knife off her belt, and prized the lock. No luck.

Frustrated now, certain she was missing out on seeing something important, she cast her glance about and saw a rock that Rowan had been playing with yesterday. Ivy hefted it in her right hand. Then took aim and—*crack!* The lock popped off. She smiled and flipped open the box.

Just as the door opened and Nurse walked in.

Ivy realized immediately it didn't look good. Rose's things strewn everywhere, the lock busted on the floor, and her with her fingers inside the box. Disappointingly, it only contained keys.

"What are you doing?" said Nurse.

"Nothing," Ivy said, aware it was a ridiculous thing to say.

Nurse strode across the room and took the box from her. "You must not touch."

"I was only looking," Ivy said, ashamed. She felt very young.

"These are your sister's things. Leave them be."

Embarrassment made Ivy bristle. How dare the nurse speak to her this way? Did she not realize Ivy's father was the most powerful man in all of Almissia? She drew herself up tall. "These are my sister's things," Ivy said, "and my sister asked that I come here in her stead. She did not say, however, that I had to be commanded by *you*. Forget not that you are her servant and so *my* servant."

Nurse glared at her briefly, then dropped her eyes and said, "Rowan has been asking after you. Would you come and play with her in the hall?"

"As soon as I am dressed," Ivy said, pleased she had won the game. "Go on, leave me be."

Nurse left without another word.

Ivy hadn't had a moment's peace all day. Nurse had gone to visit her sister, so Ivy had full responsibility for Rowan. What a handful the child was! Demanding games, whining endlessly for food, losing her temper over the slightest frustration, and pissing over herself—and Ivy's shoes—in a forgetful moment. One thing Ivy knew for certain after today was that she never wanted children of her own. She'd sooner poke her own eyes out than have to endure that burden daily.

Finally, when Rowan had found herself keenly interested in watching the cook gut the deer for the evening's meal, Ivy had slipped away somewhere quiet. She ended up in the chapel garden, taking deep breaths of late-afternoon air laden with the scent of flowers. She sat on the grass and drew up her knees, resting her forehead gently on them. Breathing in, out. The clatter of the hall seemed very far away. The afternoon wind rushed through branches in the distance and was cool upon her cheeks.

"Ivy?"

She looked up. Wengest stood by the garden gate, smiling.

"Hello," she said, returning his smile.

"Have you lost Rowan?"

"Rather on purpose. I'm sorry."

He laughed and let himself into the garden. "Rose wears that same weary expression when Nurse isn't about. May I sit with you?"

"Of course."

He folded himself up on the grass next to her. She saw him glance quickly and slyly at the top of her dress, where her breasts strained against the fabric. Well, they were magnificent, after all. Will Dartwood had said so, and plenty of other men had been enamored of them in the last few months. She shifted so she was leaning back to show off their size and shape to full advantage.

Wengest, however, was looking up at the sky. Ivy's eyes followed his gaze. Both deliberately not watching the other: She knew this game. A buzz of bright heat was growing between them, and Ivy could have laughed. What fun! Wengest wanted her. He *wanted* her. Even though she was his sister by marriage. There wasn't enough room in her heart for the vain pride the thought aroused.

"I've often thought if sunset only came once a year, everybody would stand outside to watch it," Wengest said, "but because it happens every day, we don't bother."

And here he was, trying to impress her with his observations. He was a king, yet not so very different from the young men she had dallied with. She dropped her head and looked up at him from under her eyelashes. "It's very pretty. Sad to take one's eyes off something so pretty."

He smiled at her, responding to her flirtation. "When I first saw you there, with your head on your knees, I thought you must be crying. But I can't actually imagine you crying," he said. "You are always so happy."

"I am full of happiness, Wengest," she said. "But I had my head on my knees thinking." She frowned a little . . . prettily, she hoped. "I have things on my mind."

A silence. Then she continued, in a low voice, "Do you want to know what's on my mind?"

Wengest shifted so he was looking at her face-on. "Yes. Tell me."

Her heart sped up, as it always did when she crossed the first line of a man's defenses. "You," she said, on a hot breath.

Feeling the first bite of the fire, he dropped his gaze and shook his head. "And why would I be on your mind, Ivy?"

Careful now, don't go too far. "Because you are gracious and kind and handsome. And I think my sister is very lucky to call you her own. I should consider myself very lucky, if I were she. And I should do whatever I could to *please* you."

Wengest glanced at her again and Ivy saw desire in his eyes. But his reason overrode it, and he said nothing.

Ivy was about to push a bit harder against his resistance when a loud shout broke the afternoon quiet. Rowan barreled through the open gate and threw herself at Wengest.

"Raaaar!" she shouted. She brandished a wooden plate in one hand and a stick in the other.

Wengest laughed and caught her around the waist. "Slow down, soldier."

"I'm not a soldier. I'm a warrior queen. Like Bluebell."

Wengest's laughter immediately dried up. "Ah, I see. Well, warrior queens don't tend to make friends easily, and they almost never marry. So perhaps you should play with your poppets instead." He gave her head a rub. "Go on, off with you. Ivy will take you back to the kitchen."

Ivy suppressed a sigh and stood up to take Rowan's hand. As they left, she glanced back over her shoulder at Wengest, who sat on the grass watching them. She recognized the look in his eyes and she swayed her hips a little in response. Sighere had called her a pain in the arse, and Heath had said she was barely a woman. Well, neither of them was a king. Wengest was, and he wanted her. She knew it.

Ivy didn't see Wengest for three days after that, and often found herself wondering whether he was avoiding her on purpose. Tupping a servant girl was one thing, but climbing aboard one's sister-in-law was quite another; perhaps he thought it easier to be blind to her rather than battle his conscience. She tried to get on, keeping busy with Rowan, but the longer she went without seeing him, the more convinced she became that she had to have him. Lying in bed those three nights, she imagined him sliding his rough hand under her shift to close over her breast, pressing his hot tongue into her mouth. She would tingle from her toes to her navel with the thoughts, while Rowan slept unknowingly next to her.

Then on the fourth night, late, when she should have been sleeping, she found herself hanging about by the door of her bower, gazing at Wengest's bower across the way. There was light flickering under the shutter. He was awake. But would she be welcome? No, she was being a fool. He was avoiding her for a reason. She wanted to stamp her feet. Why should Rose be the lucky one who got to marry the king of Nettlechester? Of course she would have been too young a few years ago, but now she was marrying age. Queen Ivy. It sounded divine.

Footsteps caught her attention. The serving girl came into view, making her way down from the kitchen quarters. Ivy's heart started; she was about to duck inside, then changed her mind.

Instead, she stepped out and hailed the serving girl with a raised palm. Her heart sped a little with fear and excitement.

"Princess Ivy?"

"I expect you're going to visit the king? To lie with him?"

The girl gulped. "I . . . No . . . No, of course not. I mean . . ."

"Go away. He is married to my sister, and I won't have a piece of rubbish like you soiling her husband's reputation. Leave now or I'll tell Rose, and she'll put you and your family out of Folkenham."

The girl put her hand over her mouth to suppress a sob and turned on her heel and ran. Ivy waited until she was out of sight before turning back to Wengest's bower and, with determination, striding toward the door.

As she pushed it in, she heard him say, "Edlyn?" So the serving girl had a name and he'd bothered to learn it. He rose in her estimation.

"My lord," she answered, emerging into his sight and closing the door behind her. His bower was richly decorated with tapestries and furs, lit by two tallow candles that smoked greasily. The candlelight glinted dimly off golden cups and ornaments that were mounted on the wall or placed on the dresser and table. Coals in the hearthpit glowed low and warm. In the middle of this sat Wengest, wearing only his undershirt and an expression of surprise.

"I sent her home," Ivy said, as though it explained everything.

"You won't tell Rose?"

Ivy almost laughed. He was worried his infidelities had been discovered. She shook her head. "I didn't come here to spy on you. I came here to give you what you need." She untied the front of her shift and pulled it off her shoulders, so her breasts were free.

"No, no, no, Ivy," he said, gathering the blankets around him. "You don't understand."

"Help me understand, then," she said, knowing she was glorious half naked in the firelight.

"I don't . . . I wouldn't . . . Edlyn and I, we don't . . . I can't risk a royal bastard. You understand?"

Ivy struggled to comprehend. "Then what . . . ?"

"She pleasures me. While Rose is away. I'm a man and I'm full of desire, but she"—he indicated his groin—"you know."

And now Ivy was back on firm ground, because she understood "you know" as only a young woman could.

She sank to her knees next to the bed. "Then let me do that for you. I'm longing for it."

"Ivy, you're Rose's sister."

"Rose isn't here. I am." She climbed up on the bed and dropped her breasts in his face. A moment later the back of his knuckles was grazing her nipples. "Ah, yes, you know you want to."

She wriggled her way down his body, lifting his nightshirt slowly to reveal two hard hairy white thighs, and then a cock the size of which she had never seen before. It looked angry, red, surrounded by wiry hair. She almost fainted with desire.

"Ivy," he said, half a protest, half a gasp of pleasure as she fastened on to him with her mouth. To her bafflement, he leaned over and extinguished both lights—William always wanted to watch. Wengest groaned like an animal, and Ivy was warm with pride and vanity. The second-most-powerful man in Nettlechester, spilling his seed in her mouth. Why, that made her practically the most powerful woman in the land, and all without lifting a sword.

Not a real one, in any case.

Afterward, she snuggled up under his arm, and he seemed happy to stroke her hair in the dark and kiss her cheek, though he assiduously avoided kissing her mouth. Just as she was drifting to sleep, he spoke, his voice booming after the long silence.

"Ivy, you must never, ever tell Rose."

She roused herself and sat up. Her eyes had adjusted to the dark, and she could see his face contoured by gray hues. His dark brows were drawn down low. He looked so very serious that she experienced a pang of fear. "Oh, no. Of course not."

He lifted his hands to cover his face and sighed deeply, a sound so desperate it took her breath away. "What have I done?" he said.

"Nothing. You've done nothing bad," Ivy said, stroking his arm. "We're having a little fun, that's all."

"You're Rose's sister."

"It's nothing."

"I love my wife, Ivy."

"I know, I know," she said, twinging with jealousy all the same. "But she's not here. And I'll never tell."

He sighed again and Ivy grew impatient. He'd been taking his pleasure elsewhere a long time, if Nurse's observations were anything to go by. And it wasn't as though Rose were pining for Wengest. "Listen," she said, "I'll tell you something funny, and I know it will make you feel better."

He uncovered his face and fixed his gaze on her. "Go on, then."

She smiled, absolutely sure she was doing exactly the right thing. "Rose has a lover, too!" She giggled, waiting for Wengest to laugh as well. It was a joke, after all: both of them, getting on elsewhere then feeling guilty and furtive about it.

A vacuum of silence followed her laughter, however, slowly icing over her veins.

"She has a lover?"

"Yes," Ivy said. "Well, I think so. I mean . . ."

He sat up. "Who is it?"

Frightened now, Ivy became guarded. "I don't know his name. I don't know him. I don't really know anything."

"Then why do you say she has a lover?"

"I saw them together." Her pulse hammered in her throat.

"You saw them . . ." Words stopped up in his mouth. "Maava and all his angels, how long has it been going on?" He ran a hand through his hair. "Is Rowan even mine?"

"Of course she is," Ivy said in a rush, desperate to undo the damage. A joke? Was she mad? "She looks exactly like you. And I'm sure it was only the one time."

Wengest gently pushed her off the bed. "Go," he said to Ivy. "Forget what happened here tonight."

"Only if you forget what I told you," she said.

He shook his head. "Go. You are far too young to know what you're doing."

Ivy laced her clothes and cast one desperate glance back to Wengest on the bed. "She loves you. You ought not—"

"I said go!"

Ivy bit her lip hard to stop herself from crying. Then the door was swinging shut behind her, and she was outside in the cold evening air, wondering what she had done.

chapter 22

"Put the sword down, Bluebell," Ash said, her hand on her sister's forearm. The slight man stood silent and unyielding in front of them in the dim, cold inn room.

"No. Not until he says who he is and why he's been following us."

Rose agreed. "We know nothing about him, Ash. Let Bluebell handle this."

But Ash *did* know something about him. She knew he wouldn't hurt them, she knew he was important to her somehow, and she knew he was growing impatient with Bluebell.

"I won't speak until the weapon is sheathed," he said in a soft voice that belied the steel in his good eye.

"And I won't put away the Widowsmith until you speak," Bluebell countered. "Come on, fucker. Why were you following us?"

He sealed his lips together, looking almost like a child refusing to tell. Ash could have laughed, only she was so annoyed with Bluebell that the corners of her lips wouldn't lift. "Please, sister, you must trust me. He won't harm us, I feel it strongly."

Bluebell turned her gaze to Ash. "I feel the opposite."

A thrill of ice passed through Ash, gone before she could make sense of it. "Let him go. Trust me."

Bluebell hesitated and Ash studied the man more closely. He was older than her by ten or fifteen years, clean-shaven, with hair thinning on his temples and small pale hands. His bad eye was permanently fixed to the right. If he was afraid of Bluebell, he didn't show it.

"Please," Ash said, rubbing Bluebell's forearm. "Please."

Reluctantly, Bluebell sheathed her sword and sat back. Ash saw the man's shoulders untighten slightly. So he had been afraid, after all.

"What is your name?" Rose asked.

"Unweder," he said, confirming Ash's premonition.

"I am Ash," she said. "These are my sisters Bluebell and Rose."

He nodded at them in turn, but soon returned his gaze to Ash. He offered no more words, but Ash sensed he was willing to speak if she asked the right questions.

"Have you been following us?" she asked.

"I've been following *you*," he replied, and a jolt of heat went to Ash's heart.

"Why?"

"Because you make me curious."

"Why do I make you curious?"

He raised one eyebrow, and Ash wondered coldly if he knew about her Becoming, as Eldra had.

"I'm curious because you know what you are but you do nothing about it," Unweder said.

"And what am I?"

"An undermagician."

Rose and Bluebell exchanged glances.

Ash's heart thudded. "No, I am a counselor in the common faith." She held the edge of her green cloak up, as if to provide the evidence.

"Then you have ignored the wishes of the Great Mother because, I assure you, you were born for undermagic."

His words fell on Ash like sheeting rain on parched earth: soaking in quickly, but threatening to flood. Of course it was true, and she had always known it. In those long years at Thridstow, pretending to be less than the elders, she'd known all along that a fire grew inside her that could burn the study halls down. Unweder's words were both liberating and terrifying.

Ash became aware that Unweder—and Bluebell and Rose—were

all waiting for her to answer. "I don't know how to be an undermagician," she said at last.

"You need only a good teacher."

Bluebell butted in. "Enough of this nonsense. Prove to me that you don't mean my sister harm."

He spread his hands. One of them jerked meaninglessly, as if under the control of a careless puppeteer. "I can prove nothing."

"Then why were you trying to get into the room?"

"I knocked. Nobody answered. I was concerned that she was hurt."

"I didn't hear you knock."

"Bluebell," Rose said, "we were asleep."

"I would have heard," Bluebell said. "I sleep with my ears open."

"I believe him," Ash said. "We were tired. We hadn't slept for two days."

Bluebell harrumphed, but Ash could tell she was backing down now. Unweder was too small and weak, too half blind and hand-palsied, to pose a physical threat.

"Unweder," Ash said to him, "we seek an undermagician named Eldra. Do you know of her?"

"Yes, I do. I can direct you there easily. She lives many miles to the north of me. Perhaps you'll travel with me to my house. We can talk a little more of undermagic before you continue on your way."

Ash turned to Bluebell, who shrugged. "I expect you'll do what you want," she said.

"Rose?" Ash asked.

"If he knows the way, that can only be of use to us."

Ash turned back to Unweder. "We would be very grateful if you joined us."

He nodded, and Ash sensed he was hiding a sly smile. "Very well," he said. "We'll travel together."

Rose slept lightly, determined to be awake before dawn so she could see Rowan in the little bronze loop the old woman had given her. She woke repeatedly throughout the night, then finally rose while it was still dark to go and wait outside, leaving her sisters sleeping, passing the neighboring room where the strange Unweder slept. She found a long wooden bench behind the back wall of the inn and sat there to wait. The morning chill prickled her cheeks, and she shrank from a cold wind that found its way up the alley between the inn and the next building. Clouds lay on the horizon, but as they flushed orange she knew the sun was rising. She untied the seeing-loop from her belt and held it up to her face. The block of ice had softened, was starting to melt. Rose watched as the water gathered in the loop, suspended there by magic. Once the ice had turned to water, the surface rippled and the image formed: tiny, but perfectly clear.

Rowan, in her bed. She slept, long dark hair spread out around her. Ivy was curled on her side next to Rowan. Rose studied her daughter's sleeping face for long minutes, her soft cheek and black lashes. Then the sun got too high, and the water frosted over and began to solidify. Moments later, it was a block of ice again, cold to the touch.

Rose fought a sense of disappointment. No, not disappointment—just a feeling of not being deliriously happy. She'd looked forward to this moment ever since the old woman gave her the seeing-loop. The hard ache of missing Rowan had intensified, day by day, since they'd parted. But seeing her child was no substitute for feeling her hot, impossibly light body in her arms, breathing in the sweet-salty scent of her skin.

Still, Rowan was safe. There was no question. Bluebell had put her finest warrior in charge of her safe trip back to Folkenham. Now that she was home, she was no doubt being treated kindly. Even if Ivy wasn't particularly patient, Nurse was there. And Wengest loved her madly, Rose was certain of that. Rowan was a happy, safe, pampered little girl and Rose would see her again in a few short weeks. So why had she fixed the seeing-loop on Rowan, when she could have fixed it on Heath? It had been three years since they were last together, and it might be another three years—or more—before they could be together again. If she could see him every morning in his bed at the stronghold, that would be some comfort . . .

She leaned heavily back on the wall behind her. It wasn't fair. Was it too much to ask, to know the people she loved most were happy and safe, when she was destined to be apart from them?

❖ ❖ ❖

Bluebell didn't take her eyes off Unweder. She made him ride a long distance from Ash, and kept her eyes fixed on his slight shoulders. It was their second morning with the undermagician in their retinue. The cold water in her guts told her not to trust him, but Ash was determined to have him around. Bluebell couldn't make sense of it. Her sister had never shown any interest in men. That this man with his crooked eye and thin, crooked fingers could command her attention worried Bluebell. He was an undermagician: Could he enchant her? And if he'd enchanted Ash, what was stopping him from enchanting Bluebell, too? The experience with the witch in the wood, with her mud wall held together by magic, had terrified Bluebell. She liked to be able to know her enemy; or at any rate to see him coming.

Or going.

She glared at Unweder's back.

Rose rode up beside her. "The dogs are a long way back."

"They always catch up."

Rose nodded, looking behind her again. Bluebell sensed it wasn't the dogs she was worried about. "What is it?"

"Nothing."

"Good, then," Bluebell said, and they rode side by side in silence up the wide, grass-edged road awhile.

Then Rose said, "I saw Rowan in the seeing-loop this morning but she wasn't in the same bed. She wasn't . . . anywhere I recognized."

Ah, so this was the problem. Bluebell glanced at Rose. Her eyes told the story: She was panicking. "You see, this is why I didn't want you to have that thing in the first place."

"You never told me not to take it."

"I thought about telling you. But you're not a good listener."

Rose's eyebrows twitched downward.

"Rowan will be fine. Wherever she is, she's probably with her nurse, who takes good care of her; or her father, who adores her; or her aunt, who . . ." Bluebell trailed off, struggling to think of a single good thing about Ivy. ". . . who is her aunt," she finished.

Rose sighed, her gaze going out across the long grass. "I wish I wasn't so far from her."

"Have you asked Ash?"

"She says she can't see or sense anything."

"Then stop worrying."

"But she said herself, she has little control over what she sees." Rose's voice dropped. "She wasn't telling me everything. I'm sure of it."

Bluebell smiled. "Rosie, don't make problems where there are none. Listen to me. Perhaps they discovered her bed full of bedbugs and sent her to a different bowerhouse. Perhaps she was having such fun playing with Cook's little blond son that Nurse let her sleep there the night." She could see Rose's shoulders start to relax, so she continued. "The most you have to worry about is the intentions of a four-year-old cook's son."

Rose smiled weakly. "Thank you, Bluebell. That makes me feel a little better."

Bluebell dropped her voice. "What do you think of Unweder?"

"He's an ugly little man, is he not?"

"I don't care how he looks. I care that he seems to have some hold over Ash."

Rose watched his back for a while, then her eyes flicked to Ash. "Ash doesn't make bad decisions," she said. "Ever."

Bluebell turned this thought over in her mind. It had truth about it.

"He's unlikely to try anything despicable as long as you're around, Bluebell. He wouldn't dare."

"My sword is little use against magic."

"Magic isn't always bad."

Bluebell nodded. "I will watch him closely. As for you, stay close to Ash. Distract her from him. Be a good sister and talk girlish nonsense with her."

"Would that put your mind at rest?"

"Yes."

Rose smiled. "Then we have done each other a favor this morning." Rose touched her horse's side lightly with her foot to urge it forward. Bluebell hung back, at the rear of the retinue, never taking her eyes off Unweder, even for a moment.

❖   ❖   ❖

Ash woke to a light mist of rain. At first, she tried to keep sleeping, screwing her eyes shut. The rain lifted for a few minutes, but then intensified. She sat up to look for her moleskin in her pack.

That was when she noticed Unweder, lying on his side in the rain, very still, but eyes open. Looking at her.

She frowned. At first she thought she had misread the direction of his gaze. But then he blinked slowly, and she understood he was studying her carefully. The fire was low, giving his face a faint amber flush. She didn't want to speak and wake her sisters, who were both already under their waterproof skins. So instead she lay back down. He kept his good eye on her. Not sexual interest, nor even curiosity. Just watching her and blinking slowly.

She wasn't afraid of him, and she understood he wasn't afraid of her, either. Not the way Eldra had been.

She closed her eyes, wondering if he would watch her all night, while she slept.

Sleep slipped beyond Rose's fingers. No matter how many times she listened to Bluebell's reassurances again in her head, the cool itch of doubt persisted. She dozed, startled herself awake, wondered how close to dawn it was, dozed again, falling into troubled dreams where something had been lost and forgotten, something as vital as blood. Light rain washed over them on its way to the sea and she woke before dawn, sticky with humidity under her moleskin cloak. She sat up, fumbling at her waist for the seeing-loop.

The light paused a moment behind the world, holding its breath. Or perhaps Rose was holding her breath.

Then the ice melted and shimmered and there was Rowan, lying on her side in a different bed again. She was on the move for some reason. And this time she was awake and crying, big openmouthed sobs. Nobody was there to comfort her.

The hot rush of fear made Rose's joints loose. She didn't know what to do with her hands; they seemed suddenly too big for her body. She clambered unevenly to her feet, gasping Bluebell's name.

Bluebell sat up, pale eyes open and hand on her sword.

"Something's wrong. Rowan's crying," Rose said.

Ash stirred as well. Unweder slept on.

"Rowan always—" Bluebell started.

Fear made Rose speak too sharply. "No, Bluebell. She's somewhere strange and she's crying. Something's happened. I have to return to Folkenham."

Bluebell sighed in exasperation.

Ash shook off her blanket and came to put her arm around Rose. "I think she should go."

"What could possibly have happened to her, Rose? She is in the care of her father, your husband, the king of Nettlechester. We are days away from Eldra, days away from . . ." Bluebell stopped, ran her hand through her hair. "Very well. Go. Be with your child." She cast a dark glance at Ash, who kept her expression neutral.

Rose was already gathering her things. "I hope you're right, Bluebell. But if I stay and tomorrow morning she's in another different bed, distraught and alone, then I will have made the wrong decision, and I'd be another day away from her." Rose's voice caught on a hook in her throat. *Please, Great Mother, protect my baby.* She was gripped by a powerful longing for Rowan's body: for her plump arms and sturdy knees, her impossibly elastic cheeks. She let out a little groan. "What is going on?"

Bluebell stepped forward, gathering Rose in her arms. Rose sagged against her sister's sinewy body. "She will be well, you will see," Bluebell said.

Rose straightened, brushing Bluebell's hair out of her mouth. "Thank you," she managed. Then she was running for her horse, running to find Rowan.

The sun was moving toward the center of the sky when Ash asked to stop and rest. Bluebell glanced around. Wide rocky fields riven by a narrow stream that ran, cold and urgent, over flat brown stones. A chestnut grove on a hill close by, the green leaves fluttering in the sun. She peered at it carefully but could see no movement, so she reined Isern in and dismounted.

Bluebell walked, then watered Isern. She fed her dogs while Ash and Unweder ate. Bluebell wasn't hungry, so she took a brush to Isern's mane and tail to look busy, even though her object was to watch her two companions. They talked quietly about the weather, the horses. Bluebell could tell they were dying to speak of other things, but daren't while she was there.

Then Unweder said, "You must excuse me a few moments," climbed to his feet, and headed up the hill to the grove.

Bluebell watched him, then turned her attention to Ash, who was rethreading the leather lace on her right shoe.

"Where's he gone?" she asked.

Ash shrugged.

Bluebell narrowed her eyes, turning her attention back to Unweder. He disappeared into the trees. She patted Isern's flank and whistled for her dogs, who were madly snuffling in rabbit holes, then went after Unweder.

"Leave him be, Bluebell," Ash called behind her.

But Bluebell ignored her.

In the shade, the temperature was a skin-shiver cooler. She couldn't see him, but she heard him humming and followed the noise. What was he up to, sneaking off to hide among the trees? Did he intend to perform some evil magic on them? Her hand went to her hip, fingers grazing the grip of her sword lightly. He came into view, standing very still with his back to her.

She gestured to the dogs to sit and crept up to him slowly, listening to his humming, growing more suspicious. She couldn't see where his hands were: no doubt in front of him casting his spell. Just as she was about to grasp his shoulder, he sensed her approach and half turned with a gasp.

Bluebell stifled a laugh. Not casting a spell. Pissing.

"Should I have asked permission?" he said, turning his body away with impossible-to-conceal embarrassment.

"Don't mind me," she said, "I've seen men piss before."

"You frightened me," he said. "I've got it on my shoe now."

"A bit of piss on your shoe isn't going to slow us down," she said, folding her arms. "I didn't mean to frighten you. I wanted to see what you were doing."

"Why?"

"Because I don't trust you."

Unweder raised one eyebrow and spread his palms languidly. His good eye met her gaze; his bad eye gazed off into the distance. "I don't care."

"If you fuck with my sister, I'll cut you to pieces."

"I intend no harm to Ash. She has a rare talent and I only want to help her."

"Why?"

"Because she needs my help."

"That's not what undermagicians do. Undermagicians only care about themselves. They don't make friends, and they live as far from one another as possible."

"It isn't always true."

"Enough people believe it to be true."

"Enough people believe that women can't be warriors or kings. Is that true as well?"

She didn't answer, choosing instead to stare at him and see if he would squirm.

"You should ask Ash about the dream," he said.

"What dream?"

"Her dream. Ask her about it. And perhaps ask her why she hasn't told you."

"She tells me everything," Bluebell said, madly trying to remember if Ash had mentioned a dream recently.

Unweder lifted a shoulder. "Then I suppose you needn't ask her." He smoothed down the front of his tunic. "We should be moving on. There's an inn off the road about two hours from here. My destination and yours aren't far now." He moved away, through the trees, while Bluebell watched him with a churning gut. He was slippery. In her world, she knew where things were, and they either stood still or moved slowly. But he slid about like an eel between rocks. And she didn't like it. She called her dogs and went back down the hill.

Later that afternoon, with Unweder far enough ahead of them to be out of earshot, Bluebell pulled her horse up close beside Ash's and said, "Unweder said to ask you about the dream."

Ash's eyebrows shot up. "He did?"

"What dream does he mean?"

"I haven't spoken to him about any dreams." But Ash was being evasive, and Bluebell could tell.

"Is there something important you're not telling me?" Bluebell said, trying not to sound threatening but suspecting she failed. She had never acquired that cloak of nicety that padded conversation.

"I . . ."

Bluebell saw Unweder turn his head, glance over his shoulder at them, then turn away. Was that a smug smile on his face? Bluebell's gut itched.

"Tell me. If there's something wrong and it's important, you should always tell me."

"You don't understand, Bluebell. This is not something you can solve by pulling out your sword."

"Then there is something wrong?"

Ash kept her gaze in front of her. "No."

"What is it?"

"Nothing."

"Then why are you so pale?"

Her voice dropped to a whisper. "Because I am afraid."

"Of him?" Bluebell gestured toward Unweder. "Just say the word, and I'll get rid of him."

"No, not of Unweder. I'm afraid of myself."

Bluebell realized she wasn't going to get further with Ash. It wasn't the right time: too much noise and movement. "I'm sorry you're afraid, Ash. And I'm even more sorry you feel you can't tell me something so important it makes your skin pale and your eyes haunted."

"Don't be angry."

"I'm not angry. I'm sad."

"Don't be sad," Ash said, with less conviction. "Put it out of your mind."

Bluebell nodded. "Of course. It's your choice whether you trust me with your secrets. So long as you know you *can* trust me." Her eyes went once again to Unweder and she had the uncanny sense he knew what they were talking about, and that he was laughing at her. "I can't say, though, whether you can trust him."

"I believe he wouldn't hurt me."

Bluebell smiled tightly, and didn't say what she was thinking: *I believe he* would *hurt me.*

By the afternoon of the fourth day with Unweder, Bluebell had prevented Ash from speaking more than a few sentences with him. Every time Ash sat down and asked him a question, Bluebell would interrupt, find her a chore to complete, or sit so close she couldn't talk freely. Ash knew Bluebell was being protective, but Ash didn't need protecting. Not from Unweder. He knew about her dream—Bluebell's questions had alerted her to that fact—and yet he wasn't afraid of her. He hadn't run or demanded she take herself off in exile. He could help her; she was certain of it.

So when Unweder announced they were drawing close to his home, the disappointment was heavy in her belly.

"Already?" she said as she reined in her horse next to him. Bluebell had made him ride ahead of them the whole way.

He pointed along the road in front of them. "In ten miles you'll reach a road that forks. Head west. The plains open up after the rocky heath. A tall standing stone will tell you that you are near Eldra's home. Head north a little way and the path will appear, running up a hill. Though I should tell you, she is notorious for protecting the way."

Ash thought about the corn dollies she had seen in her vision and shivered softly from the inside.

Bluebell gazed up the road, then back to Unweder with her mouth in a hard line. She nodded once. "Thank you."

Unweder looked as though he was fighting a chuckle.

"We should take him safely to his front door," Ash said.

"He can manage," Bluebell replied.

Unweder glanced at Ash. "It's only a mile from here. Perhaps Ash could accompany me while you rest?"

"Yes," Ash said, at the precise moment Bluebell said, "No."

"We should be on our way," Bluebell continued, with a steely note of warning in her voice.

Ash, made bold by the days of frustration, dug in her heels. "Bluebell, I am going to take Unweder home."

"Then I'll go with you."

Ash knew Bluebell's will was inexorable. "Very well."

Unweder inclined his head politely. "This way," he said.

They followed him down a narrow path that was little more than a track beaten into the grass. Tall trees grew on either side of it, spring saplings competing for the sun. A deep, green smell surrounded them, ancient deadfall between layers of mud. For some reason, the smell made Ash feel calm, as though the bubbling anxiety in her soul was ebbing away. She took deep breaths of it.

Within ten minutes, Unweder's house came into view. It sat in a hollow, with a narrow, lichen-spotted stone path leading toward the front door. Bare trees crowded close around it, and fallen leaves clung to the roof. Green and yellow mold bloomed in patterns on the thatch.

"Here it is," Unweder said, reining in his horse at the top end of the path. "Would you like to come in?"

Ash looked to Bluebell. "Please?" she asked.

"I'll wait here with Isern and the dogs," Bluebell said.

Ash dismounted, her heart speeding a little.

Unweder indicated the front door. "I'll take my horse around to the stable. Let yourself in."

Bluebell dropped her voice to a whisper. "If you're not back out in five minutes, I'm coming in. I've already lost one sister from this journey. I won't lose another."

Ash swallowed guiltily. "Give me ten."

Bluebell nodded.

Ash advanced down the path. A cool breeze moved past her, shaking the hedgerows. It seemed winter still clung around his house: The hedges were so bare, she could see the fine gray twigs inside. She pulled open the front door, and cold ash swirled up from the hearth-pit. The house was narrow: The walls seemed only a few feet apart. It smelled of woodsmoke and rosemary, and faintly of mice. Vines had grown through the shutter slats and died, leaving brown skeletons behind. The only light came from the open door, illuminating long wooden benches crammed untidily with objects, bent floorboards, and a narrow rectangular bed built into a corner of the room.

A shadow moved across the light, and Ash turned to see Unweder.

"That was quick," she said.

"I'll let him walk about for a while and tend to him later." He pulled a stool over next to the hearthpit and bent to stir the ashes. "Pass me a log and some kindling."

Ash looked around and saw a basket full of kindling beside the woodpile behind the door. She brought him a log and an armful of sticks. He arranged them in the hearthpit. His movements were considered and precise, almost gentle. He didn't have the strength in his upper body that a man like Heath had, and it made him seem almost effeminate. Only he was not womanish, either. Sex seemed almost a ridiculous proposition with Unweder.

"Will you sit?" he said, gesturing to the other side of the hearthpit.

"I'd best not. Bluebell is expecting me."

"Your sister is a bully."

"That's her job."

He smiled. With a noticeable effort, he stilled his hands. Then he held his fingers over the fire and rubbed them softly against one another. The kindling burst into flame.

"How did you . . . ?"

"You could, too."

Ash's heart thudded. "I could?"

"You have no idea of your power."

"If I'm so powerful, why can I not control it? Why could I not even reassure Rose her daughter is safe, or see if my father will survive this elf-shot?"

"You can't control it because you haven't focused it yet."

Ash considered him. The flames loaned a warmth to his skin that was usually missing. "I have so much to ask you."

"Go on then."

She laughed. "I have about a minute left."

"Then ask me your most pressing question."

She thought hard, then said, "Why are you not afraid of me?"

"Should I be?"

"You mentioned the dream to Bluebell, so you must know of it. Eldra sensed it on me. My Becoming is blighted, and I am a danger to others."

He shrugged. "I am curious about you. About this latent ability that fills you."

"It doesn't fill me," Ash said. "It overflows."

A thumping at the door. "Come on, time's up," Bluebell shouted.

Ash glanced to the door, then back to Unweder.

He dropped his head and stirred the fire with an iron poker. "Go. Don't upset Bluebell. She already hates me."

"She's only trying to protect me."

"You'll be back," he said.

"I don't know if I will be."

"You will."

"Have you foreseen that?"

"No. You'll be back because you have nowhere else to go."

Ash swallowed hard. "Goodbye," she said. "Thank you for your help." She opened the door. Bluebell stood waiting.

Would she be back, as Unweder said? The thought filled her with a deep, dreadful thrill, and she suspected he was right.

chapter 23

B luebell woke with a prickling sense of something being amiss. Almost immediately, she realized Ash wasn't next to her in the bed. She sat up and looked around. They were in a tiny, stuffy room in an inn less than a day's ride from Eldra. Ash was nowhere in sight. Frowning, Bluebell climbed to her feet and pulled on her cloak. She cracked open the door. The village was quiet; the sun hadn't yet fully risen. She would have heard if Ash had been dragged out against her will, so she assumed her sister had slipped off as silently as possible. Trying not to be missed.

Bluebell closed the inn door behind her and headed down the shady path toward the stream they had crossed yesterday. Ash had been secretive and strange since she'd met Unweder, and Bluebell didn't much care for it. She demanded nothing more of Ash than her loyalty and honesty, and now she doubted she had either. Somehow, half the story was missing.

Across the stream, in the tangled shadow of a willow tree, Ash stood very still. A finger of yellow light broke over the horizon and caught the corner of Bluebell's eye. She shielded her gaze and watched Ash a moment, then approached.

Ash, sensing her, snapped into awareness and opened her eyes.

The ground shook under Bluebell's feet, dislodging a small rock that tumbled into the water. Bluebell faced her sister across the stream. Beloved Ash, somehow a stranger.

"What are you doing?" Bluebell called.

Ash shrugged helplessly. "I'm sorry."

"Come over to this side," Bluebell said, gesturing with her hands. "Talk to me."

Ash picked her way over the stepping-stones and came to Bluebell's side.

"Why are you sorry?" Bluebell asked. "What are you doing out here?"

Ash sighed, and sank down to sit on the soft undergrowth at the edge of the stream. The sun over the horizon flushed the treetops yellow-bright. "Can you see them, Bluebell?"

Bluebell cast her eyes around, alert. "See who?"

"Of course you can't see them. Only I can. The unseen world, teeming with elementals. I can see them all. I only have to focus a little . . ." She held her thumb and forefinger half an inch apart. "And there they are."

Bluebell crouched next to her. A bold blackbird fluttered down low to look at them. "Are these the elementals you called to help me at Shotley?"

"Yes."

"But they helped. So they are good?"

"They are neither good nor bad. They don't like me, but for some reason they have to do what I ask. When I can make the magic work."

"So this is magic?"

"Undermagic. Unweder is right; I've known all along. I should never have gone to Thridstow. I am an undermagician, by birth, just as you are a warrior. There is nothing else for me."

Bluebell considered this carefully. She knew what it was to be born for something. "But you once told me it affected you, made you sick."

"It's all still balancing out. Some things make me feel sick, some don't. But I can feel a little black spot on my soul. Like a flower of mold on bread."

"Then perhaps it's not right. Perhaps you shouldn't do it."

Ash's gaze was far away. "I don't know if I can stop."

"Then try."

Ash turned to smile at Bluebell. "Perhaps you are right, sister. But there's something more I have to tell you, and I promise you won't like it."

Bluebell sat back, crossing her legs in front of her. She was suddenly desperate to piss, but didn't want to interrupt Ash now that she had decided to talk. "Go on."

"The dream."

"This is the business Unweder spoke about?"

"Yes."

"So there is something you haven't told me?"

"Yes, I'm sorry. But I've seen my Becoming in a dream. And it is blighted."

"Blighted?" Bluebell repeated, an ancient dread shuddering in her belly. "Are you sure?"

"Yes. Again, I have always known it in some ways. Perhaps you have always known it of me, too."

Bluebell thought of the intense protective instinct she had always had toward Ash. Was it just sisterly love or was there a creeping shadow of fear that somehow she was marked?

"I am destined to take thousands with me unless I slip into exile," Ash said. "Eldra knew. She sensed it when I traveled to her in my mind. She told me not to come near her."

"But . . ."

"That's right. I'll have to leave you to meet her alone."

Bluebell was torn. She had already lost Rose to some nonsense, and now she was to lose Ash. She wondered how much Unweder's influence was pressing on Ash's mind. But more than anything, she felt a deep pity for her sister, who was so young and so fragile, and yet somehow had to endure such a heavy load. Her heart squeezed. "Are you sure?" she said again.

"I am," Ash answered, her voice catching on a sob. "The only way I can be certain this horrible event won't happen is if I take myself out of the world. If I am alone, then I cannot hurt anyone."

"Where will you go?"

"I don't know."

"Go home to Almissia," Bluebell said. "We have land to the northwest, hunting land. You can have whatever you need: gold to pay someone to build you a house, a servant, anything. You are a king's daughter. If this is truly meant to be your fate, then at least suffer no hardship. Return to Blickstow and tell Dunstan. He will organize it all for you."

Ash palmed tears off her face. "Thank you, Bluebell. But all the riches in the world cannot buy me happiness, if I must be away forever from those I love."

"Forever?"

"How else can I be certain?"

"I don't know about forever," Bluebell said. "Maybe the path that takes you on this Becoming may one day be behind you. I will never stop hoping for your return."

Ash smiled weakly. "I hope you are right, sister." She patted Bluebell's thigh. "But you must let me find my own way. I will not return to Blickstow. I can no longer risk being in places where there are many people. As soon as I have led you as far as I can, I will find a place near a small village, perhaps by the sea."

"In Almissia? Under your father's rule?"

"Maybe. I don't know."

Bluebell bit her tongue. "How far can you lead me?"

"I'll feel the limit. Eldra will start to resist me. I've sensed every undermagician in every hut and hole since we crossed the border into Bradsey, prickling under my skin, pushing me away."

Bluebell gazed at her sister's face: her fine skin and liquid eyes. She struggled to understand. Her world was plainer than Ash's, painted in broader brushstrokes. But she would let Ash go for now, and later, when Father was well again, she would find her.

As the day grew warmer and brighter, the pressure grew stronger and harder in Ash's mind and heart. The time was drawing close: time to leave Bluebell, time to take up her exile. This moment had been coming since she first understood the dream, but that made it no easier to accept. But despite the guilt at leaving Bluebell alone, despite the despair at separating from her family, there remained a small tingle of excitement.

The farther north they went, the more elementals came out to see her pass by. It became easier for her to communicate with them in her mind, and she didn't feel so sick afterward. Clearly, this was a power the Great Mother had given her. All she needed to figure out was the reason for her power, and how to use it best. And she wouldn't get those answers from Bluebell.

But she knew where she might get them.

The pressure didn't come solely from within, though. Slowly, as they made their way up the road, she felt Eldra's resistance to her. As Unweder had said, Eldra had protected the way to her house fiercely. Along the way were charmed stones, woven mats buried under a thin layer of dirt, cotton ribbons tied in trees. Bluebell didn't notice these things, but Ash certainly did. A fine web of Eldra's magic, stretching out thirty or forty miles from her house. Ash was certain her presence was felt along those silken threads; Eldra knew she was coming.

It wasn't until the crossroads Unweder had spoken of that Ash simply couldn't go any farther. As she tried to turn her horse to the west, her ears started to ring loudly.

"What is it?" Bluebell asked when Ash pulled up.

"I . . ." The pain in her head was sudden, intense, and she gasped.

"Ash?"

Ash dismounted and ran back down the road. Her stomach heaved and she bent over to vomit. When she looked up, Bluebell was behind her, holding Ash's horse by the reins. "I take it this is as far as you can go?"

"It is." Her heart twinged.

Bluebell nodded. "Be safe, sister."

Ash took the horse's reins. Bluebell put her arms around Ash's middle and squeezed her tightly, then let her go and took a step back. "Send news if you can."

"Bluebell, I . . . I don't know what's going to happen. I don't know if I should contact you. I don't . . ."

"You are my sister. You won't ever fall out of my life completely. I have faith we will see each other again. In happier times." Bluebell glanced off to the road that headed west. "I will travel better alone."

"Yes, without Rose and me to slow you down. But do be careful."

"I'll be with Eldra by noon tomorrow."

"Be careful with Eldra."

"She's my father's sister."

"She's an undermagician."

Bluebell fixed her in her gaze. "As are you. Apparently." She grew suddenly intense, hunching up like a great spider preparing to attack. "Ash, now that your power is growing, can you tell me if Father will recover?"

Ash pinched her brain for the answer, but it slipped away. "I'm sorry, Bluebell. I don't know. I hope so. But I'm still not so good at seeing the future." She was getting better at commanding the elements, though. She said it again in her mind. *I command the elements.* A cool shudder of pride.

"I hope Eldra can help," Bluebell said, sounding uncharacteristically unsure.

"I believe she can," Ash said, squeezing her sister's hand. "Take care."

Bluebell squeezed her hand in return, hard enough to bend the bones. "You also," she said. Then she was pulling away, returning to her waiting dogs, to Isern, to her future as king of Almissia.

Ash felt she was choking on the emptiness as she watched Bluebell move off to the west. Then she wiped away her tears and looked back toward the south. It was time to return to Unweder.

Bluebell found it easier to travel without her sisters. She only had herself and her animals to account for, so she could push herself a little farther, a little faster. Still, she had to find a place to stop for the night. She was in the wilds of Bradsey now, a chaotic landscape of rocky heath punctuated by ancient gnarled groves strangled by vines and thick with moss. No inns for miles. She didn't want to sleep in the open, so when night fell she took herself into one of the groves and found a small clear area, where it looked as though lightning had struck a tree and burned down all the saplings. It smelled of old ash and dirt. She sent Thrymm and Thrack to bring her a rabbit and started a fire. She gutted the rabbit with her knife, fed the innards to the happy dogs, and spitted the rest on a spear to roast. As she sat with her back against the struck tree, listening to the sounds of night and the crackling of the fire, she realized her body was aching. No, her ribs. Her ribs were aching. She couldn't remember how she'd hurt her ribs.

Then she understood. She hadn't suffered any physical injury. Her ribs were hurting because she was unhappy. Today, she had lost her favorite sister. Hundreds of miles away, her father lay under an enchantment. And her body was aching from the weary pressure of these sodden clouds.

Thrymm sat up, ears pricked. Bluebell was instantly on alert. "What is it, girl?"

Then she heard it: a crack in the undergrowth, between the trees. Somebody was approaching.

More than one somebody. The dogs ran to her side, watching as four men emerged—from different directions—and formed a loose semicircle around her. Behind her was the mound of deadfall. There was nowhere to run.

She dropped the rabbit in the fire and leapt to her feet, the Widow-smith in her hand. She whistled the dogs forward and ran at one of the men. The dogs took one down, barking and snarling furiously, but the other three raiders flanked her immediately. She slipped between them, trying to make them approach her front-on so she could protect her back and sides. Cold steel flashed and she felt searing blood pouring from her ribs. Her heart thundered behind her eyes. Why hadn't she put her mail on? Where was her helm? The first raider dropped his arm a little too low and Bluebell judged her timing perfectly, slicing vertically into his head. The blade became momentarily embedded in his skull, losing her a fraction of time. She warded off another blow, but it glanced off her arm. More blood. The wound in her side pulsed hotly.

She swung, with precision and speed, right across a raider's knees. He fell forward, nearly tripping his friend. Thrymm was on him a moment later, tearing out his throat. Only one left. Bluebell pulled all her strength toward her, crippled his sword arm. He dropped the blade with a clang. Bluebell lifted her sword to bring down on his head. A moment later he had a knife in his hand and plunged it into the soft flesh between her shoulder and collarbone, then withdrew it with a satisfied grunt.

The force and speed were still in her arms as she split his skull in two. Then she dropped her shield and sheathed her sword, dismayed by the amount of blood she was losing. It covered her hands. She looked around. Across a raider's body, about ten feet away, lay Thrack.

"Oh no," she said, hurrying over. She placed her hand over the dog's ribs. No movement, no breath. "No," she said again, and tears squeezed from her eyes. "Come on, girl, breathe." She couldn't distinguish the dog's blood from the raider's. Thrymm was there now, whining softly. Bluebell touched the dog's head with her bloody fingers. "I'm sorry, girl. She's gone. She's gone." Bluebell coughed out a sob. Thrack had been with her for eight years. "She's gone," she said again, sitting back on her haunches and letting herself cry. The wound in her shoulder had stopped bleeding on its own, but the one in her side was leaking blood alarmingly. What was she supposed to do? There was no help anywhere nearby. If she could get Isern to take her to Eldra tonight . . . She didn't much like the idea of traveling in this much pain, but feared that to spend the night here without help could mean she didn't wake up in the morning.

She looked down at Thrack's body again, then reached bloody fingers to touch the back of the dog's neck. Thrack had loved being scratched right there. Bluebell sniffed back tears and snot, and stood. "We're going to give her a hero's send-off, Thrymm," she said, glancing around for fallen sticks. She had to move a little way into the grove, breaking off twigs and small branches, then bringing them to the center of the clearing. She used her ax to chop larger branches. She took each raider's sword to form a rectangle, then between the blades she began to build a funeral pyre, one layer at a time, small enough for the body of her beloved dog. All the while, she ignored the wound in her side, fearing to see how much blood she was losing.

She was too far from help and she knew it. She wouldn't make it to Eldra's and she had no idea in which direction the nearest village was. They had left the last of civilization behind that morning. So, out here in the wilds with her dogs and horse, she would probably die alone. To distract herself, she kept building the pyre, until it was as high as her hip. Thrack lay very still on top of the raider's body. Bluebell bent to scoop her up and laid her gently on top of the pyre. Then she soaked the pyre with Ash's fire oil, lit it, and stood back. Her knees were weak, so she sat. A slow ache pulsed in her side, a growing darkness moving up her chest, rib by rib. Cold shuddered inside her, very low, between her navel and her spine, making her legs shake.

She pulled her knees close and leaned back on a tree trunk. Thrymm sat next to her, leaning her warm body against her. Bluebell put her hand on Thrymm's head, felt the smallness and lightness of the dog's skull, and thought about her own smallness and lightness, her own impossible ephemerality. The fire bloomed, pressing its pattern of light against her eyes. Then her eyes were closing, the coldness growing. The thought glimmered on the edge of her mind: Perhaps it had been a mistake to come here. Perhaps she should have let her father die and taken up her place as Almissia's leader. Now there would be nobody left to rule. Only Ash knew of her plans for Rowan, and Ash had taken herself into exile.

An immense sadness gripped her. Not despair. Just sadness that the dark was coming before she was ready for it. She would have moaned, but there was no breath left in her lungs.

Amber light fluttered. A sound—a soft, sucking wind—passed her ears. She wasn't dead. Firelight flashed and faded as she struggled to open her eyes. Hoofbeats approaching. More raiders, perhaps. They would finish her quickly. Still her fingers stretched out sightlessly for her sword. She tilted her head back and opened her eyes. The moon was silvery blue, just on the other side of full. A strong wind drove streaky clouds across it. The moonlight moved, the firelight moved, her vision wavered. The whole world appeared to be shaking to pieces, and the hoofbeats and barking grew closer. She thought of Sighere: Had he gathered her retainers and come to look for her? What use was their help now? She was mortally wounded.

Next to her, Thrymm started to whine. She tucked her tail between her legs and trembled against Bluebell's side. Bluebell tried to focus. The sound was coming from every direction at once, like an army approaching but at high speed.

A flash of gray-white between the trees. Then on the other side. Bluebell blinked hard, trying to clear her vision. A horn sounded in the dark, a great echoing war horn. It thrilled her to her core, sending warmth pulsing through the cold dark inside her. She forced her eyes open. The world swung into sharp focus.

From the trees, a ghostly rider burst into the clearing. Behind him came a retinue of riders and dogs made of gossamer and shadows. The head rider galloped toward her, pulling up suddenly. His horse reared up on its hind legs and whinnied loudly. Bluebell sat, unable to move, staring up at him. He dismounted with a thud, as though he were flesh and blood. Bluebell was at eye level with his thigh. She saw every detail of his clothing—the stitched shoes, the leather straps around his gaiters, the hem of his cloak. But all of it was pale and silver-gray, there but not quite there. He crouched in front of her. Her heart hammered, making the blood pump quicker from the wound at her side.

"Bluebell," he said.

"Who are you?"

"Your father's father. Sent by the Horse God."

"Am I to join you?"

He shook his head. "It is not your time. You have many more battles to fight."

"I am mortally wounded."

He removed the glove from his right hand and reached it toward her side. As he touched her, a brilliant white light exploded into her mind. She could see now this was both her grandfather and the Horse God himself, eight feet tall and wearing his horned helm, traveling with his Wild Hunt. Her veins swelled, thrumming with sublime fire. The pain in her ribs was searing, but then when he pulled his hand away, it disappeared completely. She touched her skin with bloody fingers. She was whole again; the wound was gone.

At once, the coldness that had been making its claim on her withdrew. She could see and hear clearly. The rider climbed back on his horse and looked down at her. "Save my son. Save Athelrick."

"I will."

"And Bluebell," he said, lifting the reins, "beware your sister."

"Beware my . . . ?"

But he didn't hear her question. With another blast of his war horn, he was galloping away. The other riders streamed behind him in ghostly shades of silver and gray. Hooves thundered, shaking the ground. Dogs barked wildly. Bluebell watched them go until the last group of dogs disappeared into the trees. She was almost certain she saw Thrack among them.

Bluebell woke when dawn scraped the sky. Her clothes were bloody and stinking, but the skin over her ribs was smooth and well. She had dressed the other wounds last night, and neither of them was bad enough to stop her riding. So she ate and took to the road, Thrymm obediently, if dispiritedly, at Isern's heels.

The rocky ground grew smoother, the groves farther apart. Here and there, stones had been arranged in circles a few feet high. She didn't see another soul on the road. The plains opened up, vast and flat, covered in tussocky grass and wildflowers. Finally she came to the standing stone Ash and Unweder had told her of. She left the road and headed directly north, uphill. Long past the time when she should have seen Eldra's house, Bluebell began to worry. Had she missed it? Impossible, surely, if it was—as Unweder said—out in the open.

But then Unweder had also said Eldra was notorious for protecting the way.

Bluebell doubled back, then followed the same route. Still nothing. Thrymm sat down and whined softly. If only Ash were here . . .

But sometimes she and Ash could communicate without words, so perhaps she had a little of that magic in herself. She grunted at the thought of it, wanting so badly to be back inside a life where things were exactly as they seemed. Nevertheless she doubled back again, this time paying very close attention to the sensations in her body. There. A slight prickling behind her forehead. She shook her head and stared hard into the middle distance. And there it was. There it had always been. A little hut with lime-washed walls and a round, thatched roof. The path was right in front of her, right under Isern's hooves.

Bluebell urged him forward, up the hill. Six tall figures made of straw stood on either side of the path. They made Bluebell's gut twitch, almost as though they were looking at her. Isern began to shy, dropping his head and snorting. Thrymm hung back.

Bluebell dismounted, left them there, and continued on foot. She walked right up to one of the figures. Dead beetles were its eyes. Bluebell blew hard into its face. It didn't move.

But she didn't see the one coming from behind her. It put its rough arms around her waist. Her skin crawled. She drew her sword and spun around, calling out and cutting it in two. Then she slashed the others in half, as insurance, whistled for her dog, and stalked up the hill to her aunt's house.

The door was only shoulder height and painted green. Bluebell pushed it open and peered into the dark, smoky inside. A woman sat by the hearthpit, weaving with straw. She didn't look up.

"Eldra?" Bluebell asked.

"Ugh. You stink of horse magic," Eldra said.

"I—"

"Close the door, you're letting the light in," Eldra said. "We have a lot to discuss."

CHAPTER 24

Wengest and Rowan had been gone for three days, and Ivy was starting to worry. The morning after her encounter with Wengest, she had woken to find the bed next to her empty, and Nurse nowhere in sight. Wengest's bower, too, was empty, and she was forced to acknowledge they must be together somewhere. She was met with stony silence from Wengest's retainers, and her meals were brought to her wordlessly in her bower every day.

Wengest had clearly ordered everyone to tell her nothing.

By the fourth day, she had grown sick of waiting in her bower and walked down to the gatehouse to see if she could charm somebody into divulging something. Once again, she was met with resistance. So she went down the slope and walked for a little while around the base of the fort. She saw travelers and traders come and go; the whole world buzzing on as it always had.

Ivy felt young and foolish. She wished she had never pursued Wengest, and she certainly wished she had never said anything about Rose's infidelity. It was so clear now that it had been the wrong thing to do. Most of all, though, Ivy felt afraid, because the consequences seemed as though they would be very serious. Bluebell would punish her without mercy. Her hopes of a happy, comfortable life would flee from her fingertips.

Her foot hit a soft patch of ground, and she stepped back and swore softly. Cow shit. Her silk slipper drenched in cow shit. She slipped her shoes off and threw them on the ground, then found a place to sit and put her head in her hands to cry. It wasn't her fault! It was Rose's fault. Rose should never have taken a lover. Rose was a queen; she should have known better. Perhaps Bluebell would be angrier with Rose than Ivy. Perhaps Ivy would escape blame altogether. Right now, she wanted to be back home in Fengard with Uncle Robert and Aunt Myrtle. She was sick of being herself.

Hoofbeats in the distance drew her attention. She looked up and saw a small retinue approaching. She recognized Wengest's standard. Wengest was back! Relief flooded her body. She stood and strained her eyes to see Rowan, sitting on Nurse's saddle. But there was no Nurse, and certainly no Rowan. Wengest was returning only with two soldiers.

She hurried down toward the road to greet them. Wengest barely slowed when he saw her.

"Wengest!" she called as they thundered past. "Where is Rowan?"

"Go back to your bower," he grunted, without a backward glance.

Ivy stood on the road in their wake, tears welling in her eyes. He wouldn't have harmed the child, would he? No, of course not. Nurse hadn't returned, either. They were somewhere together. But why take them away from Folkenham?

Ivy swallowed hard. It was to punish Rose, wasn't it? And Ivy knew she needed to be far away from Nettlechester when Rose returned.

Her bare feet were soft on the hard road. She returned to her bower and immediately began to throw her clothes and shoes into her pack. Sighere had left for Blickstow nearly a week ago. She wished she'd gone with him. But she wasn't afraid to travel alone.

The door to her bower burst open and Wengest stood there, surrounded by sunlight. She froze, a linen shift rolled up in her hand.

"Ivy," he said, not meeting her eye.

"Wengest," she replied. She began to understand he was ashamed of what they had done. If he was angry at her, it was partly because he had lost his head with her. "Where is Rowan?"

"With Nurse."

"And where is Nurse?"

"With Rowan." He folded his arms in front of him. "They are both safe and comfortable. I love my daughter, Ivy. I would not punish her for her mother's wrongs."

Ivy felt compelled to defend Rose. "Only a little wrong, surely." She held her index finger and thumb a little apart. "No more wrong than what you were doing with the serving girl. Or with me."

Angry redness spread up his neck. "Don't you dare compare our situations! I am a man and a king. She is a woman. A mother."

Ivy shrank back.

He took a deep breath. Collected himself. "I can't have you here," he said.

"I'm going," she replied. "I'll leave today."

"You can't travel alone."

"I don't mind. I—"

"I am organizing something. Prepare yourself to travel in the next few days. In the meantime, stay out of my sight."

"I will," she said, stinging with shame and guilt.

He nodded curtly, then left.

Ash hesitated at the top of the path, looking down at Unweder's house. The chill of the gully was on her cheeks. Here, it was cold like winter, as though spring had passed Unweder by. The hedges were bare, and a few mottled-brown-and-yellow leaves still hung from the branches. She had a sense of standing on the edge of a precipice. And yet what was she to do? She couldn't be alone. Not forever. And she was certain he could help her understand her power. If she had to be in exile, and if he had said he would welcome her back, was this not the perfect place to be?

She went down the path and knocked at the door. No answer. Knocked again. Then gently pushed it open.

"Unweder?" she said softly. Inside, the house was warm. Embers still glowed in the hearthpit. Unweder wasn't here. She felt lost suddenly, as though it was a sign and she wasn't meant to be here. She turned, intending to leave.

On the long bench, several small jars stood in a line. Curious, she approached. She picked one up. Empty. The others, too, were empty. She wondered what they were for. She wondered what kind of under-magic Unweder practiced. She put the jar down and turned away from the door. Hanging from nails around the house were small charms and decorations: pottery shapes on ribbons, small mirrors, straw and feather weavings. She approached and lifted from a nail a long piece of string with a tiny clay pot on the end. It had a cork in the end. She put her fingers over it, then changed her mind. Unweder might be annoyed if she spilled whatever was inside. Hanging it carefully on its hook, she looked down and saw a large wooden chest. The latch wasn't closed. She reached for it to open it.

The door swung open. "Don't touch that!"

She whirled around, heart thudding in her throat, red-faced with guilt and embarrassment. Unweder stood there with a brace of rabbits in his good hand.

"I was going to put the latch down," she stammered.

He strode over and pushed the latch down himself. "Promise me you won't touch that. Everything else is yours to see and explore. Just not that chest." He was short of breath, and she wondered if he had sensed her and run back from wherever he was.

"I'm very sorry. I didn't mean to offend you. Your things are private, of course."

"I trust you." He went to the bench and laid down the rabbits. "I'll explain later."

"You don't need to explain at all."

He smiled at her. "I'm so glad you're back."

She smiled too, cautiously. "You don't mind?"

"No. You are very welcome to be here and to stay as long as you need to. I can make you a bed on the floor here by the hearthpit."

Ash wondered if she should doubt his intentions, but she pushed the thought away. If Unweder had any sexual desire in his body, it was slight and it was buried. She recognized this about herself, too: She was not formed for love and family as other women were. "I will earn my keep," she said. "I can hunt and fish. I can grind flour and make bread. Whatever you need."

"We can work together," he said, carefully putting the little jars aside. "When you've settled in. I expect you need to grieve the loss of your family."

She frowned. "They're not dead."

"They are dead to you, no? You can't see them again?"

Words stopped up in Ash's throat.

He approached. His tone was gentle. "I don't mean to be cruel, but you need to understand what you are doing. What you have already done. You have left the world as you know it. And now you will build a new world, starting in here with me."

Ash felt afraid of him then. His insistence weighed like lead, and she had a desperate urge to run away.

But then he smiled again. "There's no right way to feel, Ash. Take your time. I am quiet and I am out a lot during the day. You take your time deciding what you want. And you can leave whenever you like, though I would be sorry to see you go." He indicated the rabbits. "Would you care to help me prepare dinner?"

The routine tasks helped. Skinning and gutting the rabbits, preparing the turnips and carrots, chopping and boiling and stirring. Then, when the stew sat in its pot cooking and thickening, they sat opposite each other by the hearthpit and drank a cup of mead each. The smell of meat and spices made her stomach pang.

"Last time you were here you said you had many questions," he said, "though you only had time for one."

"Yes, that's right."

"Would you like to ask me another?"

She shifted on her stool, crossing her ankles in front of her. Her bare feet caught the fire's warmth. "Very well. Why can't I control this power?"

"Give me a specific example."

"My sister Bluebell has been asking me for weeks if I can see my father's fate. I get glimmers, but no clear picture. And yet, when I was in Thridstow, I often had visions of other people's fates. People far less important to me."

"All undermagicians have the sight, lesser or greater, and none of them seem capable of turning it on themselves with much success. But the sight is only ever a forerunner of what is to come, the power that eventually fills you up and comes direct from the Great Mother as her gift to you. Some do grow better at prophecy, but it is not everyone's gift." He shrugged. "I'm the same. I get flashes, often trivial. Nothing of moment, and nothing when I most want to know."

"Really?"

"Oh yes."

"Does it not drive you mad with frustration?"

"No. That isn't my gift. I stopped trying to develop the ability a long time ago, and if you stop trying it will wither away. You may feel the occasional dull urge, or you may try to bend your mind to it and make yourself ill. Either way, if it's not your gift, there is nothing you can do."

For some reason, this thought filled Ash with incredible relief. She imagined Bluebell asking her to see the future, and simply saying, *I can't. That isn't my gift.* But then she remembered Bluebell wouldn't be asking such things of her ever again.

"What is your gift?" Ash said.

"It's complicated. I'll explain another time. What do you think yours is?"

Ash bit her lip. "I'm not sure."

"You have no idea?"

"I have an idea, though I'm frightened to say it in case I'm wrong. In case you form expectations of me I can't fulfill."

"I have no expectations of you."

Ash dropped her voice, though she didn't know why. "I can see elemental spirits."

"Good."

"And I can . . . I can tell them what to do."

He went very still, though he was still smiling at her. "Also good. Very good. A very useful skill to have."

"What does it mean, though? Why would I have this power? They don't like it. They seem both fascinated and repelled by me, but my voice controls them as forcefully as a yoke on their necks."

A short silence. Unweder considered her in the smoky room. "I can't answer that now. But as you focus and develop your talent, it will become clear."

"Really?"

"Really. Focus on what comes easily to you. You will learn other abilities, but you are formed for something by the Great Mother's intentions. If it is elemental control, then let it be that, and relax."

Knotted muscles in her back began to release. He could help her. He already had. He had a wide view, the perspective she had been lacking. That those fools at Thridstow had been lacking. That her sisters, despite their good intentions, had been lacking. Unweder knew. Unweder could help her.

Exhaustion, mental and emotional, made her bones weak. She ate a little, then Unweder made her a bed and she curled up in it gratefully.

In the morning, before Ash opened her eyes, she was aware she was somewhere new by the smells. She remembered the previous day, the pain of leaving her family behind, and tried to burrow back into sleep where nothing hurt.

But it was full daylight, and Unweder was nowhere to be seen. She rose and went to the door to look outside. No, she was definitely alone.

She turned and caught sight of the chest Unweder had forbidden her to touch yesterday, and frowned.

It seemed he didn't trust her after all. He had put a box padlock on the latch.

Late-afternoon shadows and a tired horse told Rose she had to stop. Since she had drawn closer to the border of Nettlechester, the roads were busier and the inns more frequent. She paid a stable hand to take her horse and found a bench at the inn to order a meal and a drink.

The serving woman who approached her was trailed by a small girl, perhaps a little older than Rowan. Rose's heart twinged, seeing the child's poreless skin and liquid eyes.

"Hello," Rose said to the little girl.

She sank behind her mother's skirts. The serving woman put a hand in the child's hair. "It's all right, little one," she said. She smiled at Rose. "A few of the patrons have been annoyed that I have her here with me tonight. She's caught the rough end of a few tongues."

"But she's only a child."

"She's slowed me down. But my husband's away and my sister offered to look after her, but then she got sick." She shrugged. "I couldn't leave her at home alone."

"Of course not."

"It's only one night. Her father's home tomorrow."

"Are you helping Mama?" Rose said to the little girl.

She nodded enthusiastically. "I've been carrying plates."

"Good for you."

As she waited for her food, Rose watched the serving woman and her child. Here she was, a queen. She wore gold brooches and beads from exotic lands far away. And she would exchange it all to be a serving woman in an inn on the road out of Littledyke, who had her child with her and the child's father coming home tomorrow.

What waited for her back in Folkenham? She had almost changed her mind, a day out of Bradsey. She had almost headed for Stonemantel, to find Heath and tell him what had happened. Because an awful suspicion was growing inside her that Wengest had moved Rowan away from her deliberately. Every morning, Rose studied her daughter in the seeing-loop. She had finally come to rest in a rough-looking bed in a shadowy room, and was always alone and crying. Calling out, sobbing. Rose was certain she saw her little mouth forming the word "Mama" over and over, and she had to put the loop deep in her pack so her heart didn't break. But if Wengest had moved Rowan, what was the reason? Where had he taken her?

The hot nerve quivered in her heart. Her eyes followed the little girl and she felt tears slipping down her cheeks. Deep breaths. Perhaps it wasn't as bad as she feared. Wengest would never hurt Rowan. Some benign explanation awaited her, surely. But until she knew what that explanation was, she would keep moving as fast as she could toward home.

❖   ❖   ❖

Willow liked a simple life. Her days started early, before Heath was awake. She stole away every morning in the grainy dark before dawn to pray outside the front gate, begging the angel voices to come to her. Sometimes they did, with a whoosh of gray wings clattering and a tumble of words falling sharp and golden through her senses. And sometimes, there was nothing but the grindstone of her own brain. Afterward, though, she would return to the farmhouse and stoke the fire, make the morning's bread, tend to her father and his soiled bed-clothes, then start the dinner. She and Heath fell into a comfortable, if not companionable, routine. They spoke to each other little and he spent most of his days outdoors, tending to horses and hunting food. At night she slept on the floor of her father's room while Heath slept by the low-burning hearth.

On this particular day, she woke with a prickle in her senses that told her today would be different somehow. A vague wariness infused her as she slipped past the sleeping Heath and let herself out into the burgeoning morning. She paused a few moments on the doorstep, glancing around her. Nothing moved that didn't always move, like the branches and leaves and waking birds. Yellow light lay just beyond the horizon. Sweet floral smells were damp in her nostrils. Seeing and hearing nothing out of the ordinary, she moved off up the front path and made her way across dewy grass to the front wall and gate. She checked behind her once more, then decided that surely this prickle simply meant that Maava was working in her and that he or his angels would speak directly to her this morning. Excited, she was light of step as she made her way to her usual place on a collapsed pile of stones, sat, and withdrew her triangle to pray.

Maava, my lord and protector, speak to me this day that I might—

A small cry made her lift her head. At first she was put in mind of a baby bird, but when she heard it again she realized it was a child. She rose and followed the sound, across the rutted muddy path and into the woods. She strained to hear, wondering what great work Maava was calling her toward. The cries were hitching, uneven, and then one mournful word emerged. "Rabbit."

Willow found him a few moments later, a little dark-haired boy whose eyes roved and fixed on nothing. She caught him about his thin shoulder and said, very softly, "What ails you, child?"

He turned his face to her. It was covered in snot and tears. "Rabbit," he said again.

Had he lost a pet rabbit? That hardly seemed grave enough to be the work of Maava, but she told herself to follow and trust, gave him a little push ahead of her, and said, "Show me."

Their feet crunched on leaf-fall and popped on dead twigs. The boy navigated by brushing his fingers over tree trunks, and Willow came to understand he was blind. A blind child! The angels were certainly at work here.

Not too far distant, in the woods but well hidden, they came to an encampment. Willow's heart grew cautious as she saw the long figure of a sleeping man lying on a worn moleskin. She hesitated while Eni pressed forward. When he realized she wasn't behind him anymore, he turned and said, "Rabbit."

So the man's name was Rabbit. She advanced warily, then got her first good look at the man.

Not any man. As her gaze focused and she looked beyond the travel dirt and pale sickliness, she recognized her stepbrother.

"Wylm!" she cried, hurrying close now and kneeling at his side.

His eyes flickered, then opened. She took note of his sweating upper lip, the febrile gleam of his eyes, then remembered the dream she'd had about him and blushed despite herself.

"You must help me," he said. He extended his left hand, and she could see a festering wound barely covered by a filthy bandage.

Willow realized he was seriously unwell. "Can you walk? You must come with me back to the farm."

Then his eyes focused on her. He drew his brows together and said, "Willow?"

"Yes, it's me. The farm is only ten minutes' walk. Can you make it?"

"No, no. I cannot. I . . ." He trailed off, licking his lips.

Willow glanced back toward the house, even though the view was obscured by trees. Heath was there. Maybe he could come and fetch Wylm.

Eni was close, almost leaning against her arm. His eyes darted around like fish in a pond. "Who is the boy? Is he blind?"

"Yes," Wylm said. "I have rescued him. We have traveled so very far and now I fear I will not survive this infection."

"You will, for I have been sent here by a force greater than illness and death. Wait here. I will get what I can for you. I think . . . I think I know how to treat an infected wound." Countless times the little cuts she caused on her own body had grown red, and once one had even filled up with a volcano of pus. "My sister Ash left medicine."

"Anything you can do will help me, but I must ask you, please . . . don't tell anyone I'm here."

"Why not? Heath may be able to—"

"You must listen to me, for I am desperate and death is near. Don't tell them."

Willow opened her mouth to ask again, then stopped, chiding herself. It was no use asking questions when he was so ill. If he had good reasons, he could tell her when he was well. She was vaguely aware that Bluebell didn't like Wylm, and perhaps it was something as simple as that. So she said, "Very well, but I have nobody to tell."

"You are alone?"

"Heath is still with me, but Bluebell and my other sisters have left."

He visibly relaxed. So it had been Bluebell he feared. She supposed many people did.

"Still," he said. "Don't—"

"I'll say nothing. Now rest and I will return as soon as I can."

He nodded, closing his eyes.

Willow hurried back through the woods to the farmhouse. Heath was still asleep, but he stirred and rolled over when she came in. Any moment he would open his eyes. She went to the shelf above her father's bed where Ash had put the pots and potions she used. The little stone pot full of oily balm was there. She had been instructed to use it if her father had developed any infected bedsores, but so far the king had been magically free of such things in his unnatural stasis. She also found the pot of honey and crushed coriander seeds that would take down Wylm's fever. Willow put the pots in her apron then tore the bottom off her father's cloak for a bandage. In the kitchen, she seized the rest of yesterday's bread and some cold pheasant that had spent the night under a linen cloth. With these things and a skin full of clean water, she was halfway out the door when Heath woke.

"Willow?" he said blearily.

She paused, heart hammering. Why did she feel so guilty? This was Maava's good work she was performing. "I'm going for a walk," she said, with cool righteousness.

"Very well."

Then the door was slamming closed behind her and she was outside. Dawn had cracked over the horizon and golden light flooded among the trees in the wood. Into the forest she went, as Maava intended.

Think. Think. Wylm tried to clear his foggy brain. Bluebell was gone, but Heath was still here. He couldn't ask Willow to take him in, although shelter and a fire and medical care were the stuff of his desperate fantasies. Willow said she had some of Ash's medicines and Ash had studied such things so perhaps, perhaps he would survive this. Then what? If Willow healed him and then revealed his presence, he was still foiled. He wanted to take Eni and flee, but he could barely sit up, let alone walk. No, he had to make this situation go his own way somehow and if only his mind wasn't so darkened with feverish clouds . . .

He slipped into delirious sleep again, pinned beneath fiery cliffs, watched over by a formless shadow. Then flickered once more into wakefulness, hearing her footsteps returning.

"Hello?" she called. Her voice was soft, girlish. She had food. Medicine.

"Hoy," he managed in return. "This way."

She emerged through the trees a few moments later. Straight-backed, long-limbed like Bluebell, but in every other way different. A strange distractedness to her gaze, as though she were listening to voices nobody else could hear.

"Here," she said, kneeling with him, "take some of this. It's honey

and coriander and some other medicine Ash knows about." She hesitated, then unstopped the bottle and held it out to him.

"How much?" he asked.

"I'm not sure," she said, faltering. "All of it, perhaps?"

He struggled to prop himself on his elbows, and she tipped the pot
to his lips so the medicine dripped into his mouth. It tasted sweet at
first but left a bitter aftertaste.

"How long have you had the infection?" she asked, indicating he
should lie down again. She reached for his hand and unwrapped the
wound.

Wylm tensed against the expectation of pain. She was not gentle.
"It has been nearly a week since I received the wound. It looked a little
better for a time, when I had it in seawater every day. But traveling on
land with the lad, fiddling with dirt and ropes . . ." He winced as she
turned his hand to the light to look at it closely.

"And your fever?"

"Three days now." Or was it four? Or two? Time melted into itself.
He knew he had seen Eni eating leaves this morning. They must have
run out of everything.

"Let me clean this wound and dress it. It may hurt. Tell me about
the boy, and how you came to be here in the woods, while I work."

Wylm turned his face away, gritting his teeth as she poured water
on the wound and started dabbing at it fearlessly. The pain was like
fire. Worse than fire. He didn't want to tell her anything. He still
thought he might run the moment he was better.

But then she leaned forward, and a triangle on a chain slid out from
underneath her dress and he remembered the time he'd seen her praying. Remembered what she had said earlier about a force greater than
illness and death, and in a moment of clarity like the sun piercing the
clouds, he knew how to turn this situation to his advantage.

"I found Eni at his dead father's house—a friend of Bluebell's—on
a millet farm just out of Blickstow. He can hear, but he understands
almost nothing. His eyes don't work, either. A blind orphan? I couldn't
leave him. It would have been wrong in the eyes of . . . well . . ."

Willow frowned, concentrating very hard on the task in front of her.
"Grit has embedded itself in the wound. I'll have to dig a little."

"I trust you," he said. Excruciating pain followed, but then relief as white-yellow fluid poured from his hand and onto the blankets beneath him.

"This millet farm, was it manned by a fellow named Sabert?" Willow asked.

"I didn't ask his name."

"A stocky dark-haired fellow?"

"He was in his death throes when I encountered him, but yes, that seems a good description."

"I met him there once," Willow said, "many years ago when I was a child. I rode there with Bluebell. He seemed kind. It is sad that he is dead. I think I remember a small boy. This must be him."

"Yes, it must."

"You have grown, little one," she said to Eni kindly, then turned her attention back to Wylm. "You mentioned seawater."

"I cannot tell any more tales," he said. "I am tired."

Willow nodded. "I am sorry. I'm wearing you out." She wrapped the wound more gently, and he had to admit he already felt in less pain, in less hot fog. "Will you consider coming back to the house with me?"

Wylm concentrated hard to make sure the false words came out as smooth as truth. "I cannot. Bluebell hates me. I know she is your sister but she found out I . . . Willow, can I trust you?"

"I . . . yes. Yes, you can."

"She found out I still practiced the trimartyr faith of my homeland." He had, in fact, never practiced it, but he knew enough of the lore to convince her. "How could I not? Was I to accept eternity in the Blacklands simply because of whom my mother married?"

Willow froze, her little mouth a round O of surprise. "You do?"

"And I know you say Bluebell isn't at the house, but every pair of ears that hears about me is also a pair of lips that will tell her, and she will find a way to punish me. So I must stay here, and I must trust you because I think . . . I *know* that you, too, are one of Maava's good children."

"I am," she said boldly, quickly. "I do owe my sister loyalty, but my greater loyalty is to Maava and always will be. Here, I have brought you food and clean water and will do so morning and night until you are better and I will never, ever tell."

He smiled and she didn't smile back. It was odd. As though thoughts of her religion had robbed her of the ability to attend to social niceties.

She climbed to her feet, touching Eni on the head. "I'll be back," she said. "Fear nothing."

"I don't," he said. But he was lying.

Nothing felt as good as doing Maava's work, and day after day Willow returned to Wylm—morning and night as promised—and fed him and Eni. Wylm's color began to return; the wound grew less hot and pustulant. Freed from constrictions on what she said, she enjoyed retelling stories from trimartyr law for Wylm and Eni, and she reflected on what a liberty it was to be able to speak freely to somebody about her beliefs. She hadn't had such freedom since she last spoke with the trimartyr preacher who had converted her.

On the fourth morning, she grew tired of her own voice and he was sitting up and brightening, so she asked him about the sea journey he had alluded to on the first day.

He hesitated for a while before speaking, as though measuring his words carefully. His dark, intelligent eyes met hers smilingly. "Will you not be bored by men's business?"

"Not in the least. Here, give me your wounded hand. I will clean it while you speak."

"Eni," Wylm said to the boy, "go find some kindling for tonight." He waited for the boy to shuffle off then put his hand in hers. "Some things will upset him to hear, perhaps. Let me remember: I had been at sea for two days, then on the river for two before I came here. Eni and I were captured by raiders, and taken to King Hakon's lair on Ravensey."

Her mind reeled. "No! King Hakon is real? I thought he was just a character made up to frighten children."

"As real as you or me. And a nightmare to look at."

"Go back. Why did he capture you? I don't understand."

"They thought for some reason that Eni was Bluebell's son. The dead man, Sabert you called him, he was her lover."

She felt her face warm at the word "lover" and hoped he didn't notice. "Is Eni my nephew, then?"

"I don't know. He hasn't any of the noble beauty of your family." He looked away. "Forgive me for saying something so bold."

The flush in her cheeks intensified. She focused very hard on her work. "Go on. Hakon. What happened? Is he a monster?"

"He certainly looks monstrous. In any case, we made ourselves free. I am certain that Maava was guiding my hand when I managed to escape the island with Eni on a fishing boat. The first day was fair, but then gray clouds rolled in and the sea surges tossed us this way and that."

Willow turned his hand to catch the morning sunlight and see if she had cleaned it properly. Satisfied, she washed it with clean water again and held it still a moment for the morning air to dry it. She became very aware that it was Wylm's hand she was holding. Wylm whom she had dreamed of, who was now telling of his heroic escape from the monstrous Crow King. "Go on," she said.

"I left in such a flurry of panic. I packed blankets and skins, but forgot we needed water. When the rain started, the boy was cold and wouldn't stop shivering, but at least we managed to collect enough water to drink."

Willow glanced around, aware that she had stopped hearing Eni's footfalls. He traveled well without his sight.

"I had to manage the sails with a wounded hand. The rope got away from me once in a stiff wind, pulling the wound open again. I thought it would never stop bleeding."

"Hold still," she said, unstopping the pot of lotion she had brought with her and slathering it on.

"I knew where you had gone. Eni's father told me."

"Eni's father? But you said—"

"Yes, he told me everything before he died from a wound Bluebell herself inflicted in a jealous rage."

Willow's heart thudded to a stop. "What?"

"He told me . . ." His voice dropped, as though he was afraid somebody may be nearby listening. "He told me Bluebell had confessed to having poisoned her father on purpose because he was going to convert to the trimartyr faith."

Willow couldn't speak, as though her lungs were reluctant to draw in the air upon which the awful words hung.

"I'm sorry, Willow. I know you think highly of your sister."

Did she think highly of Bluebell? She found her terrifying, unyielding, yet with an uncommon kindness toward Willow. There was nothing confusing or hidden about Bluebell, and Willow found it almost impossible to believe that she would kill her own lover and then try to kill her father, especially as she appeared to be going to great lengths to heal him.

Or appear to be trying to heal him. Who was to predict what heathens might do? She tried to make her heart hard.

Wylm continued his story. "I sailed that little boat for days down the west coast of Thyrsland, looking for landmarks. It is a desolate coast, Willow. Gray mud and the skeletons of trees. A journey through a dead place. But I brought the boat in at the mouth of a muddy river, the Gema River, two days' journey north of here on foot."

"You walked? In your condition?"

"I walked." He nodded. "I walked with the boy. And I grew more and more ill. But I found you. At last." He looked at the bandage. "And you have helped me."

"You need to rest," she said, reluctantly releasing his hand. She needed to get away, needed time to think through all he had told her.

"Thank you, Willow," he said, and he looked uncertain though she wasn't sure why. She didn't understand men very well and she couldn't read his expression.

At that moment, Eni came stumbling back through the trees crying with an open mouth. He was covered from knees to nose with thick mud.

Willow climbed to her feet quickly and grabbed him. He resisted her a moment, then allowed himself to be comforted. "What happened? Did you fall?"

Eni sobbed wordlessly, but the tears in his trousers and the scrapes on his palms told the story he couldn't.

"The poor lad. He usually gets around so well for a blind boy," Wylm said. "I will take him down to the stream later and—"

"No," Willow said quickly. "Heath doesn't know him. I will take him home with me and give him a warm bath and tend to his scrapes." She could feel his ribs under her comforting hand. "And give him something to eat. You need to rest, and rest you shall. I will bring him back when I return with your evening meal."

"But what will you tell Heath?"

"I will lie for the good of a hungry child," she said, putting some steel in her voice.

Willow touched Eni lightly on the arm. "Eni," she said, "would you like to come inside with me? I can make you some food."

Eni swayed slightly. "Rabbit?" he said.

"That's me," Wylm told her. "That's what he calls me. Rabbit needs to sleep. Rabbit is sick," he said to the boy.

"After you've eaten and had a warm bath, we will come back and sit with Rabbit for a while," Willow said. "All right?" She reached for his hand, and he let her take it and pull him to his feet.

Wylm was already turned on his side, eyes closed. "Sleep now," he said. "I must sleep."

"I'll be back," she said.

"I know," he answered.

Eni dragged his feet across the road, so Willow used her warmest voice. "I know you don't want to leave Rabbit, Eni, but I will make you some warm porridge and wash your clothes and clean up those scrapes." She leaned closer and wrinkled her nose. "Yes, you are quite smelly. You can help me hang out your clothes on the lemon tree behind the house. It's a lovely sunny day." She remembered he couldn't see, and couldn't think of what else to say. But she did notice he had settled.

She opened the door, gears in her head turning over. Maava wouldn't want her to lie if she didn't have to, but neither could she tell Heath the truth. Wylm's story about Bluebell didn't fall outside the realm of possibility. Bluebell loved blood; everyone knew that. Somebody so enamored with death was out of tune with Maava's love. And certainly, Bluebell more than anyone was invested in keeping the trimartyr faith out of Almissia. What wouldn't she do to ensure that she became queen? *Come to me, angels. Maava, send your emissaries. I need to know the right thing to do.*

But no angels spoke, and when she looked at the dirty, skinny boy in front of her, she decided to choose the humane thing. She sat Eni at the hearth. Heath was nowhere to be seen, but he had started a fire before he headed out and oats were already cooking in a hanging pot. She stirred the pot, all the while studying Eni's face. He looked nothing like Bluebell. The ring on his finger, her father's insignia, was the only thing that suggested he might be related to her. She wasn't sure what to think.

Willow bent next to him and began to untie his shirt. "Come on," she said, "I'll give you one of my father's shirts."

When Heath returned, Eni was sitting in one of the king's shirts eating oats, skinny scabbed knees and shins emerging from the bottom, in a sunbeam near the back door. Willow was rubbing lye soap on his grubby clothes over a tub.

Heath paused, looking at Eni curiously. Willow's pulse seemed thick in her throat.

"Willow?" he said, not turning from Eni. "Who is this boy?"

"I don't know," she said. "I found him wandering in the woods this morning while I was out looking for mushrooms. He's blind and simple and injured and lost."

Heath knelt in front of Eni. "What's your name, boy?"

"Rabbit," Eni said.

"I don't think he knows his name," Willow answered, "but with your permission, I will walk to the village with him this afternoon and see if I can find his mother."

Heath climbed to his feet once again. "Just be careful. Don't tell anyone who you are or where you are staying."

"Of course not."

Heath was halfway over the threshold when she called him back.

"Heath?"

"Yes."

"Do you think . . . Who do you think did . . . that . . . to the king?"

"I don't know."

"Do you think it might have been somebody close to him?"

His eyes narrowed slightly. "Do you?"

"I don't know. Just like you. I don't know."

Then Heath was on his way, and Willow went back to scrubbing Eni's clothes and listening for angel voices to tell her whom to trust.

chapter 25

Bluebell closed the door, shutting out the daylight. Eldra's hut had only one narrow window, tightly shuttered, and a dirt floor under the rushes. The hearthpit was literally a pit dug into the ground. Bluebell had to duck under a low beam to get into the room. Eldra stood to greet her, and Bluebell saw straightaway that the older woman was crippled: Her hips didn't align, and one of her feet was twisted outward. She would never be able to travel.

Eldra held out her hand to Thrymm. "Ah, lovely girl," she said. Thrymm licked her hand gingerly. "You sit by the fire," Eldra said, rubbing her head, "while I talk to your master."

Thrymm sat back and watched carefully while Eldra turned her attention to Bluebell.

"So you are my niece?" Eldra said.

"I am Bluebell."

"You didn't know you had an aunt, did you?" She had very clear blue eyes and pale skin that was remarkably unlined. Her hair was gray at the temples, but otherwise brown.

"No, I didn't."

"But your sister knew."

"Rose said you had spoken to her. In a sending."

"I did." Eldra spread her hands. "Not that she listened to me." She moved toward Bluebell, her leg dragging behind her. Bluebell stood very still as Eldra stopped in front of her. The older woman stood only as high as Bluebell's breastbone. She looked up at Bluebell with her piercing gaze, and her nostrils flared slightly.

"You're the image of your father."

Bluebell felt the corner of her lip twitch into a smile. The comparison had been made so often, by so many, and still she found it pleasing. But then she realized Eldra's mouth was turned down.

"You and Father . . ." she started.

"There isn't much love there," Eldra said. "You must have guessed that. Did he ever mention me?"

Bluebell shook her head.

Eldra's eyebrows lifted. "Not once, eh?"

"No."

"And why do you think that is?"

"Knowing my father to be noble in thought and action, I would guess it was to protect you in some way."

"Protect *me*?"

Bluebell nodded. "Blood is important to him."

Eldra snorted. "Spilling it, perhaps." She limped back to the hearth-pit to poke the coals. "I suppose you'll be wanting to eat."

Bluebell's stomach grumbled. "I have food in my pack."

"There's cold salted rabbit under the cloth on the bench. Bread there. Cheese there." Eldra waved her hands vaguely and sat down.

Bluebell realized if she wanted to eat she had to fix it for herself, so she went to the bench and uncovered the food, assembling it on a plate. "Is there anywhere for my horse to stay?"

"There's a shelter, down the hill toward the stream. You can take him down there later. But sit with me now. Tell me why you are here."

Bluebell glanced over her shoulder. Eldra's back was turned to her. "Don't you already know?"

"Your other sister, the poisoned one, had an idea in her head about your father. I couldn't grasp it with both my hands. Besides, reading minds isn't my skill. Thankfully. I can't imagine anything worse than being privy to the nonsense that plays out in most people's heads."

Bluebell brought her plate and sat opposite Eldra, with the fire between them. The firelight made her aunt's pale skin warm.

Her aunt. Bluebell tilted her head slightly and considered Eldra.

She could see a lot of Willow in her aunt's face: the distinct widow's peak, the wide flat cheekbones.

"What are you looking at?" Eldra grunted.

Bluebell set to her food. "Family resemblance to my sister Willow," she said through a mouthful. "Rose and Ash look like my mother. Ivy is fair like me, but . . . pretty."

"You might have been pretty if you'd chosen a different path."

"How do you know what path I've chosen, if you can't read minds?"

"I may live alone, but I still travel and trade. I could hardly escape your fame. Besides," she added grudgingly, "you are family, and I have found out what I can about you all."

The rabbit meat was salty and sweet. Bluebell relished it, licking the bones clean. Then she wiped her fingers on her tunic and put the plate aside. "Father is sick, elf-shot. You will heal him."

Eldra's face was passive. "Will I?"

"Yes. Because you are an undermagician and he is your brother."

"What if I can't heal him?"

"You can try."

"What if I don't *want* to heal him?"

The question made no sense to Bluebell. "He is family. He is the king of Almissia. For the love of your own blood, and for the sake of peace in Thyrsland, surely you would try."

Eldra took a deep breath, then let out a huff. "Well, then."

"You are lame. Can you travel? I can try to get a cart from—"

"I can travel. Don't you mind about that. I can travel fast and well. Faster than you."

Bluebell frowned, not sure what she meant. "If that's so, then we can leave tomorrow."

"You are not my commander, young woman." As Eldra said this, a shadow crossed her brow and a swirl of embers lifted from the hearth-pit, then settled again.

Bluebell realized her heart was beating a little faster.

"You are wrong about Athelrick. He hasn't hidden me to protect me." Eldra shook her head, working her lips against each other as though she had tasted something bad.

Bluebell kept quiet, not wanting to ask. Not wanting to know.

"How old do you think I am?" Eldra asked.

"I know not."

"Sixty winters."

Bluebell shrugged. "Happy birthday?"

"Your father is fifty-eight winters, is he not?"

"I don't see what . . ." But then she did see what Eldra was trying to say.

Eldra was firstborn.

"Ah, yes," Eldra said, wagging a crooked finger. "Now you understand. I am a woman, and Athelrick is a man. I had first claim on the throne of Almissia, but he took it from me." She closed her fist, made a snatching gesture. "He doesn't believe women can rule."

Bluebell scrambled for a way to make sense of this. "The king of Almissia must be a warrior. Your father was a great swordsman, and Athelrick has no peer. Perhaps they believed it was not safe to have a king who couldn't lead an army into battle."

"A *queen*, Bluebell. Try as you might, you'll never have a prick." Eldra's lips curled into a smile. "A battle-ready warrior queen, who trained as hard as any man, who understood the strategies of war, who could charge herself with supernatural energy . . ." Eldra trailed off, her eyes turning to the fire.

"You?" Bluebell asked.

Eldra indicated her hip. "It was in a skirmish with those dogs of Nettlechester. Your friend Wengest's uncle knocked me off my horse, speared me through the pelvis, and kicked me down a ravine. I lay there six days, my body shattered, then finally dragged myself to help when I realized nobody was coming for me. When I got home, they had already crowned Athelrick king."

"They would have thought you dead."

"I wasn't when I turned up. Obviously."

"By then it was too late, surely. For the stability of the kingdom." Bluebell's mind worked, trying to make sense of it. "He would have known himself the better protector, the better warrior because he was whole."

"Believe what you like. You know in your heart what is fair."

Bluebell stared at Eldra in the dim, smoky firelight. The fire popped softly. She could hear the thrum of her pulse in her ears. Finally, she said, "Will you come?"

Eldra raised her gaze to meet Bluebell's. "I won't do it for love."

"Then do it for money. I can pay you well."

Eldra gestured around. "I live simply."

"Then do it for curiosity."

Eldra shrugged.

"What can I offer you?"

"Why do you want to save him? When he dies, you will be queen."

"My father's life is more important to me than my own ambitions."

"Really?"

"Of course."

A pause. "I am impressed." Eldra smiled mischievously. "I presume, though, that you don't intend to hand the kingdom over to me now that you know the truth."

Bluebell trod carefully. "Nobody in Almissia would know you or trust you. But you would be welcome to live with us in Blickstow and be part of the family, and use your skills to help keep the peace in Thyrsland."

"And you would let me do that?"

"Yes. Of course."

Eldra's eyes grew dark, birdlike. "It's more than your father ever offered. Why do you think that is?"

He was ashamed at how he treated his sister, but also terrified that if she was too close she could gather enough support to challenge him. "You will have to come with me, make him well again, and ask him yourself."

Eldra nodded. "Well, then. I suppose I will."

Relief spread warmly behind Bluebell's eyes. "We can leave in the morning."

"No, we can't. We must travel at night."

Bluebell sat forward, shaking her head. "My horse can't travel at night."

"He will, and so will I. Only at night." Eldra smoothed her skirt over her legs. "I will pull the strength of the Earth Mother herself from the ground tomorrow during the day, and we will leave once the sun has disappeared behind the world. We will travel nearly twice as fast as you could travel. The horses won't tire, though you may." Eldra smiled, a little cruelly. "You'll have to guard me during the day while I renew myself, and we'll travel all night while my body is at its strongest."

"Are you saying you can overcome your lameness with magic?"

"Well enough to travel. But most important, I can enchant the horses for speed and night vision. Ah, I see it in your eyes. How useful that would be in battle. But Athelrick thought not."

Bluebell ignored this, saying instead, "It's night. Can we leave now?"

"I need to renew myself. In the daytime. When the sun's warmth is in the ground."

"I don't understand."

"You will come to understand. Where is your father? Back in Blickstow?"

"At a flower farm, outside of Stonemantel."

"We can be with him within a week."

Bluebell's heart leapt. "Really?" Then a darker thought. Was he even still alive?

"It depends on how much magic I can draw out of the ground. But I think it should be an easy and fast trip. You must rest tonight, though, because there won't be much rest for the next week."

"My horse," Bluebell said.

"You go on. I'll get myself ready."

When Bluebell returned, Eldra had cleared a space for her to unroll her blankets on the floor. She stretched out her long frame while Eldra continued to potter about, gathering things and placing them in an embroidered pack. She closed her eyes and told herself to sleep, but it was much later, when Eldra had taken herself to her little bed under the lowest roof beam and the fire in the hearth had grown low, that she finally drifted off into a dream where Father wasn't really Father at all, but a gray-haired stranger who said one thing, but meant something quite different.

❖ ❖ ❖

Bluebell woke to the smell of dirt and ash, light pressing on her closed eyelids. She opened her eyes. The shutter was open and letting in a dazzling beam of bright morning light. Bluebell sat up.

In the beam of light, Eldra had cleared the rushes next to her bed and was digging. With her fingers.

"What are you doing?" Bluebell asked, her voice catching on sleep.

Eldra looked up. "The soil is very loose. Don't worry. I've done this before."

"But why are you digging?"

"This is how I renew myself with the Earth Mother's magic."

Bluebell's memory twitched. She had heard of such a practice, whispered with suspicion by those who opposed undermagic. *They bury themselves alive.*

"Can I . . . help?"

"I am quite capable of doing this myself, as I have done many times before."

As Bluebell watched, Eldra climbed into the pit she had dug and, sitting up, began to cover her legs and lower body.

"How do you breathe?"

"Don't believe all you've heard. I don't bury my face or arms." She packed the soil down hard and continued to scoop more in. "The sun will sit on this spot for an hour and warm the ground, and I will be in here, renewing, until nightfall."

"Renewing?"

"It is a kind of deep sleep, so I won't hear or see anything until I wake. In here I am safe; on the open road, I am prey to every under-magician in Bradsey."

"I won't let anything happen to you."

Eldra harrumphed. "And well you shouldn't. I'm doing you a very great favor."

"You are doing your brother a favor."

Eldra stopped for a moment, fixing her in a glare. "Oh no, I am not." Then she kept working, filling in her pit, finally lying down and scooping the last of the dirt onto her chest. "Make yourself food, and get the horses ready in the afternoon. Try to get some more rest your-self, if you can. I have to go under now."

"All right."

She closed her eyes and soon grew very still.

Bluebell stood and went to the pit, looking down at Eldra. Her pale face was relaxed. In the bright sunlight, Bluebell could see the little imperfections in her face. Fine wrinkles, little pale hairs growing on her chin. Bluebell watched her for a few minutes. She knew that, if somebody watched her with this intensity while she was sleeping, she would wake up. But Eldra didn't stir.

The little house was very quiet. She could hear birdsong from outside, far away in the woods. She glanced around, went to the bench, made food, ate it. Still the house was dark and quiet. She thought about going outside to chop wood, or find water, or . . . something. Anything rather than waiting in here with the deathly quiet.

She sat heavily by the cold hearthpit. It wasn't the quiet that bothered her; it was her thoughts. Her father had displaced Eldra as the heir to Almissia's rule. She tried to tell herself that it might have been the same had Eldra been a brother, crippled by battle, unable to lead an army. But she knew with sinking certainty that this wasn't the case. Eldra's other talents more than made up for an infirmity of the body. And then, rather than having her near so he could take her counsel and honor her, he had allowed her to slip into undermagician exile. He had allowed her to slip beyond the edge of his family's memory. And as much as she loved her father, Bluebell knew that was wrong.

Well, when Eldra cured him, she would ask him about it. The thought cheered her a little, and she sat back to wait in the soft quiet morning.

Bluebell saddled and packed both horses before sunset, then went back inside to find Eldra awake and risen, brushing dirt out of her hair.

"Ah, there you are," the older woman said.

"The horses are ready."

"Very well. Now, where have I put my pack?"

Bluebell reached for the embroidered bag, which had leaned beside the bench all day. Eldra moved to take it from her, her gait easy and fluid.

"You can walk."

"Yes, of course." She put her pack over her shoulder. "But only if I've spent hours buried in warm ground. It's not worth it most days."

Bluebell couldn't imagine it. If her body wasn't whole and healthy, she would do anything to make it so. Her hand unconsciously went to her side, where the Horse God had healed her.

Eldra saw the movement, and her nostrils twitched. "Ah, that's where the smell is coming from."

"Smell?"

"Horse God magic. Raw and gamy. The smell of a frightened weasel or distant pig shit. Faint, but there."

"The day before I came to you, I was attacked by four raiders," Bluebell explained. "They wounded me mortally. But the Horse God came, in the guise of your father."

She snorted. "That old fool. I suppose you should count yourself lucky then." Then, to her surprise, Eldra softened. "I'm glad you didn't die."

"So am I," Bluebell said with a laugh.

"But you can be sure every undermagician in every direction will be able to smell you. And that will make some of them angry."

"Why?"

"Because we spend endless hours and moments of delicate and finely balanced work gently coercing the Earth Mother to bless us with her magic. Then the Horse God bestows his instantly and with baffling partiality." She pointed to Bluebell. "Of course he loves you. You send him many souls."

Bluebell raised her hands. "I tire of magic, Eldra. I can't see it and I don't understand it. Are you ready to leave?"

Eldra tipped back her head and laughed loudly, way down into her belly. "Well, then. Let's be on our way."

Outside, the long afternoon shadows were dissolving into night. Isern looked at Bluebell uncertainly, and she rubbed his cheek. "All will be well, my friend," she said to him.

Eldra had her hands on the flank of her horse, muttering something under her breath. Then she approached Isern and Thrymm to do the same.

"Come," she said, climbing into her saddle with ease.

Bluebell patted Isern and mounted. She gently touched her heels to Isern's sides and the horse moved forward, as sure-footed as he was in full daylight.

Eldra smiled across at Bluebell, then shouted, "Go!"

And the horses began to gallop, flying over uneven ground as though it were smooth and flat. Soon they were galloping out across the plains, Thrymm fluid in their wake. Isern showed no signs of being tired or unsure of where he was going, and Bluebell relaxed into her saddle and let her aunt lead the way.

Eldra took her by a different route than she had come. She skirted the edge of the darkened woods Unweder had led them through, cutting instead across plains bracketed by trees and punctuated by standing stones. The waning moon was bright in a cloudless night sky, lending its uncanny silver light to the scene. As they skimmed along, Bluebell had time to take in only quick impressions. The broken tooth of a giant's tower glowing white in the moonlight; a huge black tree spreading its branches like a magician calling down magic from the sky; a small enclave of lime-washed huts like Eldra's built in the shelter of a crumbled ruin. The air smelled of damp earth, approaching rain, and the sweet-sour scent of night-blooming flowers.

It felt to Bluebell as if she traveled in a dream through this landscape of undermagic. She let her mind drift: to Ash, to her father, to Rose. Were they well and happy, so far out of the circle of her influence? She glanced ahead at Eldra, whose riding cape was streaking in the wake behind her, her plump behind bouncing in the saddle. Bluebell smiled. She liked Eldra, despite the fact she was an undermagician. Perhaps it was the effect of shared blood. In any case, Bluebell intended to ask her to come to Blickstow when Father was well again. She would do her best to make them settle their differences, even if it meant Father had to concede a little land to Eldra. It wasn't right for the king's sister to be living in a mud hut in the middle of the wild wasteland.

After a few hours, weariness crept into Bluebell's limbs. She didn't need much sleep: perhaps only an hour or two, but Eldra refused. "If we stop or slow down now, I have to cast the spell again and it takes up more energy. We'll be slower, I'll need longer to renew tomorrow, and my hip will start to ache. You must keep going."

So Bluebell kept going. Past midnight when the silver-gray landscape was so deserted it seemed as though she and Eldra were the only two people left in the world; through the hours when the grass grew slippery with dew and the night wind settled and sank. By the time the sky began to lighten, Bluebell's eyes were flaky with sleep, and the wheels in her mind had slowed to a grinding pace.

"We can stop here," Eldra said. "Have a little rest while I dig the pit."

Bluebell dismounted. They were in a quiet valley dotted with gray rocks and a few broken saplings. The sun slanted down on them, illuminating Eldra's gray hairs.

Bluebell spread out her blanket and fell gratefully into sleep, only to be woken up prematurely by Eldra. She opened her eyes. The sun was up, so perhaps it had been two hours, but she felt as though she had only blinked.

"Already?" she said.

"I have to get into the ground while the sun's first light is on it." Eldra's face grew serious. "You will stay awake, won't you? I can't defend myself."

"Of course." Bluebell climbed to her feet, shaking herself awake. "Do what you have to."

While Eldra buried herself, Bluebell went to her pack and pulled out her byrnie and her helm. She armed herself and sat on a rock near Eldra, who had already become smooth and quiet.

She watched birds fly over. She watched the wind move in sunlit patterns across the long grass. She heard a stream in the distance and grew thirsty. She found her water bottle and drank deeply. She wondered if it would be safe to leave Eldra for a few minutes to refill it; she decided it wasn't. She went through Eldra's pack, instead, and drank some of her water. Then she looked through the objects in Eldra's pack, and couldn't make sense of most of them. A rabbit's paw, a piece of round glass, a string of amber beads with dried blood smeared across them in a pattern, a dozen tiny cotton bags filled with dry herbs, a strip of parchment that smelled odd and familiar at the same time, and twigs and stones that looked as if they couldn't have been deliberately kept.

Bluebell returned to her rock. Eldra was motionless. Birds, wind, stream. Nothing had changed. Her eyes grew heavy, so she stood and began to pace. Isern and Eldra's horse were sleeping, Thrymm was sleeping, Eldra was sleeping. Only Bluebell was awake, pacing and pacing, waiting for the day to end.

Bluebell was eager for night to fall. But of course, with night came more travel, and no rest. She let Isern carry her, following in Eldra's supernatural train, but couldn't sleep for fear she would fall off. Besides, Eldra sounded a cautionary note before they began to move.

"The next two days take us through dangerous territory."

"Raiders?"

"Undermagicians."

"You're an undermagician."

"We are nearing the sea. The west coast of Thyrsland is a wild place, and those most interested in wild magic have gathered here. We are passing through a cluster of spiderwebs. We are surrounded on all sides, so there is no point in trying to go unnoticed. They will sense us."

"I have little defense against magic, Eldra. My sword appears to mean nothing to them."

"Between your sword and my magic, we can survive. Perhaps they will leave us alone. Come. To the sea."

They turned to the west. The headwind was strong, gusting through Bluebell's hair and shaking the branches on the bent trees that lined the gravel road down toward the ocean. The prevailing winds in Thyrsland came from the west, from the Great Ocean that raged for thousands of miles uninterrupted by land. In winter, the wind sometimes swept right across the country, bringing freezing rain to the calmer seas of the east coast. In summer, the wind came laden with balmy warmth from unseen southern lands. Tonight it was brisk, rank with seaweed, jumping down her throat when she opened her mouth to yawn. From time to time, a brief shower of rain passed over them, leaving a clean cold odor in its wake.

Around the middle of the night, Bluebell spotted a dark figure standing very still ahead of them.

"Ignore anyone you see!" Eldra called back to her, her voice made weightless by the wind.

They galloped toward the figure—a small child—and he raised his arm as they drew close. "Hey, now! Stop! Stop!"

Bluebell leaned forward in her saddle.

"I am dying! You must help me!" he called.

"It's a trap," Eldra shouted to her.

"Hey, now! Hey, now!"

They were drawing level with him and Bluebell risked a look to her right to see him more closely. She could make out no facial features, only a smooth gray surface. Her skin crawled.

"Hey, now!" he called again, and the voice came not from him directly, but from around him. Then, as they galloped past, his face lit up brilliant white, flashing once like lightning. He fell to the ground and was revealed to be only a creation of sticks and cloth. The flash stayed on Bluebell's eyes as they moved on.

They saw two more thralls on the road—lures for the unwary who would slow to stop and talk and be drawn into dangerous magic. Bluebell kept her eyes on the road, ignoring their questions or their pleading. Eventually they rounded down toward the cliff path, and the ocean came into view. Wild and green-black in the moonlight. Far, far out to sea, she thought she could see a tiny light, tossed this way and that, but when she looked upon it directly, it was gone.

The roar of the waves on the shore was deafening as they traveled south down the cliff path. Bluebell hung tight to Isern's reins, longing for the night to be over so she could sleep, knowing it would not be enough to purge the weariness from her limbs.

❖   ❖   ❖

As dawn light began to stain the sky, Bluebell found herself galloping down a steep road where the cliffs melted into a wide gray beach. The smell was thick and rancid. Black seaweed formed long mounds, with rotting fish tangled inside it. The bones of some large sea creature— bleached ribs and a skull caved-in and unrecognizable—lay half buried in sand. A great stone arch rose out of the cold currents, and the blue-black waves sucked and swirled through it loudly. Eldra had slowed, and Bluebell reined Isern in next to her.

"Is it time to rest?" she asked.

Eldra nodded. "I think I'll use the sand."

Bluebell's gut clenched. It wouldn't take long for Eldra to dig a hole in the sand. "I need at least two hours' sleep," she said.

Eldra fixed her in her piercing gaze. "The cycle must not be broken or slowed."

"But if you were digging in hard ground, I'd have two hours. Are you trying to punish me deliberately?"

Eldra pointed to the ground. "Lie down. Sleep."

Bluebell slept. For what seemed like a minute. Then Eldra was waking her again. "Come, I have to get into the ground. Wake, Bluebell. And beware of undermagicians."

"What should I do if one comes to speak to me?"

"Don't answer. Say nothing." Eldra was pulling sand over her legs and lying down. "And don't let them touch me. They'll try to steal my magic, and then you'll be stuck in the middle of nowhere with a lame woman who has no way to heal your father."

Bluebell fed and watered the horses, who then drooped their heads to sleep. For a while Thrymm was awake, too, but gradually she nodded off in Bluebell's lap. Gusts of wind picked up fine sand and blasted her face and hands. Her lips were dry and salty. The waves gathered and released, over and over. A flock of seabirds arrowed through the stone arch.

Bluebell watched them, mesmerized, alone at the gray edge of the world.

The slide into grainy sleep and out again was probably only momentary, but when she opened her eyes, she found herself looking at two bare feet in the sand in front of her. She jerked her head up, her eyes lighting on a tall, plump man with a wild black beard and two small black eyes.

She jumped to her feet, hand at her hip. Thrymm was up with a growl. Sleep fell away, but everything seemed too bright, the ocean's lonely roar too loud.

"Who are you?" the man said, in a gruff voice. He wore a necklace of seashells and bones that clattered softly when he moved. His ragged, filthy clothes smelled like stale sweat and piss. A large pink-white blister sat on his bottom lip, and his teeth were brown.

Don't answer them. Say nothing. Instead, she drew her sword and gestured that he should leave.

He lifted his head and sniffed the wind. "You smell like horse magic."

"Fuck off," she said, frustrated that he wasn't afraid of her.

He ignored her and turned toward Eldra, hand outstretched. Bluebell leapt in front of him and brought her sword down sharply, stopping short of his wrist. He looked at her, the wind picking up a long strand of his black hair. Then he sniffed again, and his eyes went to her ribs.

Bluebell's skin prickled.

He edged back toward Eldra. Bluebell drew her mouth down hard. If he was determined to die, then there was little she could do to stop him. She lunged, running him through his heart, and he crashed to the ground. Sand stuck to his blood, congealing into gory clumps.

He raised his hand, almost as though he was reaching out for Bluebell's help. She took a step back, too late. He pointed his finger and poked the air hard and Bluebell's side roared with pain. Then he collapsed to the ground and the pain eased to a dull, throbbing ache.

She tore off her byrnie and pulled up her tunic. There was no longer whole, white flesh over the wound the Horse God had healed. Rather, there was a long red mark. Bluebell poked it gingerly and then winced with the sharp pain. She ran her hand over it. Still smooth. Not open or bleeding as it had been that night. Gingerly, she smoothed her tunic over it again and shrugged into her byrnie.

The body in front of her couldn't stay here. She bent and grasped the undermagician's wrists, and dragged him down to the sea. Her side throbbed lightly. She waded in up to her thighs. The water was cold and the sand shifted under her feet. His blood smoked into the water, and she gave him a heave so the tide would catch him and carry him out to sea. She watched for a few moments, gulls screeching above her, the gray sky heavy and the sea licking her knees. He drifted out, resembling nothing more than a tangle of black seaweed.

Bluebell returned to the beach, kicked over the bloody scuff the undermagician's body had made, and sat down to wait for Eldra, her wound a dim, warm, inescapable ache at the edge of her consciousness.

Chapter 26

The tall pillars of the entrance gate to Folkenham made Rose's heart lurch. Beyond those gates was her answer to what had happened to Rowan, but she didn't know whether that answer would be a happy one or an alarming one. A late-afternoon rainstorm was blowing in; the wind lifted her hair off her neck and promised her only cold. She spurred her horse forward, deaf to the greetings the gatehouse guards called to her, deaf to the considerate questions of the stable hands, hearing only her own pulse hammering in her ears.

She walked up to the bower—her bower, the one she shared with Rowan—and pushed open the door. Her heart knew not to expect Rowan and all her noisy chaos, but seeing the tidy, quiet room with her own eyes still gutted her.

Ivy sat in a chair by the bed, working on an embroidery ring. Ivy looked up, then scrambled to her feet, dropping the ring. Her face was pale, and Rose feared the worst.

"Where is Rowan?" she said. Her words sounded as though they were coming from outside her. Everything in the room seemed too bright, as though it had gathered a halo of nightmarish light. She pushed her toes hard into her shoes, desperate to feel grounded.

Ivy put both her hands up, palms out. "She's well. She's unharmed."

"Where is she?"

"I don't know."

Rose blinked fast. "Then how do you know she's well and unharmed?"

"Because Wengest took her."

Ivy's answer deepened the darkness that had been growing around Rose's heart since she first noticed that Rowan was missing. Even when she had been worrying, she had believed somewhere in her body that everything would be well. But that belief had been misguided. "He took her?"

Ivy nodded.

"And they are coming back?"

Ivy shook her head. "Wengest is back. Rowan is . . . not."

A hollow emptiness opened up in her stomach, sucking the breath out of her. "Then I shall go to Wengest and demand he take me to her." She hurried to the door on tingling feet.

"Wait! Rose!" Ivy caught her sleeve.

Rose considered her sister's face in the soft afternoon light. She looked like a child, afraid of someone. Then Rose realized: Ivy was afraid of her. "What is it?" she asked, suspicion foiling her attempts to sound gentle.

Ivy licked her lips. "Wengest knows."

"Knows what?"

"About . . ." Ivy averted her eyes. "That you have a lover."

Rose's stomach turned inside out. She grasped Ivy's hands to stop herself from falling. "How could he . . . How did he . . . ?"

"He doesn't know it's Heath. He only knows you have a lover. *Had* a lover."

"But how could he know?"

"I saw you with Heath. In the woods."

Rose brought her attention back to Ivy's face, dropping her hands. "Ivy. No."

"I'm sorry. I'm sorry!"

Rose's body was falling apart. The worst had happened. The very worst. "No! Do you not know I'm a peace offering between Wengest's kingdom and Father's? You have put everything at risk."

Ivy stood back, her face growing impassive. "No, Rose. You took a lover. *You* have put everything at risk!"

Fury coiled in Rose's guts. She drew back and slapped Ivy hard across the mouth. Ivy staggered back, her hand over her face, blood trickling between her fingers.

"You bitch," Ivy spat.

"I don't have time for you now. I have to go find Wengest. I'll let Bluebell deal with you later."

Ivy's pupils shrank to pinpoints. Rose slammed the door of the bower behind her, took a moment to catch her breath, to slow her thundering heart. Her fingers tingled hotly from slapping Ivy.

She looked up toward the hall. Wengest. How dark would he be? How long did he intend to keep Rowan apart from her? She screwed her eyes tight and took four panting breaths, then headed up the hill. She was not so afraid of Wengest that she wouldn't fight him to get her daughter back.

Rain spattered over her as she walked the last few feet to the hall. She pushed open the tall, carved doors, letting in the late-afternoon light. A spitted deer was roasting over the fire, and the hall was filled with smoke and the smell of cooking. Two servants were setting up the tables for the evening meal, and Wengest stood in a dark corner talking quietly to a man she recognized as his cousin Gunther. Her heart hammered on her ribs.

"Wengest?" she said, much more slowly than she had intended.

His head snapped up. At the sight of her, his mouth set itself in a small, hard line. He said something quietly to Gunther, who nodded and moved away, walking past Rose with a smug expression on his lips.

"Out, all of you out!" Wengest called to the servants, who heard the threat in his voice and dropped the table they were moving into place. They scurried from the hall.

Then the door swung shut and it was just Wengest, Rose, and the roasting deer. The black fury on Wengest's brow had her wishing to swap places with the deer.

He strode toward her, dressed beautifully in blue and gold, with silver pins across his chest. In the firelight, he was handsome and stern and noble. Her husband. Not since her wedding day, when she had gazed at him with mingled apprehension and excitement, had she seen him look more like a king, with the power to bend anyone to his will. His dark glamour unhinged her knees.

"Where is Rowan?" she asked, breathless.

"I have taken Rowan and her nurse away from Folkenham, and I will not be telling you where they are. I love the child dearly and will see no harm comes to her, but—"

"She's missing me." Rose already knew this for a fact from Rowan's swollen eyes and tearstained cheeks.

"I expect she'll be used to being away from you."

"No, she's used to being *with* me."

"It seems to me you are often keen to be rid of her."

"That's untrue." *Was* it untrue? She thought about the unrelenting nature of motherhood, how she had longed to be alone with Heath, how she had traveled north from Stonemantel without Rowan as Bluebell had asked, with little protest.

Wengest held up his hands. "I won't bicker."

Rose swallowed hard. "So when are you going to tell me where she is?"

He smiled bitterly. "When you tell me who your lover is."

"I have no lover."

"Ivy thinks otherwise."

"Ivy is a little fool."

"She said she saw you with another man. Fucking."

Rose had never heard him speak so directly of sex. For some reason it frightened her—a sign that reason had no more use to him, that passionate rage had replaced it.

Wengest paced a few moments, then planted himself firmly in front of her, his voice returning to a normal pitch. "This is very simple. I am enraged that there walks a man in this land who has known my wife so intimately. I can't live with it. It fills me with a wrath so dark I cannot see its center. If you name this man, you can have Rowan back."

Rose scrambled for answers. "I have no lover," she said, but it sounded hollow even to her ears.

"Do you understand, Rose?" Wengest said, enunciating each word clearly. "You must choose. Your child, or your lover."

"It was nobody. Somebody. I don't even remember his name. It was just the one occasion." Her words stumbled over one another.

He shook his head slowly. "I am no fool, Rosie," he said. "You are not the kind of woman to take a random stable hand to bed. Who is it?"

A voice in her head was shouting at her, *Tell him! Just tell him! Get your baby back!* But fear held her tongue. Her throat was so dry she could barely ask her next question. "What are you going to do to him if I tell you?"

"I'll kill him, of course," he said.

His words, delivered so casually, turned her blood to ice.

"So name him. And I will give you back your child."

She opened her mouth, but no words would come out.

"Name him."

Wengest would never hurt Rowan. And as long as she still breathed, Rose could find a way to see her again.

"Choose, Rose," Wengest said, doubt creeping into his voice. "Your lover or your child."

But he would hurt Heath. He would kill Heath. No matter that Heath was his nephew—his favorite nephew. Hatred would bend his heart. He might not do it with his own hand, but it was certain Heath would not survive.

"Choose!" he shouted.

"I won't tell you his name," she said, her ribs bursting, her throat stopped up with sobs. "I won't let you kill him."

His face twisted. He was a monster now, with fiery cheeks and heavy black eyebrows and a raging mouth. She had made him angry; angrier than he was before. Before, his wife had simply been with another man. Now she had revealed she *loved* him.

"You are not a fit mother," he said, spittle flying from his lips and landing hot on her cheek. "And while I live, I shall make sure you never see my daughter again." He slammed out of the hall and left Rose in the darkened room, falling on her knees, sobbing into her hands.

❖ ❖ ❖

Ivy knew she couldn't be here when Rose returned. Her sister's rage and pain were too raw for Ivy's liking. So she threw her things into her pack and buckled it, closed the bower door behind her, and went the long way around the hall and into the village. She had a few coins left to pay for a room at the big lime-washed alehouse on the main street, and then she would persuade a trader to give her passage back to Fengard. She hated her sisters; all of them. She would be glad to go home and pretend none of this had ever happened. How dare Rose hit her? If keeping Rowan was that important, Rose should have kept her legs crossed. It was bound to come out sooner or later that she was having Heath on the side. Rose should be thanking Ivy that she didn't name Heath, nor allow the seed of doubt to grow about Rowan's paternity.

The alehouse wife eyed her lip warily. "What happened to you?"

Ivy touched her mouth. The ring on Rose's hand had cut across her bottom lip, and it had been almost impossible to stop it bleeding. "Never mind," she snapped. "Hand me my keys."

She went up the wooden stairs and let herself into a tiny room with white walls and fresh rushes. She propped open the shutter to let the last of the afternoon light in, then curled up on the bed to cry. She cried like she hadn't cried since she was a child, miserable and self-pitying, nursing a stinging lip and an equally stinging shame that would not go away.

She lay there for maybe an hour or so, as the rain intensified and the room grew dark and her stomach started to rumble. She thought she'd best clean herself up and go downstairs for food. She lit the lamp and rummaged in her pack for her little bronze mirror. What a mess! She wiped the tears and snot off her face, touched her wounded lip gingerly with her tongue, and cursed that she didn't look as pretty as usual. She needed to find somebody to take her home, and how could she do that with a mouth puffed-up and bloody? She ran a comb through her hair hard, pulling out knots. Then there was a knock at the door.

Curious, she cracked it open. Wengest stood on the other side. In the light of the hallway, he looked tired and damp-eyed. Had he been crying? Did men cry? Kings? She squirmed with embarrassment for him.

"I need to speak to you," he said, clearly making an effort to control himself.

Ivy opened the door wide and stepped aside. He came in, back erect, dark hair loose and flowing over his shoulders.

He glanced around the room. "Why are you here?" he asked.

"I couldn't be with Rose. I want to go home. I'll find a passage to-morrow and—"

"You're not going home."

She drew her brows down. "I'm not staying here."

"That's right. You're not staying in Folkenham. But you are staying in Nettlechester."

Heat crept up her chest. "What? Why?"

"Two years ago Bluebell offered you in marriage to Gunther—"

"Gunther? He's a hundred years old!"

He continued as though he hadn't heard. "—and I have been delaying on making a decision because you are young and I didn't want to foist a silly wife upon my cousin. But under the circumstances, a peace deal between Almissia and Nettlechester should be sealed as soon as possible. Gunther likes what he sees, and so he has agreed."

"What circumstances? Are you putting Rose aside? Bluebell will kill you."

Wengest leaned forward, drilling an index finger into her shoulder. "Don't threaten me with your sister. Bluebell is wiser than to punish me for Rose's mistakes. It is the will of your family, it is my will, and that is that."

Ivy's mouth opened and closed, but words wouldn't come. *Couldn't* come. She had always known this would happen one day. In fact, she had relished the idea from time to time: a wealthy husband, the keys to her own household, nobody telling her not to boss the servants so much. But this revelation was so unexpected. Why hadn't Bluebell mentioned it to her? She had hoped she might be married to a good-looking man. Certainly a much younger one. "I want to go back to

Blickstow first," she said, scrambling for time, "and talk to Bluebell about it."

"Bluebell had best do as I say if she wants peace to hold," Wengest said darkly. "She has no love for you. You know she won't break the agreement."

Ivy's bottom lip trembled. He was right. Damn him. "I'll tell Gunther what we did!" she shouted. "You are not so noble and strong. You have a prick like a twig!" It was a silly insult. He had a prick like a branch and he knew it.

His cheeks flared warm in the dim light. "Gunther has seen your preening ways and wouldn't care how many others you had turned your hot eyes on, so long as you bear him five fat sons before you are twenty summers old. His first wife gave him none, so he will be keen."

Ivy gasped, thinking about her tidy figure, stretched forever out of shape.

"I have a guard downstairs. Don't try to run away." He rubbed his hand over his bushy black beard, his voice softening. "You are a princess and you must do as your family dictates, as my Rowan will one day. I wish you no ill, only that you would accept your fate with hope in your heart. Gunther has ridden home to the shorefort at Seacaster to prepare your lodgings. My retainers will come for you in the morning."

Tears flowed again, pouring down her cheeks. She imagined he might take her in his arms and comfort her. But he did not touch her. With an awkward nod, he turned and left.

Rose was ready at dawn to leave, alone in the stable with the door propped open, breathing the scent of dew-drenched morning and fresh hay. She hadn't slept more than a few fitful hours, her mind a whirl of plans, adopted and abandoned equally swiftly. She was not about to stay here in Nettlechester, but neither could she return to Blickstow, to a life she had been displaced from five years ago. She didn't even know if there was still room for her at the family compound. In the end, there was only one thing she could decide on: go back to the flower farm and tell Heath. He couldn't fix anything, but she longed for comfort and she knew he would give it to her.

She hoped, too, for Bluebell's compassion. Oh, there was no doubt Bluebell would be angry, but she was loyal to family and surely she would fix things. Wengest couldn't keep Rose from her own child forever.

Once again she shuddered with the sorrow. Where was her baby? Was she missing her mama? Asking for her every hour? Crying? Did she think Rose had abandoned her? The pain of this thought was so acute she had to stop saddling her horse and bend over double, clutching her belly.

"Queen Rose?"

She turned. Coelred, Wengest's first retainer, stood there. She stood up tall, forcing herself to meet his eye, fingers clenched around the reins. "Coelred?"

"Wengest sent me to pass you a message, my lady."

She smiled tightly. "Am I still your lady, Coelred?"

His head drooped a little. "Your quarrel is not with me," he said quietly.

"Go on, then," she said.

"You are to pass this on to Bluebell. The future of our kingdoms relies on you doing so."

Her blood cooled. She braced. "I will."

"You are not to see your child again if peace between our kingdoms is to hold. Now that you have broken the bonds of peace with your . . . actions"—he cleared his throat and glanced away—"you must give up your daughter."

A rough wind shook the eaves of the stable, threatening to freeze her face with an expression of shocked misery on it forever. "Must I?"

"I am sorry," he said.

"A child should be with her mother," Rose said, her pulse hammering in her throat. "It is the natural way of things."

"Will you pass this message to your sister?"

Rose swallowed hard. Licked her lips. "Yes," she said softly. *And may Bluebell bring her entire army down to Nettlechester to punish Wengest for it.*

"I wish you well," he said, nodding once.

She turned back to her horse, tightening the saddle. When she looked back, he was gone. She mounted and urged her horse forward, out of the stables, down to the road and out of Nettlechester, hoping with every nerve in her body Bluebell would see things her way.

CHAPTER 27

Bluebell tried not to notice the twinge of pain in her side when she set off riding that night. If anything, she was glad it kept her from falling forward in her saddle into sleep. The night passed in a blur of movement and shadows, and the twinge became a throbbing pain, pulling sharply if she moved too suddenly. Rain came, but it didn't slow them. Bluebell's tunic grew soaked under her byrnie. With a hot sense of alarm, she started to believe the moisture she could feel dribbling down her side might be blood. But there was no chance to stop and take off her clothes to see, so she kept her eyes ahead and kept going. At first light, while Eldra dug her hole in the muddy slope under an ash tree, Bluebell gingerly pulled off her byrnie, wincing as she stretched. She pulled up her tunic to see a cut about the length of her outstretched hand, curving around from under her rib. It wept blood slowly.

"Have you hurt yourself?" Eldra said, peering at her.

"It's an old wound that's reopened."

Eldra looked at her sharply. "The one the Horse God healed?"

Bluebell nodded.

"Curious. Perhaps he's not as powerful as he thinks, eh?" She smiled smugly.

"Perhaps." Bluebell didn't tell Eldra about the old magician for fear she would know Bluebell had been asleep on the job and not trust her enough to continue.

"It doesn't look too bad. Do you want me to dress it?"

Bluebell thought of the sleep she'd miss, and sighed. "I suppose you should."

She sat while Eldra cleaned and dressed the wound, then waited under the tree in the rain while Eldra put herself into the ground for the day. Her side throbbed and throbbed. Pain was nothing to her. She had felt pain before and would no doubt feel it again. But pain laced with fear of magic was different, because she didn't know what to expect. It could get worse, stay the same, get better, or kill her . . . She had no way of predicting the outcome.

So she paced to take her mind off it, and reassured herself that within a few days she would have brought Eldra to Athelrick, which is what she had set out to do. In fact, it was all she could do. If Eldra couldn't heal him, then Bluebell would have to accept it.

The day passed in a blur. Her brain was a whirl of birds' wings, no thought settling long enough for her to think it through properly. The weariness and pain sapped the strength from her limbs, so she could barely pull herself onto Isern that night.

Eldra, her clothes caked with mud but otherwise well and limber, narrowed her eyes. "Are you well enough to travel?"

"We can't stop," Bluebell said.

"That's right."

"Then let's go."

The night unfurled, as the nights before it had. The dark woods blurring past her, the thunder of the horses' hooves as they sped supernaturally forward. But tonight, the searing thorn under her ribs was different. Breaking into the rolling rhythm of movement was an insistent, wretched pain. She felt a trickle, and wondered if it was sweat or blood. Her head pounded, the road unfolded—gray with grim shadows—beneath her . . .

She wasn't aware she'd lost consciousness until she regained it, brittle as crushed glass in her mind. Eldra's face was above hers, her lips pursed so dark furrows formed around them. Eerie night shadows gathered on her brow. Bluebell's heart hammered.

"What has happened to me?" she said.

"You fell. Don't move." Eldra inched up Bluebell's heavy mail byrnie, then the tunic, and gasped.

"What is it?"

"This wound," Eldra said.

Bluebell struggled to sit up, caught a glimpse of dark gore, and was pushed back down by Eldra. "No. Don't look at it. How has this happened?"

"A magician, on the beach," Bluebell said. "He must have undone the spell."

"Why didn't you tell me?"

"He got close while I was . . . sleeping. I didn't mean to sleep."

Eldra shook her head gravely. "We can travel no farther tonight. I will have to use what magic I have in me to heal you."

"You can heal me?"

"With the amount of power I have pulled from the ground today, I can undo the second spell, so the first will hold. But be warned: These two magics do not mix well. You will be sick for a few days. And every magician for miles will smell you. You'd best never return to Bradsey."

Bluebell lay back on the cold ground while Eldra raised her hands and began muttering her incantations. She closed her eyes. No, she would never return to Bradsey. She could happily live her whole life without seeing another undermagician.

She thought about Ash, and sighed. Ash would become one of them, with shadows on her brow. Would she smell Bluebell and shun her? She listened to the wind in the trees while the hot pain cooled in her side, then withdrew altogether. When she opened her eyes, Eldra sat, head bowed, next to her.

"Eldra?"

"Sleep. We can travel no farther tonight. I am spent."

And although she longed to get back to her father, the idea of a full night's sleep was sweeter than honey. She rolled out her blanket and remembered nothing more until morning.

❖ ❖ ❖

It had become clear to Ash that Unweder did not like the rain. Cooped inside on gray days, he wandered from one side of his tiny house to the other, growling about the weather and peering repeatedly out the shutters with his bottom lip pushed out. On fine days, he was gone with his hessian bag full of clattering pots in the morning until late afternoon, when he would return with a rabbit or a pheasant or pockets full of wild mushrooms for their meal. Ash would cook while he tidied up his things, and then they would eat together and talk. Every time Ash asked Unweder what she should be doing to develop her skills, he told her simply to rest and think and recover from the loss of her old life. "Until your mourning is complete, you won't be able to access the full extent of your power."

Although Ash didn't reveal to him that her mourning would never be complete, she understood this was one of the tenets of undermagic. Earthly attachments interfered with the craft. This was the reason so many undermagicians lived alone. Unweder had taken her in and seemed keen to share his knowledge, but Ash was not so foolish as to think he acted from entirely unselfish motivations. She held back a quarter of a breath in her lungs, knowing eventually he would name the price she had to pay. She had already decided that she wanted his knowledge so badly, she would pay it.

Two days of rain cleared to sunshine on her seventh day with Unweder, and he woke her early with a gentle nudge of his toes.

Ash looked up, blinking sleep from her eyes. He had opened the shutters and a cool morning breeze stirred in the branches outside, making the sunlight move on the wooden floor.

"Come," he said. "I want to see what you can do, and there's no better time than early morning."

Ash propped herself up on her elbows. "You want to see what I can do?"

"Yes," he said, fixing her with his good eye. "The elementals."

Her heart picked up its rhythm, and she fought a smile of pride. "Then let me show you."

She threw back her blankets and found her shoes, tied them on, and climbed to her feet. Unweder had gathered his hessian bag and waited by the open door. She joined him and they stepped out into the dew-soaked morning filled with birdsong, crickets, and the sounds of animals in the woods finding breakfast. Her own stomach rumbled but she had to catch the dawn, when elementals were most active. Unweder took her up his front path, then around the back of his land, down a slope thick with slippery, damp leaf-fall, then through crowded elm trees and down to the overgrown edge of the stream where they drew their daily water supply. The sun filtered through the trees and made diamonds on the water. Ash removed her shoes and left them by the side of the stream, then tucked up her skirts and waded in up to her ankles. The water was cold and clear. She could see the rocks in the bottom, the bright-green weed pulled softly on the current, tiny fish darting around. She looked up at Unweder, who stood on the bank with his arms folded, smiling.

She smiled back, then closed her eyes, breathing in deeply. She could feel them around her. The air teemed with invisible movement. Rather than opening her eyes and trying to see them, she found one with her mind—a muscular movement in the air. It communicated with her wordlessly, tensed against her hold but not struggling.

"What is it you want from me?" Its words were not words, but a shape in her head. She understood it with the hindmost part of her mind.

Ash thought about what Unweder had said. This was her gift. She didn't have to concentrate so hard; she didn't have to exert herself so much and make herself sick. Now that she had stopped trying to develop her ability to prophesy or heal or any other thing, she could allow her body to do what it had been born for. To control elementals.

She felt her lips moving, but no words came out. Her thought was enough. The water began to swirl around her ankles. She pushed her toes in among the cold stones to anchor herself, and the water shot up around her, surrounding her but not touching her. She stood inside a funnel of swirling water. Then, merely by dropping the thought, the water dropped, splashed loudly, then was still again.

She opened her eyes. Unweder was looking at her, mouth agape.

"Well?" she said.

Still he didn't answer, the expression of astonishment frozen on his face. Ash wasn't sure whether to be proud or frightened. Her pulse thudded past her ears. She had done it so easily. So easily. Was the fact that she was away from her family already working? Or was it simply that she had the focus and confidence she lacked before she met Unweder? A mild swirl of nausea pulsing in her belly and joints was the only aftereffect. That and the tiny cool finger on her heart, but that was surely only fear of the unknown. Soon, undermagic would be known to her, and that would stop, too. Elation swelled inside her.

"Ash," Unweder said at last, shaking his head, "I had no idea. I suspected, I hoped, but you have exceeded my imaginings of your power." He sounded sincere, not envious, though there was a hard gleam in his good eye.

"It was easier today than ever," she said, knowing she sounded young and over-enthusiastic, but not caring to check herself. "I only had to think and the elemental moved."

He moved down to the water and offered her his hand to help her out. She came back to the bank and sat down in the grass to let her feet dry, noting that her knees shook a little. He crouched in front of her. "What does it feel like?" he said.

"It feels wonderful," she confessed.

"I mean, how do you do it? What happens in your mind?"

"I find them with my thoughts. I can see them, too, and they never look happy. But they do as I ask without delay and then are relieved when my mind releases them."

"Any element?"

"Water, earth, trees . . . they are the only ones I have tried."

"Spirits?"

"I'm not sure that I understand."

"The spirits of the dead?"

Ash's blood cooled. "I don't know. I haven't tried."

Unweder sensed her fear and backed away from the question. "You will learn more about yourself over the coming years. But I must tell you, your ability is rare and strong. The Earth Mother has blessed you."

"I wonder what reason she had," Ash said.

"I doubt there's any reason, Ash."

"But there must be. Some task I am to fulfill or . . ." She trailed off, aware that Unweder was shaking his head.

"Do not seek or expect reason in undermagic," he said. "Things are as they are, and undermagicians pursue their own aspirations."

Ash frowned. "But that seems so—"

"Selfish?"

"Yes."

Unweder stood, stretching his arms above him with a sigh. "Everyone is selfish," he said. "Everyone. Whom should we serve but the person we are and must always be?"

Ash listened to him and didn't respond, wondering if he was right. Bluebell made much of serving her family and her kingdom, but by doing so she served herself. She looked up at the sky through the trees. The sun was being eaten by a blanket of gray cloud.

"Rain coming," she said, pointing upward.

Unweder glanced up then grimaced. "I am cursed this week."

"Unweder," she ventured, "perhaps now we are out here and it is still fine, you can show me your talent? You can explain to me what the Earth Mother blessed you with?"

He made a dismissive gesture with his hand. "Oh, I do many things."

"But you must have a special interest. You said yourself that—"

"I am very experienced. I am a master of many skills. Too complicated to explain now. You focus on your abilities. You can see you've already gained power by taking your mind off other things. Don't worry about me." He held out a hand to help her up. "Come. Let's return to the house and breakfast."

She followed him back through the woods as the first spits of rain clattered on the brown leaf-fall, unconvinced by his dismissiveness, suspecting that he was deliberately holding something back from her.

It was one thing to convince Willow he was a trimartyr like her, but quite another to convince her to side with Wylm over her sister. Wylm had listened to her endless sermons, had prayed with her and comforted her when she cried that Maava's angels were disappointed with her for not being a good enough pilgrim, but he hadn't yet tested where her allegiance lay. Then, however, it became apparent that Willow was interested in more than just healing him and sharing with him in trimartyr love.

One evening, as the fire began to crackle and she began to talk about heading home, he had caught her looking at him. He knew what that look meant, even if she didn't. He was in some ways stupidly flattered. Was Wylm the only thing that had ever made her think about something other than Maava? His male pride was not so useful to him, however, as her girlish loving heart might be.

Because he needed an ally, even if that ally was his enemy's sister. If she was thinking with her heart rather than her head, then all the better.

Now Willow had a calling. An injured man and a blind boy waited for her in the woods. Relied upon her for food and medicine. She was gone before dawn most mornings, her apron heavy with supplies for them. Sometimes when she arrived, they were still asleep and she sat and watched them both. Well, mostly watched Wylm. The rise and fall of his chest, the faint purplish tinge of his closed eyelids, the way his long fingers curled by his cheek. After giving them breakfast, she would head back to the farmhouse to tend to Heath and her father, spend a few hours praying, then be back in the woods at dusk. To her delight, Wylm started to heal. By the end of the first week, the wound's edges were dry and pink, and his fever had ebbed away. He seemed as delighted with her as she was with him, and they spoke about the miracles of Maava; he even once compared her to Liava, the doomed mother who died with her twins upon the fire so that others might hear the way of the light.

"You are so patient and kind with Eni," he said, eyes crinkling at the corners with a smile, "as Liava must have been with her children."

Oh, she had glowed for hours after he'd said that.

The next day, though, she was in Father's room, trying to concentrate on prayers rather than replaying that moment over and over in her mind's eye. Indeed, it seemed her mind's eye had developed its own will and wandered often to the woods and to Wylm's side. Outside, a light drizzle had moved in, and her father's room was very quiet and still. Stuffy. She tried not to worry about Wylm in the rain. She tried not to think about him. She bent her head and closed her eyes.

Maava, great and good, give me the strength to resist these waking dreams that come upon me . . .

But then she remembered. The other things that came into her mind unbidden were angels' voices. Could it be that these flashes of her mind's desire were actually given to her by angels? By Maava himself?

And if that were so, what about the dream, the one where Wylm had saved her from the raiders, like a fiery angel with a holy sword?

The door to the room opened, letting in a strong smell of woodsmoke and baking bread. Willow looked around to see Heath standing there with Eni.

She hurried to her feet. "Oh."

"Isn't this the boy you returned to the village?"

"Yes. He must have found his way back."

"Willow, we can't have people knowing where we are."

Willow put her arm around Eni's shoulders. "I know, I know. But nobody knows who I am, don't worry. Nobody knows about . . ." She didn't say her father's name, gesturing with her head instead.

"Rabbit sleeping," Eni said.

"Is that right?" Willow said, lightly, reassuring herself that Heath could have no idea what they were talking about. "Come, let me take you home."

"Be careful," Heath said, frowning, as she took Eni through the kitchen and out the front door.

His tone of voice made Willow bristle. Be careful? That was precisely what she was doing. Taking care, and not of a bunch of heathens. What did he know about care? "I know," she said gruffly, closing the door behind her.

"You mustn't come here looking for me," she said to Eni, but he didn't seem to understand. He shuffled along at her side, feeling the way with his toes adeptly.

"Rabbit sleeping," he said again.

Wylm was indeed sleeping. It was best for him to sleep, to give his body time to heal. She ached to sit next to him and be there when he woke, but Eni was restless so she took him down to the edge of the stream where they found rocks and oddly shaped twigs, and he was happy and quiet for an hour or so, his hand in hers.

"Come now," she said. "Let's take you back to Rabbit."

As they made their way through soft leaf-fall and between the saplings, the fluttering of angel wings started in her ears. A breath became caught between her lungs and her lips, choking her. She tried to breathe in, but could only pull in a series of loud wheezes.

"If you can speak to him with your mind, you can trust him."

I don't understand, angel, Maava's minion. I don't understand what you mean.

"Speak to him with your mind, as you speak to us."

A thousand sharp, chattering voices rushing around her. Wylm's sleeping back came into view and, without pondering further, she focused her mind on him and said inside her head, *Wake up! Wake up!*

His shoulders twitched and he sat up with a gasp.

Willow smiled, waving at him. He waved back, a bewildered expression on his face.

I can speak to him with my mind! She pushed away the sly thought that it was just a coincidence, or that he'd heard her footfalls. Because they were linked somehow. Destined to work together, in Maava's name, for the good of Thyrsland. She knew this as a fact as well as she knew her own name. She felt light.

"Eni came and found me at the farmhouse," she said, closing the last distance between them and sitting down.

"I must have dozed off."

"It's good for you to sleep. Your bandage has come loose. Let me fix it."

He offered her his hand, and she slowly unwrapped the bandage.

"It looks much better."

"I still can't close and open it properly. It's tight and hot."

"Yes, but you are no longer dying of a fever," she said, wrapping the wound again and tying it neatly. "And that is to be celebrated."

He smiled at her, and wings flapped past her ears. The angels had delivered their message and were no doubt satisfied with her. Perhaps they were going straight to the Sunlands to tell Maava. The idea of being thought well of by both Wylm and Maava was the dearest happiness she could imagine.

"You have a warm heart and a happy nature, Willow," he said, "but I need to be able to defend myself, and until my hand is properly better . . ." He glanced at the sword, lying in its scabbard, that he slept beside.

"It isn't your sword hand," she pointed out.

"But it is. I'm left-handed."

How wonderfully *uncommon* he was. "It will be better in a week or so."

"I need it to be better now," he mumbled, but she didn't push the conversation any further.

"Is it your father's sword?" she asked.

He shook his head. "My father wasn't much of a swordsman. He was a trader. No, I stole this from the Crow King."

"Never! How brave you are."

"I did what I had to." He unsheathed the sword, and she could see runes carved into its grip, the evil troll magic of the raiders.

Then her breath caught. This was the sword she had dreamed of. More proof, if any were needed, that they shared a miraculous connection blessed by Maava.

"What is it?" he asked, peering closely at her face. "You look as though you've seen a ghost."

"I dreamed of this sword . . ." she said, then couldn't finish her sentence because the rest of the dream had been so unsettlingly intimate.

"You did?" His eyes were eager now. "Then destiny . . . Maava's will . . . is working in us both."

She reached out and touched the grip of the sword. He closed his own hand over hers and held it there one moment . . . two . . . three, his eyes dark and steady on hers.

"You know what this sword is for?" he said, his voice soft but urgent.

She shook her head.

"To kill Bluebell."

Of course. Of course it was, and the *rightness* of this knowledge made her heart hot.

"I know it was made by Hakon and I know he is a heathen, but can we not use his heathen magic for Maava's greater good?" he continued. "To punish those who would still the tongues of trimartyrs?" Wylm's index finger gently stroked the back of her hand. Once. Twice.

Willow's pulse slammed in her ears. Yes. *Yes.* She had had her tongue stilled by Bluebell and she had accepted it and let her own truth be subsumed.

Then his hand withdrew, but already the wheels of some great engine had started turning within her body and her mind. Angels shrieked, and hot oil ran in her veins.

"I should go," she said, shooting to her feet.

"Come back soon," he said, sheathing the sword.

She couldn't form another sentence, not even to reassure him she'd be bringing bread at dusk. Her body and brain were too bright with heaven's blaze to stoop to anything as low as language.

Rose's journey east to Stonemantel took three and a half days. At first, the blackest of clouds had possessed her, so she shook and sobbed like a madwoman, drawing the pitying stares of those who passed her on the road. The weary limbs and muscle aches of being in the saddle for hours every day took their toll, and she slept poorly at night so that daylight seemed to her too bright, too unforgiving. She made a habit by the second night of reminding herself Rowan was not dead: She was safe, in the care of her nurse. There was still hope; in fact, there would always be hope. So she said this word over and over, "Hope . . . hope," as she made her way toward Heath.

The stable door was ajar as she walked her horse through the front gate in the late afternoon. The flowers were blooming in wild profusion, their scent heavy and deep in the damp air. Bumblebees careened around her. She led the horse to the stable and ran into Willow coming in through the front gate.

"Rose!" she said with a gasp.

"Willow? Are you well?"

"I am . . . Yes, I am well. But where is Bluebell?"

"She's not back yet?"

"No."

Rose did the calculations in her head. Of course Bluebell wasn't back yet, and if she'd thought about it—if she'd had any room left in her mind for rational thought—she would have realized that. "Bluebell and Ash went ahead without me. I imagine they will return very soon." Rose began to unbuckle the horse's bridle, but Willow stopped her.

"You look tired. Have you been traveling a long time?"

"Nearly four days. Why?"

"Let me take care of your horse. You go inside and wash and eat. Heath is there."

Rose's heart hitched. "I would be so grateful."

"Go," said Willow, taking the horse's reins. "It will make me most pleased to do this for you, sister."

Rose blinked back tears, this simple human kindness almost too much for her. She nodded, touched Willow's shoulder lightly, then turned to hurry over to the house.

The door flew inward, and Heath was there. Heath, the only person in the world from whom she could draw comfort.

He looked startled. "Why are you back before your sisters?"

"Oh, Heath," she started and began to cry. "It's such a mess."

And he folded her in his arms, against his broad chest, and she let her body shake with sobs. The smell of him was intoxicating: rain and damp earth and his own musky perspiration through his woolen tunic; his stoked heat, his body's reality, his Heathness. She breathed huge lungfuls of it, wishing that time could stop and this embrace would be the last of all events in the world.

But already he was pulling away and indifferent air was pushing its way between them and time continued on its way toward loss, and age, and death, and he asked her to tell him what had happened. Through choking sobs, while he held her hands clasped in his own, she unfolded her story. His sea-colored eyes were full of love and compassion, but he winced when she told him Wengest had vowed to kill him if he discovered his identity. When she had finished, he pressed her against him again and she could hear the rapid beating of his heart.

"My only hope is that Bluebell will somehow force Wengest to give Rowan back," she said.

He hesitated before speaking, and Rose sensed his doubts. "You must remember," he said carefully, "nothing is more important to Bluebell than the peace between Almissia and Nettlechester."

Rose pulled back and looked at him, the black fear creeping once more into her heart. "But Rowan's our blood."

Heath rubbed her shoulder softly. "Perhaps you are right, Rose."

The defeat in his voice was too much for her to bear, and she collapsed against him and wailed. "My baby, Heath, where is my baby? What if I never see her again?"

He made circles on her back with his palm and shushed her softly, but she drew little comfort. The inescapability of her situation was a hot, heavy thing in her brain. When his voice rumbled in his chest, it took her a few seconds to comprehend what he was saying to her.

"I'm sorry?" she said.

"I said, you are released from your marriage now, Rose. We could leave. Together."

Her heart hammered and her knees felt weak. She opened her eyes. Beyond the deep red wool of his tunic she could see the hearthpit smoking, a finger of light from beyond the door, the closed entrance to her father's bedroom. Everything tensed as though waiting for her to respond.

"We could go and find my father's family in the north. You wouldn't have to be Queen Rose or Princess Rose. Wengest wouldn't know; Bluebell wouldn't know. We could disappear and have the life together we've always dreamed of."

She stepped back, pressed her palms into her forehead.

"What do you say, Rose?"

"I feel as though you have just handed me the sweetest fruit, wrapped in poisonous leaves."

"I don't understand."

Of course he didn't understand. He might be Rowan's father by nature, but he shared no bond of the heart with her. It was nothing for Heath to let Rowan go and run away to Bradsey.

"Heath, I must stay in this life and fight to have Rowan back."

He nodded, his expression softening with understanding. "I see. Well, then I shall stay in this life, too, as you say, and I will do whatever I can to make that happen."

Wild happiness, which had veered so close, now fluttered off on its mad wings. Always beyond her fingertips. She allowed herself to be comforted, but felt the sting of knowing that Wengest loved Rowan more than Heath ever could.

Willow woke in the night, and listened for a moment. Something had woken her, some soft dreamlike noise.

It was coming from the main room, where Heath and Rose slept. She sat up and was about to rise to check on them when she recognized the noise. She had heard Ivy and William Dartwood make those noises, in the bed right next to hers back home in Fengard. Willow had pretended to sleep, but really she had watched from under her eyelashes, horrified and curious all at once, as Ivy applied herself to the puzzling task with more bounce and vigor than Willow had ever seen her muster.

Willow listened to Heath and Rose until they grew silent, and then her mind turned to Wylm and to the dream she'd had, and a soft shifting feeling began to tickle between her legs. She tried praying for the ability to control her thoughts better, while allowing her hand to stray down to rub at the tickle. *Stop, stop, stop,* she said in her mind. She wasn't a bitch in heat like Ivy. Why was this happening to her?

Maava, help me. I am succumbing to sin. The tickle grew to a violent ache under her fingers. *Please, Maava, I don't want to be like my sister. Make this feeling go away.*

Oh, the feelings that shuddered through her then. Her breath sucked back into her throat and her legs flipped around like the tail of a fish drowning in air. Then stillness. And guilt.

What was wrong with her? *What is wrong with me?* Silent angels. She rose, cracked the door to the main room open. Heath and Rose slept by the dying light of the hearth. She crossed the room on silent feet and went outside. On the dewy grass she sat, pulled out her knife, and inched up her skirt to reveal her white thigh, luminous in the moonlight. Here. She would cut here. And the blood that flowed would tell the angels she was sorry.

"Heathens fornicate, trimartyrs spawn dynasties."

The voice came to her just as she pierced her own flesh. Her heart slammed and she cut further, longing for the voice to continue.

"Maava made the love act pleasurable so children might be born."

Children? Willow remembered the number of times Ivy had gone to the village witch for abortifacients after her dalliances.

She pushed the knife against her flesh once again. *Tell me more. Tell me everything I need to know, angels, for the love of the great Maava. I will do whatever you ask.* She scored three lines on her thigh, but the angels had stopped talking. She breathed deep, letting the warm blood drizzle down her leg, and set her mind to the angels' words.

Heathens fornicate. Yes. Rose, Heath, her twin. Bluebell, if Eni's father was to be believed. *Trimartyrs spawn dynasties.*

Her blood, Wylm's blood. Trimartyr blood of the royal family. Were it to be mixed, a trimartyr child might be born. One that would unite Thyrsland under the holy triangle.

She sighed, closed her eyes with deep contentment. This was why the desires of her body were so insistent. Maava *wanted her* to lie with Wylm. Their entwined destinies demanded it. Now she understood her purpose in this world. Not to bear arms like Bluebell, but to bear a child. A miraculous child. Many people wandered the trimartyr path for decades before understanding their part in Maava's great plan, but here she was, just on the threshold of womanhood, and she already knew what she must do.

How good fortune had smiled on her.

CHAPTER 28

luebell was relieved to cross the border into Almissia. The lawless realm of the undermagicians was behind her, and she had returned to a place where things were as they seemed. She endured the long days pacing with very little sleep, and the strange swift nighttime travel, knowing they were drawing close to the end of their journey. At the other end, a possible cure for her father waited. Sleep waited.

They took the rutted track around Stonemantel toward the flower farm on the sixth night of travel, while clouds covered the moon and the air was still and smelling of damp earth. Bluebell's ribs expanded; the darkness of the last few weeks began to lift. She didn't entertain the thought that Eldra couldn't cure Athelrick: Eldra was able to enchant herself so she could walk, make the dog and horses speed like hares, and reverse the sand magician's spell. An elf-shot would be easy for her to remove.

They unsaddled their horses in the dark stable and the animals, now released from the enchantment, collapsed into sleeping heaps. Eldra herself began her walk from the stable with a smooth gait, but was limping again by the time they reached the front door. Inside, the air was warm and smoky. Sleeping bodies. Rose had returned already, and lay encircled in Heath's arms. Idiots. The urge to lie down among them and close her eyes for blissful hours was so strong that Bluebell had to shake herself. She hadn't come on this journey to let her father languish another moment under his enchantment.

"Father is through there," she whispered to Eldra.

Already their arrival had woken Heath, who sat up sleepily and said softly, "Bluebell?"

Bluebell ignored him, opening the door to the king's bower and leading Eldra in. Willow was asleep on the floor, but scurried out with one stern look from Bluebell. A few moments later, Rose was there with them.

"Bluebell, I need to talk. Wengest has—"

Exhaustion made Bluebell sharp. She held up a hand. "Not now. Father first. Then sleep, then your problems with Wengest tomorrow. I see you're taking comfort where you shouldn't already."

Rose was about to bite back, but then she stopped and looked closely at Bluebell's face. "You look utterly exhausted."

"I have survived on an hour or two of sleep a day for nearly a week," Bluebell said. She thought about introducing Rose to Eldra, but the older woman was absorbed in her examination of Athelrick.

Rose turned her eyes to Eldra, and Bluebell gestured that she shouldn't interrupt. "Go," she said. "We'll talk later."

Eldra wrinkled her nose as though she'd smelled something bad. "I'll need complete quiet."

Rose withdrew reluctantly, and Bluebell stood back as Eldra sat on the edge of Athelrick's bed.

"He's very gray," she said. "Too many cares, I imagine. Being a king." She gave Bluebell a grim smile.

"Can you feel the magic?" Bluebell asked.

"Oh, yes. It's not even very strong. If it had been stronger it might have killed him. But I should be able to remove this easily."

Bluebell's knees buckled. "Oh, thank fuck."

"How long do you say he's been like this?"

"Nearly five weeks."

"Then it will take time."

"How much time? Weeks? Months?"

"Days. And when he wakes, he will have no recollection of time having passed. It will be as though he had just put his head down to sleep, closed his eyes, and opened them again."

"He'll be confused then."

"Momentarily. But he will wake with all his faculties."

Bluebell couldn't control her smile.

"Hopefully," Eldra concluded.

"Hopefully?"

"There's always the chance that the magic leaving will simply kill him. I don't know. Some undermagicians leave a barb inside the elf-shot, so that its removal is fatal. It depends on whether the person who gave it to him wanted him dead."

Bluebell's gut tightened. "And will you be able to tell us who elf-shot him?"

"As the magic leaves his body, it will reveal its secrets. Don't worry."

Bluebell turned this over in her mind. If the elf-shot killed him, then Almissia would lose its king. But he was no king in this state.

"So, you want me to go ahead?" Eldra asked.

"Yes," Bluebell said grimly, "whatever the cost."

Eldra's gaze held Bluebell's for a few moments. Bluebell was not good at reading people's subtle cues, but she thought she could see admiration in Eldra's eyes.

"I'll get started then. I'll be here with him for the whole process. Go about your lives."

Bluebell left the room, stumbling into Rose who was waiting. Willow was nowhere in sight, but Heath was preparing food in the kitchen.

"Bluebell . . ." Rose started.

"No, Rose. No. Not you now. Sleep now."

Rose's eyes grew glassy with tears. Bluebell might have softened under any other circumstances, but weariness had stripped her softness away. She rolled out her blanket by the fire, lay down, and, while the household tiptoed around her, slept.

❖   ❖   ❖

Grithbani. Wylm held the sword upright, eyeing the runic inscriptions coolly in the dawn light. The randerman had told him each rune had powerful magic, and that when the time for combat with Bluebell was near, they would glow. He squeezed the hilt, sharp pain seizing his hand. Gritting his teeth, he forced himself through the pain, squeezed harder.

It was no use; he couldn't do it. Even beyond the pain there was a physical obstruction. The sword simply wouldn't sit in his hand properly.

He sheathed the sword and rewrapped the wound, glancing around to find Eni with his eyes. The boy had grown confident as he learned the landscape of the woods, and was off in the distance crouched on the ground, marveling over something he had found with his fingers.

A thump of footsteps drew Wylm's attention. He turned, tense as ever. It was Willow and she was running. He was growing used to her strange, unpredictable behavior. Her veering from being completely engaged in their conversation to being off in some distant place in her head, her strange gray eyes almost without pupils. He was used to her constant tic of drawing triangles on her chest with her fingers, of saying Maava's name as though she were clearing her throat with it lest he choke her. But in all this time he had never once seen her run.

"What's wrong?" he asked as she drew closer.

"She's back," Willow gasped. "Bluebell is back."

Wylm's stomach turned to water. His ears rang, and he had to sit down so he didn't fall down.

Immediately he hated himself for such weakness. What kind of man was he, to collapse like a pisspants child at the mention of his stepsister's name?

Willow crouched in front of him. "Are you well? You look pale. Has your fever returned?"

"When? When did she get back?"

"Just now. She woke me. She came in with an old woman I don't know. Looks heathen, covered in charms, mud in her hair."

An undermagician. Bluebell had gone to fetch herself an undermagician to heal Athelrick. All would soon be undone, and here he was unable to hold the magical trollblade destined to kill her. *It's too soon. Too soon.* Destiny rushed upon him while his breath was still flat in his lungs. He barely noticed that Willow had pulled him against her shoulder and was stroking his hair.

"Don't be afraid of her," Willow said.

"I'm not afraid," he said through a mouthful of her straight brown hair. What was she doing? Up until this point, she had become skittish at anything close to physical contact between them. A good trimartyr virgin. "Does Bluebell think the old woman can cure her father?"

"I don't know what Bluebell thinks."

"Perhaps her spells won't work."

"It's in the hands of Maava now." And off she went into her strange, silent whispers, as though she had left this clearing and the woods behind.

He let himself be held. Willow had bent so easily to his will, her brain so malleable from years of trimartyr worship. He'd remembered a few prayers and proverbs, and she had fallen over herself to side with him, to provide him food and medicine and take the boy from time to time so he could rest or scheme or practice swordplay with his mutilated hand. He had never viewed her as anything more than an object to be placed where he needed her most, but her hands had moved down his back now and he caught a smell of her sweet skin and a glimpse down her dress to the upper curve of a slight breast. How like Bluebell she was with her hard surfaces and athletic limbs. But how unlike Bluebell, too. Vulnerable and innocent and not of this world. Something stirred in his loins, but he was smart enough not to mistake it for emotion; it had simply been a long time since a woman had touched him.

Gently, he pushed her away. She seemed disappointed. "Willow," he said, "I need you to keep a very close eye on Bluebell. You need to tell me if your father wakes. The moment it happens."

She nodded solemnly. "Of course."

"And be careful when coming to give us food. Don't let her see you or follow you. She's sharp. Sharper than you can imagine."

"I know my sister well enough."

"Nobody does. You can think her the sharpest and the strongest person in the world and still you'd be underestimating her. She is a monster. Never forget it."

Already her thoughts had wandered; he could see it by the way her pupils shrank.

"Go, then," he said. "Be my eyes and ears."

"Do you not want my comfort?"

The question startled him. "I . . . The greatest comfort you can give me is to assure me I am safe from Bluebell until my wound has healed."

She nodded once. "But you have the sword."

"Yes. All will be well when the time comes, but I need it not to come. Not yet."

"I will be your eyes and ears," she said solemnly, then left. He watched her go, then turned once again to his sword. No matter what pain, no matter that he opened the wound again, he must master this weapon. And soon.

Not now, Rose, not now. How many times had Bluebell said that since her arrival? Rose understood her sister was tired: the dark shadows under her eyes were proof of that. But then she woke and took her dog out and refused company: "I'm too tired to think straight. Ask me about it tomorrow."

Rose knew she should wait. Time would not affect the outcome, and she needed to approach Bluebell in a good mood. She even considered waiting until their father was recovered, but the urgency pressed itself too hard upon her heart.

Bluebell spent the rest of the day in the king's room with Eldra, whom Rose had not yet spoken with. Bluebell kept everyone away. Frustration upon frustration as the whole day passed and Rose was no closer to resolving the anxious misery in her heart.

There was the consolation of Heath, of course. They left the house separately, discreetly, and met in the woods to spend hours together. But they did not touch and kiss and make love. Rose was sick and cold for the loss of Rowan. They talked, and there was only one topic of conversation. How much she missed her daughter and couldn't believe this had happened to her. How sorry he was that she was in pain.

The next morning, Rose stood in the kitchen grinding grain for bread. Willow had carefully unpicked the stitches in Rose's forehead then said she was going out to collect herbs for a salve. Heath had gone to tend the horses. Rose had grown frightened of solitude: being alone with her thoughts was a form of torture. As she worked, she became aware from the prickling of the hairs on the back of her neck that someone had entered the room. She turned to see Eldra standing there, watching her. Rose's skin went cold. She had once seen Eldra in a dream, and now she stood here in the flesh. Small, pale, and with a very focused gaze. She seemed a thing of the night, out of place in the morning light.

"Good morning," Rose said, trying a smile.

"I told you to kill Wengest," Eldra said, with no returning smile.

Rose's mouth strained at the corners. "Yes, you did. Four years ago."

"Perhaps you should have listened." Then she limped off, opened the kitchen door, and left.

Rose held her breath, but she didn't return.

That meant Bluebell was alone with Father.

Rose carefully placed the heavy quern-stone on the wooden bench, wiped her hands on her apron, and went to the bedroom.

Bluebell sat next to the bed, her arms stretched out in front of her, hands clasped, and her face on the bed. Was she sleeping?

"Bluebell?"

Bluebell looked up, blinking. Yes, she had been dozing. But she looked less tired than the day before.

"Not now, Rose," Bluebell said.

"Yes, now. Eldra isn't here. You've had a proper night's sleep. Now. It's urgent. It's a disaster."

Bluebell's face softened. She reached out to touch the angry line on Rose's forehead. "It's healed, then?"

"Yes, thanks to my sisters as much as the witch in the forest."

Bluebell nodded. "Go on. What do you need to say to me?"

Rose held her breath, couldn't speak for a moment. Until Bluebell knew and decided what she would do, hope was still alive that Rose would get Rowan back. Slowly, carefully, she said, "Wengest has discovered that I have not been faithful."

Bluebell sat upright. "He has?"

"Ivy told him."

"How did Ivy know?"

"She . . . she saw us. Before we left to head north. But Wengest doesn't know it was Heath. And he still thinks Rowan is his."

Bluebell's mouth tightened. "Do you see what you have done?"

But Rose wasn't in the mood for listening to lectures. The next part came out in a rush. "He's taken Rowan away and he won't tell me where she is. He can't do that. He can't separate a mother and her child. It's not fair. And he says to tell you that peace will hold between Nettlechester and Almissia only if I never see her again."

Bluebell frowned. "So peace will hold?"

Rose's heart thudded. Already, she knew how this discussion would end. "He says so. Yes."

"Then you can't see Rowan."

"But she's my baby," Rose sobbed.

Bluebell sighed, spread her hands apart. "I am sympathetic. Of course. But I have to balance the desires of your heart against the lives that will be lost if we go to war with Nettlechester again."

"It's not a desire of my heart. It's a need."

"Same outcome."

"I'll die! I'll die if I can't see her! Wengest is terrified of you. He's terrified of Almissia. You could make him do whatever you want."

"But Rowan will be alive and well. Wengest adores her. She has a nurse that she knows and loves."

"She'll miss me."

"She'll . . ." Bluebell stopped herself.

"Go on, say it," Rose said, anger clouding her vision. "She'll forget me. That's what you were going to say."

"No, I was going to say she'll adapt," Bluebell said. "She's very young."

Rose's body felt light and grainy, as though she were becoming as transparent as she would be in Rowan's mind. A thing half remembered. The pain in her heart was more intense than it ever had been; she thought it might kill her. Bluebell wanted her to let Rowan go.

"Maybe, in a few years, Wengest will have cooled down," Bluebell said. "You're right. He is afraid of us, and when the edge has worn off his anger we can ask him again about you seeing your daughter."

"Years? Do you realize what you're saying to me?" Rose's voice sounded hysterical, and it frightened her. She had lost control of everything. The threads of meaning were unraveling and slipping from her fingers.

Bluebell pulled herself to her feet, towering over Rose and grasping her upper arms. "I told you, Rose. It gives me no joy to say that, but I told you over and over again that no good would come of fucking that man. If you had only listened to me, Ivy wouldn't have seen you, and wouldn't have had something to say to Wengest. Do you understand this? *You* did this to yourself. *You* couldn't control yourself. *You* put Rowan at risk of losing you."

Rose gasped. Half of her wanted to scream at Bluebell. How did she dare to say such cruel things? If Rose's love for Heath was so destructive, then why did it feel so good and pure? But the other half of her realized with horror Bluebell was right. She had put herself first. She *always* put herself first. She had expected Bluebell would go to war with Wengest, never thinking deeply about the people who would die. Die and never live again, because she was in love with her husband's nephew.

Bluebell released her. "I'm sorry that you are sad, Rose. But you have thought of nobody but yourself. I'm not going to rescue you now."

Rose doubled over, face in her hands. The nightmare was too real to comprehend.

"Accept your lot and make the best of it," Bluebell said, opening the door for her to leave. "And for fuck's sake, stay away from Heath. Wengest will kill him if he finds out." She gently pushed Rose out of the bedroom. "Don't let your selfish desire doom him as well."

Then the door closed and Rose stood on the other side in the empty house, her world in pieces at her feet.

Bluebell blamed herself.

She should never have let Heath come with them. Yes, it would have meant letting the truth about her father's illness spread a little wider, but she should have realized the idiots couldn't keep their hands off each other. No doubt they would say to each other that love was a mighty force, mightier than armies. But love wasn't mighty; love was just selfish. And now Bluebell's plans for Rowan were scattered to the wind.

She turned over on her other side. Sleep wasn't coming easy tonight. Rose lay next to her, finally asleep after sniffling and crying quietly for hours. Willow was on the other side of the hearthpit. Eldra had simply lain down next to the king to sleep. Heath was in his usual corner, keeping a respectful distance from them.

Ha! A respectful distance might have helped.

It was hard for Bluebell to be furious with Rose, whom she loved, and much easier for her to be furious with Heath. Certainly he was a good soldier, and had fought by her side from time to time. But she had asked him to do only one thing, and he hadn't managed it. The most important thing. He had defied her absolutely. It might have been for the best if Heath was named as Rose's lover; then he would be Wengest's problem.

But no. It remained important that Wengest believed Rowan was his. It was the only thing protecting the child. One glimmer of auburn in her hair and Wengest would realize the truth.

Bluebell sat up and glanced across at his sleeping form. No doubt they'd want to be together now that Wengest had put Rose aside. Then there would be more bastard babies to deal with. She kicked off her blanket and crossed the room to stand over him. Nudged him with her toe. Firmly.

He startled awake, blinking back sleep. Looked at her curiously.

"Get up and ready to leave," she spat.

Heath climbed to his feet and Bluebell waited while he pulled on his shoes and rolled up his pack. Then she gestured for him to follow, as she led him outside into the dew-drenched night.

She took him through the front garden and out under the carved wooden arch, her bare feet growing damp. Then she leaned back on a pillar and he stood in front of her, wordless. He knew what was coming.

"I specifically asked you not to—"

"I know!" he said, holding up both hands.

"Then why did you?"

"Because Rose specifically asked me otherwise."

She studied him in the gloom. His face gave away nothing about what he was thinking, but she knew he was afraid of her. "And why should I not put you to the sword, just as Wengest would if he knew?"

He took a deep shaking breath. "Because I have been a loyal and hardworking soldier."

"That's true. Mostly. But a loyal soldier might have kept his cock in his trousers when told to."

"Have you never loved, Bluebell?"

She smiled grimly. "You sound like Rose. Yes, I have loved. I love Rose. I love all my sisters. My father, of course. I have friends whom I love dearly. I have even desired. Don't look so shocked. But my love and my desire have always been subject to my duty. I have great power, great wealth, great fame. These things are not just granted to me, an accident of my birth that I sit around and enjoy without responsibility, as Wengest does. I earn them. I live for my kingdom and I would die for it. Every breath I draw, I draw for my king, for Almissia, for the greater good of Thyrsland. If I didn't, I'd be crippled by my guilt. And I am constantly amazed that nobody else in my family feels that way."

He dropped his head. Was he ashamed? He ought to be.

"I would give up my life, Heath, and have my body burned to ashes that travel forever on the cold wind. You and Rose, you wouldn't even give up each other."

"I'm sorry."

"You have to go."

"Of course. Back to Folkenham? Or would you have me back in Blickstow?"

"Neither. You have to go into exile."

His head snapped up.

"You are no longer my soldier and, under threat of death, you are not to return to my kingdom or your uncle's kingdom."

"Bluebell—"

She held up her hand to stop him. "No excuses. No pleading. Rose and Rowan's safety is at stake now. You need to be far, far away from them both, and far away from Wengest lest he has a moment of acumen and realizes Rowan isn't his. This dangerous game is over. You will leave now and you will not look back."

He set his chin, and looked like nothing so much as a boy pretending to be brave to impress his father. An owl hooted in the trees, a lonely sound. "I will go," he said, "but not because you threaten me. I'll go because I love Rose and I would do anything to keep her and our daughter safe."

"Whatever you want to believe about yourself is fine with me," Bluebell grumbled. "Go find yourself a wife. Have babies. Have a life. Rose is never going to be yours."

She could see her last remark had hurt him, as intended.

"Will you tell Rose why I've gone?"

"I don't know. Probably."

"I couldn't stand her to think I didn't care for her."

Bluebell frowned. "Rose is not yours to worry about anymore. I can take care of my sister; better than you ever could. You led her into danger and misery."

"I cared only for her happiness."

"Well, perhaps spend the next few lonely years thinking really hard about that," Bluebell said dismissively, "because I've never seen her look so unhappy."

She watched him go to the stable, then she crept back inside, careful not to wake anyone. Rose was still asleep, oblivious. Bluebell had a sharp pang of sympathy for her sister. No doubt the loss of Heath would hurt her, but she would be better off. Perhaps Bluebell could see if the elders in Thridstow would take Rose in Ash's place at the study halls. Certainly, Rose needed something to do with her time.

Bluebell crouched next to Rose a moment and stroked her hair gently. "I'm sorry," she whispered. Then she lay down, and finally slept.

chapter 29

Ash sat by the hearthpit, scrubbing a dress in a tub full of water and soap. She'd been wearing it yesterday afternoon, down by the stream, practicing her elemental magic. A rock had shifted under her feet and pitched her to the ground. She'd cut her hand on a sharp stone, and her dress had gotten soiled with blood and mud. As she scrubbed it, she thought about the three dresses she had brought with her from Thridstow, and how they would be her only dresses now for a long time to come. She would no longer be visiting Blickstow for festivals, getting new clothes from the king's dressmaker. She had a rust-colored dress, a plain blue dress, another blue dress with gold piping, and her green cloak. That was it. As for shoes, she would have to keep repairing the ones she owned. Thinking about these things made her eyes feel heavy with sadness. Her old life disappearing behind her, into the hall of memory. A new, strange life with Unweder, with her uncanny power, and with only one pair of shoes.

"You take a long time to wash clothes," Unweder observed. He had been agitated this morning, pacing, watching her work, organizing and reorganizing the jars on his bench.

"Is there something wrong?" she asked him, for the third time that morning.

"No. I said no before, and I meant it."

His body made lies of his words. His lithe arms were drawn close to his ribs, his shoulders hunched.

"It's not raining." Though the dark chill in the air promised something different.

"I don't care about rain. I don't want to go out today." He paced some more.

She wrung out her dress and stood. "I'm going outside to hang this on a tree. I'll be back to empty the tub."

She made it halfway out the door when Unweder grasped her wrist. "Don't come back for a little while."

"I'm sorry?"

"I need . . . I need the house to myself today."

"I'm sorry. You only had to say." What was she going to do, out of the house all day? Walk in the woods, perhaps. Plot the whereabouts of the different elemental types. "I'll come back for the tub."

"No, no, never mind. I'll do that. You go."

She was curious, but everything Unweder did made her curious. She had to tell herself to be grateful that she had somewhere to stay and someone to guide her in her next learning journey. He would reveal himself to her eventually, she hoped.

He closed the door behind her as she walked up the front path to an elm tree with a low branch. She spread her dress on it evenly, glancing at the sky. No sunshine and no wind. She had a feeling she'd be drying it by the fire tonight. With a last glance back at the house, she headed into the woods.

It was hard to tell without the sun, but Ash guessed it was midmorning. The chorus of birdsong had died off a few hours ago, and now there were just one or two bird cries, deep and far away. She stepped lightly through the layers of leaf-fall, breathing the green smell of it, running her fingers over the smooth bark of the elm saplings. The clouds parted a little, letting in weak sunlight. She sat on a log and closed her eyes, sending her mind out searching for elementals.

The woods swarmed with them, but she tried to keep her mind quiet so they wouldn't notice her, so she could observe them gently.

She sensed them in the trees, in the rocks, in the earth, in the cool damp air. For an hour she sat there, feeling them with her thoughts, keeping herself veiled. The Earth Mother's minions, the spark of the divine in every natural thing. Then she opened her eyes. The sun had gone behind cloud cover again, and a distant rumble told her a storm might be on its way.

She walked a little farther in, wandering in no particular direction. She had a strong inner compass and knew she'd find her way home. Every quarter mile or so she would stop and sit, observing the elemental activity around her for a long time, learning its contours. There were more elementals in areas of the woods where there were lots of saplings and new growth; fewer where dead logs and leaf-fall choked the grass. By midafternoon, when her stomach was growling for more than the currants that she'd picked off their bush, she became aware of a dead zone in the woods. At first it was simply a faint ringing in the part of her mind listening to elementals. But as she drew closer, the ringing gave way to a numbness. It made Ash think about the times she had slept on her arm, and how poking it afterward gave her a strange feeling of unfamiliarity. This numbness was there in the elemental field, yet ought not be, as though everything in the area had been put to sleep unnaturally. Curious, she followed her instincts toward it, forgetting about her inner compass, forgetting about the storm gathering beyond the woods. One foot in front of the other, listening with her mind.

The wind picked up, whipping at the strands of hair that had escaped her plait. The thunder rumbled closer. Rain started to spit.

And Ash saw where she was. She had found the edge of the dead zone, and it was about a dozen yards from Unweder's house. She had come around in a circle.

How had she never noticed before? There were no elementals around Unweder's house. Or if they were here, they were silent. Silenced. She looked at the sky. The clouds were bruised with holding in the deluge that was about to start. She'd been gone for hours; surely Unweder wouldn't mind if she came back a little early. She could always ask, in any case.

So as the freezing rain started to pour, she ran around the side of the house and to the front door. Her dress was lying on the grass, strewn with leaves. She would have to get it later. She cracked open the door and said softly, "Unweder? I'm sorry, but it's raining."

She moved inside the dim house, closing the door behind her. The hearth was stoked, but Unweder was nowhere in sight.

"Unweder?" she said again.

No answer. A scurrying noise above her had her looking up sharply. The flick of a rat's tail disappearing over the beam.

Unweder was definitely not here. She sat by the fire and pulled off her shoes, propping them up to dry. Then she unbraided her hair and brushed it by the fire, drying off, warming up. Wondering where Unweder was. Wondering why no elementals lived near him. Wondering . . .

The chest. The one she wasn't supposed to touch. The padlock was on the floor; the latch was open.

Promise me you won't touch that.

She looked around her, licking her lips.

Promise me you won't touch that.

If she just flipped up the lid, had a quick look . . .

Promise me you won't touch that.

But she had never promised, had she? She hadn't said the actual words, *I promise I will never look in the chest.* And Unweder wasn't around. And if she was going to stay with him, she needed some answers about what he did. Didn't she?

Ash went to the door, looked out. Rain bucketed down. Unweder wasn't dashing toward the house to escape it. He'd probably found a place to shelter in the woods.

The chest waited. Her hand on the rim didn't even look like her own: It looked like the hand of a bolder, less obedient woman.

She opened the lid. It creaked softly. She glanced around again, then knelt in front of the chest and peered inside.

Her first instinct was to recoil, because the chest was full of dead animals. But there was no smell of decay, no lines of ants or maggots. The smell was almost pleasant: the warm fur of a favorite pet, slightly damp. She gingerly reached in and pulled out the body of a crow. Its head lolled to one side. Its fine skeleton was light between her fingers, its feathers gleaming and black. The residue of warmth in its body suggested it had just been killed, but she didn't see how. Nor did she see a mark on it that would indicate how it had been killed. She placed it carefully to one side, then looked again at the tangle of slack paws and soft faces. A rat lay on top, and she pulled it out to look at it. Again, it was warm. Ash glanced up at the roof beam, where she had seen the live rat earlier. Its little face peered over the beam, whiskers twitching, looking at her.

"Sorry," she said to it, "I hope this wasn't a friend."

She put her hand into the chest with her palm flat. The animals in it were definitely dead, but felt as warm as though they were living. As though they were about to draw breath again any second and shudder into life. Badgers and rabbits, swallows and skylarks. What were they for? Did they have something to do with the dead zone around Unweder's house? Ash replaced the crow and the rat as she had found them and closed the lid, leaving the latch exactly as it had been. She sat back down beside the hearth to listen to the storm clatter overhead, but then began to grow guilty and anxious. If Unweder came back and found her here alone, after specifically telling her to leave for the day . . . Would he know, somehow, that she had been poking around in his things?

She climbed to her feet and went to the door again. Rain fell heavily. She wanted to take her moleskin from behind the door, but Unweder had seen her leave without it. So she went out into the soaking rain, so that she could come back later and pretend she had never done anything wrong.

Three hours later, she decided it was finally safe to come back. The storm had long since cleared, and she'd found a place to sit in weak sunshine to dry off a little. But she was cold and her skin was puckered with wet when she came home.

Unweder sat on a stool by his bench, pouring a hot mixture into his little jars. "Ah, you're back," he said.

"I'm soaked," she replied.

"The fire is warm. Take your wet dress off."

She did as he said, stripping down to her linen shift and hanging the dress over the back of a chair. She sat by the fire, stretching out her fingers. The warmth was welcome and comforting.

"Have you eaten?" he said.

"Nothing but currants since breakfast."

"I'll cut us some cheese and bread."

Ash glanced at the chest. The latch was down. The padlock was closed.

He took his time cutting up the food, putting it on plates. Then he came to sit by her. They ate in silence a few moments. Ash felt her pulse thudding hard in her throat. She wanted to ask him about the numbness around his house, but was judging a way to say it that wouldn't give away that she had been snooping.

Then he said, casually, "I know you went into my chest."

Ash's head snapped up, her mouth opening to deny it. But she couldn't deny it. It was true. So instead she said, "How do you know?"

He shrugged. "I'm not in the mood to tell you."

That's when she realized he was angry at her. The pupil in his good eye was shrunk to a pinpoint.

"I'm so sorry," she said.

He waved away her apologies. "It's good to know I can't trust you. I won't be polite about locking things from now on."

Ash squirmed with the shame. She wished for nothing less than to disappear. "I'm so sorry," she said again, quieter. But he didn't respond.

The hearth wasn't yet cold when an angel's shout woke Willow. The figures of her sisters lay around her. Bluebell snored softly. Rose's hip was a silhouetted hillock on the other side of the fire.

What is it, my angels?

But they gave her no words, just shouts and yelps and growling sentences of ominous babble. She closed her eyes, chasing sleep, but then she felt that tickling again, down low inside her. She hadn't done what they said. She hadn't taken Wylm inside her and made the child that would one day rule Thyrsland. Was it any wonder they would torment her sleep?

She had tried, boldly holding him and stroking his back.

Don't be a baby, Willow. She had seen Ivy do it. Not once had she stroked William Dartwood's back to get him interested. She flipped over, screwing her eyes tightly shut. A frightened virgin. That's what she was.

Maava, one god, only god . . . What was it she needed so desperately to ask him? She was afraid even to put the thought into words, lest the cruel laughter start again. But there was only silence, and she ventured again to reach for her lord in her mind. *I am falling in love with Wylm,* she said in her mind. *If this is wrong in any way, give me a sign.*

She tensed against the sign coming. Two owls hooting in the dark perhaps, or a shooting star overhead. But no sign came. She waited, and still it didn't come.

Be bold. Be bold for Maava. Quietly, she turned over, folded back her blanket. Climbed to her feet and was out the door in silent seconds.

She found her way to him in the dark. He and Eni were both sleeping. Their fire was still burning, and she could see Eni in the dark, on his back, his face in repose giving no sign that he was blind or simple. Just a beautiful, skinny boy.

Willow knelt next to Wylm, her hands in her lap. She gazed down at his face by firelight. By Maava's light, he was gorgeous. She focused her mind as she had that other time. *Wake up.*

His brow furrowed in his sleep, then his eyes fluttered. Brief fear, chased by recognition.

"Willow?" he said, in a croaking voice.

She put her finger to her lips, remembering the performance she had seen Ivy give. She took his hand and placed it on her breast. Only she didn't have breasts like Ivy's, and the movement seemed awkward.

Wylm allowed her to rest his hand there. Then she felt his fingers flex as he closed his hand over the curve. His eyes seemed very dark. In one quick movement, he rose on his elbow and pulled her down next to him, his arm locked around her waist. Her back was pressed up against his chest.

And she realized a swelling chorus of voices was bearing down on her. The heat of his body was the only thing holding her together, because as the angel voices rushed through her, gushing up between her legs and through her stomach and then pouring out her eyes and ears, her body began to shake. Shake as though her joints might disconnect one from the other and her limbs might spin off into the dark and she might never find herself again and so she stayed in her body and burned, while Wylm's hand moved up her leg and gathered her skirts and Wylm's fingers gently stroked the underside curve of her buttock and Wylm's fingers probed her gently and found her slick and wet and Wylm's other hand grasped her breast through her dress and Wylm's lips were on her neck and Wylm's body pressed against hers so she could feel the hard heat of his erection and the foreign yet welcome thrill of him as he entered her body and moved so that she rolled her eyes back and her head and the angels and the voices and the exploding white-hot spangles of Maava's love snagging on her flesh and in her throat and the slow darkness bleeding into the edges of everything . . .

"Willow?"

Ears ringing.

"Willow?" It was Wylm. She was lying on her back; he was bent over her, gently rubbing her face.

She opened her eyes.

"You blacked out," he said. "You frightened me."

She beheld his beauty in the dark. He was half undressed, his hair a mess—a glorious gorgeous mess. She reached for it, tangling her fingers. "I'm well again now," she said, realization hard upon her. What had she done? But under the panic was a sense of certainty. Maava had led her here.

Maava had led her here, Maava had put the feelings of longing into her body, and that meant she and Wylm were meant to be joined that way. It was Maava's will and she would serve him by bearing and raising the child as a true soldier in Maava's righteous army.

"Willow, we really shouldn't have—"

"It's all right, Wylm. We won't do it again." She had his seed now. All was well.

"I'm sorry. I . . . haven't felt the touch of a woman for . . ."

"You need not be sorry." She smiled at him. "But I must go back to my bed beside the hearth."

He nodded. She felt his eyes on her as she left. Willow pressed her hands over her stomach. Ah, she could feel it already. The spark of life, and she the mother of a trimartyr king.

CHAPTER 30

The four walls of the bedroom grew closer together every hour. Bluebell stood, paced, leaned, while Eldra sat very still, her hands flat on the blanket over Athelrick's chest, wordless. It was the third day. Athelrick lay as though dead, just as he had before Bluebell had left to find Eldra. Outside, the sun shone brightly. Bees and butterflies dazzled in the air. Inside the dim room, the air was humid and stale.

"Can you tell me anything?" Bluebell asked.

Eldra smiled serenely. "You should get out. You aren't any use to me. In fact, your pacing is very distracting."

Bluebell planted her feet firmly on the floor, arms folded. "I'm not going anywhere."

"That dog of yours will need exercising."

"I'll send Willow out with her."

Eldra raised an eyebrow. "You trust her?"

"Willow? She's just young."

"No, there's something closed off about her. Something cold and hard beneath the warm skin. I tried to prod inside her mind—"

"I wish you wouldn't. Do you prod my mind?"

"Not much to prod," Eldra said with a laugh. And then more kindly, "Bluebell, why would I? You are a monument, not a shadow."

"Should I be worried about Willow?" Bluebell said lightly.

"Willow does not hold our gods as her own," Eldra said, lifting her hands and then placing them in another location, barely an inch from the first.

"That is every person's right. All gods are the same god, with different names for different seasons and times."

"I think you will find that the trimartyrs are something quite different."

"Well, Willow isn't a trimartyr," Bluebell said.

Eldra resumed her silent work, and Bluebell watched her for a while. She had expected instant results, one way or another. A declaration that Athelrick couldn't be cured, or an immediate improvement. Not this endless . . . nothing. Bluebell didn't like the barb of doubt in her heart. Eldra had no love for Athelrick. What if she was making it worse? Leading them on? What if she had made the elf-shot in the first place?

So she stayed close when she could, and continued to live in doubt and fear. Only when Athelrick's eyes were open and seeing again would Bluebell release her breath.

"You're pacing again," Eldra said.

Bluebell realized she was right. She leaned against the windowsill. The shutter was open a few inches, letting in a warm beam of sunlight on Bluebell's back. "I'm sorry."

"I'll tell you something," Eldra said. "This elf-shot was not administered by an undermagician."

Bluebell stood straight, ready to pace again, then checked herself. "No? How can you tell?"

"It's been rather poorly done. It's undermagic, yes, but bought undermagic. Probably from a traveler or a peddler. I'm almost certain that the person who did this to your father didn't mean to."

Bluebell's gut clenched. "What do you mean? This was an accident?" The idea that there would be nobody to eat steel over this caused her physical pain. She needed to spill enough blood to wash the nightmare of the past long weeks away.

"No, not really an accident. But I don't think it was an actual assassination attempt. I think it was a little curse that has had unexpectedly large consequences."

"Who did it?"

"I don't know yet. But I will soon. As the magic leaves him, I will know everything."

"Even if he dies?"

"You have revenge on your mind, I take it?"

"Yes."

Eldra said nothing.

"You will tell me when you know?"

"You are ruled by the Horse God. I expect I will tell you, and I expect we might both regret it. But you should consider your actions carefully."

Bluebell shrugged. She'd had weeks to consider her actions. Her father was the king; somebody had tried to kill him. There was nothing else to be done but avenge him. Blood could only be paid in blood.

Eldra returned to her silent vigil, and Bluebell turned to put her hands on the windowsill, leaning her head on the shutter. "Fuck," she sighed, closing her eyes. A rustle in the gorse bush below the window made her eyes fly open. She pushed the shutter aside and peered out, only to see Willow disappearing hurriedly around the corner of the house.

"Hey!" Bluebell called. When Willow didn't return, she strode out of the room and flung open the front door of the farmhouse. "Willow!" she called again, rounding the corner of the house and finding Willow sitting there, hands in her lap, her back against the wall of the house. Her lips were moving silently.

Bluebell approached warily, her recent conversation with Eldra still fresh in her mind. Willow looked up defiantly. Dandelion seeds flew past on the wind, one of them tangling itself in Willow's hair.

"What?" Willow said.

"Were you hanging around the window of Father's bedroom?"

"Yes."

"Why?"

"I want to know what's happening with him."

"You only have to ask. I keep nothing from anybody."

"I want to be near him while he's sick."

A prickle of apprehension. "You're welcome to come in while Eldra works."

"I don't like Eldra. She's . . ."

"She's your aunt. She's family."

Willow nodded. Bluebell looked down and realized Willow was holding a silver triangle on a chain between her fingers. Rage boiled up inside her.

"What's that?" she demanded, although she already knew and of course so did Eldra.

Willow's fingers shook, even if her voice was bold. "You know what it is, and so you know what I am."

"For fuck's sake, Willow. You're the daughter of a heathen king! Maava's not going to want you in his flock."

Willow's face grew red and she struggled for words. "Don't say that. Don't ever say that!"

"So what were you doing? Praying for Father's soul?"

Willow clamped her mouth tightly and nodded.

"Because he's sick, or because Eldra is an undermagician?"

"Both."

What on earth had Uncle Robert been doing with these girls? Letting one of them chase men and the other chase Maava? When Athelrick was better, her first priority was to get them out of Fengard and back into service to their family.

"You're young," Bluebell said gruffly. "You'll grow out of this nonsense."

"I won't. My soul belongs to Maava."

"I thought you might have the strength for arms, but I see I'll have to marry you off. A heathen husband might put you straight."

Willow's eyes flashed steely silver, and Bluebell wondered if she had gone too far, if she had taken too much pleasure in the threat.

"Go on, get out of my sight for a while. I can't deal with this now," she said, kicking the wall. She leaned over and snatched the chain from her sister's fingers. "And give me that. We'll talk about this when Father is recovered."

Willow clambered to her feet. "Give it back!"

"No." Bluebell held the chain above her head, out of Willow's reach. "Go on. Take Thrymm for a run. Don't come back until suppertime. I don't want to look at you for a while."

Willow met her eyes angrily, and Bluebell was put in mind of Eldra's description of her. Something cold and hard beneath the skin. They stood like that a moment, frosty in the spring sunshine. Then Willow dropped her head and slunk off toward the house. "Come, girl," she said to Thrymm, who was scratching flea bites in the dust by the door.

Bluebell watched as Willow disappeared out the front gate, and she remembered the warning she'd received from the Horse God. *Beware your sister.* Her gut stirred with bad feelings. She never thought she'd find herself feeling so much doubt about her own family.

When the sun set behind gray clouds and the first showers of rain came down, Rose began to pace. Heath had been gone when she woke, and Willow had told her that Bluebell claimed he'd gone to Stonemantel for the day. If that was so, then he should have been back hours ago. Heath was her only comfort in a cold world and she relied upon him heavily, even if it was only to see him and not touch him. She had already made enough excuses to go out the front door and search the gate and the road beyond for signs of him. Now she dropped excuse-making and stood with her shoulder in the threshold, gazing openly outside.

"It grows cold, sister. Close the door," grumbled Bluebell. She sat by the fireplace, eating deer stew, her long legs stretched out in front of her.

"Does it not trouble you that Heath isn't back yet?"

Bluebell kept eating, wordlessly.

"If it was one of us, you'd be worried."

"Heath can look after himself."

"But what if he's been attacked by raiders? Or thieves? If he was on his way to town, then he would have had coin to steal."

"What makes you think he's gone to town?" Bluebell still hadn't looked up. Willow, who sat across from her, pretended not to notice their conversation. She concentrated very hard on mending the rip in her skirt. Rose prickled with suspicion.

"Where else would he have gone?"

Bluebell silently finished her meal and took the bowl to the kitchen bench. Rose watched her back, trembling.

"You should go out and look for him. He might be on the side of the road hurt," Rose said.

"I'm not going out to look for him."

"Then I'll go."

"And where would you look?"

"Along the route to Stonemantel. He went to Stonemantel." She swallowed hard. "Didn't he?"

Again, the silence. Rose closed the door and leaned her back against it. Bluebell turned around to face her from across the house. Willow put aside her sewing and watched. Rose's pulse fluttered at her throat.

"Where is Heath, Bluebell?" Rose asked, her voice constricted.

Bluebell's mouth was hard. She folded her arms. "He's gone."

"Gone? Where?"

Bluebell shrugged.

Rose grew mad with infuriation. "Answer me!"

"I can't answer you. He's gone."

"You sent him away."

"It was his choice."

The words stung, as they were no doubt intended to. But she gathered herself. "And what choice did you give him? Leave or die?" Even that wasn't enough. She wanted him to say he would die for her. How could he fear Bluebell so greatly? She was only a woman.

Bluebell uncrossed her arms, gestured to Willow with a tilt of her head. "Out," she said. "This is between me and Rose."

Willow left swiftly and wordlessly.

When they were alone, Bluebell said, "Heath knew leaving was best for you and for Rowan. That's what he said."

"Did he say anything else?" A declaration of eternal love? A promise to return? But Bluebell was already shaking her head and she knew that Heath would not be so foolish as to say such things in front of her. "But you told him to go, didn't you?"

"I suggested it. Yes."

Rose could feel her face contorting from the effort of holding back angry sobs. "And do you love me, sister?"

"More than you know."

"You say that, and yet you have barred me from my two greatest happinesses!"

Bluebell opened her mouth to speak, but then changed her mind. Instead, she crossed the room and laid her hands on Rose's shoulders. "I can say nothing that I haven't said before," she said. Then she walked past Rose and out the door, letting it close behind her.

Rose gave in to her sobs. Willow returned a moment later and gathered Rose in her arms, but Rose took no comfort. Emptiness, nothing but emptiness waited for her. Long, hollow years. The two stars by which she guided herself forever hidden.

Ash rose before Unweder and crept out of the narrow house and down toward the stream. Every few feet she stopped and reached out with her mind, searching for the border of the dead zone around Unweder's house. When she found it, she stood with one foot inside it and one foot outside. For the first time, she looked closely at the dead and dying trees that surrounded Unweder. If a tree grew beyond the border, it was fine and well, and its supple limbs and green leaves spread into the dead zone without harm. That's why the extent of the blight around her had been so hard to see at first. But inside the border, everything was spotted yellow, or shriveled to brown. The rocks were slimy with moss. The pools of water that sat after rain were stagnant and smelly. She had thought that Unweder might be keeping the saplings in check near his house, but she realized now that no new trees could grow in the dead zone. The leaf-fall was thick and greasy. Whatever had happened to the elementals around Unweder's house had made them unable to perform their duties.

Ash closed her eyes and quieted her mind, then reached out for a tree elemental with inaudible words. She asked it to go over the border into the dead zone and immediately felt its resistance. Its weightlessness grew dense, dragging away. This was more than resistance; this was fear. The kind of mute primitive fear cattle exude when on their way to the slaughter. She released it with a snap, and it disappeared into the bark with an almost-audible crack. She didn't want to be responsible for sending the elemental into that silence. She opened her eyes and was surprised to see Unweder standing ten yards away, very still, watching her. A slight speeding of her heart. A little fear and a little guilt.

Ash stepped back over the border and approached him. "Good morning."

"What are you doing?"

"Practicing."

His good eye considered her unblinkingly for a few moments; then he sighed and spread his hands. "Things don't grow well around my house, Ash. I take it you've noticed?"

"Yes, I have."

"I have to move every six or seven years. Everything turns to dust around me, and eventually the wood in the house starts to rot."

Ash turned this over in her mind.

"Do you know what it is?" he asked, and she could tell he was trying to guard the hope in his voice.

"There's a numbness around your house. No elementals. As though they've been suffocated."

His eyebrows shot up. "I see." He glanced around him at the yellowing leaves, the autumn that held even in spring. "Is it possible to get them back?"

"I tried to make one cross over into the dead zone. It was terrified. I let it go."

Unweder's attention returned to her. "You let it go?"

"I did."

He smiled weakly. "You're a compassionate woman, Ash. That's a rare quality in an undermagician."

She couldn't tell if this comment was meant as a compliment or a criticism, so she didn't reply. Questions burned inside her. Why did this dead zone follow him about? What had he been doing to create it? Or was it something about him that frightened elementals away? Or destroyed them? She didn't ask any of them, because she was still afraid of upsetting Unweder after being caught snooping yesterday. So she held her tongue, and they gazed at each other across the dying wood.

Finally, he said, "I think it's time I told you what I do."

Ash nodded calmly, despite a flash of excitement.

He beckoned her forward and she went to him. At first she thought he was offering his hand to her—which was odd because he rarely touched her—but then she realized he was holding one of the little glass pots that he used.

"What is it?" she said.

"Take it."

She did as he said.

"Now uncork it and drink it."

She hesitated and he grew impatient.

"Go on," he said. "What reason would I have to poison you? Would it help you to know that I drank this same draught yesterday and it helped me to see you prying in my chest?"

Curiosity won her over. Was it some kind of seeing potion? She uncorked the bottle and put it to her lips. The liquid was greasy, foul-tasting. She swallowed it, screwing up her face involuntarily, then handed it back to Unweder.

"No, don't close your eyes," he said. "Keep them open."

She had been expecting something to change in her brain, pictures to overlay themselves or distant voices to become audible. But instead, she felt the changes in her body. An awful, squirming feeling in her stomach, her muscles, her bones. As though they were becoming soft and pliable and she was in danger of falling over and never rising again. Her heart panicked and she reached for Unweder, who stepped back and let her pitch forward. Strange muttered words surrounded her, and she realized they were Unweder's. In the moment that it took her to fall to the ground, her body experienced an excruciating sensation of compression and she assumed this was death crushing her.

But it wasn't death. Because the next thing she knew, she had spread her wings and lifted off, leaving the ground far behind. She was light, made of airy bones and weightless feathers, a tiny hot heart tapping away inside her. Up she went, up above the blighted wood, and now she could look down and see the lichen-covered roof of Unweder's house disappearing as she sped on above the world, toward distant trees and plains, then circling back again, then down and down, called by Unweder with his strange mutterings, then soft as snow landing on the undergrowth.

"It's going to hurt, Ash," Unweder said, his voice distorted and muffled by her bird ears. He crouched before her, seeming a giant with heavy hands and a head made of rock. But then the pain returned, worse this time, as her bones and sinews grew dense and heavy. She cried out, but heard only a bird's squawk. Then her own voice returned, and she was lying curled on her side in the leaf-fall, her entire body feeling as though it had been hammered from within.

Unweder helped her up. She'd been sure she couldn't stand, but was surprised to find her feet were firmly on the ground. She gasped, staring at him. She hadn't realized such magic existed in the world.

"Sorry it was such a short flight. I only had a little potion left."

"You can turn yourself into a bird?" she asked.

"Any living creature," he said. "I was watching you from the roof beam yesterday."

"You were the rat?"

"Yes."

"And the animals in the chest?"

"I steal their form. They are dead, but must be kept safe and whole by magic. If I had destroyed the swallow while you were up there, you too would have been destroyed." A cold breeze rose up and stirred the leaves at their feet. He shivered. "Let's go inside. I think the rain is coming back."

They went inside, and Unweder fed the fire in the hearthpit while Ash sat and gathered herself. Her body was recovering; she felt like herself again. But her mind was reeling. She glanced at the chest, knowing that her bird form was in there somewhere, dead but not quite dead. In an unnatural sleep.

Unweder sat across from her, knees apart, and Ash flooded him with questions. How was it done, how many times had he done it, how long could he stay a bird or a beast, what was in the potion, and so on. It seemed Unweder had been performing this magic for many years, and sometimes spent whole seasons as a hawk or a stoat or some other improbable thing. He had seen the world as nobody else had, but the cost was dear. The potions he drank were made by compressing the spores of a rare moorland fungus, which he spent most of his days wandering to find, and one dry winter might wipe out his supply altogether. After a second barrage of questions, Unweder held up his hand. Ash waited while the fire popped softly, and the rain began to fall.

Finally, Unweder said, "I have a question for you. Do you think the elementals have left because of my magic?"

"They haven't left," she said, certain of it, though unsure how she was certain. "They are in an unnatural sleep. Like the animals in the chest."

"No, no. The animals in the chest are dead."

"How did you kill them?"

"I catch them then suffocate them; then when there is less than a quarter of a breath left in their lungs, I bind them with magic so they are still, so that all the grains of dust that are them, that make them, suspend and hold. They don't rot; they don't get softer or stiffer. They simply . . . stay."

"So they aren't really dead."

"I've stopped them living. That's death, isn't it?"

Ash realized she was repressing a shudder. There was something horribly macabre about what he was telling her. "When you bind them, the magic must be leaking out around the house. It's suspended the elementals as well." *Stopped them living.*

He nodded. "Can you bring them out again?"

"I don't know. It's as if they aren't there. Perhaps when I'm stronger, better at my craft. Or perhaps if you release the animals, they—"

"No," he said quickly, sharply. "I can't risk . . . Ash, there are things I need to tell you and I can see you already think me a magician of death. But nobody blinks to kill a deer for food, or a rabbit for its skin."

"I suppose you are right." Her words held more conviction than her heart.

He dropped his head, and her skin prickled lightly. He was about to tell her something she wouldn't like. She found herself leaning closer to the fire. The rain intensified outside, hammering on the roof.

"There are others," he said. "They can't all be kept in a box. I prefer small animals, ones that aren't hunted, that are overlooked by most. It gives me freedom. But I've been every kind of animal."

"Where are their bodies?"

He pointed between his shoes. "Under the floor. A horse. A wolf. And . . ."

Her feet went cold.

"I aspire to higher and higher forms. If only my body held together properly, I would hunt a dragon and become one."

She shook her head forcefully. "There are no dragons left in Thyrsland."

"I know there is one. I have seen it with the eye of my mind, and I am certain it lives and breathes on the rocky edges of the known world." He turned his own hands over in front of his face. "I do it for good reasons, Ash," he said. "It isn't just a whim to change my shape and form. I am experimenting right on the edge of undermagic. I ask the oldest question known to mankind: Where is the border between life and death?"

"Life and death?"

He nodded, holding her gaze with his good eye while the sightless one wandered to the corner of the room. Here it came, the thing she didn't want to hear. "I have lived for a hundred and twelve years," he said, his voice soft. "When this body wears out, I will simply go and find another."

Ash's ears rang as she comprehended what he meant. She pointed at the floorboards. "You mean . . . ?"

"The man I . . . became, yes. He is under there with the horse and the wolf."

"What happened to your old body? Your original one?"

"I left it to die in the woods. And the second. And the third and fourth. I was a woman for a while." He smiled.

Ash fell to silence. Unweder had just admitted to murdering for his undermagic, so that he could unnaturally prolong his life. He had just admitted a preserved corpse lay under his floor. These, of course, were the reasons for the silence in the elemental field. Elementals were natural; Unweder's magic was unnatural.

Could she stay with him now that she knew his dark secret? Where else could she go?

"Do you see why I need you, Ash?" he said, jolting her back to herself.

"To stop your house from rotting?" she asked.

"No. To stop *me* from rotting. Every time I change bodies now, it gets quicker. As the trees around me die, as the house starts to sag and mildew, I grow sick. I have been in this body only eight years, and already I have lost the use of an eye. My left hand grows palsied, and my right is soon to follow. I need life around me again. I need the elementals back."

Ash couldn't answer.

"I know what you're thinking, but I never prey on good or decent people. This is the body of a vagrant drunk. Before that it was the body of a murderous whore."

This is wrong.

"It's no different from your sister hacking up anyone who annoys her. I am discovering things that nobody ever has before." He rose, then came to kneel before her, reaching for her hands and closing them in his. She noticed his fingers were cold, clammy. "Ash," he said, "I'll share it all with you."

The prickle of curiosity. And desire. To be part of something so enormous. To live an unnaturally long life. A moment of incredible significance was upon her, heavy and thundering and real.

"Why me?" she asked.

"I followed you for many days. I saw with my inner eye only a tenth of the strength inside you. You and I, we are a match for each other. We are probably the only people who will ever understand each other. I don't want you for a wife. I don't want you for my bed. I want you to share the terrible wonders of undermagic with me."

"I'll stay," she said.

"Will you? How much can I ask of you?"

Ash thought about her life before now. It seemed she had viewed the world through a knothole. "Ask me anything."

"The potions . . . I can do without them if I have something else.

Just a little vial of it. Perhaps once every year or so. Something even thicker with magic, something to bind to the essence of the animals whose forms I steal. Something I would not need to drink but only to smear a single dot on my tongue."

"What?" she asked, already knowing what his next words would be.

"Your blood."

Willow stood in the kitchen, grinding meal to make dumplings for the afternoon's stew. She had spent the morning with Wylm and Eni by the stream, enjoying the sunshine. What a strange little family they made. Willow had started teaching Eni a basic trimartyr prayer, and he had managed the first "Hail, Maava," to her immense surprise and delight. The twin pleasures of being with Wylm and being a good soldier for Maava had made her giddy and light. Returning to the house, to her heathen sisters and undermagician aunt, had made her feel oppressed and overly warm, as though she were coming down with a fever. How she longed to get away from them. For good.

But Bluebell and Rose were nowhere to be seen and Eldra was locked away with Athelrick and her foul magic. Willow got on with her chores, longing for the time when she could go back and be with Wylm again. She hummed in her head, listened to the faint whisperings of the angels, and tried not to think about what Bluebell intended for her future. Maava would find a way to help her, given the importance of the child she was carrying. The fire in the hearthpit had gone cold so she filled it with kindling and used her flint to light it, pocketing the flint in the front of her apron along with the little jar of fire oil she carried about with her when cooking.

A creak in the quiet. She looked up to see Eldra peering out of the king's bedroom. She fixed her gaze on Willow. "Where's Bluebell?"

"I don't know."

"I need her urgently. Get her for me."

"Is it the king? Is he better?" Her heart thudded dully.

"Just get her."

Willow dropped her pestle and flew out the door and toward the stable. Rose, who was gathering herbs in the garden, saw her and straightened her back.

"Willow? Are you all right?"

"Eldra wants Bluebell."

"Bluebell went to town this morning. She should be back soon."

"She said urgently."

Rose frowned, leaving her basket on the ground. "I'll come."

Together they hurried back inside. Willow hung about by the door of the bedroom while Rose went in.

"What is wrong?" she asked Eldra.

"Where's Bluebell?"

"She's out."

Eldra sighed, ran a hand through her white-streaked hair. Willow had only seen Eldra in passing, but she had never seen her look flustered before.

"What is it?" Rose urged.

Eldra ushered Rose into the king's bedroom, closing the door partway behind her. Willow inched a little closer to listen.

"The spell is lifting, and I know who did this to Athelrick."

Spell? What heathen nonsense was this? Bluebell had poisoned him, hadn't she?

"Who?" Rose said, breathless.

"The queen."

"The queen?"

"His wife. Gudrun."

Willow's heart iced over. The awful woman, Willow's aunt, dared to blame Gudrun, Wylm's mother, for some kind of deadly magic? It was beyond belief. But a hotter, more urgent thought broke through her righteous outrage: Wylm, his mother, Eni . . . Good Maava, Bluebell would kill them all.

She began to run.

chapter 31

Willow burst out of the house and was about to start across the field to the stream when Bluebell rode through the front gate, her long hair streaming behind her. Willow hesitated. Should she stay and see what happened when Bluebell found out? Maybe Rose would convince Eldra not to tell her. For it was certain that Bluebell would want to kill Gudrun, and everybody knew it. Wylm would know it.

Bluebell saw her and called out, and there was no chance to escape. But then Willow had an idea.

She ran over to Bluebell and said, "Athelrick is recovering."

Bluebell's eyes popped. "What?"

"I'll look after your horse." She took Isern's reins. "Go. Quickly."

Bluebell dismounted and ran toward the house. Willow watched until she had gone inside, then led Isern quickly toward the stream. Wylm and Eni would need a strong mount to get away.

Bluebell's heart was too big for her chest. She slammed into the house to see Rose standing uncertainly in the hallway to Athelrick's room.

"Is he well?" she said, and it came out as though it were all one desperate word.

"Bluebell, whatever you hear—" Rose started, but Eldra interrupted.

"He isn't well yet, but he will be in a matter of hours, or at least by morning."

Bluebell's body went limp; her legs shook under her. "Oh. Oh, thank the stars. Thank the stars." She fell to her knees next to her father's bed and took his hand. Already a little pink was returning to his cheeks. He looked not so much like a breathing corpse.

"But, Bluebell," Eldra continued, and Bluebell's shoulders tensed once again, "I know who did this."

Bluebell's head snapped up. In her relief, she had forgotten that burning question. "Who?" she asked.

Eldra didn't answer immediately, exchanging a look with Rose.

Bluebell's skin prickled. Searing wrath flared in her guts. "It was Gudrun, wasn't it?" Already she was on her feet, hand at her hip. Her fingers itched for the weight of her sword.

"Don't rush off to do anything regrettable," Eldra said. "Wait until Athelrick's awake, at least."

"I'm going to kill her," Bluebell said, because they were the only words she could say. There were no other words in the world. "I'm going to kill her."

"She's your stepmother," Eldra said, but even through the crimson fog of her anger, Bluebell could see the slight amusement at the corners of her aunt's mouth.

"She tried to kill the king. *Nobody* survives that."

"Whoever did this did not intend for him to die."

"I don't give a fuck. I'm going to kill her."

Bluebell pushed past Rose, who stood aside wordlessly. She hoped Willow hadn't yet unsaddled Isern. In two days she could be in Blickstow, with a pool of her stepmother's blood at her feet.

Wylm was carving a dog—a skinny one—out of a twig for Eni, who was sitting by the side of the stream with his feet making circles on a flat, mossy rock. Something about carving made his hand and wrist feel better, more able. The small movements trained him for the large ones, he was certain. Every day, he was growing stronger. His destiny as *kyndrepa* could not be far away now.

The thought made him hollow with fear.

He looked up through the sun-dazzled branches to see Willow approaching, with Bluebell's horse. Curious, he stood, casting a shadow over Eni, who sensed the change in light and looked around.

As she drew closer, the look on her face made Wylm's blood tingle. "What is it?" he asked.

Willow caught a breath. "My aunt says she has removed an elf-shot. She says she has taken away Athelrick's bad magic. Why did she say that? Bluebell poisoned my father, did she not?"

Blind fear. "Athelrick is recovered?"

She shook her head. "Not yet, but soon. Wylm, Eldra says your mother made Athelrick sick."

Wylm's heart turned to ice. "No. Oh no."

"Is it true?"

Wylm wanted to bat her away and not answer her needy questions. But he needed her as an ally more than ever. "I . . . no, of course. Of course it is not true. But they will say anything, these murdering heathens. Has your aunt told Bluebell?"

"She was heading inside just now. But if she is the murderer, she will know it isn't true."

Panic flapped like raven wings in his head. The time had come and he wasn't ready yet. His hand still throbbed and wouldn't curl or uncurl properly, but he needed to stop Bluebell before she killed his mother. "It will not stop her acting. To hide her dark deeds."

"Yes. I thought that. I brought you her horse," Willow said. "You and Eni can get away. Back to Blickstow to warn your mother."

"No, not Blickstow." Bluebell's retainers were looking for him. He had to draw her out elsewhere. He seized Eni by the wrist and pulled him to his feet. "Come on, boy," he said.

"Where are you going?" Willow asked.

He shook his head, clearing his thoughts. "I need you to tell Bluebell you've seen me. Tell her I have Eni and I've gone to Blickstow."

"I thought you said you weren't going there."

"I'm not. I'm going to take Eni home."

"I don't understand."

"I have no time to explain. You must trust me. I will protect this boy with my life." Or rather, Bluebell would protect the boy with her life. The instant she discovered he had Eni, she would head directly for the millet farm to find out what had happened to her lover. And she wouldn't know he'd be waiting with his magical sword and his living, breathing shield. He lifted Eni into the saddle and then mounted behind him. Willow stood anxiously, not comprehending.

"I will explain all on the other side of this," Wylm said, surprising himself by feeling pity for her. "For now, I need you to stall Bluebell for as long as you can. I need a head start. Just say, *Wylm has Eni and he's gone to Blickstow.*"

"I'll do anything for you," Willow said, on one breath.

"This is all. This one sentence, but it must be perfect. *Wylm has Eni and he's gone to Blickstow.* Nothing more or less than that."

"Wylm has Eni and he's gone to Blickstow," she said.

"Good girl." Wylm leaned down to offer her a kiss, but she missed the signals, staring up at him instead with her strange, flat eyes.

"Goodbye, Willow," he said.

"Be safe," she said.

"I hope to see you again," he said, and found that there was some truth in the statement. "And I hope it is a happy occasion." Then he urged Isern forward.

Stall Bluebell for as long as you can. Willow had no idea how she was going to do that, especially as she could hear Bluebell already, from fifty feet away, screaming, "Where is my fucking horse?" from inside the stable. Her instinct was to run away; Bluebell was frightening and dangerous, and something about the situation felt wrong in her guts. Why would Bluebell be so angry if she herself was the poisoner? Could Wylm have lied to her? That could not be; he was the father of the miraculous child. The angel voices inside her head were intensifying, overlapping and swirling together, so that she could make out no words. She had to think despite them and it was hurting her brain. She only knew she had to trust Maava, who had chosen Wylm for her. Something serious was happening, and she had to play her part in it.

She approached the stable warily. She would tell Bluebell that Isern had slipped out of her hands and galloped away. Yes. Then Bluebell would go looking for him and . . .

Then she realized it was simpler than that. She kicked the stable door shut and dropped the big wooden latch.

"What the fuck?"

Willow stood back, pulse jumping in her throat, while Bluebell began to swear and kick the door.

"Who's there? Who did this?"

"It's Willow," she called, in a steely voice.

"Willow, open this fucking door. Don't give me any of your trimartyr nonsense. I will do what I have to do. Mercy doesn't apply in this situation."

Willow realized Bluebell thought she was trying to protect Gudrun. "I have a message from Wylm," Willow said.

Silence. Willow was glad she couldn't see Bluebell's face.

"He says he has Eni, and he's heading to Blickstow."

"Eni?"

"Yes, the little blind boy. We rescued him. I know what you did." Then Willow clamped her hand over her mouth, reminding herself not to tell Bluebell too much.

"Wylm has been here?"

Willow didn't answer; she had just remembered the flint in her pocket.

"Talk sense to me, girl," Bluebell said. "What could he possibly know about Sabert and Eni? Wylm is not our friend. His mother tried to kill the king, our father."

"No. Do not say it. *You* did. You did it." Willow built the little pile of kindling at the stable door in seconds, barely recognizing her hands as her own. Then she took the flint and struck it. A spark jumped into the kindling. A little orange flame. Smoke. She fanned it with her apron. It singed the bottom of the stable door. Black streaks. Bluebell was still demanding answers. A generous splash of Ash's fire oil and . . . there. Then the flames caught and held.

Dropping the flint, she turned and ran, angels shrieking at her all the way.

❖   ❖   ❖

When Bluebell smelled the smoke, any questions about Wylm and Sabert and Eni dropped away. The horses were already uneasy, shifting restlessly, snorting, ears flickering. Bluebell kicked the door as hard as she could, but it wouldn't budge. She screamed Willow's name several times, then realized the girl had gone. The stable was wood, and it was a clear, dry day. She didn't have much time.

Bluebell went to the shutter at the back of the stable and pushed it open. Punched it off its hinges. She put her hands in the opening and pulled herself up, but could already see she wouldn't fit through. Choking smoke swirled up behind her. By now, the horses were whinnying loudly, rolling their eyes and kicking at the stable walls. She slid back down to the ground. The door was on fire; if she tried again to kick it down, she would burn. Embers were falling into the straw all over the floor. Bluebell frantically stamped them out. The flames were curling around the door now, moving up into the stable and licking up the doorframes. The door suddenly sagged, and she realized the latch had given way.

Bluebell turned to the horses. Of the five of them, she chose the calmest and, coughing until her throat was raw, saddled it and held tight to the reins as it strained and whinnied. When the door fell in, she might have a few seconds before the fire leapt across the opening, and she wanted to be prepared. As the smoke filled the stable, she realized that flames were no longer the greatest threat. She tore a strip off her tunic and tied it gently around the horse's eyes. She went through the motions, slipping the bit between its teeth, talking to it quietly. Then she held the horse still long enough to mount it, its ears working back and forth. But Bluebell stroked its neck firmly and calmly. The horse, like her, would smell the fresh air and run for it. The door sagged again, with a crashing thump, as the wood around its hinges burned through. Bluebell's body was tensed like a bow.

"Bluebell!" It was Rose.

Bluebell gasped in relief. The horse tried to throw her. The heat from the fire made her face feel raw. "There's a water trough and a bucket behind the—"

"Already found it." Then a puddle of water spread under the door.

Bluebell held tight, coughing and spitting. More water. The flames began to subside. The door was safe to approach, so she let the horse have its head. "Stand back!" she called, and her mount and the other horses bolted for the fresh air. Rose waited on the other side, her face streaked with soot. Bluebell gulped the clear afternoon air, galloped out the gate, and then slowly and calmly brought the horse back to a walk and circled it around to the gate, where Rose waited. "Thank you, sister," she called.

"What happened?"

"Willow did it."

Rose's eyes rounded. "Willow?"

"She's gone to Maava. And was talking about Wylm. Has Wylm been here?"

"No. I would have told you if he had been."

"Then there's something suspicious going on." Bluebell untied the horse's blindfold and wiped her sweaty, soot-streaked hands on it. "Willow said she's been talking to Wylm."

"I haven't seen Wylm around here—though Heath mentioned a little boy who showed up from time to time to see Willow."

Bluebell's heart jumped. "A blind, simple boy?"

"Yes. And Heath said Willow often disappeared without warning, taking food with her. You don't think . . . ?"

Wylm. Wylm had Eni. "I have to ride. Now."

Rose opened her mouth to speak then stopped.

"I suppose you're going to tell me not to be rash. Not to go to Blickstow and kill my stepmother?"

Rose shook her head. "I'm going to tell you to do what's in your heart. Of all the people I have known, Bluebell, you are the only one who always knows the right thing to do."

Bluebell smiled despite herself, despite the smoke and the rawness in her chest, despite the mystery of Wylm and Eni, despite Willow's stinging betrayal. "Yes. I do. And Father's mercy will leave the whole kingdom exposed," she said. "I'll leave Thrymm here to guard you and Eldra until Father wakes. Look after her and she'll look after you.

Round up those horses when they've calmed down, and make sure all the embers are out."

"You're going directly to Blickstow?"

"Almost directly." If Wylm had Eni, that meant something had happened to Sabert. The thought made her flinch. "But my path and Gudrun's are destined to meet now. She can't escape her fate."

Late evening. Light under the shutters making a yellow band across the pale branches of the ash tree that Willow had been cowering in since dusk. Hissing, spitting voices in her head.

"You killed your sister. You murdered her."

No, no. I had to! She is a murderer. I had to save the life of the little boy. He might be her son; my nephew.

"You care nothing for the little boy. You want the man. You burn with desire for him. Whore! Murderer! Sister-killer!"

My sister is a heathen.

"She was *a heathen. Before you killed her."*

Willow tilted her head to one side and thumped her ear, in the hope that the voices would drop out the other side.

"Leave her be. She is doing Maava's good work. Bluebell would have been a heathen queen."

Yes! Willow breathed again. This voice came from time to time, stronger than the others. She liked to imagine it was Maava himself.

"She carries a child within her who is fathered by the rightful heir of Almissia."

"Her sister burned to death."

I had to do it.

"She had to do it."

Willow groaned. She didn't have to do it. Wylm only asked her to stall Bluebell, not to kill her. Not to slay the monster. The voices in her head whirled on, but she started to suspect that her own thoughts were infecting her. That one of those voices—the one calling her a murderer—was actually her own. Her hands trembled on the branch in front of her. They were covered in dried blood. She had cut herself so much today and it had flowed freely down between her fingers, making them stick together. Bloody handprints marked her route up the tree. The wounds along her wrists stung, reminding her that she was real and still in the world.

Finally, the light went out in the house. She was about eight miles south of Stonemantel, outside a house she didn't recognize, full of people she didn't know. But there was a horse tied up under a shed just on the other side of this tree, and that was what she wanted. Only Wylm could give her the comfort she needed, and she knew where she could find him.

Since Rose had lost Rowan and then Heath, the days flowed as slow and formless as cold honey. So when Eldra said it had been twenty-four hours since Bluebell left, Rose was puzzled.

"Has it?"

Eldra turned from the open shutter and looked at Athelrick, lying still between them. "A full day since I removed the elf-shot and still he hasn't woken."

Rose went over it in her mind. After helping Bluebell out of the burning stable, she had cleaned herself up and sat by the fire, dozed then slept, prepared food, and washed her dress in a tub . . . Yes, she supposed it had been a day. One full cycle of the sun.

Eldra sighed. "There's nothing more I can do. I suppose we wait." She nodded at Rose. "I'm going for a walk. You'll stay with him? He oughtn't be alone."

"Of course," she said.

Eldra limped off. The shutter was still open, letting in a late-afternoon breeze that stirred the hangings on the wall. Rose sank forward, her arms folded on the bed, her chin resting on them, listening to Father's rhythmic breathing. She wondered how close Bluebell was to Blickstow by now. Perhaps another day away. Would that day also pass as though it hadn't? Would every day from now on be indistinct, blurred with misery and longing?

The covers moved and Rose lifted her head. Had she imagined it? Father had been still for weeks. She watched him a moment. Then he stirred again, his hand fighting the tightly tucked-in blanket. Rose sat back and watched in amazement as he withdrew his hand and then let it come to rest on top of the blanket. She realized she was holding her breath. She released it and said, "Father?"

The word sat expectant in the quiet room for a moment, then another and another.

And then he said, "Bluebell?" A statue coming to life: his eyelids fluttered, opened.

"No. It's me, it's Rose," she said, happiness flooding warmly into her heart for the first time in days. "Bluebell is . . . You'll see her soon, my lord."

"Where am I?" He licked his lips and coughed. His pale-blue eyes seemed strangely unfamiliar after so long closed.

Rose leapt to her feet to pour him a drink of water from the pitcher by the door. "Just outside Stonemantel. You've been sick. We brought you here to cure you."

He drank the water gratefully, dribbling some of it into his beard. But instead of being oblivious to it as he had been the last few weeks, he cursed lightly and ran his palm over it. He handed the cup back to Rose. "I am so tired, Rose," he said.

"Sleep a little longer, my lord. There's no hurry. Now you are yourself again."

He lay back, looking at the ceiling a few moments. Then his eyelids dropped softly closed. A minute later, he turned on his side. A man sleeping. Not an enchanted king. Rose began to cry, her heart blocking up her throat. If she couldn't be happy for herself, she could at least be happy for her family. For Bluebell.

The spell was broken at last.

CHAPTER 32

The first night had been one long bad dream for Wylm, waking up every twenty minutes certain that Bluebell would find them and kill him in his sleep, before he could get his hand on *Grithbani.* They had camped in a ditch away from the road, but still he couldn't shake the feeling. So this evening he was a little more relaxed. He'd found a cave in a hill high above the treetops. He'd tied the horse to a tree on the flat near the road—it was exhausted and would likely not last another day, as Wylm had pushed it harder than he'd ever pushed an animal before in order to stay ahead of Bluebell— and then helped Eni up the rocky slope and into the cave. It was shallow, dark, musty. They had eaten only a few mushrooms early in the day, and Eni was whining from the cold and hunger.

"I'm sorry, Eni, but I dare not light a fire," Wylm said. "There's a monster following us and we can't risk discovery."

Eni quieted. This story, about them escaping together from a monster, had worked on the child brilliantly. Though now, at night, Wylm felt sorry for him. He slipped off his cloak and put it around Eni's shoulders, pulling the boy close. Eni laid his head in Wylm's lap so that Wylm could stroke his hair the way Willow did, and there was something soothing about this very human touch. Wylm remembered his own father, who would hold him still on his lap once a week to clean his ears. It had been Wylm's favorite time of the week, sitting between his father's strong knees, enveloped in his manly warmth.

Perhaps Wylm could have been that kind of man, one who was gentle with children and animals and craved no power or influence in the world. But no. His father, after all, could never defend himself in a fight, would never have had the gumption to kill somebody, especially somebody like Bluebell. Wylm needed to be a different kind of man. He stilled his hand.

He looked out of the mouth of the cave, over the treetops and down to the road in the gray dark. The black shape of a rook, late to bed, flew past, its caw echoing around the rocks and out across the fields. A sign from Hakon and his randerman? Wylm shuddered. Rooks were considered portents of death.

Tomorrow was the day. If he had Eni, then Bluebell couldn't hurt him. Wouldn't hurt him. It would give him the time and freedom to land the killing blow.

He felt about for the sword and unsheathed it. Fear and wonder caught on his ribs, and he noticed a faint phosphorescent glow on the runes. The time was drawing near, then. A battle with Bluebell approached. He hefted the sword in his hand. His grip was not what it should have been; it didn't sit where it ought. But still, here it was, his glowing trollblade, forged to kill Bluebell. He thought he could smell the randerman's burning herbs on the wind, and he allowed himself a little smile.

Eni startled, letting out a moan in his sleep. A nightmare. Wylm smoothed his hair off his brow. "Shhh, Eni," he said. "Soon there will be nothing to worry about." His eyes went to the silent road again. "Tomorrow I will slay the monster."

There was no need for secrecy, so Bluebell took the Giant Road, the mighty artery that led to her hometown. The road bustled with trade and travel, and the inns took advantage of the extra traffic and the longer days. The world was a whirl around her, but Bluebell was trapped in her own grim reality.

"Do you have a room?" she gruffly asked the alehouse wife. The inn she'd stopped at as soon as the sun set was large, but also very popular. The bar was full.

"For you, my lord, we will find a room," the woman answered. She shouted some orders at a kitchen boy, then returned her attention to Bluebell. "Are you hungry? Can I offer you food?"

"Have you seen a man and a boy traveling together? The boy is blind. The man is a slippery weasel with black hair."

"No, I haven't. Would you like me to ask around?"

"If you would. And put out the word to those who pass through that Bluebell is looking for them."

"I will, my lord. Now do you mind me asking you how goes the king?"

Bluebell's eyes narrowed. "Why? What have you heard?"

"There have been rumors from travelers that he has long been away from Blickstow, that some were saying he had gone mad."

She was naïve to think that such rumors wouldn't start. "He is well." The words didn't give her the buoyant happiness she had expected to feel. "He will return soon to Blickstow."

The alehouse wife smiled with genuine relief. "Really? Well, I shall let everyone know. Please, my lord, find a spare seat and I'll bring you food and ale, compliments of the alehouse. Your room will be ready very soon."

In a corner, opposite an elderly woman mopping up the last of her soup, there was a spare stool. Bluebell strode over and sat down. The woman looked up, opened her mouth to say something, but Bluebell raised her hand in warning.

"Don't speak to me. I have a lot to think about."

The woman's mouth twitched, and she quickly finished her meal and vacated her seat. Bluebell leaned forward on her elbows, considering the people around her, drinking, talking, eating, laughing in the warm light of the lanterns and the roaring fire. The smell of smoke and sweat and dogs. Everyone seemed so unburdened by cares, but she knew it wasn't true. Everyone had worries, everyone struggled. It was just that Bluebell's struggles bore more weight. Fates of kingdoms rested on her decisions.

Three impulses pulled her in three different directions. Kill Gudrun. Get to Sabert's farm and find out if he was unharmed. Find Wylm and Eni. The last she could do little about. She could waste days or weeks or more trying to find them. Once the other things were sorted out, she could use the king's resources to track them down. Eni was defenseless himself, but Bluebell could mobilize a king's army if she had to.

If Wylm thought holding Eni to ransom was going to stop Bluebell from killing Gudrun, then he was wrong. He could send a ransom note if he wanted, but Bluebell couldn't read, and besides, it would likely arrive after Gudrun was already dead. Perhaps he would send Willow to stop her. Perhaps that's why Willow had taken her horse and locked her in the stable. Damn Willow. She'd become a trimartyr and betrayed her family without a breath in between. Bluebell could forgive many offenses due to Willow's youth and innocence, but trying to burn her sister alive was not forgivable. She could never trust Willow again, and so there was little to be done but to lock her up somewhere in Blickstow and let her rot.

But Sabert's farm was only half an hour from Blickstow. She could stop and look in on Sabert. Maybe she would find him there, with Eni, both well and happy, and Willow's story would be revealed as a lie to frighten her out of killing Gudrun. The idea gave Bluebell a warm feeling in her stomach. Her food arrived and she ate it with a good appetite. This time tomorrow, it would be over. Gudrun would be gone, Father would be recovered and on his way home, and life could resume as it had been once, when things were good.

Before Athelrick had loved Gudrun. Before Willow had turned trimartyr. Before Rose had lost her child. Before Ash had exiled herself. Before Eldra had told her the truth about her father.

She reached for her ale to drown out her thoughts.

Ash's eyes flew open in the dark, her heart thudding. She could see her own pulse as her eyes adjusted to the lightless house. Why had she woken? The strangled half of a dream slipped away from her. Something about Bluebell.

She rose. The hearthpit had burned down to warm embers, so it must be well past midnight. She went to the door and opened it quietly, gazing out into the dark. Cold air. Bare trees. Stars obscured by shredded clouds. Somewhere out there was her sister, and she was in trouble. Ash felt it low down in her stomach. She tried to concentrate her mind and reach out, but received only frustrating half images. Somebody lying in wait. The image was daylit, so it hadn't happened yet. Bluebell on her back, open to attack. Was it raiders? No, somebody closer to home. Ash's mouth was dry. Bluebell went to war and Ash had never felt this way. Why now, unless . . . Unless she really was seeing Bluebell's death?

"Ash?"

She turned to see Unweder behind her.

"I had a dream."

"Do you remember it?"

"No, but it was a premonition. My sister is in danger."

"Which one?"

"Bluebell. I think . . . I think somebody is trying to kill her."

He smiled in the dark. "Isn't somebody always trying to kill her?"

"But this time, I think he's going to succeed."

Unweder took her arm gently, closing the door. "Bluebell may be in danger, but that is how she lives her life. Nobody can kill her."

"Then why do I feel such a sense of dread?"

"Nightmares do that. The shadows wait everywhere at night. You'll feel differently in the morning."

She allowed herself to be led back to her bed, where she sat, holding her knees, while Unweder stood over her. "You aren't part of their lives anymore, Ash. If you are to do your work here, if you are to develop the command of the ability that I know you have in you, you simply must disconnect from your family."

"But how can I? The same blood flows in my veins as my family's."

He flinched at the word "blood." It was a sore point between them that she hadn't yet agreed to his request. While she knew it would hardly hurt and she would not miss such a small gift of her blood, she was still not sure how much she could trust a man who killed for magic.

He shook his head. "Undermagicians don't care much for family. Perhaps you don't want to be an undermagician."

She watched him go back to his bedroom. The outside air had made the room cold, so she lay down and wrapped herself tightly in her blanket. She thought about what Unweder had said, and perhaps he was right. Perhaps the sour taste of the bad dream had made her premonition seem worse. Perhaps it was time she let go of her family.

Or perhaps there was one last thing she could do for Bluebell.

At first light, Wylm took one look at Bluebell's horse and realized it would kill the beast to go farther. He considered saddling it anyway, taking it as far as he could until it dropped dead, but pity stirred in him unexpectedly. He, too, knew what it was like to be exhausted, to want to lay down his burden and rest.

He gave the horse some water and let it free. He wouldn't need all this gear anyway. Just bread and water for him and Eni for one day. Everything else, he could figure out later.

He grasped Eni's hand firmly. "We are walking. Hold on to me tight. The monster may be here."

Eni tightened his grip on Wylm's hand. They walked as the sun rose and peaked. Later in the afternoon, Wylm noticed Eni tilting his head this way and that, like a bird. Perhaps he recognized the sounds and the smells; they were very close to his home. It was a fine day, and the ground was firm underfoot. Soon the millet fields came into view, a sea of green undulating gently with the warm southerly breeze. It didn't seem like a day when anything bad could happen, and he took heart. He had all the advantages. She didn't even know he was here. He simply had to find a place to hide until she came.

Then he frowned. *If* she came. What if she went directly to Blickstow? What if the well-being of her lover was less important than taking revenge? The thought bit him coldly. Even now, his mother could be hours away from her brutal death.

Breathe. Breathe. He couldn't defend her without risking his own life. Mother would want him to live and be king, and with Bluebell out of the way, he could.

The farmhouse came into view, and Eni tensed.

"Yes, you know where you are, don't you? How can you tell without seeing?" Wylm took a deep breath of the air, but could not smell anything distinctive. Earth and animal shit. Perhaps that was enough for Eni to recognize his home. "But we must be careful. We have to hide a little while. Very quietly."

"Papa," Eni said, and Wylm had a pang. Surely he wasn't so simple that he thought his father might still be alive? He glanced at Eni's face. No, it was sad, lost. Wylm forced steel into his heart.

"Papa's not here. The monster killed him. Now the monster must die." He spotted a chicken coop, directly parallel to the farmhouse's back door, about twenty feet away. He flipped up the door and crawled in. It smelled of chicken shit and damp hay. He opened one of the boxes and found an egg for him and one for Eni, puncturing them with one of his knives so they could drink them. Then he took the child into the house, where Eni went into paroxysms of anxious whimpering, remembering the feel and smell of the place. Wylm found a position, behind weevil-ridden flour sacks beside the door, for himself and the child to sit and wait. Should Bluebell enter the farmhouse, he would be able to see her before she saw him. He thought about the back of her neck—smooth and white—and shivered slightly. He hoped she wouldn't be too long coming.

Rose spent the day outside. First washing all the blankets down at the stream—Bluebell and Heath were gone, and Willow was nowhere to be found—then finding trees with low branches in the sun to dry them. The sky was wide and blue. A light wind down low made fast-moving shadows across the grass and lifted the fluffy seeds of dandelion clocks so that they tumbled past, catching in Rose's hair. The sun was warm on her back, and Rose had a strong desire to keep walking, not to return to the dim house just yet. So she'd started up the edge of the stream, searching for mushrooms between the trees and rocks. Willow had disappeared, Eldra never cooked, and Athelrick would have his appetite back, so that afternoon's dinner was her responsibility. She realized it was the first time she had been out of the house since Heath left. Being out made her feel lighter. As though she could breathe.

By the time she came back, the sun was low in the sky and the house was quiet. Bluebell's dog, Thrymm, looked up when she came in.

"It's quiet in here, girl," Rose said, dropping the mushrooms on the bench and wiping her hands on her skirt.

The dog's tail thumped. Rose went to the bedroom door to look in on her father and Eldra.

Eldra was not there, but more important Athelrick was not there, either. The bed was empty. At first she feared something bad had happened, but then she realized that the fresh clothes, boots, and sword that Bluebell had insisted they bring from Blickstow were gone. He was up. He was dressed. That morning when she'd last seen him, he'd been asleep still, snoring softly. But now it seemed he and Eldra had gone out. Perhaps hoping, as she had, that fresh air and sunshine would do him good. If only she could get a message to Bluebell that Father was awake and risen. That grim face might actually break into a smile.

Rose was tired from her day's work and wandering, so she lay down crosswise on her father's bed. Thrymm climbed up to lie next to her, head on paws. Rose rested her hand lightly on the dog's head, closing her eyes.

She must have drifted into a doze because when she opened her eyes, Thrymm was sitting up, ears pricked, whining softly.

"What is it?" Rose asked.

Thrymm barked once then leapt off the bed and ran toward the door. Footsteps beyond the bedroom. Rose sat up, embarrassed that Eldra and her father might find her sleeping before supper was made.

But it wasn't Eldra or her father. Standing at the door to the bedroom, his hands being savagely licked by Thrymm, was Heath.

For a horrible, too-bright moment, she thought she was dreaming. But then he smiled and opened his arms and she was pressed against his chest, breathing the clean-earth scent of him. He was warm and hard and real. "What are you doing here?"

"I've been camped in the woods since Bluebell told me to leave. I couldn't go without saying goodbye. I saw horses leaving earlier today. Your father. He's better?"

"Yes, he is. They took horses? Do you have any idea where they were going?"

"No."

"They can't have gotten far. Father has been sick a long time, and Eldra would have trouble staying horsed. She has a terrible limp."

"She had no limp."

Rose pressed her lips together, curious.

"I saw you returning to the house alone," Heath continued. "I figured it might be my only chance to see you. Before I go."

"Where are you going?"

"North. My father had relatives on the very northern coast of Thyrsland, in Bradsey. They don't know me, but they may take me in for a while."

"They are First Folk?"

"Yes. I know nothing about them." He rubbed his chin, a few days unshaven and already ginger. "I'll be able to grow my beard at last." He smiled—but when he saw that she didn't, he dipped his head. "I'm sorry."

The northern coast. Icy-cold seas, the ever-present danger of raiders, widespread poverty. "So we really aren't to see each other ever again?"

"Bluebell is right. For Rowan's sake. For your own. And for mine."

She dropped her head on his chest once again, heard his heart thudding. "How is it that love, so pure and so true, cannot be allowed to survive?"

He stroked her hair and her back. "I don't know, Rose. All I know is that I will always love you. Through every cold day of winter and every long day of summer. I will always love you."

She turned her face up to his and he kissed her, gently at first, then gathering in passion, his tongue and hers seeking each other out. Desire stirred again among the cold ashes. Heath stood back, sent Thrymm from the room, and closed the door.

"I don't know when Eldra and Father are coming back," she said.

He smiled and reached up to drop the latch across the door. Then he moved toward her, his hands unpinning the brooches that held her dress together while his mouth remained pressed against hers. Her dress fell to the ground. She pulled off his tunic and they collapsed on the bed together, struggling half out of clothes. Her shift was tangled around her waist, his trousers around his ankles. His hands squeezed her thighs, her fingers grasped his back. His mouth found her breasts: too rough. She flinched. He gentled and desire made her deaf and blind. There was only the bright light and ringing music of passion. He was inside her, kissing her and kissing her, his body crushing her sweetly. Every sensation in her skin was amplified in her blood, echoing through her body and her breath. She clamped her legs around his hips and gave herself up as she had never given herself up before. When he came, she realized she was weeping silently. He kissed the tears from her face and held her while her blood pressure returned to normal and her knees grew solid once again. Afternoon light fell through the open shutter, making a square on the bed that fell on his skin and the blanket. She burned the image into her mind, in case it was the last time.

The very last time. Her soul held its breath. She knew the goodbye would come.

"I should go," he said at last, "before Athelrick returns."

They dressed and let Thrymm in. The house was still quiet. Rose opened the door and peered out. No movement from the stable, with its burnt-out door. No movement on the road beyond. "You'll need a horse and money," she said to him.

"I don't need anything. I'll be fine."

Rose shook her head. "Take a horse, and I'll give you what coin I have."

Heath looked as though he might protest, then changed his mind and sighed. "I should be able to look after myself."

"You have provided me such joy and comfort, my love. Material things are the least I owe you."

He nodded, and she fetched her purse to give to him. He collected the spare clothes that he'd left behind, and then they stood awkwardly together at the door.

"I don't know what to say," he said at last.

She opened her eyes. "Goodbye. And I love you."

"Yes." Then he was walking away, toward the stable. A few minutes later he emerged, mounted, and lifted his hand in a wave. Tears ran down her face and dripped from her chin. She shuddered as he disappeared out the front gate. A lumpen cold possessed her. She put her hands over her face and she could still smell him. "Goodbye," she said, kissing her own fingers as passionately as she had kissed him. "Goodbye."

chapter 33

sh paid close attention to the prickling tingles of her pre- monition. She had not woken free of dread, as Unweder had suggested. Rather, she was sure that today was the day Bluebell would die. Every second seemed heavy with it. The tension was soft, though persistent, in the morning, but by the middle of the day it clutched firmly, and unreadable runes danced across her field of vision. Ash knew what she had to do; she just didn't know when she had to do it. She barely listened to a word Unweder said to her that day, but he seemed to have decided to let her be preoccupied. As the sun passed full height and began the slow slide toward setting, the tension became acute, a hard sharp thing in her stomach.

She stood, began to pace.

"What is it, Ash?"

"I have to go."

"You have no illusions of riding to Bluebell's rescue . . ."

"To the woods," Ash said. "I have to go to the woods. I know what I have to do."

Unweder nodded. "I won't stop you."

Ash left the house, trembling with fear. The danger was so close to her sister now, and Bluebell had no idea. No idea at all. Ash went out of the dead zone and down across the stream to the densest part of the wood, where she knew the elementals were thick in the trees and on the ground. She sat on a rock and focused herself, closing her eyes and taking note of the movement around her. She had a little sprig of angelica that she'd pinned to her dress earlier in preparation, and now she crushed its oil onto her fingers and wiped it across her eyelids, and on her temples. She breathed. The elementals gathered at a distance, curious but wary.

"Keep my body safe," she said, and felt their grudging compliance in the way they moved in closer, sitting around her ankles.

Ash put her hands on her temples, gathering her mind between her fingers. *There it is. There.* She lifted her hands and pointed them south, toward Bluebell. She felt the pull and snap when her energy, her focus, her talent with elementals left her body as a bright ball of light and went rocketing through the woods. In her inner eye, she could see the trajectory it took as a dreamlike journey among magical beings. Tiny creatures with leaves for eyebrows, cracked rock for mouths, twigs for hands, stood to watch. And whenever the bright thing slowed, she would order an elemental to pick it up and propel it forward again, south, the force of her mind too much for them to resist.

Finally, she began to feel Bluebell was close. But closer still was Wylm, her stepbrother. Ash knew immediately that he intended to kill Bluebell, but there was no mind left for her to worry or wonder. She dropped the bright ball just outside the dark house he hid in. Elementals in the area came cautiously close, and she pulled them closer and held them with her mind. She felt a great, gleaming pair of eyes watching her from across miles and mist. An echo of her dream of Becoming. She held back any fear, using her energy instead to hold the elementals close, despite the wave of formless exhaustion that threatened to pull her down to the undergrowth.

Ash waited.

Bluebell arrived at Sabert's farm as the afternoon shadows were starting to grow long. Her back ached from a long day in the saddle, but her blood felt electric as she dismounted outside his house. Everything seemed very quiet, but she told herself not to worry. There were many reasons a house might be quiet. She tried the door and found it swung open easily. Not locked.

There were many reasons a house might be unlocked.

"Saba?" she said as she entered. "Eni?"

The smell told her immediately Sabert wasn't here, and that he had been gone a long time. A rotten piece of meat sat liquefied on the table, surrounded by chunks of mold-covered bread. She opened the little door to the bedroom, peering in at the bed where she and Sabert had so often taken their pleasure. Nobody there. No Sabert. No Eni. Just the smell of old piss.

So perhaps Wylm did have Eni. But where was Sabert? Bluebell started looking in cupboards and nooks, then outside the back door in barrels and troughs, realizing that she was now searching for a body. Sabert's greatest fear was to die and leave his boy unprotected, and now it seemed that had happened.

A whistling sound rushed past her ear and something thudded into the wooden wall beside her. Bluebell had her sword in her hand before she'd even glimpsed the knife sticking out of the wall, before she'd even turned to see who had thrown it.

It was Wylm. And he had Eni held tight against his body.

"Eni!" she called.

The boy looked around sightlessly, his mouth upside down with frightened sadness. This expression enraged her, even more than Wylm's useless attempt on her life.

"What the fuck are you doing?" she asked Wylm.

With his free hand Wylm drew a gleaming sword from its sheath, then held the cruel edge of it against Eni's neck. "Drop the Widowsmith," he said, in a slow, measured voice that told Bluebell he was shitting himself and trying not to show it.

"Prepare to die," she said.

He leaned gently into the blade, breaking the skin on Eni's neck and releasing a thin trickle of blood. "Drop the Widowsmith," he said again.

She dropped it. She had a knife in her belt, another at her ankle. There would be a chance to kill him yet.

"Let the child go."

"Is he important to you, Bluebell? Do you love him? I find it hard to believe that there's a heart inside you."

"He's the son of one of my friends," Bluebell said. "I won't let you hurt him."

"Ah, your *friend*. The thick-necked farmer I killed."

Her gut clenched. There was no time now for sorrow. "What do you want?"

"I want you to fear me, Bluebell, for I am the *kyndrepa*. Do you know what that means?"

She spread her hands as though nonchalant and exaggerated a shrug. "Limp dick?"

Wylm laughed bitterly. "I see I can't threaten you. I'll tell you this then: I want you to promise me that you won't hurt my mother. Then Eni will be safe and so will you."

Fuck. She should have known this would be his demand.

"If I hear you've hurt her, I'll kill this child."

"And when do I get Eni back?"

"When my mother and I are safely in Tweening."

She looked at Eni's face; she thought about Sabert, about her long-dead friend Edie. "Very well," she said.

Wylm started to back up, gestured with his head toward the door. She backed out and he followed her, half dragging poor Eni. He pointed to a gap in the hedge that surrounded the garden. "Go. That way. Don't look back."

She spread her hands in front of her, smiling, and continued to walk backward.

"Turn around!" he demanded.

"Back off, then."

He shuffled away a few feet, pulled Eni roughly against him. "Turn around!" he cried again, his veneer of calm beginning to crack. "I'll kill him."

Eni began to sob: big openmouthed sobs. "Rabbit," he cried mournfully.

Bluebell's heart started. She turned and ran for cover, intending to vault over the hedge. She felt movement behind her, was achingly aware of her unguarded back, her vulnerability. She half turned, then stumbled at the hedge and landed hard on her stomach. Bright-hot disbelief flooded her. It was happening. She was down, unarmed. She flipped over in time to see Wylm standing over her. She could see the strange runes on his blade glowing with preternatural pale fire, and she wondered if she was dreaming, if her spirit was already uncoiling from her body ahead of her death. For no well-placed kick, no late-minute gathering of a knife from her ankle, could help her now. He was too close and she was on her back. The moment was bright and heavy. Eni ran away toward the house, whole and unharmed. Mother-less, fatherless. She looked up at Wylm again, her face twisting with anger. Her heart was beating so hard that it seemed the ground was shaking underneath her. She ripped open her tunic and said. "Through my heart. Make it quick."

He smiled at the sight of her breast. "Ah, they aren't made of iron after all," he said, raising the sword.

The ground shook again, and this time Bluebell knew it wasn't her heart. The movement was enough to knock Wylm off-balance. He caught himself by plunging the sword into the ground beside him, shouting with a pain she didn't understand. It gave Bluebell enough time to sit up, but not to get up. He had the blade in a bloody hand in front of him a moment later, but this time the hedge began to shake, the long tendrils of marjory vine that grew over it standing erect as though lightning had struck the ground. He could have killed her then. He had time and proximity, but the vine's movement distracted him half a moment more than it should have. A second later the vine shot out and tangled around his ankles. He fell on his side, dropping the sword, breaking his fall with his arm, which twisted into a sick angle beside him. Bluebell had his sword in her hand in a second, standing above him. Their situations reversed. Only Bluebell wouldn't delay with fancy speeches and observations. She drew up her arm and plunged the blade deep, deep into his heart. He had time to gasp, then to say, "Have mercy on my mother."

He had time to hear her say, "Fuck you."

Then the steel stopped his heart beating and he convulsed and went still.

Bluebell released the grip and stood back. She wiped her nose with the back of her hand and stood a moment, catching her breath, breasts still bare in the sunshine. The vine had withdrawn back into the hedge; the ground was still. Bluebell closed her eyes. "I love you, Ash," she said, then pulled her tunic back together and went inside to look for Eni, leaving Wylm's body for the ravens to relish.

Ash had sat for so long, mind and body separated, that the insides of her eye sockets had gone icy cold. She held out long enough to hear Bluebell's message of love, and then began to pull her light back toward her. Only her light wasn't so bright anymore, and she was weary from holding it apart from her. She sought out elementals, who began to pass her along, away and away from that field near Blickstow. *I'll always love you, sister,* she said, though she wasn't sure if her lips moved here in the woods, or if she said it only with her mind, all those miles away. She fluttered in and out of knowing, finding her light on the ground and having to ask again and again for the elementals to pick it up, pass it along, send it shooting north to Bradsey. The elementals cared nothing for her; they only did something if ordered. If she blacked out for a minute, she would find herself once again dull and unmoving. Exhaustion overwhelmed her. She felt her mind and body drawing back together. Slowly. Too slowly . . .

The road northeast out of Folkenham had been wide and well traveled, but the eastern route to Seacaster, where Gunther had his hall, was narrow, rutted, and crowded in by twisted trees. Ivy knew the trees were bars and she was entering a cage: She was a pretty bird for Gunther to admire, feed, and show off to others, but, nonetheless, captive. The conviction persisted, even after the trees scattered and cleared, and she and her retinue—two of Wengest's warriors, although not his best—came out across the wildflower moors that led to the sea. Seacaster was a bustling port town and shorefort built on a tall clifftop. Gunther commanded a small army of his own and the town was heavily fortified. Even from this distance she could see the great, high walls obscuring from view everything that was inside: the town and hall and bower that would constitute her new life. Her breath sat flat in her lungs.

They crossed the bridge that had been lowered over the deep ditch surrounding the town, then under the gate and into the crowded town square. Everywhere the smell of fish and seaweed. Ivy felt as though she were choking on it.

The town seemed dark and damp compared with the bright warmth of Blickstow, or the wide lanes of Folkenham, or the summery freshness of Fengard. She tried to cheer herself by remembering that she would soon be a duchess, the most important woman in Seacaster. All of these plain-faced people at the market would soon recognize her and have to smile at her, have to acknowledge and respect who she was. For now, she kept her head down as the horses sidestepped people and carried them around to Gunther's stables.

She dismounted and stood at the entrance to the stable gazing out at her new home. Gunther's hall was small, and the bowerhouses around it few. How much luckier had Rose been in marriage, just because she was older. In fact, Bluebell, as the first daughter, ought to have been married to Wengest, but of course nobody thought that a good idea. And if they could change the rules for Rose, then why not for Ivy? She would have been a much better queen of Nettlechester.

A tall woman with long, gray-streaked hair was hurrying toward them, and Ivy presumed this was their welcome. She stood up straight and squared her shoulders.

"Princess Ivy of Almissia," the woman said, and Ivy noticed she did not smile. "I am Elgith, and Gunther has sent me to show you to your bower."

"Thank you," she said, glancing behind her at her retinue, who were conversing with the stable hands. Even though she didn't know them or like them, she felt the twinge of leaving them behind. That was it: her last link back to her old life. She felt it stretch and snap as she walked from the stables to the bowerhouses with Elgith.

"Where is Gunther?" Ivy asked.

"In the hall. He'll see you afterward."

Ivy didn't like the way Elgith spoke to her, as though Ivy were lower than she. She didn't like the way the woman didn't smile, either, or offer her any kind of welcome befitting a princess of the most powerful kingdom in Thyrsland. She would make it her first piece of business to tell Gunther and have the woman put out of service.

Then the door to the bower swung open and Ivy gasped. Where the outside had been dark and spotted with lichen, the inside was clean and lime-washed, with smooth wooden floorboards and a thick red rug. The walls were hung with gleaming objects: gold-hilted swords, golden trays and cups, everything bejeweled in garnet and amber, richly colored tapestries and elaborate silverwork candlesticks and lanterns. A large oak dresser was swamped under several bolts of cloth—blue and gold-shot, and deep red and amber.

"These are for you," Elgith said grudgingly. "I am a seamstress by trade, though now I am in Gunther's service. This afternoon I will measure you and make you some new dresses. Gunther says you like dresses."

"I do. And shoes."

"I can take you to the shoemaker tomorrow."

Ivy had opened the door of the dresser, and she found inside a box full of new things: a bone comb decorated with garnet, a bronze mirror, gold brooches joined with a long string of colored glass beads, a necklace of jet and amber.

"These things are all for you. A welcome present from Gunther," Elgith said, flatly.

Ivy was already unpinning her dress and repinning it with the new brooches. "They're beautiful." Then she turned and saw the bed. Low and wide, covered with thick blankets and sheepskins. Her heart fell. This was where she would be sleeping with Gunther. Giving up her body to Gunther. She tried not to shudder. Perhaps it wouldn't be so bad. She glanced back at the bolts of cloth.

"Come," Elgith said, "Gunther is waiting for you."

They left the bower behind and crossed the small distance to the hall. The sea breeze was gusting hard now, setting the flags on the gables fluttering madly. Then they were inside again, in the dim firelit hall. Three servants were setting up the tables under Gunther's direction. When he heard the door close behind them, he looked up and smiled.

Ivy tried. She really tried not to see the age in his face. But even in the low light, she saw the gray hair, the deep lines, the jowls. As he reached his hand for hers, she almost recoiled at the knotty veins in his hands. She'd thought him younger than her father, but perhaps she was wrong. Ivy took a deep breath and forced her fingers into his. He pulled them to his lips and kissed them. She applied a smile.

"Gunther," she said, with a short nod.

"Ivy, I am so delighted to have you here. We are setting up a grand feast tonight, in honor of your arrival."

A little warmth bloomed under her ribs. "A grand feast? In my honor?"

"Yes. You will bring sunshine and beauty and youth to Seacaster." His eyes turned to Elgith, and something like regret clouded them. "You may go," he said.

"As you wish, my lord," Elgith replied.

"Yes, you may go," Ivy said, and waited for a *my lady* from Elgith, but none was forthcoming. Instead, Elgith pulled away and let herself out of the hall.

Ivy turned to Gunther with a raised eyebrow, expecting him to notice Elgith's slight. Echoes in the hall, wind battering the shutters, salty air sliding in through the cracks . . . but no response from Gunther. He merely looked at her quizzically.

Finally, Ivy said, "She's been very rude to me. You ought to put her out of service."

To her surprise, Gunther waved away her comment. "You'll want her around. She's a fine seamstress and she will be a good friend to you."

"I hardly think—"

"Ivy," he said, in a voice more forceful than she had expected. "Elgith has been a faithful companion to me for many years. I am not putting her out of service."

And Ivy knew that, of course, Elgith had been sharing his bed. No wonder she hated Ivy.

"It matters little if Elgith didn't welcome you warmly enough," he said, the tenderness returning to his voice. "Tonight the whole town will welcome you. May I hold you, my dear?"

She hesitated, not sure for a moment what he meant. Then she said, "Of course," and opened her arms and closed her eyes. Best to get it over with.

He gathered her against him. He smelled of stale sweat and seaweed. His fingers stroked her hair gently, then fell to her back and moved slowly around to the sides of her breasts. She could feel the stiffening of his cock through his tunic, and her body tensed.

"Don't be afraid," he murmured. "I know you are new to the world of love. I will be gentle with you."

A sob rose in her throat. The cage snapped shut.

Ash didn't know how much later she woke, on her blanket next to the fire in Unweder's house. Her head and eyes ached as though every inch of the inside of them were bruised. She could barely find the energy to move her eyeballs to find Unweder. Luckily he wasn't far away. Sitting on his stool at her side. When her eyes opened, he leaned forward and put a cool hand on her forehead.

"Close your eyes and stay very still," he said.

"What happened?" she mumbled.

"You did dangerous magic."

"I saved Bluebell."

"And I saved you."

Ash turned her memory over. "I sent my mind out."

"And you couldn't get it back," he said. "I found you on the ground in the woods, breathing shallowly, but quite unable to respond. Lucky for you, I'd seen such a thing before. I changed to bird form and flew around looking for your mind. A little glowing ball in the undergrowth just a mile south. I could have swallowed it whole, but I didn't. I brought it back for you."

Ash would have nodded, but she couldn't move her head. "Thank you," she said, knowing there would be a debt to repay, knowing what that repayment would be.

"You might have died, Ash, or been nothing but a breathing corpse for life. You simply cannot do something so dangerous."

"I had to."

"I tried to tell you this yesterday, but you wouldn't listen. Perhaps now you will." His voice grew softer. "You can't live in two worlds. If protecting your sisters—and I note you have four and they are all trouble-prone—means performing such dangerous magic, then you need to think very clearly about what you are risking, and what you are gaining. Life does go on beyond this house, Ash. It does. But we are not part of it anymore. To try to be both the old Ash and the new Ash means you will literally be split in two."

Tears gathered at the corners of her eyes, searing her eyeballs.

Unweder, uncharacteristically tender, stroked her hair. "Ah, there," he said. "What you did was brave and you demonstrated enormous power and ability. But no more of that now. No more."

Ash sniffed back the tears. Unweder was right. She had to sever that last connection or go mad. Her Becoming was not to be with her sisters; she had to let them go. "Yes," she said, "no more."

"Now, Ash. Now that I have saved your life, perhaps you could help me with—"

"Yes," she said quickly. "Yes you can have my blood, but on one condition."

He frowned a little, two small lines appearing between his eyes. "What condition?"

"No murder. Animals, yes. But people. No."

He blinked once, then nodded. "Let us make it so."

Only an hour later, while Ash sat by the hearth with a bandage around her forearm where her blood had been spilled—not painlessly, but not horrifically, either—Unweder banged into the house with a high color in his cheeks and a huff of excited breath.

"Ash, come and see."

"See what?"

He beckoned her to her feet, and she rose—still unsteady from her adventures—and followed him to the door.

Outside his house, a riot of plants had sprung to life. Vines and leafy trees, flowers and deep hedges. As she watched, she could almost see it growing, inch by inch. The dead zone was no more.

But then her second sight shifted and she saw them. Thousands upon thousands of elementals, amassed like an army outside her door, looking at her expectantly with their wild pagan faces. As though waiting for orders.

She gasped.

"What is it?" he said, his good eye urgent.

"You can't see them?"

"See what?"

"There are so many! Thousands!" She remembered bidding them to help her, enslaving them with the force of her mind. "It's an army. I've summoned an army by accident."

His eyes widened, but he was still smiling. "They must have smelled your blood."

Ash thought about her Becoming, her fear that she was doomed to take innocents with her. Was this how it was to unfold? A careless thought, an army of magical beings to make it real? Panic shimmered through her veins. "We must get away from here, Unweder." And then an idea. The dragon in her dream; the dragon in Unweder's aspirations. "We will go west. We will hunt that dragon."

"You would help me?"

"Yes, I would." Not so that he could take the dragon's body. So that she could kill the creature and reclaim her Becoming.

He nodded, hooked his arm through hers. "We'll leave tomorrow," he said.

"No," she replied. Tomorrow wasn't soon enough to start the process of cheating her own fate. "We leave today."

Just inside Blickstow, on the first laneway past the guardhouse, there stood a blacksmith's shop where Seaton, Sabert's brother, lived. Sabert and his brother didn't get along—*hadn't* gotten along, Bluebell corrected herself—but his wife never bore a child who survived past the age of five and she had taken an interest in Eni's welfare. Bluebell knocked on their door with Eni under her arm just as the sun was setting behind the giants' ruins.

Seaton's wife opened the door. The clang and hiss of the forge echoed out into the laneway.

Seaton's wife curtsied. "My lord."

"I come as Sabert's friend," Bluebell said. "He is dead. There is nobody to take his son." She thrust Eni forward. "He doesn't know much, but he needs to be loved." Bluebell's voice almost broke and she kicked herself inside. "Will you take him?"

The woman took Eni's hand. "Yes, of course. For how long?"

"I don't know. Forever, if you'll have him. I'll make sure there is money given to you every month to help with his upkeep. But he is clever enough to learn a few small jobs."

"Forever?" Seaton's wife glanced around. "I'll have to check with Seaton."

"Take him tonight. Feed him and give him a soft bed. Talk to your husband. I will be back tomorrow to hear your answer. You'll have to forgive me. I can't stay. I have to go and kill someone."

Seaton's wife nodded nervously.

Bluebell crouched in front of Eni, touching his soft cheek. "All will be well for you now, child. You aren't to worry."

"Bluebell," he said, and Bluebell couldn't stop herself from smiling.

Willow found the millet farm as night was closing in. She was exhausted, filthy, stained with blood and dirt, but the worst were the voices in her head. Echoing voices bouncing around like mirrors within mirrors. Some of them loved her, some of them hated her, and she didn't know who they belonged to. She cried out in her head over and over for Maava's guidance, but it didn't come. Just this confusion of worship and abuse, until she didn't know herself. All she knew was that she had to find Wylm and Eni. Wylm could make the bad voices go away, she just knew it.

She tied the horse to a beam and dismounted. The door was wide open so she went in. "Wylm? Are you here?"

"Whore. Murderer."

Her blood fluttered. She needed him. "Wylm?"

She went through to the back door, then looked out into the garden. A dark shape on the grass. She cried out.

"Wylm!" She ran toward him. A rook, which had been sitting on the hilt of the sword that protruded from his chest, took to the sky with a clatter of its wings. She bent over him. Blood. So much blood. "Oh, Maava. Maava, no. Don't let it be true!"

She laid her head on his chest and wept, calling over and over for Maava to help her, to stop her from losing her connection to the world completely. But the voices were gone now. There was just the sound of crickets and her own ragged sobs.

"Good to see you, my lord."

"Blickstow has been too empty without you and your father."

"My lord, may I talk to you briefly about my case with my neighbor?"

Bluebell left her horse with the gatekeepers and stalked through town. From Seaton's forge to the family compound, she had to fend off the greetings and supplications of many people. She stopped them all with a gentle wave of dismissal and a promise that she would be able to talk to them soon.

The rage was boiling inside her. Gudrun had started this. She had poisoned Bluebell's father, and then her son had nearly killed Bluebell. Gudrun wouldn't be closing her eyes to sleep in her soft bed tonight. She would never sleep again.

Bluebell didn't go around to the gate, climbing the fence into the compound instead. Father's hall stood tall and mighty against approaching dusk. A shiver of night on the wind. There was the bower she'd had Dunstan set up for Gudrun. Bluebell drew her sword, hungry for the kill. Nothing and no one could stop her now. Not Wylm's pleas for mercy. Not Willow's schemes. Not even Rose's veiled appeals to her inner sense of good and right. Her heart hammered a steady rhythm in her chest; the surge of her blood made her feel more alive than she had ever felt. Clear. Bright. Juicy.

The padlock was not on the door.

Bluebell's guts contracted. She kicked open the door. No padlock, but still Gudrun was here, sitting on her bed, packing a bag. She looked up and saw Bluebell and shrieked, scrambling up on the bed and whacking her knees on the post.

Bluebell lifted her sword and advanced, point-first. "I know what you did," she said.

Then the sharp point of a sword was in Bluebell's own back, pressing against her spine. Enraged, she swung around, flipping her wrist and bringing the sword up to cut the head off the bastard who was trying to take her moment from her. The clang of steel on steel as his sword stopped hers with such force that she caught her breath.

"Father?"

"Put it away, Bluebell. That's not how to fix anything."

In her tunnel-visioned moment, Bluebell hadn't seen them here in the bower: Athelrick and Eldra. Her heart thudded, her sword still pressed down against his. A moment passed, and then another. He was old; he had been asleep for weeks. He was no match for her unwell. He might not even be a match for her when he was well anymore. The desire to kill Gudrun was so fierce that a fog of it had clouded her mind.

She glanced at Eldra, who raised an eyebrow. In challenge, perhaps?

Then back to her father, who met her gaze with his own. Her father, her lord, her king.

Sick with it, squashing down a rage that wouldn't fit behind her ribs, aware that Eldra was watching her and judging her, Bluebell dropped her sword.

CHAPTER 34

Bluebell let herself into the stateroom. She and her father had spoken barely a dozen words to each other since the day she had arrived back in Blickstow, but he had sent Dunstan to tell her she had to meet with him. She was dressed in her mail, freshly oiled by her steward, with the king's colors on her sash. She veered between apprehensive and defiant, but ultimately his word was her directive.

She closed the door behind her. Athelrick sat at the table in the middle of the room, his hands folded in front of him. Around him the walls were hung with rich furs and elaborate tapestries, gold and silver, and amber and garnet objects befitting a king. His hair was clean and combed, his gray beard trimmed close to his face. He was dressed beautifully in a deep-red tunic and yellow cloak. Nothing about his body or face hinted that he had been so long out of the world. But the deep line etched between his brow told of the wife he'd had to send home to Tweening in disgrace. Try as she might, Bluebell could not feel sorry for him.

And try as she might, Bluebell could not feel the overwhelming joy she'd expected to feel when he was well again.

"Thank you for coming, Bluebell. Are you well?"

"Yes, my lord."

"Any news from your search party?"

She had deployed a group of three men to search Almissia for Willow, who had disappeared after the incident with the stable.

"No. She isn't anywhere to be found."

"You think she'll turn up?"

Bluebell shrugged. She wasn't concerned, because if Willow was dead, that would save her some trouble. She couldn't put her own sister to the sword, but the girl would rot in a jail for life for treason. Less pleasant.

"Don't stop looking for her."

Bluebell opened her mouth in a biting retort, but of course she couldn't rely on her father to make sensible decisions about those who tried to kill them. "They will find her," she said instead.

He nodded, then tilted his head to the side and said, "You've been avoiding me."

"I have not."

"You have. You make excuses when I enter the room, you don't show up for meals. Dunstan said you ran away from him when he saw you in the hall the other day."

"I didn't run from him. I was late. I was meant to be at Seaton's house for a meal, to visit Eni."

He ignored her excuse. "I realize that you and I disagreed over Gudrun, but you understand that it looked bad enough that you killed her son."

"I was defending my life!"

"I know that, but your reputation hangs in the balance. Those who hate you would gladly see you as a monster, one who kills off members of her own family. Killing a woman of nearly sixty winters while she was unarmed? You don't want that hanging around you forever."

"That's not why you stopped me. You stopped me because you still loved her. Even though she tried to kill you."

His body sagged, almost imperceptibly. "She did not intend to kill me."

"So you've said. So she said. She *intended* to get you to turn on me."

He waved away her remark, regaining his kingly bearing. "She is gone. I have put her aside, and she has returned to her home where she has to live forever with what she has done, and how it led to the death of her son. That is punishment enough."

Blood would have been nicer. "If you say so, my lord. I have something to ask you."

"What is it?"

"I want to take my hearthband and get out of Blickstow. I want to retire poor Isern and get a new horse. And I want a remote post, maybe up at the Littledyke stronghold. I need time away from"—she dropped her head, choosing her words carefully—"from the family."

He smiled tightly. "I'm afraid you can't. Not just yet. You have to represent Almissia at Ivy's marriage next week."

"Why me? Nobody wants me at a wedding."

"Who else can go? I have already been away so long from matters of state. Willow is missing, Ash has taken herself off among the undermagicians, and Rose hasn't returned from taking Eldra home."

Bluebell was surprised to hear him say his sister's name. Athelrick and Eldra hadn't fought, but the air between them had remained icy the whole time she was here in Blickstow. Then, at dinner in the hall one night when Athelrick had said something about Bluebell's destiny as queen, Eldra had stood wordlessly and hobbled out, leaving only an awkward silence in her wake. And now Bluebell winced as she remembered Eldra's last conversation with her. "I see you do whatever he says. I don't think I'll stay here in Blickstow, after all." She had demanded a cart and a retinue, with Rose to keep her company. No more traveling fluidly and swiftly in the night as she had with Bluebell and then, of course, with Athelrick. Just a crippled old woman who seemed determined not to reconnect with her family. Rose had been surprisingly happy to leave Blickstow. Bluebell had thought she'd stay and bruise herself begging to be reunited with Rowan. More than once, Bluebell had wondered whether she had an ulterior motive for going so easily.

"So will you go?" Athelrick said, stirring her out of her reverie.

You do whatever he says. She nodded. "You are my lord and king. If it is your wish that I should go, then I will go."

"Bluebell," he said, his voice soft, "I am your father. I ask you as my daughter. I don't order you as your king."

She dropped her head and he stood and came around the table. One hand on her shoulder, his free hand under her chin turning up her face to meet his gaze. In his eyes she saw his love, his strength, but also his humanity. He had made mistakes. He didn't always know what was right.

And yet, she didn't have the give in her to excuse his behavior. The way he had treated Eldra and Gudrun had made her doubt him. She didn't want to be in a world where she doubted her father, but doubt him she did; and that made life smell different somehow. She forced a smile. "I am glad you are well again, Father," she said.

"You will go to Nettlechester for me?"

"Can I drink too much at the ceremony and disgrace myself?"

He laughed softly. "Of course."

Bluebell nodded. "Then, yes," she said, "I will go for you."

EPILOGUE

G udrun was woken by thumping, dogs barking. She sat up, pulling a shawl around her shoulders and listening fearfully.

Finally, the door to her bower opened. "My lady," a voice said.

"Yes, Olaf, what is it?"

"A young woman stands at the entrance to the house. She won't speak to anyone but you."

Gudrun rose and came to the door of her bower. The dogs still barked. "A young woman?"

"She won't tell us her name."

Gudrun shouted at the dogs to be quiet. "Stay close by me," she said to Olaf.

"I will."

Across the cold floor and past the cold hearth. The open front door let in icy air. There would be snow before long. Outside stood a woman, a hood and cloak covering her from view, a canvas sack over one shoulder. Not quite tall enough to be Bluebell. Gudrun let her body relax. Maybe she would eventually come to believe that Bluebell wouldn't one day hunt her down and kill her.

"Who are you?" Gudrun asked.

"Make your guard go away."

"I . . ." She turned to Olaf, then gestured him away with her head, but noted with comfort that he stood a short distance away, under the beam to the kitchen. "He's gone," she said to the girl.

The girl pulled back her hood with one hand. Gudrun recognized her at once.

"Willow?"

"I am not alone," she said.

Gudrun peered out into the frosty darkness. "What do you mean?"

With her free hand, she unfolded the front of her cape to reveal a belly stretched to bursting.

"You are with child?" Gudrun breathed. "Come in. Come out of the cold. You poor thing; you must be frozen."

Willow lumbered into the house and lowered herself onto a seat, placing the canvas sack on the floor beside her, but hooking her foot around it guardedly.

"Do you have nowhere to go? Who is the father of this child?" Gudrun asked. She eyed Willow's belly and decided she could not be more than a day or so away from giving birth. Memories of the excitement and discomfort of being this pregnant with her own infant son flooded back, followed by a liquid pang, remembering he was gone.

Willow fixed her in a cold gray gaze. "This is Wylm's child."

Gudrun's heart stood still.

"Will you help us?"

"Of course," Gudrun said, words falling over one another. "You will both live here with us and the truth will come to light in its own time. My son! Oh, I am happy for the first time since I can remember. But nobody knows about the child but me? You haven't told?"

Willow shook her head. "No, nobody knows."

"Because as my grandchild, as Wylm's child . . . this baby couldn't be more vulnerable."

Willow smiled a hard smile, which gave Gudrun a moment's pause in her joy and excitement. The younger woman reached down and untied the canvas sack, pulled the drawstring. "No, not vulnerable at all," Willow said, drawing a sword in the dim firelight. "For here is his father's sword."

Read on for a sneak peek at

SISTERS OF THE FIRE

❖ ❖ ❖

We hope you have enjoyed *Daughters of the Storm*. We're pleased to present you with a sneak peek of the next book in the Daughters of the Storm series, *Sisters of the Fire*. Enjoy!

PROLOGUE

R owan kept many secrets. Some were big and some were small. Some she had been told to keep, and some she kept to protect herself. By the time she was seven, she had so many secrets that she decided to draw a special code to remember them all. After supper one evening, she took off into the sapling grove behind the house with her bone-handled hunting knife and a stick of charcoal from the fire. Carefully, while the day cooled off the land and the evening breeze thickened in the oaks of Howling Wood, she drew her diagram in the corner of the fence Snowy had built.

She mustn't tell Papa about the sword her aunt Bluebell had given her on her seventh birthday. And *absolutely*, should she ever see her mama again, she mustn't tell Mama that Bluebell knew where she was all along. Mama was represented with a soft round outline, indistinct as she was in Rowan's memory; Papa was a strong square.

She mustn't tell Sister Julian that Snowy took her hunting every afternoon when she was supposed to be practicing her sewing, and she should certainly never mention how her bow shot was finer and more accurate than her stitching by a hundred miles. She drew Sister Julian with her headscarf over her eyes, to indicate she wasn't allowed to see the beloved elm bow Snowy had made for Rowan, precisely the right size for her child's hands. "Sapwood for the back, heartwood for the belly," he'd said, stroking the inside curve. "Let the world believe you fearless, but keep your heart soft."

She mustn't tell Bluebell about the prayers to Maava she said every night, just as Papa asked her to. And of course, she mustn't tell Papa about the prayers to the Great Mother and the Horse God that she said every night, just as Snowy asked her to. A long straight rectangle for Bluebell, with her dog at her side.

Pleased, Rowan sat back to consider her drawings. Her hands ached a little from carving, and her fingers were black with the charcoal she had rubbed into the lines.

But how to represent the last secret, the big secret? Perhaps she didn't have to. Once, she'd overheard Snowy telling Sister Julian that Rowan had forgotten about her mother already, and it was better that way. But she had not forgotten; she curled up against her mother's back every night. All it took was to close her eyes and send her shimmering self (that was what she called it—she didn't know the real word, or even if there was one) out and above the world, where it found Mama and plummeted toward her like a hawk hunting. She found the warm curve of her mother's back, and she pressed herself against her and slept dreamless every night. Woke up in her own bed every dawn. She knew Mama was sad, but Rowan had no way to tell Mama she was there or to comfort her. Anyway, Mama had another child now, though Rowan couldn't see him, just feel him when he was there in bed with Mama. The three of them all curled together, a family that nobody could see.

It wasn't the only time she sent her shimmering self places, either. Some nights she flew over the Howling Wood, looking for the source of the beautiful singing she heard from time to time. But then the wood coiled in on itself like a labyrinth within a labyrinth, and she couldn't find it. She would never stop looking, though.

That was Rowan's very own secret.

CHAPTER 1

The music and laughter and free-flowing mead made her father's hall seem so alive that Bluebell could hardly believe this feast was to mark a death: the king's counselor, Byrta, who had served their family for sixty years. But for Bluebell and her hearthband it was a party, a chance to catch their breath and eat heartily after the privations of life on the road.

"And then I sat on him," Gytha was screeching, "until he said yes!"

A loud roar of laughter went up, and Bluebell gulped her mead and laughed with them. Gytha, the only other woman in her retinue, was telling the story of how she had convinced her new husband to marry her.

"I suppose you'll be off having babies now," Sighere, Bluebell's second-in-command, said. "Just when your spear arm was becoming legend."

"Depends on who has the greater claim on my womb: the Great Mother or the Horse God." She shrugged, took a gulp of her drink. "What will come will come." But Gytha had already been to see Bluebell to ask how to avoid a pregnancy, something Bluebell herself had avoided since—when had she started fucking? Sixteen? Seventeen? A long time, in any case. Gytha didn't want to leave the road any more than Bluebell did. Life after the road was dull and circumscribed, waiting around to die.

Bluebell glanced around the room. Firelight and smoke and movement. Her eyes were drunk and exaggerated everything, and she smiled at nobody and everybody. The wise women of the village crowded around a table near the hearth—their bones so cold from age that even summer couldn't warm them—telling happy stories of Byrta's life and laughing in defiance of death. The rest of the crowd was made of old warriors, young stable hands, musicians and tale-tellers, Byrta's friends from town, and others who had known and loved her—many of whom were unused to being in Athelrick's hall and were full of marvel and excitement rather than mourning. It was a happy occasion.

"Where's that little serving wench?" Ricbert slurred.

"Over there," Lofric said, pointing across the crowd to the other side of the hall.

Bluebell's men had become infatuated with one of the new hall girls. She was tiny, perhaps a foot shorter than Bluebell, with curling ringlets and a poppet's face, but enormous breasts.

Ricbert stood, holding up his empty cup. "Hey there! Hey!" And when she didn't hear over the din, he put down his cup and lurched off after her.

Sighere was straight-backed, alert.

"Relax," she said. "Enjoy yourself. No harm will come to us today."

"Your father," he said. "The king. He's nowhere to be seen."

"He probably went outside to piss."

Then there was a shriek and Bluebell saw that Ricbert had picked up the little serving girl and was carrying her back to where the hearthband was sitting. Indignant, the girl dumped her jug of mead all down his back. The other men were laughing and whooping, calling to Ricbert to toss the girl to them. They began to pass her around, lifting her over their heads and crowing about how strong they were.

Bluebell finished her drink, stood up, and boomed, "If you are so keen to lift a woman over your head, try it with me!"

Lofric placed the woman on the ground, and she scurried to the fire.

"Come on, then. Lofric? Ricbert? No?" She spread her arms. Bluebell never drew attention to her sex. She was sure, for the most part, her men thought of her as they might think of another man. She was a more powerful soldier than any of them, taller than all but Sighere, and made them call her "my lord" rather than "my lady." But it was the sign of a craven spirit in a man to exercise his power over somebody weaker outside of battle, and she disdained it furiously. Would they be so cruel to children, or to dogs?

"Ricbert," she said, with cold threat in her voice. "I want you to try to pick me up."

Ricbert knew better than to defy a direct command. Sheepishly, drunkenly, he took a step forward and reached for her. Thrymm, Bluebell's dog, leapt to her feet and growled low.

"Down, girl," Bluebell said.

Ricbert's arms went around Bluebell's waist, and as hard as he pulled her up, she planted herself ever more firmly on the ground. It was no contest. She was bigger than him, and he was drunker than her.

"Anyone else?" she asked.

Gytha laughed and piled on with Ricbert, then it became a joke and they were all crowding around her, falling over one another as they tried to pull her off her feet. Thrymm barked nervously and Blubell laughed and laughed as they failed to move her. She was made of stone. She brought down her arms with one swift movement and swept them all off. Some landed on the floor among the rushes and the dogs. A crowd that had gathered laughed and hooted, and Sighere put a cup of mead in her hands and she called them all fuckers under her breath and sat down again.

"He's not back," Sighere said.

For a moment she didn't understand what he meant, but then she glanced up at the high table and realized he meant her father hadn't returned.

"I'll see if I can find him," she said, and patted Thrymm's flank so the dog would follow her.

Bluebell slipped out of the hot, noisy hall into the long summer twilight. If her father had sought peace, he wouldn't have headed to town, but rather around toward the stables. She followed the path and saw him soon enough, standing under an oak tree at the top of the hill, looking out over fields beyond the giants' ruins. The oak was thick with foliage except for the topmost branches, and a dozen rooks had perched up there: black fruit. The sky was washed yellow-gray as the day finally gave way, late as it always was this time of year.

"Father!" she called, and he turned and waited for her to join him, patient and still. Thrymm ran down to him and licked his outstretched hand.

"Are you unwell?" she asked as she approached over the dewy grass.

"I suffer from what every old man suffers when a good friend dies," he said.

"And what ailment is that?"

"An unshakable feeling that my death is near."

The cold touched Bluebell's heart, but she pretended to laugh his comment off. "Byrta was fourteen years older than you. A crone. You are still—"

"I am not *still* anything, Bluebell. I have seen sixty-two winters. I have old injuries that ache more with each passing year. Byrta lived to an old age because she had a life indoors, in quiet rooms and soft spaces. I have worn my body out in service of my people. I cannot be too far behind her."

Bluebell realized that her father's morbid ramblings were his way of grieving. Four years ago, he had fallen into a deathly sleep for many long weeks; he already knew the darkness that was coming. He had never been the same since. He had lost some of his steel.

"You are still hale," she said gently. "You are still our king. My king."

"But if there was a war, Bluebell, could I lead the army? Or would you do it? I'm good for visiting shearings and settling land disputes and placating people who think they've paid too much tax, but not much else." His eyes went back to the fields laid out all around the town of Blickstow, crops of different shades of green ripening in pro-fusion. "It's already over," he muttered.

"Nothing is over," she said.

"I had hoped to die by steel, not by winter."

He turned back to her and she saw the deep lines on his face, the sag of his eyelids and the silver of his beard, and felt a pang.

"Death will come to you, too, one day," he said.

Bluebell's spine stiffened. As it did, she could feel the strength and suppleness in her muscles and joints, and she dismissed her father's words without letting them settle inside her. "If death comes for me, Father, I'll cut its fucking head off."

Athelrick laughed, light returning to his eyes. "That you would, my girl. I can imagine it all too well. Well, at least I can say I raised a good child."

"Five good children."

His smile retreated. "Well."

"Three, then. Ivy and Willow were a waste of your seed, I'll admit that."

He nodded. "Ash," he said. "I want her back. I always thought she would take Byrta's place. She trained for it."

"She never finished her training. And now she's taken herself into exile, and we aren't to reason against that. She believed it the right thing to do."

Her father's expression told her he disagreed, but he didn't pursue the point. "You know I have eyes all over Thyrsland looking for her."

"You should leave her be."

"I only want to know where she is. I won't bring her back against her will. But I liked it better when I knew where you all were. What you were all doing. I long for us all to be reunited. How long will Rose stay with her aunt? I expected her to return ages ago."

Bluebell bit her tongue so she didn't interrogate his choice of words. "Her aunt." Why not *my sister*? He had refused to explain their estrangement, and there was no point in pressing him now. Bluebell wouldn't mention his bastard grandson. Instead, she said, "Rose fears your disapproval."

"As she should. She behaved foolishly, but not all is lost. She gave up Rowan; the peace still holds. For now."

For now. Nettlechester, long their foe, was in the protracted process of converting to the trimartyr religion, as Tweening already had. If Littledyke also went down that road, nearly half of Thyrsland would have adopted the cruel faith. A faith that said women couldn't rule.

"Had you given thought to Rowan's future?" Bluebell asked suddenly. "One of King Blackstan's sons might make her a good husband, and secure Littledyke."

"Ask him next time you go north. How old is the girl now?"

"Too young to wed. Seven, I think. But a promise might be made. If Wengest is amenable." Wengest, who was too stupid to see Rowan wasn't from his seed.

Athelrick nodded, opened his mouth as though about to say something, then thought better of it.

"Go on," she prompted. "You can tell me anything that's on your mind."

"It would be much easier if *you* wed."

But Bluebell was already shaking her head.

"And if you had your own heirs."

"They wouldn't grow inside me. Everyone says my womb is made of steel," she joked.

"Bluebell . . ."

"The Horse God made me this way."

"Take a year out, while I'm still alive—"

"No babies." Bluebell's pulse was thudding in her throat. He had never said it directly to her before, though of course it had been implied a million times. His wistful mood must have made him say it. He was grieving. He felt old and longed for his family to be biddable little girls again.

Not that Bluebell had ever been biddable.

"Rowan will be a good queen. She's in good care and far enough from the trimartyr fervor of her father's court," Bluebell said. "I go north as soon as the mourning is over. I will send ahead to Blackstan for a meeting." She glanced up to the hall. "Will you come back inside?"

"I am enjoying watching the day dwindle," he said. "I'll be along in my own time."

"Very well." She turned and began up the path.

"Don't forget," he called after her urgently, "that you will die one day."

"Don't forget," she replied, without turning around, "that you are still alive."

CHAPTER 2

The Howling Wood, at the bottom of Greyrain Range, was dense and gloomy, and Skalmir's first glimpse of his little house at the end of a long working day always made him smile. Out into the long sunshine after a shadowy day tracking, trapping, hunting, into the fresh air after the cold tang of blood by the stream then the choking air of the smokehouse. Yes, he was muddy and bloody and his hair smelled of smoke, but inside were clean clothes and sweet-smelling herbs hung from the ceiling beams and, of course, Rowan. His dogs wrestled and growled around his feet, happy.

Skalmir opened the door and there was Rowan, sitting by Sister Julian. The shutters were all open to let the afternoon breeze in, and yellow sunlight hit Rowan's hair and found auburn highlights. She looked up at the same time as Sister Julian. Rowan's first instinct, he could tell, was to bounce out of her seat and hug him hard around the middle, winding her little legs around his ankles and demanding he walk around the house with her hanging off him, a limpet—her favorite way to greet him. But with Sister Julian's eyes on her, she sat still.

"Snowy!" she cried instead. "You're home!"

Strike and Stranger jumped up on her lap, wagging their tails happily.

"That I am, little one," he replied, sitting at the freshly lit hearth and taking his boots off.

"Good afternoon, sir," Sister Julian said, eyes returning to her stitching.

"Good afternoon, sister."

Sister Julian came from the village daily to mind Rowan, to teach her to sew, and to tell her stories about Maava, the god of the new religion that hadn't quite spread as far as the Howling Wood. She rarely spoke more than a few words to Skalmir, but seemed kind enough with Rowan, and Wengest had insisted on hiring her for Rowan's care and instruction.

"I'll clean myself up. You may go," he said to her.

She nodded, but he couldn't see the expression on her face below the headscarf she always wore over her long, fair hair. He sometimes wondered if she was embarrassed by him, as if the fact of her being a spinster and him being a widower meant they should never look at each other directly.

"Rowan, can you water the dogs?" Skalmir made his way across the room and through to the back door, which opened on overgrown weeds and a stone slab with their water barrel on it. He ladled water over his head and hands, then stripped to the waist and left his clothes in a bundle for Sister Julian and Rowan to wash tomorrow. A robin chirped above him, and he glanced up. "Good afternoon to you, too," he said.

He ran his eyes along the length of the eaves, checking for loose parts and gaps where the rain could get in. He had built this house with his own hands ten years ago, when his wife Mildrith had been expecting their first child. He knew every nail, every inch of oak and elm, every handful of mud, every flat stone collected from the stream. He had never worked so hard as he worked that year, watching his wife's belly grow, keen to keep them all warm. But the first child had not survived the birth. The small anteroom off their bed chamber remained empty. No, not empty: hollow.

By the time Mildrith's belly swelled again, they were raising Rowan together, King Wengest's daughter in hiding, deep in the ancient woodland reserved for Skalmir's work as king's hunstman. This time the birth was more brutal, and neither his child nor his wife lived through it.

But the house still stood, sturdy as ever.

Skalmir found a sunny bank of grass to lie on and closed his eyes, filling his lungs with afternoon air.

A few moments later, Rowan was there, flinging herself on top of him. "She's gone! Today was very long," she declared.

"Why is that, dear heart?" he asked, spitting her long hair out of his mouth.

"Because Sister Julian is very old and very boring."

"She's the same age as I am," Skalmir said, although even he found it hard to believe that a woman of only thirty could have such a pinched face.

"Yes, but you're my lovely Snowy and she is just an old bore." Rowan wriggled off him and grabbed his bare arm, trying to pull him up. "Take me shooting."

"I don't want to go out again."

"In the sapling grove, then. Please. I've been sitting still all day and I'm *dying*."

He dragged himself to his feet. "Go on then. Get your bow."

With an excited yelp she hared off inside again, while Skalmir waited with the afternoon sun on his bare shoulders. The sapling grove had once been land cleared for farming. Mildrith had had the Great Mother's touch with plants, and her small vegetable and herb patches weren't enough to keep her busy. She had wanted to grow food to sell to the markets. She had wanted to be busy and productive, and raise her child to be the same. After her death, Skalmir replanted the space with saplings, so he wasn't reminded every day of the dreams that had died with her. Now it was Rowan's favorite place to go: safe and close enough to home, but still wild, with its rabbits and its chatter of birds and gleam of insect wings.

The door slammed behind her again, and a moment later her hand was in his and they were walking the muddy path into the sapling grove, the dogs at their heels. Sparrows pipped in the low branches.

"So what did you learn today?"

"How to be a good trimartyr," she said grimly. "Which is a great deal the same as how to be a commonsense good person, but far more boring and with lots of talk of death by fire."

"Well, always remember, nobody sees inside your heart. You may believe what you want to believe." Though Skalmir hoped she believed in the old ways.

"I know, Snowy. I can keep all of the gods in my head at once. Don't worry."

He didn't worry, not really. Rowan was almost preternaturally able to present the perfect face to every person she encountered. With King Wengest she was the demure princess; with Bluebell she was the raging warrior-child; with Sister Julian she was the patient trimartyr pupil. Skalmir liked to think she was herself with him. Somehow his grief and Rowan's had found in each other a sweet harmony. They both knew Rowan wasn't his, that one day she'd be taken from him, but as far as Skalmir and Rowan understood life, that was the nature of loving someone.

He stood by her in the dying afternoon light as she shot arrow after arrow into a painted target he had built for her out of a larch log. Every afternoon she would do this, for hours. He sometimes believed she wouldn't stop if he didn't tell her to. She didn't tire of it, or grow bored, as she did with everything else. She was all focus and energy, running back and forth to fetch her arrows and unleashing the whole quiver again and again. Then, in the evenings, she would sit happily by the fire after supper to replace arrowheads and mend fletchings and wax her bowstring.

"Give me a challenge, Snowy," she said after a while. "I'm sick of shooting at that target."

"All right," Skalmir said, grasping her hand and walking her up a hillock. "See that ash over there?"

"That one?" she asked, pointing with an arrow. "With the ivy growing up it?"

"Yes. The lowest branch is very narrow, but you have a clear shot. Can you hit it from here?"

She nocked the arrow without a word. Became still. He never saw her so still as she was when shooting.

With a soft swoosh the arrow sailed away and thudded into the branch.

"Well done!"

She pulled out another arrow. A soft rustle in the undergrowth behind them caught her attention. Skalmir had time to register the fact that a rabbit had emerged from its hole a hundred feet from them—moving, half hidden by wildflowers—before the arrow had left Rowan's fingers and found its mark.

She gasped. "Did I hit it?"

The dogs, trained for precisely this task, streaked off after it. Skalmir and Rowan began to run back through the undergrowth, the long tickling grass. Skalmir found the little body, warm but limp, Rowan's arrow protruding from its back.

"I hit it!" she shouted. "Snowy, I hit it. I caught us dinner. And from so far."

"Not only that, it was moving," he added, trying to sound more encouraging than astonished. He reached out to stroke her hair, but she ducked away, too full of excitement for affection, and snatched her rabbit off him.

"Now you can show me how to skin it and gut it, and then we'll roast it with some turnips." Already she was heading back to the house, her proud little spine straight and square, quiver bouncing over her shoulder, the dead rabbit dangling from her hand.

Skalmir followed, brimming with pride, even though she wasn't his to be proud of.

Late, late in the night, a boom of thunder woke Skalmir from a confusing dream about a deer that could speak, once it had taken an arrow to its brain. He blinked in the dark and saw the flash of lightning through the cracks around the shutter. Another boom. Rain hammered down.

He turned over, told himself to go back to sleep, but then remembered that Rowan liked to sleep with her shutter open on warm evenings, and it had been cloyingly warm at bedtime. So he kicked the dogs off his feet and rose to open the door between their chambers. Yes, the shutter was open, and the rain was gusting through it in swells. Another bolt of lightning momentarily blinded him, leaving a flash on his vision. He closed the shutter. Tomorrow he and Rowan would have to take out these wet rushes and put new ones down. He turned to where she lay, sleeping on her side. In the dark, he could make out her white nightgown, her shoulder rising and falling with her breath.

Skalmir went to her bed and crouched down. It seemed she had slept through the thunder. Gently, careful not to wake her, he reached out to stroke her shoulder.

She was icy cold.

Puzzled, his heart speeding a little, he let his hand rest there a few moments. She was definitely breathing. So why was she so cold? The shutter had been open but the night was muggy. He reached under her blanket to feel her back. Again, icy.

Now he began to doubt himself, doubt his eyes. She was as cold as the dead, so he shook her lightly and said her name. "Rowan?"

She moved. Of course she moved. She was breathing, she was alive. She made a small mumbling sound, then said, clear as a bell, "Mother?"

Skalmir didn't know what to say. He couldn't answer. If she was dreaming happily about her mother, he would not be so cruel as to remind her that she was stuck here in a dark, ancient wood with him, and would perhaps never see her mother again. Wengest had put Rose aside—Skalmir didn't know why for certain, but the rumors were of infidelity—and ordered her never to see her daughter again if peace was to hold between Almissia and Nettlechester.

Rowan's question hung there in the dark, unanswered. But she was breathing regularly and deeply again, and still as cold as frost under his hand. He pulled her blanket up higher and tucked it around her tightly, trying to warm her up. He was surprised she remembered her mother; perhaps she only remembered her in her sleep.

Skalmir stood. Leaving her small, sleeping body behind him, he closed the door and let her dream.

PHOTO: © KIM WILKINS

KIM WILKINS is the author of *Daughters of the Storm*. She was born in London, and grew up at the seaside north of Brisbane, Australia. She has degrees in literature and creative writing and teaches at the University of Queensland and in the community. Her first novel, *The Infernal*, a supernatural thriller, was published in 1997. Since then, she has published across many genres and for many different age groups. Her contemporary epic women's fiction is published under the pseudonym Kimberley Freeman. Wilkins has won many awards and is published all over the world. She lives in Brisbane with a bunch of lovable people and pets.

kimwilkins.com
Facebook.com/KimWilkins2014

About the Type

This book was set in Palatino, a typeface designed by the German typographer Hermann Zapf (b. 1918). It was named after the Renaissance calligrapher Gíovanni Battista Palatino. Zapf designed it between 1948 and 1952, and it was his first typeface to be introduced in America. It is a face of unusual elegance.